Everwinter

Elizabeth Baxter

For Mark

You know why

Prologue

Variss, 731 AD

The king had gone mad.

Captain Harn Yorgesson had suspected for a long time, but now he was sure. Why else had the king brought them on this trek? Why else would he not tell Harn where they were going? These days the king consulted only with that accursed monk. The Great Warrior alone knew what poison that man had been pouring into the king's ear.

Harn shook himself. What right did he

have to question the king? He was a captain of the Royal Guard of Variss, sworn to obey. He would do his duty even though every step he took up this gods-forsaken mountain intensified his dread.

"Captain," said sergeant Tarl. "When are we going to call a halt? If we don't stop for food and rest the injured men will die."

Harn cast his eye over the line of soldiers. Many of them carried small injuries: cuts, bruises or torn muscles. But the three worst injured — those caught in the rock-slide two days ago — were being hauled on crude stretchers slung from the exhausted shoulders of the others. Anger twisted Harn's mouth. The king refused to send the injured men back to Variss, leaving only two choices: bring them along or leave them on the mountainside to die.

"I'll consult the king," he said.

Harn waited at the side of the trail until the king's party caught up to him. As always, the king and monk were deep in conversation. For a moment, Harn thought they would walk right past without even noticing him, but as he came abreast of the captain, the king's gray eyes snapped up.

"Captain Yorgesson. Is there a problem?"

Harn bowed. "Sire, we need to make camp for the night. My men are weak and exhausted. Many sustained injuries in the rock-fall. They need food and shelter."

The king stared at him for a time, and then shook his head. "No. We don't have time to stop. We must reach our destination before nightfall."

"And what is our destination, sire?"

The king gazed up to the mountain's peak. "The gods." He took the monk's arm and moved on, leaving Harn alone on the trail.

Harn pinched the bridge of his nose, beating back a headache. His gaze wandered along their route, showing him nothing but the endless vista of the Sisters. Although the spring weather had been kind, they'd had plenty of other dangers to contend with. Wolves and bears, creatures normally shy of humans, had become aggressive, plaguing the party through the mountains. And there were other creatures as well. Creatures that stalked just beyond the edge of the firelight. Creatures Harn had no name for. Once, Harn would have scoffed at the stories of ghosts and ghouls that haunted the Sisters. Fairy stories, he would have said. Tales to frighten children. But now he wore a protection charm around his neck like the rest of his men.

So far, Harn had lost nine soldiers. Nine dead and the king did not care.

King Beorl Godwinsson was not the king Harn had once loved. He was no longer the shrewd, brilliant young general who had won Harn's loyalty all those years ago. *That* King Beorl had refused to leave even one injured soldier on the field when he led his army at the battle of Mother's Ridge. *That* King Beorl would have wept at the injuries the men sustained in the rock-slide.

But no longer.

Now a hunger Harn could not comprehend drove the king of Variss. Since the monk had arrived in Variss a little over six months ago, the king had begun to change, gradually becoming somebody Harn no longer recognized.

The princess had seen it. She had done her best to halt the growing influence of the monk over her father. But whatever hold the foreigner had gained seemed unbreakable. The princess had refused to accept her father's new gods and been banished. Harn's guts still twisted at the memory. He remembered standing with the princess and Lidda, her maid, on that last afternoon. He remembered the shock and fear in the princess's eyes. He'd so wanted to go with her, to turn his back on Variss and ride off with her into the south. But he hadn't. He was a king's man and his vows held him chained. Six months had passed with no word. He wondered if the king ever thought about his daughter, ever wondered where she was or what she was doing.

"You all right, captain?" said Sergeant Tarl, frowning at Harn in concern.

Harn shook himself. "I'm fine, Tarl. Come on."

4

They marched in silence. After a while, the trail ended and the soldiers halted in confusion. The monk pushed to the front of the group and knelt on the ground, forehead pressed into the dirt, as though praying to his strange gods.

Harn scowled. He disliked any god that put a man on his knees. The Great Warrior taught all men to face him with head high and sword in hand.

The monk took a map from the pocket of his robe and unrolled it on the ground. Leaning close, he studied the map for a long time.

"I knew it," he whispered. "All the searching, all worth it. I've found it!" His bony finger pointed upwards, at Black Seza towering above them. "There."

Harn sucked in a breath. Black Seza, the tallest peak of the Sisters, had a dark reputation. Lost souls walked her summit, the tales said, and none who climbed her pitted flanks ever returned.

The king conferred hurriedly with the monk. After a moment, he turned to Harn. "Captain Yorgesson, that is our road."

What would be his punishment if he refused? What would happen if he ordered his men to abandon the king and his mad plans? Would the Great Warrior forgive him? Probably not. A soldier never left a comrade on the field and Harn had sworn oaths to his king that bound him like chains.

"Sergeant Tarl, take four scouts and range ahead. Find us a trail up the mountain. Corporal Mannon, you take the rear. The rest of you form up in marching order. Sire, I suggest you hold your place in the middle of the line."

For a wonder, the king smiled. "As you wish, captain."

Tarl and the scouts moved out. Harn and his men waited in silence and soon heard the call of a white eagle.

Harn nodded. "That's the signal. Let's get moving."

In marching formation they began to climb. They picked their way through outcroppings of boulders sticking out of the ground like the mountain's bones, and clumps of small, scraggly brush. At times, they had to move in single file which Harn didn't like one bit. Strung out like this, they became the perfect target for an ambush.

But who would set an ambush out here? He thought. *Nothing human, that's for sure.*

He shuddered.

Tarl waited ahead. "The scouts have found a trail of sorts. It's odd, captain. The trail is paved like a road but who would build a road up here?"

Harn shook his head. He didn't want to guess. "Show me."

The road appeared through the scrub,

wide enough for a cart and paved in square-cut stones. It ran straight and true toward the summit of the mountain as if newly laid for their purpose.

Harn made the sign of the Mother at his breast. "What devilry is this?"

The rest of the troop had caught up, and now the monk and king pushed their way to the front. Seeing the road, the monk's eyes widened.

"We've found it, sire!" he cried. "Didn't I tell you we would? We are so close now!"

The king stared at the road and then up toward Black Seza's crown. For the first time since they'd left Variss, Harn saw doubt in the king's face. It flickered across his features for a moment before the mask descended again.

"Captain," the king said. "We must hurry. Dark will soon be falling."

They made good speed on the road. It sloped gently upwards along the mountain's flank, and where the ground rose too steeply, the mountainside had been cut away to make the road's passage easier. Harn marveled at the engineering involved. Who had built this? And how had they brought the materials up here, this far into the Sisters? Variss lay many leagues to the south. No other settlement existed in the Sisters. Nothing lived up here, except…

No.

It couldn't be. Could it?

The Quiet Land.

Harn shook himself. A children's story, a name to whisper around a campfire. Nothing more.

The road bent round to the east and Harn saw that a great cliff bisected this part of the mountain, blocking their path. The road ran straight into the cliff.

As Harn reached the scouts one of them said, "We can't find a way around. The road leads here and stops. If the king wants to go on, we'll have to climb."

The rock face was sheer and high. They'd need climbing gear and would be unable to hoist the injured men up. Black Seza's cloud-wreathed summit towered above them. At this angle, the jagged crags almost looked like a face leering down.

Harn turned to the king. "The road ends here, sire. There is no way around, if you want to continue we must go up."

The king regarded him. "Up? Why would we want to go up? We've found it."

Harn looked around. What was the king talking about? They were surrounded by the featureless flanks of the mountain. There was nothing else.

The monk stepped forward. His large hands roved along the cliff face, gently caressing.

"What's he doing?" Harn asked.

"Be silent!" snapped the king.

The monk seemed to be searching for something. After a moment, he stopped and pressed his ear to the stone.

"Here, sire."

The king placed his hand on the stone where the monk indicated. "You're sure?"

"Yes. Close your eyes. Can you not feel it?"

"I can!" whispered the king after a moment. "So much life! So much power! The Lords of Life are close. Let us begin."

The monk bowed then took a knife from his belt and sliced the blade across his arm. Blood welled from the cut, a sheet of red liquid that spread over his hand and dripped from his wrist. The monk wiped his arm across the face of the cliff, smearing blood across the rock.

Harn watched in fascinated horror. He was in the company of mad men.

The monk's blood gleamed in the sunlight, and to Harn's eyes, looked as though it was spreading along the stone, crawling as if alive. But that was impossible.

Around him, the men began to mutter. They had seen it too. The monk's blood moved upwards and sideways, spreading itself across the stone until it revealed a rough pattern like the outline of a door.

Harn's heart thudded. He had been in many battles and seen things that would cause nightmares for a lifetime. Yet nothing had filled him with the cold fear that drenched him now.

He stepped forward. "Sire, what is going on?"

The king tore his eyes from the door and looked at Harn. The captain stepped back a pace. A shadow danced in the king's eyes, a dark madness that jumped and spun.

"We stand at a crossroads, Captain Yorgesson. You and your men are privileged to witness the dawning of a new age. All my life I have guarded the ancient secret given to my line. Never must this door be opened, lest it release a terrible power from the other side. But Nashir has helped me to see that my ancestors were wrong. The Lords of Life wait beyond. It is my duty to release them."

Harn tried to move. As the king approached the cliff, his every instinct screamed at him to stop this. But he was rooted to the spot. Fear chained him.

The king bared his arm and let Nashir slash the blade across his skin. The king wiped his blood down the rock.

"I open the Rift. Lords of Life, I give you the freedom of this realm! I live to serve you! Bring us all into your loving embrace!"

The king's blood ran across the cliff face, seeping into the pattern of the door.

For a second, all was quiet. Harn dared to hope. Perhaps they were wrong. Perhaps all this drama was just the delusional antics of two mad men.

But then a shaft of light burst from the

door. Harn threw his arm across his face and
his men yelled in alarm. The light flared
brightly and then faded.

When Harn looked again he saw an
opening in the cliff face, a dark tunnel like a
hungry mouth.

The king went to his knees. "They are
coming! I can feel it!"

Something small and white landed on
Harn's shoulder. A snowflake.

Snow began falling all around. The men
muttered in fear. It was a warm spring day.
What was happening?

The wind rose. It screamed from the tunnel
and hit them so hard that Harn stumbled
backward. On its heel came a blizzard.

Harn had time to cry out, "Sire!" before he
was enveloped in a white blanket.

The world turned to chaos. He heard his
men shouting to each other, fearful and lost.

The king, he thought desperately. *I must
reach the king!*

He took a tottering step forward but was
driven to his knees. His clothes were sodden,
hair plastered to his head. He dashed snow
from his eyes and peered into the storm.
Ahead, he saw the shadow of the tunnel.
Something moved by the tunnel entrance. A
scream cut through the air.

"Retreat!" Harn bellowed to his men, not
knowing if any of them heard.

But he was a captain of the Royal Guard of

Variss and must save his king. He placed his hands on the ground and began to edge forward. Inch by slow inch he moved into the heart of the blizzard, crawling like a blind man.

A shape reared up before him. Then a talon the length of his arm erupted from his chest.

Who will warn Variss? He thought as pain flooded him and his thoughts spun down into darkness.

CHAPTER 1

Ral Tora, three years later

Bramwell Thornley was not, and had never been, a religious man. But now, as he hung three hundred paces from the ground, he was beginning to reassess that stance. Squeezing his eyes shut, he sent a prayer to any god, goddess, demi-god or friendly spirit that might be listening.

Let me get down in one piece and I promise to never do anything this stupid again. Please!

Above him, the spire of First Storm Tower soared into the gray sky. Clouds had gathered, ready to throw their anger at anyone stupid enough to enter their domain. A freezing wind blew from the north, howling around the tower and lifting the ends of Bram's sweat-sodden hair. He clung to the metal ladder so tightly his fingers were cramping. His nose, lips and ears felt like frozen slabs of meat. To top it all, he'd strapped his pack on too tightly and now it was digging into the skin beneath his armpits.

All in all, Bram wished he was somewhere else.

The wind dropped and Bram seized his chance to squint upwards. The tower's pinnacle rose only a few paces above him but it could have been a hundred miles away.

If only he'd kept his mouth shut! If his stupid pride hadn't goaded him he'd be safely on the ground right now. It was always the same with him — his mouth always ten seconds ahead of his brain. This morning, when Chief Engineer Rassus had asked for a volunteer to repair Old Rosella, why had he raised his hand? He should have stared at the ground and pretended he hadn't heard like Romy had.

Fool! Think before you open your mouth! He told himself. *You're an engineer, not a steeplejack!*

Shaking his head to clear the clinging threads of hair from his face, he reached for the next rung and pulled himself up. As he climbed his world shrank to a pinprick; only the ladder and his next hand-hold mattered. Nothing else.

Despite the freezing temperature, sweat beaded on Bram's forehead and dripped into his eyes, making his vision blur. He settled his boot on the next rung and felt the grips on his boots catch on the icy metal for a second — then slide out from under him. Desperately he threw up his arms, trying to find a handhold, but his gloves slid off uselessly and the weight of his body ripped him from the ladder.

With a strangled cry, Bram fell.

Panic flashed through his body. Blood roared in his ears. Then, with a grunt, the breath was punched from his lungs as the safety harness jerked him to a halt. He'd only fallen about five paces.

Bram hung there, winded, desperately trying to pull in a breath. Dots of silver light danced in front of his eyes. Unbidden, Bram's eyes swiveled downwards and he caught a glimpse of the patchwork of Ral Tora's streets, far, far, below.

Gorge rose in Bram's throat. Waves of dizziness swamped him. He closed his eyes and sucked in deep breaths then forced himself to grab the ladder and haul himself upright. His boots scrabbled against the rungs and eventually found purchase. Bram pressed his forehead to the cold metal, allowing the fear to leak out of him like water from a burst skin. It felt as though his thudding heart would shatter his ribs.

You're all right. You didn't fall, he told himself over and over.

The wind howled, sounding like cruel laughter in Bram's ears.

You're not up to this job, the wind seemed to whisper. *Go back to the menial tasks you can cope with. Only real engineers should be up here.*

Bram almost gave in. *You can't do this,* he told himself. *Go down, before you kill yourself.* But a louder voice answered, *what, and prove you can't cut it as an engineer? That you should still be an apprentice?*

Sudden anger flared in Bram's chest.

I will not give up!

Gritting his teeth, he narrowed his eyes at the ledge and climbed.

One rung.

Two rungs.

Three rungs.

Four.

At last, Bram scrambled onto the ledge and lay on his back, gasping. Triumph surged through him. He'd done it!

In front of him the pointed top of First Storm Tower rose up, a narrow spire that ended in a weather vane shaped like a cockerel. Several tiles had slipped from the roof, leaving gaps through which Bram could see Old Rosella, the great bell, hanging in the chamber below. If she hadn't commanded such affection from the citizens of Ral Tora, Chief Engineer Rassus would not have spared the labor to conduct repairs. The engineers were busy enough already.

But Old Rosella was one of Ral Tora's oldest landmarks and people measured their day by her hourly peals. So when she had failed to chime this morning, the chief engineer had sent Bram to investigate. But while the bell chamber itself was accessible from inside the tower, the roof above was too narrow and could only be reached from the metal ladder on the outside of the spire.

Bram saw the problem immediately. The hole had been letting in snow that seized up Old Rosella's striking hammer. Bram shrugged the pack of tools from his shoulders and took out what he needed. None of the tiles had fallen from the roof and smashed on the street below so all he had to do was re-position them and then nail them into place. He worked as quickly as he could, before his hands became too cold to use the hammer, doing his best to ignore the wind that tried to tear him from his precarious perch.

At last, Bram nailed the last tile into place. He put his tools away and slung the pack over his shoulder. The wind dropped and the clouds broke to let through the midday sun. The effect was startling. The dull, lifeless day suddenly came alive with beauty. Ice glistened on the roofs of Ral Tora, glittering like thousands of tiny crystals.

Holding the safety line, Bram edged forward and looked out over Ral Tora. The city spread out below like a giant's map. In the far distance Bram could see the curtain wall that protected the city, and the twelve watchtowers rising along it. Directly below Bram's perch the four quarters of the city fanned out in perfect symmetry around First Storm Tower's central courtyard. It reminded Bram of a wheel, with First Storm Tower as the hub and the streets radiating outwards like spokes.

Home, he thought.

Pride swelled in his chest. This was Ral Tora, the greatest place in the world.

Tugging on the safety line to check it was secure, Bram turned around, lowered his foot onto the first rung of the ladder and began his descent. Although Bram wouldn't have thought it possible, going down was worse than going up. Agonizingly slowly, Bram crawled downwards. Each time he moved he had to pause and make sure his grip was secure before moving on.

At length, he reached a door in the spire's side. Bram gratefully took his feet from the ladder, pushed his way through the door, and lay panting on the landing inside. The smell of old wood replaced the icy odor of the wind.

He'd reached the bell chamber and the great bell, Old Rosella, hung above him, the iron turned green with verdigris. With the roof fixed, he just had to free the mechanism and then he could get back to the ground. He unclipped himself from the safety harness and with cloths, brushes and oil, set about cleaning the cogs and springs that controlled the bell's striking apparatus. Finally, he greased the whole thing so the icy air wouldn't cause the machinery to freeze.

With tired arms Bram slung the pack onto his back and climbed to his feet. A hefty staircase spiraled around the inside of the tower. As he tottered down it, the reassuring feel of the banister helped to steady the thumping of his heart.

A voice suddenly called from somewhere below, "Hoi! Bram! What took you so long?"

Bram saw a familiar figure standing at the bottom of the stairs. He smiled. "Next time I volunteer for this, Romy, will you please give me a whack on the head?"

Romy barked a laugh and then rushed to take Bram's pack as he reached the bottom and sat down on the smooth flagstone floor.

Romy leant over him. "You all right? You look a bit pale."

Bram waved his friend's words away. He needed to gather himself.

But before he could catch his breath, another voice spoke. "Engineer Thornley, report!"

Chief Engineer Rassus stood in the

doorway, hands planted on his hips. He was a bear of a man, with bushy eyebrows and a glare to melt lead.

"Well?" he demanded. "Did you complete the repairs?"

"Yes, sir," Bram replied. "I found a hole in the roof and the mechanism had seized. It should be fine now."

"Then why hasn't Old Rosella chimed this hour?"

Bram opened his mouth and closed it again. He'd been so focused on his descent that he hadn't been listening for the bell's chimes.

Oh no! He thought. *Don't make me go back up there!*

A loud peal suddenly rang out. The clonking cacophony echoed through the tower, rattling Bram's teeth. As the last strains died into silence, Bram sighed in relief.

Rassus glanced at the tower and back to Bram. "Good work, engineer." He strode off without a backward glance.

Romy blew out a breath. "What a day for surprises! A climb that would have the best of us soiling our breeches, then a compliment from Rassus. This must be your lucky day, Bram!"

Bram raised an eyebrow but didn't reply to his friend's sarcasm. Romy's yellow hair was matted with grime, his face a patchwork of mud and soil.

"What happened to you?" Bram asked.

"You look like a street urchin who's been scrapping in the dirt."

"Charming! I trudge all the way across town to see how you're doing — without even stopping to have a bath — and all I get is insults! I've been at the north wall all day. Again."

"How's it going?" Bram asked, kneeling to tie his bootlace.

"It's the last section of tunnels that's giving us the trouble." Romy shrugged. "I suppose when they built the wall they didn't think that one day we might need to lay pipes underneath. Rassus has given me the honor of overseeing one of the digging teams. Gods, those boys can moan! Three times they had me in the tunnels, checking the measurements. Three bloody times! They reckoned the wall was going to collapse. Of course, it wasn't. I've never met such a superstitious bunch of old women in my life!"

"I'll swap you then," said Bram, straightening. "Next time Old Rosella needs repairs you can go up, and I'll look after your digging team. What do you say?"

Romy craned his head back and looked up at First Storm Tower. "No chance."

Bram laughed and they left the tower, locked the door behind them, and headed toward the center of town. They found themselves on a busy thoroughfare. People scurried back and forth, heads bent against the blustery weather. Wind-blasted olive and fig trees lined the street, black and shrunken.

The street opened out into a large park with a cluster of buildings sitting in the middle. Lamps gleamed in the windows, battling the already fading light. A sign by the gates read:

University of Ral Tora, Engineering Academy. Charter granted by Great Father Toran, year 299.

Had it really been less than a year since his graduation? It felt like forever.

The two friends skirted the length of the university precinct and entered a large square. A fountain shaped like a rearing horse dominated the center. In better days, people had sat round the square, enjoying the warm southern climate and chatting to friends. But now the water in the basin was frozen and there was no warmth to enjoy.

Nevertheless, a large group of people were gathered round the fountain, staring avidly at a man who'd climbed onto the rim and was bellowing at them. The man had a livid scar running through one eye and he'd smeared soot around his eyes, giving his face a skull-like pallor.

Romy whistled under his breath. "Great. It looks as though we've walked into the middle of a Wailer meeting. Shall we go the other way?"

"No, it'll take ages. If we keep our heads down they shouldn't bother us."

They pulled their collars up and scurried around the outside of the square, heads bowed. As they drew nearer, Bram could make out the man's words.

"Listen! The mighty ones are coming! Already we feel their power! In our pride we have forgotten the old gods and they are punishing us. If we don't repent they will send us all to Hell!"

Bram shook his head. The man was talking nonsense. There must be a perfectly rational explanation for this unseasonal weather. Old gods had nothing to do with it. Why did the Wailers have to keep stirring things up? Didn't Ral Tora have enough problems already?

"There!"

Bram looked up to find the man's eyes had fixed on him and Romy. He pointed a bony finger at them, a triumphant expression on his face.

"There! Two of the blasphemers! Two of those who ignore the will of the old gods and defile their names!"

The crowd turned toward the two engineers. An angry murmur broke out.

Bram glanced at Romy. His friend's face had gone pale.

"Let's get out of here," Bram whispered.

They turned on their heels and strode back the way they'd come. Once out of the square Bram wiped his brow and whistled under his breath. "That was close. The crowd was beginning to get ugly."

Romy snorted contemptuously. "Who do they think they are? They have no right to intimidate people, as though they own the city. The city fathers should do something about those scare-mongering lunatics."

Bram nodded his agreement and they made their escape down Merchant's Way, a roundabout route that would take them twice as long.

At last, they turned into White Road and reached their destination. The headquarters of The Honorable Guild of City Engineers was a three-story building made of good Ral Toran brick. It had a gabled roof and a large red door. Warm light spilled from the windows.

"I don't know what you're looking so relieved about," Romy said. "I bet Rassus is waiting for you in his office, wanting a full report."

Bram groaned. "You're right. No doubt he'll find something he can shout at me for."

Romy looked sympathetic. "Tell you what; let's get a few of the lads together later. I might even stretch to a jug of wine or two."

Bram clapped Romy on the shoulder. "I'll hold you to that."

Grinning, they made their way into the guild house.

CHAPTER 2

Toran's Day, the first day of the new year, was ushered in by a blizzard that battered Ral Tora relentlessly for a week. New Year was normally a summer festival in Ral Tora, celebrated by exchanging garlands of flowers. Not this year. Nobody would be dancing on the greens tonight. Instead, people would be huddled in their houses with candles lit against the evening darkness.

Even so, reflected Bram, as he trudged along the street with his hood pulled down and a scarf wrapped round his neck, people were still doing their best to observe the holiday. Where North Road met Chandler Way, a group of singers bravely chanted the lay of Toran and in Trader's Square stalls selling hot-spiced apples and mugs of mulled wine were doing a fair trade. With the streets so busy Bram arrived late at his destination: the memory pool where he'd come to pay his respects to his parents.

A stone basin fifty paces across, the memory pool was fed by carefully directed streams from the great aqueduct above. Many people stood around the pool, silently remembering. Bram took a floating candle from the stack always kept by the pool, lit it carefully and placed it on the pool's surface. As he watched the candle bob gently across the water, memories crowded in: his mother with hair as yellow as the sun, smiling at a joke. His father with the dark eyes and sandy hair Bram had inherited, his nose stuck in a book.

Bram smiled sadly. All gone now. Just memories.

Reluctantly, Bram left the memory pool and made his way back to the guild house. A woman with long black hair and creamy skin jumped to her feet as he opened the door.

"Finally!" snapped Engineer Falen. "I thought you would keep me waiting all morning!"

"What?" Bram asked, flustered by her

outburst.

Falen's green eyes narrowed in annoyance. She thrust a piece of paper at him. "Bramwell Thornley, have you forgotten the meeting?"

It took a moment for Bram to decipher the words through her thick northern accent. "I hadn't forgotten! What time are we supposed to meet the professor?"

"By Rosella's fourth chime. Which was a quarter of a bell ago."

"Oh. We'd better be going then."

Sheepishly, he followed Falen out the door and across town. He felt like a child trailing after an adult. Although roughly his own age, Falen had graduated from the academy two years ago and since then she'd played a vital role in finalizing the plans for the pipe network beneath Ral Tora.

Whilst you were playing pranks on your tutors and getting drunk with your friends, he chided himself.

They turned into the university precinct and approached a rectangular building bearing the sign: *University of Ral Tora, faculty of chemistry, charter granted by Great Father Toran, Year 305.*

"Can I help you?" said a small, aged man sitting behind a desk in the reception area.

Falen showed him their papers. "We're here to meet Professor Strand."

"Ah, yes. He's expecting you. Up the stairs, right, second door along."

They took the stairs and Falen knocked on a shiny wooden door.

A muffled voice came through the wood. "Enter."

A large room greeted them. A battered workbench filled one side, covered with contraptions of all kinds. A clockwork device hanging from the ceiling caught Bram's eye. The machine consisted of several globes and circles moving intricately around each other in a mesmerizing dance. A model of the heavens, Bram realized.

"Ah! You've found my astrolabe!" Professor Strand appeared from behind a bookcase. He had his sleeves rolled up and a dirty white apron covering him from chin to ankles. He was much younger than Bram expected, with spiky brown hair as messy as Bram's own, and wide blue eyes that darted all over the place like a startled rabbit.

"Does it work?" Falen asked. She was staring at the astrolabe with interest.

The professor shook his head. "I've not quite perfected the design yet. Mandrake is moving too quickly and Therlese is orbiting Nervandu at the wrong angle." He grinned. "But I'll get it right! And then those finger-wagging idiots in the physics department will eat their words!"

Falen smiled wistfully. "I could never get mine to work either."

"I'm sorry? What?"

Falen shrugged. "It doesn't matter. I believe you have a prototype to show us."

"Ah yes! Of course! This way, please."

He led them to the workbench on which sat two small bottles shielded behind a glass screen. Next to this was a device consisting of a flat piece of metal with a grill over it that sat upright on little legs. On the top was a button and some sort of feeder pipe.

Strand fished a pair of glasses from his apron pocket and perched them on his nose. He lifted one of the bottles, holding it up for them to see. It contained a dark liquid like treacle.

"Here's the stuff everyone's been getting so excited about!"

Falen leaned forward and examined the bottle. "Curileum?"

"The very thing. This is the first properly refined batch. Watch this."

Strand unstoppered the bottle of curileum and carefully poured some of the thick liquid into the end of the feeder pipe. After waiting for it to dribble down the pipe, he pressed the button on top of the metal contraption.

There was a whooshing noise and flame ignited. The flame spread until it covered the whole of the flat metal plate, burning gently.

"It works!" cried Bram, feeling a wriggle of excitement in his belly.

This device might be just what they needed. The plan so far was to use curileum to heat only large municipal buildings such as the infirmary, schools and government buildings. But the engineers had been working with the university to invent a device that could use curileum to heat people's homes. This might do the trick.

"How did you make this thing?" Bram asked.

Strand looked suitably proud. "The design is much simpler than it looks. This button creates a spark that ignites the curileum in the reservoir at the back. The result is a controlled fire. It will burn as long as the curileum lasts."

Bram felt a spark of excitement inside his belly. Perhaps they could really do it. Perhaps the Engineering Guild's plan to beat the Everwinter could work.

Falen chewed her lip. "Do we have enough fuel to heat the entire city?"

Strand set the bottle back on the bench. "The guild of miners reckon there's enough buried curileum in the plains to last for thousands of years. I'm told the conversion of the old sewers is coming along nicely."

Bram opened his mouth to answer, but Falen cut him off. "Coming along nicely? Hardly a phrase I would use. Yes, the pipes beneath the city are finished but now we have to connect them to the mine. That involves digging beneath the north wall. So no, it's not coming along nicely. Not yet."

Bram cleared his throat, feeling

uncomfortable at Falen's words. "So you want the engineers to begin work on this device?"

Strand nodded. "This is only a rudimentary design which I'm sure you can improve upon. Excellent! Well I think that concludes our business. Do keep me updated on developments, won't you?"

He ushered them out the door and shut it behind them.

"Do you think this will work?" Bram asked Falen as they left the university.

Falen glanced northward, toward her homeland. Bram knew she must miss home. There had been no word from Variss in three years. No word since the great blizzard that brought the Everwinter. No word from the messengers sent north. It weighed heavily on them all.

"It has to," Falen said at last. "What other chance do we have?"

Bram had no answer.

They returned to the guild house where Falen rolled out the plans on the table. Bram leaned over her shoulder, trying to decipher Strand's spidery writing.

Falen scowled at him. "I can manage from here. Why don't you go and see if Rassus has something for you to do?"

Bram hid a flash of annoyance. "We're supposed to work on this together."

"Two engineers aren't needed for this. Your skills would be put to better use elsewhere." When he didn't respond, she said, "I'll put together some ideas for improvements and then we can work together on testing them. How does that sound?"

It was the best offer he would get. "Right. But you'll let me know if you need help?"

Falen had already bent her head over the plans and didn't answer. Bram sighed and left.

Falen was right: Rassus had plenty of things to keep him occupied.

"Get to the north wall!" he barked when Bram presented himself in the chief engineer's office. "Celian's boys are working flat-out. You can oversee one of the digging teams. Can you manage that?"

"Yes, sir," answered Bram, stifling a groan. The north wall was on the other side of the city.

A miserable sleet was falling outside. The people celebrating Toran's day were quickly driven indoors, leaving the streets almost deserted. Bram pulled his coat up around his neck and hurried on. He turned onto North Road and soon found himself trudging across the Forum, the administrative heart of Ral Tora. The Forum housed the Father Hall, where the city fathers conducted the governance of Ral Tora, the House of the Guild Masters, where the complicated business of running the city's commerce went on, and the watch house of the Ral Toran City Watch.

Bram kept close to the buildings, hoping

for a little protection from the elements. Despite his best efforts, great flakes of freezing mush blew into his face and stung his skin.

At the corner of the Forum, set a little apart from the rest, Bram passed a domed building with high windows. It was in a terrible state of disrepair. The domed roof bore a hole that let in the weather and many of the windows were boarded shut. At the bottom of the building's steps, Bram paused and looked up. A cracked statue of an owl stared malevolently down at him, the symbol of Saiis, king of the gods. This building was Ral Tora's ancient temple. It had been abandoned for centuries. Although constructed of good marble by the skills of the ancient engineers, time was finally starting to claim the old building. It would not be long before it collapsed or the city fathers ordered it pulled down to make way for a government building.

It took the best part of an hour before Ral Tora's buildings receded and Bram found himself crossing the open ground before the north wall. The wall stood high and impregnable, as forbidding as a mountain. Guards patrolled the wide parapet atop the wall and manned the watchtowers rearing up on either side of the massive gates. If anyone needed reminding of Ral Tora's power, this sight would do it.

Scaffolding covered much of the north wall and the ground below had become a building site. Sacks of sand and gravel, piles of timber, racks of picks and shovels, teams of horses dragging wagon loads of rubble, all this greeted Bram as he scanned the site for Second Engineer Celian.

"Bram!" a cheerful voice called. "You've been sent to work with us peasants eh?"

He turned to find Romy approaching. At his side walked Seth, a wiry young man with shocking red hair who had been Bram's friend since childhood. Bram grinned and clapped them both on the shoulder.

"Thought I'd come and keep you two from making a mess of things."

Romy snorted, "How thoughtful! Managed to tear yourself away from our beautiful northern wildcat then?"

It was Bram's turn to snort. "Don't let Falen hear you, she'll take your head off for comments like that. Besides, she made it perfectly clear she neither needed nor wanted any help from me."

"Ah. I see. Excellent. You'll be free this afternoon, then. This little rat has talked me into going to the Toran's Day recital. You can come too and save me from an evening of boredom."

"Don't make out you're doing this from the goodness of your heart!" cried Seth indignantly. "It was a fair deal: you come with me to the recital. I do your early shift."

Bram rolled his eyes. "You still haven't

grown out of that stuff, Seth? You're as superstitious as an old woman!"

"Bugger off. You're a pair of philistines."

Bram and Romy grinned at each other. Then Bram threw up his hands. "Fine! I'll come."

Seth smiled, satisfied. "Good. We'll meet here at the end of shift."

"Agreed. Now, I'd better go and find Celian. I'll see you later."

Bram found Celian overseeing the construction of a new set of scaffolding. The Second Engineer quickly dispatched Bram to the tedious task of checking and cataloguing the supplies.

Still, it could have been worse, Bram said to himself, *at least I don't have to go into the digging works.*

He lost himself in tallies, charts and supply orders, and barely noticed as the afternoon began to wear away. As Old Rosella chimed for the third time Bram looked up to see Romy and Seth waving at him from the edge of the supply area. He hurried over to his friends.

"You ready?" asked Seth excitedly. "If we hurry we'll make the start."

They trudged toward Stonetown, Ral Tora's oldest district. Massive villas dominated this part of town and the richest citizens lived within. Passing through the winding streets, they at last reached the entrance to The Mantle, the largest of Ral Tora's three amphitheaters.

Despite the gloom of the cold day, people were streaming through the gates, carrying the traditional Toran's Day candles.

A big man dressed in the uniform of the City Watch approached them. "Don't tell me he's roped you two into this as well?"

Bram recognized Oscar, Seth's older brother. Bram shook his hand and said, "You know he wouldn't give us any peace for a fortnight if we didn't come along."

Oscar snorted. "Ha! Isn't that the truth? Come on then, let's get us some cups of wine, I'll need to be drunk to get through this tedium!"

He dodged the mock punch Seth aimed in his direction and the four of them passed through the gates. A variety of stalls were dotted around the entrance selling all sorts of refreshments. They bought themselves a hot-spiced apple and a mug of mulled wine then picked their way through the crowds to a seat near the front.

Oscar looked around at the crowd. "It's all families," he grumbled. "We must be the only ones here who aren't either a child or a parent. You and your bloody children's tales, Seth! We could be in a tavern right now!"

"Oh, shut your face!" Seth snapped at his brother. "If you stop moaning you might learn something!"

Bram smiled at their bickering. He wrapped his fingers round his mug and took a sip of the hot, sweet wine. The liquid made a lovely warm feeling that traveled down his throat and settled in his stomach.

A hush fell over the crowd. A tall woman with lush black hair wearing a white robe strode out into the middle of the floor.

"My greetings, people of Ral Tora," she said in a strident voice. "Happy New Year!"

Cries of "Happy New Year!" and "Happy Toran's Day!" echoed around the amphitheater. When the cries died away, the woman continued, "What better way to celebrate Toran's Day than to remember the life of our great forefather? Tonight's festivities will begin with *The Lay of Toran*."

The lamps were extinguished. The afternoon outside had already begun to darken so the amphitheater was lit only by hundreds of tiny candles, giving it a strange, otherworldly atmosphere. Into this flickering darkness, the woman began her tale.

"I will take you back into the distant, murky past. Older than the memory of our oldest ancestor, older than the bones of the mountains, is the history of our people.

In the elder days, Thanderley was populated by many strange and powerful beings. Humankind was weak and insignificant, scratching a living from the land in isolated communities hoping to escape the notice of the powerful creatures they lived beside.

In one such community on the southern plains lived a young fisherman called Toran. His people had long lived under the protection of one of the great dragons and in return, they served her. Toran, seeing the subservience of humankind went to his elders and asked, "Why do we serve creatures of magic? Why are we not free?"

To which the elders answered, "Because they are stronger and wiser than us."

"But we are strong and wise also," said Toran.

"It is our place to serve the great ones," answered the elders. "We must not question the way of things."

But Toran was not happy with this answer. He sought out the dragon his people served, a great queen called Teranan.

"I come to ask freedom for my people," he said.

At this, the great dragon laughed and said, "What would you do with your freedom?"

"We would learn and grow and become great."

Teranan considered for a long time. At last she said, "I will make you a deal. I will set you a task and if you complete it successfully, I will free your people and help you to teach them. Do you agree?"

Seeing his chance, Toran said boldly, "I agree."

Teranan nodded gravely. "Very well. I set

you this task: you see the river that flows from this valley? You must stop it from flowing."

Then she departed, leaving Toran to wrestle with the problem. He despaired. The river was strong and powerful. How was he to stop it from flowing? He did not have the strength or the skills for such a task. Then, watching a family of beavers at work, a plan began to form. He went to the beavers and said, "Your skills are unmatched, great builders of the river, but you struggle to feed your young when the winter comes. I have a proposal for you." And so he made a bargain with them. If they dammed the river for him, he would give them the surplus fish from each of his catches.

When Teranan returned she found that a dam had been built across the river and it no longer flowed. She turned to Toran and said, "You have completed the task I set for you. You have shown cunning and foresight. Remember that the greatest skill your kind possess is your intelligence. Use it wisely. Now, I will free your people as I promised."

And so it was that Toran became known as dragon-friend and he rode the breadth of the land on Teranan's back like the ancient gods of old. He learned many things in his travels and eventually he said, "It is time my people had a city of their own." And so he founded the greatest city in the world, our city, Ral Tora."

A chorus of hearty clapping met the end of

the woman's tale. Seth leaned forward eagerly but Romy had slumped down in his seat, scowling. Oscar was snoring softly.

Bram smiled to himself. It was going to be a long night.

CHAPTER 3

Bram rubbed at his eyes then squeezed them shut while waiting for the soreness to pass. He *hated* early shift. The words on the report in front of him blurred until they became an undecipherable muddle of black marks. After he'd read the same sentence for the fifth time he realized it was time to take a break. He stretched his arms behind him and yawned. Outside, all was dark. Although Old

Rosella had chimed her morning chorus, the sun had not yet risen.

He pushed the stack of reports away, stood, and moved over to the fireplace. The kettle was just beginning to whistle.

"Tea?" he said.

Romy sat at a desk opposite and he wasn't faring much better than Bram. He'd been staring at the same page for the last quarter bell, chin resting on his hands. He looked up, eyes bloodshot. "Why not? Are there any biscuits?"

Bram rattled the biscuit tin and was disappointed with the result. "Afraid not. Who's turn was it to get them in?"

"Yours."

"Ah. I'll get some at lunchtime. Promise."

He brewed up two mugs of the scented drink, dropped in a bit of honey to sweeten it, and passed a mug over to Romy. "What are your reports about?"

Romy screwed his face up. "Sanitation. Again. I swear if I read one more complaint about whiffy privies I'm going to scream. What do people expect? There's bound to be some leaks with all this freezing weather. We're not bloody miracle workers! Let *them* go down into the tunnels to fix the damn things and see how they like it!"

Bram winced at Romy's tirade. His friend was not at his best in the mornings.

The door suddenly burst open and Falen

strode in, pencil stuck behind one ear and a stack of papers in her hand.

"I think I've solved the problem," she announced. With a sweep of one arm she sent Bram's reports crashing to the floor then laid out her papers on the desk.

Bram shared a look with Romy, who shrugged. Bram peered over Falen's shoulder.

Falen had scribbled a diagram of Professor Strand's burner on the paper. Around the diagram, she had written little explanations of how each part worked.

"What's this?" Bram said, pointing to a small rectangular box on top of the burner.

"That's what I'm talking about," Falen replied, frowning at Bram as if he was stupid. "Strand said the main problem with his invention was keeping the flame confined as it ignites. If there is too much curileum coming through when the ignition button is pressed it sends out a jet of flame which is a fire hazard."

"So this box stops that from happening?" Bram was having trouble following Falen's line of reasoning. It was too early in the morning for thinking.

"Exactly. If we encase the ignition button in glass we can keep a small flame burning continually–a pilot light if you like–so when it's ignited, the flame will be encased within the glass and will be much safer."

"Good plan," Bram said, sipping his tea. He'd made it too hot and it burnt his tongue.

"How easy will it be to modify the gas burners?"

"Well, if we keep—"

The inner door swung open with a creak and Chief Engineer Rassus swept out of his office with a face like a thundercloud. "Message just arrived from the Father Hall," he snapped. "Emergency meeting. Come on."

He headed for the door. Bram, Falen and Romy grabbed their coats.

"Not you. You can stay here," Rassus said, pointing at Romy.

"But this meeting must be important," Romy protested. "I don't want to miss it!"

"Tough. Somebody needs to stay here until the next shift comes on. And that somebody is you. Clear?"

Romy opened his mouth and shut it again. Reluctantly he took his coat off and slumped back down into his chair, arms crossed against his chest. Bram shot his friend a sympathetic look and then hurried out before Rassus decided he should stay behind as well.

The wind outside cut straight through Bram. He shivered, hunkering down into his coat.

Ideas buzzed around inside Bram's head. *An emergency meeting! What does it mean? Perhaps there's been an accident at the mine. Or maybe some problem with the digging works? Ye gods! I hope the wall hasn't collapsed!*

Lamps burned in the Forum, leading to the

Father Hall. Rassus bounded up the steps two at a time, nodded to the guards stationed on either side of the massive iron doors, and then strode inside.

Bram had visited the Father Hall on only a handful of occasions and its grandeur still had the power to impress him. The vestibule which they entered was richly furnished. A colorful mosaic covered the floor and a huge statue of Great Father Toran stood at the far end.

Falen and Rassus did not even glance at the furnishings but strode purposefully ahead. Bram trotted to keep up.

They entered a wide audience chamber affectionately called 'The Moot'. Although it had been originally designed for receiving visiting dignitaries, the room now served as a meeting place for the city's leaders. A huge round table dominated the room, at which sat the most powerful people in Ral Tora. Yellow-robed city fathers, opulently dressed merchants and uniformed officers of the City Watch.

Father Hewin, the somber-faced Speaker of the Council was addressing the assembly. He saw the newcomers and said, "Ah! Chief Engineer Rassus, we've been waiting for you. Please, sit down."

Rassus took a vacant chair at the table and Bram and Falen seated themselves on either side. Father Hewin nodded to the guards and they swung the heavy doors shut. Father

Hewin sat down, clasping his hands in his lap. Silence descended. All eyes turned expectantly to a figure seated on a grand chair at the far side of the table.

Great Father Samarin climbed wearily to his feet. He'd been Ral Tora's leader for as long as Bram could remember. He had aged and put on weight in recent years, his hair had become as white as bleached bone and he walked with the aid of a cane. Yet his eyes were still as strong as Bram remembered, and he carried himself with quiet authority. Like the city he ruled, the Great Father's presence was as immovable as rock.

"Thank you all for coming at this early hour," he said into the silence. "But I think you will agree that it was necessary." His pale blue eyes swept the gathering. "A messenger has arrived from Variss."

Gasps of surprise echoed around the chamber. The color drained from Falen's face.

"Variss?" Rassus asked. "After all this time?"

Samarin nodded. "In the middle of the night the guards on the north gate were alerted to somebody wandering around outside. They apprehended the man and brought him straight to me. I think you should all hear what he has to say."

Samarin signaled to the guards. They swung the doors open and a man strode through. He was tall, with wide shoulders and muscular arms. A leather band tied around his forehead held back shiny black tresses. He had chiseled features and, Bram thought sourly, the kind of face women swooned over.

But something didn't seem right. The man's hands moved continually, wiping at each other as though he twisted an unseen rag. The man's deep-set eyes flicked over the assembly, skipping from face to face. His gaze stopped on Bram. Their eyes met. The hairs on Bram's neck rose. Then the man looked away and the feeling passed.

"My name is Tomas Eorlsson," the man said in the heavy, guttural accent of the north. "I come to tell you of the fall of Variss."

Falen gasped. "Explain that," she demanded.

Tomas nodded in her direction. "You and I, and others who were absent from Variss, may be the only survivors. We are exiles now. Our home is destroyed." His gaze snapped to the assembly again and his voice took on an empty, toneless quality. "Almost three years ago, a terrible blizzard descended from the Sisters. It was spring, a time when the weather is unpredictable, but we'd never seen the like of this storm. In Variss many of the old and infirm died before the tempest blew itself out. But that was not the worst. An avalanche came down from Black Seza. Half the mountain fell away. We had no warning. It buried Variss under tons of rock and ice." He looked at Falen once more. "I'm sorry."

"The king?" Falen asked in a choked whisper.

Tomas shook his head. "I don't know. King Beorl left the city before the blizzard came."

Great Father Samarin spread his hands on the table. "Terrible news. Yet not unexpected. We feared the worst, having heard nothing from Variss in all this time."

A ball of numbness formed in Bram's stomach. He'd never been to Variss. Come to think of it, he'd never been further than the Isle of Ashon, but he'd always expected that one day he would see ancient Variss, Queen of the North.

An entire city destroyed. All those people. Is that the fate lying in store for Ral Tora? Are we deluding ourselves with our grand plans to save the city? Will the winter come south and devour us as well?

Somebody coughed. Father Erris, a fleshy man who made his yellow father's robe look like a tent, leaned forward, hands clasped on the table.

"Your tale puzzles me," he said to Tomas. "You say the avalanche destroyed Variss three years ago? So where have you been all this time? Why hadn't we heard this before now?"

The question seemed to confuse Tomas. "I don't understand."

"It's a simple question. Did you visit Tirsay or Chellin? Have you been sheltering in

Esclede? And if so, why haven't they sent us word?"

Tomas fixed Father Erris with his dark gaze. His brow furrowed. "I haven't been to Tirsay or Chellin or Esclede. I brought my tale straight to Ral Tora."

Father Erris glanced around at the other city fathers and then spread his pudgy hands wide. "But that makes no sense. Why would you travel all the way to Ral Tora when either Tirsay or Chellin are many leagues closer to Variss? Why travel the length of the continent?"

For the first time, doubt flickered across Tomas's face. His hands moved furiously, dry-washing something that wasn't there. "I...I ..." he faltered, unable to find the words. "I... I was compelled to come here, to warn you. I... I cannot remember."

"Cannot remember what?" pressed Father Erris. "Where you have been for the last three years?"

"I have been...gone... for a long time. I was taken. Taken beyond, into..." Tomas screwed his eyes shut, as though unwilling to look on a memory. "My mission. To find...to protect...to find..." His words trailed off.

Great Father Samarin raised his hand to silence Father Erris, "Don't push the man, Erris. He's been through an ordeal. We'll question him further when he's had time to recover."

Tomas's eyes popped open. "I come to warn you!" he cried. "The Old Gods are coming! They have captured the north! They are coming here, to Ral Tora, because you hold what they most desire. You must not let them find it!"

Samarin laid a hand on Tomas's arm but he shrugged it off. "You have not seen what I have seen! Vias dorea! Vias dorea vo carthamon!"

He collapsed into a ball on the floor, arms wrapped around his head. Samarin waved at the guards who gently lifted Tomas to his feet and led him away.

When he'd gone Great Father Samarin said, "Anyone know what he was saying?"

"It was an ancient Varisean dialect," Falen replied in a shaky voice. She turned her engineer's badge over and over in her hand. "Translated he said, 'Save me. Save me from the demons in the ice.'"

Her words shocked everyone into silence.

Father Erris was the first to regain his composure. "Are we supposed to believe all this? Have you brought a mad man to our council, Samarin? We've no proof he is who he claims. How did he escape Variss if it was destroyed? How did he make the perilous journey here alone? It just doesn't make sense. He's either insane or a liar."

"Why do you accuse him of lying?" Falen asked. "This is the first news of Variss in all this time and you dismiss him out of hand."

"You heard his words!" Erris retorted. "Babbling about old gods and demons! Correct me if I am wrong, but isn't that the sort of drivel the Wailers spout? I think we've been duped. This is a hoax!"

Bram said, "He didn't seem like a Wailer to me. He looked terrified. I think he was telling the truth."

Father Erris snorted. "Engineer Thornley, do you really believe such gibberish? It's obvious that the Wailers are trying to infect the council with their superstitious nonsense. If you believe otherwise, you're more of a child than I thought."

Anger rose, hot and quick, in Bram's chest. Before he could stop himself, he said, "And you're narrow-minded. It's attitudes like yours that will get us all killed!"

Father Erris went as pale as milk. His piggy eyes bulged in his face. "How dare you? How dare you speak to a city father that way? I will not tolerate such insolence!"

Bram held Erris's gaze, refusing to look away. Chief Engineer Rassus grabbed Bram's arm with bony fingers.

"You overstep the mark, boy. Apologize to the father. Now!"

Everyone was watching Bram. He forced the words past a tightness in his throat. "I apologize, Father. I didn't mean to insult you."

Father Erris glowered at him. A vein in his

temple throbbed. Finally he said, "Sit down, Engineer Thornley. I think we've had enough of your opinions."

Bram did as he was told. He realized he had made a powerful enemy. *Bramwell Thornley, you dolt!* He berated himself. *When will you learn to connect your brain and your mouth?*

Great Father Samarin said, "Father Erris thinks this to be a hoax. What say the rest of you?"

Falen stood. "Great Father, if what Tomas says is true, and he did survive this avalanche, there's a chance others may have survived Variss's destruction. We'll never know unless we send a delegation to find out."

Some in the room banged their hands on the table in agreement. Many had friends or relatives in Variss.

Father Erris scowled. "Are you seriously saying we should send men — men we cannot spare — to the north to investigate the ravings of a mad man? What would it achieve? We have already sent messengers and none of them returned!"

"If there's the slimmest chance of survivors we must help them!"

"Even if Tomas is telling the truth, you heard what he said—there were no survivors! Besides, if anyone should mount an expedition to Variss it should be Tirsay or Chellin. They're much closer to Variss. It's not our problem!"

Falen's face reddened. "Not our problem? Should we just turn our backs then? Leave the people of Variss to rot?" In her anger, Falen's accent was becoming thick, making her harder and harder to understand. Soon she was likely to start cursing.

Erris sighed. "Don't be dramatic. I am only stating the facts. Ral Tora is facing her own crisis. We must focus our resources on that."

Erris's words carried weight. Many at the table nodded.

Falen muttered something under her breath. She slumped back in her chair and folded her arms across her chest. Great Father Samarin leaned forward.

"We'll vote. All those in favor of sending an expedition to Variss raise your hands."

Falen's hand shot into the air. Bram quickly followed her example. There were no others.

The Great Father nodded. "Fine. There'll be no expedition. Tomas will go to a healer, and I'll look into this being a Wailers' hoax. If so, I'll close down that scare-mongering sect for good. Thank you all for coming, I'll keep you from your tasks no longer."

Everyone began to file out.

Bram was heading for the door when the Great Father called, "Bram, wait. I'd like a word."

Bram groaned inwardly. Why didn't he keep his stupid mouth shut? Bram approached the Great Father and spread his hands innocently. "Great Father, I know I shouldn't speak to Father Erris that way, it's just—"

"That's not what concerns me. Sometimes Erris is too full of wind for his own good."

Bram grinned. "I think I'll avoid him for a few days all the same."

The Great Father nodded. "Most wise." Samarin cocked his head to the side, regarding Bram. At last he said, "I've been most impressed with you today. You've shown a rare compassion. I've a job for you. I'm putting you in charge of Tomas. I want you to talk to him. See if you can get any sense out of him. My heart tells me there's more to this than some Wailer's hoax."

Bram's heart sank. He didn't feel like being a nursemaid. "Why me?"

The Great Father placed a hand on Bram's shoulder. "You and Tomas appear to be about the same age. He'll relate to you better than a stuffy old city father."

"I'll do my best," Bram said. "I'll do my best."

CHAPTER 4

Bram padded through the corridors of the Father Hall in danger of getting lost. He'd already ended up in the kitchens — much to the annoyance of the cook — and had only found his way back with the help of a knowledgeable servant. Although he was trying to follow the Great Father's directions, the maze of rooms, corridors, landings and staircases was making his head spin.

Turning a corner, Bram entered a corridor carpeted in green. He halted, looking around. Had this place been in Samarin's directions? If so, Bram had forgotten it. Scratching his head, he sat down on a velvet-cushioned stool to get his bearings. His eyes strayed to the paintings on the walls. Watercolors of Thanderley's great cities met his gaze: Ral Tora, Esclede, Tirsay, Chellin and last of all, doomed Variss. Bram squinted up at the painting. He wondered if the massive, fortified citadel that crouched at the base of the mountains like some snarling beast was a true depiction of Variss. Falen would know. Had she ever seen these paintings?

In the distance, Old Rosella chimed. Time was marching on.

Turn right after the long corridor, the Great Father had said.

Bram strode through the door and turned right.

At the staircase, go two floors up.

At the top of these stairs, Bram found a wide landing with four doors leading off. A pair of guards stood at one of them.

Bram breathed a sigh of relief. He handed a piece of paper to a guard who read it and raised an eyebrow at Bram.

"So you're the poor bugger they've sent? Good luck, my friend. He's totally crackers, if you ask me." The guard lifted a tray from the floor and handed it to Bram. "We saved his breakfast. Perhaps you'll have better luck than we did."

Bram took the tray and mumbled his thanks. He pushed through the door backward, holding the tray against his chest. As the door opened, a cold breeze brushed his skin. Goosebumps rode up his arms.

Bram entered a lavishly furnished guest room. He edged over to the bed and set the breakfast tray down on a bedside table. Tomas had thrown the windows open and was slumped in a chair, staring out over the balcony toward the north.

The room was so cold that Bram's breath misted in the air. Incredibly though, Tomas was wearing only a thin shirt. Bram gaped at him. What was wrong with the man?

"Hello?" Bram ventured. No response. "Do you mind if I light a fire? I'm freezing."

Tomas remained silent. Bram moved over to the fireplace where a stack of logs sat untouched. He tossed a few logs into the fireplace and took flint and tinder from his pocket. He made some kindling from wood shavings, and struck a spark.

Tomas sprang to his feet with a howl. He stamped on the log, sending it skittering over the floor, leaving a black smear on the carpet.

Bram sat back, shocked.

"No," Tomas panted. "No fire. I'm burning."

Tomas's face and arms gleamed with sweat.

"Fine, no fire," Bram said, swallowing. "Do you mind if I light the lamps?"

Tomas stared at him silently. "It's you. I knew you'd come."

"Er, yes. I'm Bram. The Great Father sent me. Can I light the lamps?"

Tomas shrugged. "If you like."

Bram levered himself to his feet. He moved around the room, lighting the lamps. He pulled one of the thick blankets from the bed and threw it around his shoulders. He regarded Tomas. The Varisean had resumed his seat and was staring silently at Bram with lidded eyes.

What have I gotten myself into? Bram said to himself. *I'm an engineer, not a nursemaid!*

He picked up the breakfast tray, placed it next to Tomas and took a vacant seat. Bram moved his tongue in a suddenly dry mouth, working up enough saliva to speak.

"My name is Bramwell Thornley. I've brought your breakfast. You must be starving, especially after such a long journey."

No answer.

Bram pulled the cloth off the tray, revealing some pieces of cold chicken, a wedge of white cheese, a loaf of bread and a small bottle of mead. Bram picked up a piece of the chicken and nibbled on it.

"This is very good. Do you want a bit?"

Tomas gazed at Bram, at the piece of chicken, then back to Bram. Slowly he reached out, took the chicken from Bram's hand, and nibbled it like a rodent. After a moment, he seemed satisfied and took a big bite, swallowing without chewing.

Bram forced a smile. "That's good, isn't it?"

Tomas grinned suddenly, revealing perfect white teeth. "Yes. Is there more?"

Bram pointed to the tray at Tomas's feet. Tomas put it on his lap, tore off a big chunk of bread and offered it to Bram.

Bram shook his head. "No, you eat it. I've already had my breakfast."

Tomas dropped the bread onto the tray.

Bram held out a hand. "On second thoughts, I would love a piece of bread."

When Tomas had seen Bram eat the whole piece, he seemed satisfied. He grabbed the loaf and tore off great chunks with his teeth and then polished off the cheese.

Tomas set the tray on the floor, leaving the bottle of mead untouched.

Bram nodded at it. "Not thirsty?"

"It's liquid. Liquid freezes." He seemed to think this was explanation enough.

Bram shook his head. "It won't freeze, the temperature's not cold enough in here. This is alcohol; it freezes at much lower temperatures than water."

Tomas sat back in his chair, dark eyes flashing. "Doesn't matter, *they* could freeze it. *They* can freeze anything. Even blood."

Bram didn't know what to say. He opened his mouth and then closed it again. Tomas's gaze made him uncomfortable. Why had the Great Father gotten him into this? He leant back in his chair, drumming his fingers on his knees.

Tomas stared at him.

What am I supposed to do now? He wondered.

The Great Father wanted him to befriend Tomas. Bram tried to think of something to say.

"Do you like your room?" he managed at last.

Tomas blinked rapidly. "My room?"

"Yes, your room. This room." Bram indicated the space around them.

Tomas swiveled in his chair. He seemed to notice his surroundings for the first time. "Yes," he said. "My room. Lovely."

Silence descended. Outside a dog barked. The muffled sound of the guards' conversation came through the door.

"Your people think I'm mad," Tomas said.

The statement startled Bram. "I, er, I…"

"You're right to fear me but not for the reasons you think." Tomas leaned forward, his handsome face intense. "I've traveled a long way, through horrors you cannot imagine. Why do you suppose I did that?"

"I don't know," Bram stammered.

A small, tight smile flickered across Tomas's face. "I was given a task and I mean to fulfill it. They are coming. You don't have much time."

"Who is coming?"

Tomas turned his head and stared northwards. "Read your histories. Open your eyes. You've been blind for too long."

Bram placed a hand on Tomas's arm. "What do you mean?"

Tomas recoiled as though Bram's touch was poison. He leapt from the chair and backed up against the far wall. His eyes had gone dark, full of shadow.

Bram's heart pounded. Time to go. Slowly, he began levering himself up from his seat. Tomas sprang at him, pinning him to the chair. Hands like claws knotted in Bram's shirt and pulled his face close.

Tomas's eyelids flickered suddenly and his eyes rolled back in his head. He opened his mouth wide and a long, deep, sigh escaped. His lips curled up and the breath he exhaled stank of smoke.

"You must save me!" he said in a voice that sounded like nails scraping over slate. "Come north. Save me!"

Tomas leaned closer, his breath enveloping Bram like a cloud. "Come north! Come to me!"

Bram yelped in terror. "Let go!"

Tomas's mouth twisted into a snarl. His eyes narrowed to slits. A low moan escaped his lips.

Bram grabbed Tomas's shoulders, trying to push him off, but as his palms touched Tomas's skin, Bram wailed in sudden pain and snatched them away.

Tomas blinked. Abruptly he let go of Bram's shirt, scuttled across the room and hunched himself in a corner. He pulled his knees up to his chest and wrapped his arms around them.

Bram looked at his hands. Puckered burns covered his palms. Bram stared in horror. He heaved himself to his feet, ran to the door and wrenched it open. The guards started in surprise as he ran past.

"Did you get him to eat anything?" one of them called.

Bram didn't answer. He just ran.

CHAPTER 5

Astrid stood at the prow of the ship and watched the shore approach. The wind tore at her golden hair and whipped spray into her face, but she barely noticed. She was so near her goal.

"My lady!" someone cried. "We're almost at land fall!"

Yes, I can see that, Astrid thought. *I do have eyes.*

Astrid permitted herself a smile of triumph. They had made it! At last, this goddess-forsaken voyage was over! Nothing had gone right since the moment she had first set foot on the smooth deck of *Stormdancer*. If not for the guidance of the tashen, Astrid knew her ships would have foundered on the treacherous reefs or been lost in one of the wild storms that battered the coast. If Astrid had been a superstitious woman, she would swear her mission was cursed.

And I know who'd be the perpetrator of any curse, she thought. *May the Goddess smite that priest and his damn meddling!*

Thoughts of a tall, blond-haired man flickered into her mind. Tamardi Di Goron, High Priest of the Goddess, spiritual leader of the city of Chellin, and the bane of Astrid's life.

Even here, so far from home, the thought of the high priest made Astrid's blood boil. The arrogance of the man! The way he strutted and preened, throwing his weight around whenever he could. *She* was the ruler of Chellin, not him! She ought to have arranged for him to have a little 'accident' long ago. She would have, except the senate would start asking tricky questions.

Astrid was certain the high priest had used his powers to try to sink her ships. What else could explain them being pushed so far off course?

"My lady?"

The deep voice broke into her thoughts. Rama, Astrid's bodyguard, was regarding her with his steely gray eyes. Rama's stance looked relaxed — shoulders back and feet apart — but his hand rested on the hilt of his sword and his chiseled face was alert. A few steps behind him, Aeron, Astrid's second guard, leaned nonchalantly against a water barrel. To most eyes, he would look tranquil, paying her no attention, but after all the years he'd been by her side, Astrid had learned to spot the tell-tale glint in his blue eyes as he perpetually scanned for danger.

"Yes, Rama?"

Rama jerked a thumb in the direction of the coastline. "We'll be going ashore soon. It's time to bid the tashen farewell."

Astrid nodded curtly and followed Rama to the aft deck where a crowd had gathered. Mattack, the balding first minister, handed her the ritual scepter and salt as she came abreast of him. To Astrid's amusement, he still looked as sick as a beached kracka. Mattack had never gotten used to sea travel. To think — a Chellin, afraid of the sea!

Astrid smiled sweetly. "Still feeling unwell, Mattack?"

The first minister managed a weak smile. "Let's just say, my lady, I'll be glad when my feet touch solid ground once more."

Astrid placed her hands on the aft rail and looked out. The ocean was a rolling mass of gray water. A freezing rain had started to fall, stinging the skin as it hit and turning the sky into a muddy blanket. Through the downpour, Astrid spied the strip of coastline they'd soon be heading for.

Ral Tora, she thought, *I never thought I'd be making my first trip here under these circumstances.*

The three ships of Astrid's fleet pulled abreast of each other and then dropped anchor so they bobbed slowly up and down in the choppy waves like large, ungainly sea birds. People filled the decks of all three ships. Word of the farewell ritual had spread, and all were eager to show their homage to the tashen. Even the crews had left their tasks.

Such a superstitious lot, Astrid thought, *and who can blame them? These evil times will make beggars of us all.*

Astrid raised her arms up to the sky and let her hair whip out behind like a cloak. In one hand, she held the pot of salt, in the other, the scepter. In a strident voice she shouted, "Lords of Air and Water! We salute you! Come forth so we may pay our homage!"

The words died into silence, devoured by the wind. For a second there was stillness. Then the sea began to boil. In answer to Astrid's call, two massive creatures broke the surface of the water. Long, snake-like bodies of glistening black scales writhed, whipping the sea into white foam. Enormous, wedge-shaped heads rose out of the sea, and the beasts reared up and up until their eyes were level with the deck of *Stormdancer*.

Astrid spread her arms wide and dropped into a deep bow. "Well met, my guardians.

You have guided us faithfully on this long journey, and we owe you our thanks and our lives. Now comes the time of our parting. Long have our races been friends and long may it remain so. Go now with our blessings. Until we meet again, by the scepter of the air and the salt of the sea, I renew and seal our bargain. May you call on us when you are in need and be sure we will answer."

She touched the heads of the tashen with the scepter, and then leaned over the rail and tipped the salt into the sea. She raised her arms to the sky once more and shouted, "Tashen, hail!"

On the three ships, the people responded, "Hail!"

The tashen bowed their heads and then sank back beneath the waves.

Mattack sidled up to Astrid, screwing his face up against the rain. "Nicely done, my lady. We need the tashen, now more than ever."

Astrid nodded. "I'm grateful for their help on this journey. If not for them we would have been smashed to pieces long before we got here."

"Let us be thankful we reached our destination in one piece."

Astrid held Mattack's gaze for a moment, searching for hidden meaning in his words.

How many enemies do I have aboard this ship? she thought. *If I cannot even trust Mattack...I'm getting paranoid.*

Pushing all such thoughts away, Astrid called for Ravi, the stable master. As he emerged from below decks and trotted over to her, Astrid screwed up her resolve. Time to get off this tub. Time to put her plans into motion.

Ravi inclined his red-fringed head. "My lady?"

"I think it's time we released the dolarchu, Master Stableman. I'm surprised they've not tried to chew their way out of the hold by now."

Ravi grinned. "They've been a bit restive of late; perhaps they smelled the tashen."

"The dolarchu will be safe now the tashen are gone. Make the preparations."

"Yes, my lady." With a small bow, Ravi spun away and began calling orders.

Astrid watched the stable master go then looked at the coast again. Curling her gloved hands round the rail, she savored the hard solidity of the wood, as if it could anchor her courage in place.

Give me the strength for this, Lady.

The soft pitter-patter of rain on the deck was getting heavier, becoming a steady drumming that formed the background to Astrid's thoughts. The coastline, obscured by misty rain, seemed strange and mysterious, as though it held secrets behind its gray veil.

What awaits us there? Astrid asked herself. *Glory? Ruin?*

If she failed here the high priest would seize control of the senate, and if that happened...

I won't let it happen! I will be dead before I see that black-hearted whoreson ruling my city! I should have had him killed when he first started sniffing round the senate. If he stood before me now I'd cut out his whining tongue. I'd slice out his liver, the lying sniveling toad, I'd —

"My lady?"

Astrid jumped. "What?"

Rama lifted an eyebrow. "I said, are you ready to go ashore now?"

"Yes," Astrid replied curtly. "But I wish to see the dolarchu safely to shore first. Where is Ravi?"

"At the stern awaiting your pleasure."

"Come on, all of you." She marched off and the little entourage of ministers, guards and sycophants that always followed her, stepped into line behind.

The stable master was leaning on the rail, looking down. He waved briefly to something over the side, then bowed to Astrid. "All's ready, my lady. Chen will see them safely to shore."

Astrid followed his gaze. Below, a small boat bobbed in the waves. Stableman Chen sat in the boat, attaching a lantern to a pole in the stern of the vessel. At a signal from Ravi, Chen gathered the oars and began to row. The little boat set off.

Ravi pulled a rope dangling from a yardarm. A hatch in the ship's hull slid open and a brown muzzle poked tentatively out. It sniffed the air and was followed by a pair of large, luminous eyes, and a sleek brown head topped by two little ears. The dolarchu looked around, its nose working continually. Then it spied the lantern on the rowing boat and the beast's training took hold. It leapt into the sea and sped after the craft, its graceful body cutting through the water with ease. A second dolarchu followed the first, then another and another. Soon the boat and beasts were lost to sight amongst the gray waves.

Astrid's heart quickened. There was no going back now. She addressed her entourage. "Time to go ashore. Make everything ready."

A short time later, Astrid was scrambling down the ladder into her yacht as nimbly as a street urchin. The yacht rocked slightly as it took her weight, but Astrid paid it no heed and scrambled over to one end, where a canopy covered a cushioned area — the boat builder's effort at providing comfort for the Regal.

The people aboard *Mystery* and *Scimitar* had also disembarked, and a little flotilla of vessels bobbed on the sea, their occupants wearing looks of apprehension.

Astrid waited with ill grace as they rowed to shore. She wanted to get on with it. Several times minister Mattack tried to speak to her about their policy for this mission, but each time Astrid snapped at him until he finally gave up and went to remonstrate with the quartermaster instead.

Stupid man! Why does he fuss like an old woman?

Rama leaned over and said quietly, "That was not well done, my lady. Minister Mattack fusses to hide his fear. For this mission to succeed you need his support."

Astrid glared at Rama. *Who does he think he is?* But Rama's gray eyes didn't flinch, and her anger leaked away.

Damn the man! Why is he always right?

"Minister Mattack. Would you attend me please?" she called.

Mattack, who was giving the quartermaster a list of supplies to purchase in Ral Tora, turned in Astrid's direction. A look of injured pride flashed across his features and Astrid realized Rama was correct. Injured pride might easily turn into resentment, and that was something she could ill afford.

Astrid smiled sweetly. "I'd like to hear your thoughts on this expedition if you would, minister. Your good counsel would greatly ease my worries."

Mattack's face broke into a grin, and Astrid knew she had him. "Certainly, my lady. I am, as always, at your disposal."

Men! Astrid thought to herself. *A coy smile and a bit of flattery and they turn to jelly!*

Arranging her features into a look of

intense interest, Astrid nodded at intervals as Mattack began his flow of pompous bluster. It was only a short journey, but for Astrid it couldn't be over quick enough. When the bottom of the yacht scraped the beach, Astrid jumped up, mumbled her thanks to the first minister, then jumped over the side and waded onto shore.

As the rest of the party embarked in a statelier manner, Astrid hiked up her robe, and ran up the beach to where Chen was waiting.

"In a hurry, my lady?" Chen said with a grin, "I've never seen Mattack look so shocked!"

"Good! I'm so glad to be off that ship!"

The feel of earth under her feet made Astrid feel light-headed with relief. She felt like doing a little jig right there on the beach. Instead, she placed a long-fingered hand on Chen's arm. "How is Nallak?"

The thick-set stableman shrugged. "As well as can be expected. Their confinement in the hold has taken its toll, as you'll see."

Astrid felt a stab of guilt. She heard a reprimand behind Chen's words. Perhaps she should have left the dolarchu at home. But Astrid had brought them because they would impress the Ral Torans, and she wanted to have as much impact on the southerners as possible.

She followed Chen up the gently sloping beach. The half-frozen sand crunched and popped as Astrid walked and the wind moved round to the west, driving the rain into Astrid's face. After a hundred paces or so, the beach gave out onto dunes and hillocks covered in stunted, windblown vegetation.

In the shelter created by a fallen black pine, the dolarchu had been tethered. The beasts moved around restlessly, and whickered irritably at each other.

Chen led Astrid to the beast standing at the front of the group of animals. Astrid stared up at Nallak and smiled.

"There you are, old boy. Have you missed me?"

Nallak turned his grizzled muzzle and blew a jet of hot air in Astrid's face, a sign of his annoyance. Despite his age, he was an impressive beast. The dolarchu were the largest species of sea otter, and Astrid sent thanks to her ancestors who had decided to tame the great beasts. Astrid stroked Nallak's head, muttering apologies for shutting him in the hold of the ship.

When he was saddled up, Nallak knelt down and allowed Astrid to mount. Astrid waited for Rama and Aeron to catch up, then called a soft command to send Nallak ambling off along the beach.

Rama and Aeron came abreast of Astrid as they reached the end of the beach. A large, curving bay lay ahead. Rocks poked above the sea like jagged teeth.

"Is this the place?" Astrid asked.

Rama nodded, pointing toward the sea. "See the shadow beneath the water? That's the wreck of *The Search*. It can still be seen at low tide."

Astrid strained her eyes. Yes, there was a dark smudge beneath the water, about the right size and shape for a shipwreck.

"*The Search*," Astrid breathed. "This is where she and the boy came ashore. It begins, then."

Astrid turned Nallak around and they rejoined the rest of the party. Astrid took her place at the front of the column and, with Rama and Aeron on either side, led her people inland, toward Ral Tora.

CHAPTER 6

The corridors of the Father Hall whirled past in a kaleidoscope of color. Bram bolted down the entrance steps and skidded to a halt at the bottom, heart thudding. His hands throbbed, a steady rhythm that matched the beating of his heart.

What am I supposed to do now? He thought.

The Great Father had gotten him into this, the Great Father could bloody well get him out of it!

He trotted down Cooper's Row, turned into Saddle Street, and approached a small town house. Two watchmen stood outside. Four square windows looked out onto the street, spilling light from beneath the curtains.

As Bram approached, the guards snapped to attention.

"I need to speak to the Great Father. My name is Bramwell Thornley, a city engineer."

One of the guards nodded. "Stay here."

Bram waited, stamping his feet, while the other guard stared at him suspiciously. After a while, the first guard returned.

"The Great Father says he'll see you. Follow me."

Bram shuffled along behind him, grateful to be getting out of the cold. They passed under the lintel and into a long corridor. At the end of this they entered a small room with a low, beamed ceiling. A huge fire blazed in a hearth in one corner with two easy chairs lounging before it. Bookcases lined the walls from top to bottom and in every available space were crammed manuscripts and parchments of all kinds. A big oak table filled the back of the chamber, piled high with books in no discernible order.

The Great Father sat in a chair by the fire. Someone with their back to Bram sat in the other chair. The Great Father waved to Bram and the guard, indicating for them to wait. He handed a handkerchief to the person in the other chair and there came the sound of someone blowing their nose. The Great Father patted the other person's knee.

"There, child," he said in a gentle voice. "I hope you understand now why I cannot override the wishes of the council. I appreciate how you must feel. I'm sorry."

The person nodded and stood. It was Falen. Her midnight hair was disheveled and her uniform crumpled. She thanked the Great Father in a quiet voice and headed for the door.

Bram said, "Are you all right, Falen?"

Falen looked at him with despair in her eyes. She seemed about to say something but then swept past in silence.

"Ah, Bram," said the Great Father. "I didn't expect to see you so soon." He nodded to the guard. "It's all right, Barus, you can go back to your post. Marion has made a mug of spiced wine for you and Angus. They're in the kitchen."

Barus nodded his thanks and left.

The Great Father sighed. "Sometimes, Bram, being the Great Father feels like being a toddler. Everyone thinks you need looking after. Even though the temperature outside is virtually unbearable, Barus and Angus refuse to come into the house, or to go home. Anybody would think I am a baby, incapable of caring for myself. Let's hope you never get saddled with the job of Great Father, eh?" He cackled loudly and slumped down into the chair. "Well come in, lad, take a seat."

Bram nervously moved into the center of

the room and stood there, waiting.

The Great Father leaned forward, his elbows resting on his knees. "Bram, you either sit down or this meeting is ended right now. You can't expect an old man to stare up at you all the time. I will get a crick in my neck."

"Yes, Great Father. Sorry." Bram slid into a chair. It had been pulled close to the fire and the cushions were already warm. It felt wonderful but the heat made the burns on his hands smart. He placed them palm upwards on his knees and curled his fingers round like claws, trying to find the most comfortable position.

Samarin leaned forward. "What is it, Bram?"

"It's Tomas, sir," Bram began. "I think there's something wrong with him."

Samarin frowned. "Yes, I should say so. He obviously has some medical issues that need addressing—"

"I don't mean that. I mean, I think…There's something bad in him. Something dangerous."

"What do you mean? Bram, I think you should start from the beginning."

So Bram did. He told the Great Father of his encounter with Tomas from the time he'd entered the room to when he'd ran in terror. When he came to the part where Tomas had grabbed him, he found his voice faltering and the fear came flooding back, making his heart pound once more.

Throughout his story the Great Father remained silent, his brow creased in concern. When Bram had finished, Samarin pursed his lips for a moment. "I owe you an apology, Bram. I shouldn't have asked you to visit Tomas. His delirium is far more pronounced than I thought, and he seems more dangerous than I gave him credit for."

"Great Father, I don't think he's delirious, I think it's more than that. There's something... odd about him. He frightened the life out of me. It was like there was something else inside him."

The Great Father stared at him. He seemed to be weighing up his next words carefully. "I realize now that a healer should have seen Tomas immediately, and we could have diagnosed his condition straight away. Tomas seems to be suffering from a disease of the mind."

Annoyance rose up in Bram. He thrust his palms toward Samarin, so he could clearly see the burns. "Would a disease cause someone to do this?"

Samarin examined Bram's hands. "What have you done to yourself?"

"I didn't do it. Tomas did. He attacked me. I tried to push him off, but when I touched him, this happened."

The Great Father took Bram's hands in his and pulled them onto his lap. He peered at the burns and then shook his head.

"You say this was caused by touching Tomas's skin?"

Bram nodded.

"These burns must be treated right away."

He rose and went over to a shelf. The Great Father rummaged around for a while and pulled out a small green jar. He took out the stopper, allowing a smell like rotting tree bark to steal through the room. The Great Father wrinkled his nose.

"Ah, still good. Hold out your hands, Bram."

"What's that?" Bram asked suspiciously.

"Something to help those burns. Now hold out your hands!"

Bram reluctantly held them out, palm upwards.

The Great Father stuck his finger in the jar and scraped out a gray paste. He smeared a generous portion all over the burns on Bram's hands. Next, he fished some bandages from the shelf and wrapped them around Bram's palms.

"Change the dressing every day and keep the wounds clean. They should heal in a week or so."

A cooling sensation spread through Bram's hands, wiping away all vestiges of pain. Bram sighed. "What was that stuff?"

The Great Father shrugged. "I'm not sure. I got it from a Chellin woman many years ago."

"I didn't know you'd visited Chellin,"

Bram said.

Samarin nodded. "It seems a lifetime ago now, back when I was first elected to the council. Their Regal was keen on improving relations between Chellin and Ral Tora. So I went on a diplomatic mission, and stayed for three months. A most interesting visit. But we are straying off the point. Tomas. Once, when I was in Tirsay, I saw a man with similar symptoms. He had a rare disease that raised his body temperature alarmingly. Nobody could go near him. In the end, he died."

"And you reckon that's what's wrong with Tomas?"

"Perhaps. I'll send our best healers to him. With the correct treatment I'm sure he'll recover."

Bram began to calm. Of course the Great Father was right. There was nothing to worry about. Bram felt a little foolish to have panicked.

Samarin said, "I think it best if you don't visit Tomas anymore. I'll go and see him myself. I'm giving you the remainder of the day off. I suggest you go home and rest, then report to Chief Engineer Rassus on the North Wall in the morning."

Bram breathed a sigh of relief. He didn't want to go anywhere near Tomas ever again.

"Thank you, Great Father," he said. "I hope you can help Tomas."

"So do I, Bram. So do I."

***

Chief Engineer Rassus was in a foul mood, which, of course, was nothing new. Today it was Bram's turn to be on the receiving end. Bram had already received a roasting for being late, even though nobody had told him of changes to the roster. Now Rassus was bawling at him for the second time this morning.

Bram had just overseen the digging of a tunnel for one of the curileum pipes; a job which involved climbing down into the hole and measuring all the dimensions. Bram's work had not met the chief engineer's high standards.

"Three spans!" Rassus bellowed. His face had gone beetroot red and little bits of spittle flew from his mouth and landed on Bram. "I told you quite clearly three spans! So what do you go and do? You make it three and a half spans! Three and a half when I told you three! What's wrong with you, Bram? Why can't you follow simple instructions?"

Bram had the overwhelming urge to trip Rassus in the dirt. He kept his voice deliberately neutral as he said, "Chief Engineer Rassus, I was only doing what you've always taught me to do."

Rassus raised an eyebrow and seemed about to speak so Bram carried on in a rush, "Use my initiative, I mean. Isn't that what you say makes a good engineer? The ability to recognize a problem and fix it?"

From the scowl on Rassus's face, Bram couldn't tell if he was making any progress. He fidgeted uncomfortably.

"I, er, I… I know you told me to make the tunnel three spans but I realized that would make the pipes sit too snugly up against the walls of the tunnel. I did some calculations and I reckon if we increase the depth of the gravel layer, the pipes are less likely to crack when it gets cold. Here, look."

He handed Rassus the scrap of paper that he'd scribbled his calculations on. Rassus studied the paper. His face showed nothing, locked as it was into his perpetual scowl. He uncrossed his arms. One hand went up to scratch his chin.

"Celian!" he called over his shoulder.

The Second Engineer came scurrying at the sound of his name.

Rassus transferred his flinty gaze from Bram to Celian. He held Bram's scrap of paper out to the Second Engineer. "Make the tunnels wider and increase the depth of the gravel layer. Here, follow these calculations. That might help to stop the pipes from cracking."

Celian took the scrap of paper. "Right you are, boss." He hurried off, shouting orders to the men.

Rassus turned back to Bram. "Well, don't just stand there, boy. Go help Celian's team."

Bram mumbled a thank you and strode off after the Second Engineer. He felt a small surge of triumph. He'd been right! And Rassus had approved his plan! It was the closest Rassus ever came to giving a compliment.

The construction site reminded Bram of an ant's nest. People were scurrying everywhere carrying shovels and pickaxes, hauling pieces of timber, pushing barrows of dirt. Here and there engineers, marked out by a red band on their forearm, shouted orders and directed the operation.

Bram did not envy the workmen. They had the dangerous job of going into the tunnels dug beneath the curtain wall and laying the pipes that would connect Ral Tora to the mine in the plain. Although the diggings were supported by thick timber supports, the wall could still collapse at any time. The workmen wouldn't stand a chance. Tension filled the air. There would be no second chances. If the wall collapsed the pipes beneath would be destroyed. If that happened, the engineers' plan of pumping fuel into the city would fail.

A team of engineers were detailed with keeping an eye on the wall. They monitored it constantly, taking measurements every quarter bell to see if it had moved the barest millimeter. They kept the balance and center of gravity just right using a series of weights and pulleys. Bram didn't envy their job much either.

Second Engineer Celian stood with a team of men. Bram tapped him timidly on the shoulder. Celian turned and his ruddy face broke into a grin. "Ah, Bram. Still breathing, then? I thought Rassus might eat you alive!"

Bram managed a small smile. "Oh you know Rassus, he blustered and shouted a bit but in the end he realized I was right."

"So I've heard. It's you we have to thank for making the tunnels wider? A lot more work for us!"

Bram couldn't tell whether Celian was really annoyed or joking so he just shrugged apologetically.

Celian winked and clapped him on the shoulder. "Well done, lad. It's a sound plan."

Bram's cheeks burned. He looked down and kicked some pebbles at his feet. Celian pointed at a gaggle of men struggling with a windlass; a machine made of ropes and pulleys they used to haul dirt into the barrows.

"Bram, I'd be grateful if you'd sort that mess out. The holding strap has snapped so there's no tension on the lifting arm. If we can't fix it, we'll have to move the earth by hand."

"Yes, boss."

The foreman of the group stared at Bram suspiciously when he approached. He reached up to scratch his stubbly chin. "What can we do for you?"

Bram steeled himself. This man could be trouble. Many of the older workers resented being ordered around by someone of Bram's age.

Bram put on a nonchalant expression and shrugged. "I'm a bit of a spare part round here, everything seems under control. I noticed your windlass has snapped. Thought I could give you a hand."

The man eyed Bram, trying to find some ulterior motive behind his words. He planted his hands on his hips. "The holding strap gave way and now we can't pull the arm down far enough to fit another." He pointed to a big wooden bucket filled with stones. "That's the weight we use to balance the arm, to pull it up and down. But we can't seem to get the weight right. Every time we load it the damn thing snaps again."

Bram pursed his lips in thought. "I might have a solution to that."

Bram worked diligently with the men all morning. He made sure to never sound like he was criticizing or ordering them around. Eventually, the men warmed to him. When they finally managed to get the loading arm sprung properly the foreman even clapped him on the back and thanked him.

In the distance, Old Rosella rang. Midday. The sun was a pale yellowy haze behind the clouds. Bram paused, wondering if Celian would mind if he went to get some lunch.

"Bramwell Thornley?"

A boy of about thirteen years approached

him. He wore the blue and white uniform of the Father Hall kitchen staff. He had flour on his nose.

"You Bram Thornley?" the boy said again.

"Yeah. Why?"

The boy grinned. "Thought so. The man said you were scruffy looking."

"I'm not scruffy!" Bram cried, glancing down at his dusty clothes and running his hand through his unruly mop of hair. "What do you want?"

The boy pulled a bundle from under his cloak and handed it to Bram. "Man at the Hall asked me to bring you this." He glanced at the sky. "Looks to me like snow again. I'm off back to the kitchens, it's freezing out here." The boy sprinted away.

Bram inspected the package: cylindrical and wrapped in expensive cloth that looked like it had been ripped from a curtain in the Father Hall. He pulled the wrapping off and discovered a bottle of mead with a label attached. *I thought you would enjoy this more than me.*

Bram frowned. He could guess who'd sent it: Tomas. But why? Was this Tomas's attempt at an apology?

Bram hesitated, his eyes fixed on the bottle. The liquid inside was the color of honey, a deep gold. Nobody on the construction site was paying Bram any attention. Rassus stood over the far side of the site shouting at one of the diggers, Celian was overseeing the deliveries. Would it do any harm to have a quick taste?

Bram pulled the cork free with his teeth, held the bottle to his nose and breathed deeply. The fruity smell reminded him of summer.

Lifting the bottle to his mouth, he tipped back his head and took a sip. The mead slid down his throat and formed a lovely core of warmth in his stomach. He lifted the bottle again but then paused before it touched his lips. He would save the mead, not waste it.

Besides, Rassus would flay him alive if he smelled alcohol on his breath.

Sighing, he pushed the cork back into the bottle and went to ask Celian what he wanted doing next.

"Are you on the early shift again tomorrow?" Celian asked.

Bram nodded.

"In that case, you can knock off for the day. New supplies are coming upriver tomorrow so I'll need you here early to help with the stock-taking. Go home and get some rest."

Bram left the site and went in search of something to eat. He didn't realize where he was going until his feet brought him to the door of *The Ploughman's Nag*. This was becoming a habit. He wasn't much of a drinker, but lately he found himself in the taverns more and more. They had roaring fires and good food.

Bram pushed the door open and saw the tavern was busy. Puddles of water had gathered on the floor and condensation dripped down the windows. Smells filled the air: wet hair and clothes, pipe smoke, cooking. Bram thought he could detect roast beef and potatoes. His stomach rumbled.

"Bram! Over here!" said a voice from a table by the fire. Bram saw three faces grinning at him: Romy, Oscar and Seth. They looked a little the worse for drink. Each had a glassy look to their eyes and rosy cheeks.

Bram shook his head in mock despair. He wondered how long they'd been here. Quite a while, by the looks of it. Romy shifted over on the bench to give Bram room to sit. "What are you three doing in here?" Bram asked as he sat down.

Romy grinned. "We just got the roster and found we're all on early shift this week. That leaves today free. What better way to spend a day than in a tavern with your friends?"

Oscar curled one of his large hands around his glass and raised it into the air. His deep voice rumbled. "I propose a toast. To good friends."

"Hang on," said Bram. "I'll go and get a drink."

"No need, friend!" said Romy. He lifted a big tankard of frothy brown ale from the seat at his side. "I got you a pint. I'm immensely proud of my will power. I nearly drank it at least three times while we were waiting for you."

Bram eyed the mug suspiciously then took a sip. "It's warm! How long has it been there?"

Romy shrugged. "Thought you'd arrive earlier than this."

Oscar, whose arm was still raised for the toast, cleared his throat loudly. "Bram, stop complaining and join in, will you?"

They lifted their tankards one by one.

"Right," Oscar boomed. "Here's to friends and a long, lazy life!"

A cry of "Cheers!" went up and the four banged their mugs together so hard that ale spilt all over the table.

Bram waved over a serving girl. "What's for dinner today?" he asked her. "Is that roast beef I can smell?"

The girl glanced in the direction of the kitchen and replied, "You would think so, wouldn't you? It's actually reindeer caught from the wild herds come down from the north. We used up our last beef ration yesterday. The reindeer's good though, if you cook it long enough. Can I get you some?"

Bram nodded.

The door swung open, sending a blast of cold air into the room before it banged shut again. Three men entered and strode over to Bram's table.

"Romy Satchwell?" one of them asked.

Romy looked up at the man. "Who's

asking?"

The man glanced at his companions then cleared his throat. "I'm Jon, this is Talla and Bemis. We are from the bakery on Wheeler Road." He paused, reluctant to go on. "Er, the thing is…"

"Yes?"

"The bakery ran out of flour today. We were laid off. We've been drafted into the digging teams and some bloke called Rassus told us to report to you."

Romy's face softened with sympathy. "Oh, I see." He looked the three men up and down. "You look like strong lads, you'll be an asset to the digging teams. Unfortunately, if you've been assigned to me, it means you've drawn the early shift. Report to the guild house at Rosella's first chime tomorrow."

Jon nodded, and the three men left the tavern.

Romy watched them go, and then turned back to his friends. "That's the second lot this week. Three days ago, the lads from the chandlery were drafted in after the last of the wax was used up." The others nodded. It was the same all over the city. More and more people were losing their jobs.

The serving girl arrived with Bram's food. He sniffed at it warily, picked up a chunk of the meat and gingerly placed it in his mouth.

"What's it like?" Seth asked.

"Good," Bram replied.

"Right, that's all I needed to hear." He waved over the serving girl again and said, "We'll all have what he's having. Oh, and we need another round of ale."

CHAPTER 7

I should feel colder than this, Bram thought, as he wandered down the street.

Even though a layer of sparkling frost covered everything, Bram's skin burned and his belly glowed with heat; the legacy of the alcohol he had unwisely imbibed. Ale had flowed all afternoon and into the evening. They would all regret it in the morning. When the tavern keeper eventually turned them out, Bram had said his goodbyes to his friends and started walking home. He moved in soft, rambling zigzags, through the deserted market square and along Drake Street.

Bram looked up at the stars. The sudden

movement made his vision swim and the soft sweep of the sky began gently rotating. Bram concentrated and eventually his vision steadied. The night was clear, crisp. The stars seemed incredibly bright, like tiny holes picked in the firmament. Directly above shone Saiis, the evening star, brightest in the sky and named after the king of the gods. To the east glowed the red orb of Shir named for the goddess of sorrow and low on the horizon hung the twin orbs of Mantaro's belt, god of warriors.

An urgent thought broke through the fog of Bram's thoughts. *Stop messing around like a drunken fool! Get home before you freeze!*

He wobbled down the street. He saw people coming toward him so he stopped and waited for them.

"Who goes there?" said a muffled voice.

After staring for a moment, Bram realized he was looking at a couple of watchmen out on night patrol. No features of the two watchmen were visible through their thick fur hoods and coats. They looked like big woolly bears.

One of them gestured at Bram with a mittened hand. "What are you doing outdoors at this time of night? You know the rules."

Bram squinted at the man. "Sorry, officer. I'm on my way home."

The watchman leaned closer. "Bram? Is that Bram Thornley? Young Oscar's friend?"

"Yep, that's me," he answered, smiling

disarmingly. "Just been in the tavern with Oscar and a few friends. Trying to warm up with a little liquor, you know how it is."

In the gloom, he thought he saw the man smile. "Yeah, I suppose I do. All right, go straight home now, won't you?"

"Right you are, officer."

Bram threw them a salute and staggered off. His house sat between a butcher's and a tailor's, a solid little townhouse built of red Ral Toran brick. Once inside, Bram stumbled over to the fireplace and ran his hand along it until he found his tinderbox and a fat candle. He carefully sparked the tinder and held it to the wick while the flame took hold. The soft yellow light illuminated a small room with a rickety table, a rocking chair by the fire and a painting of Bram's parents on the wall. Bram slumped into the chair and stared up at the portrait. They were smiling. They looked happy.

Bram's thoughts drifted back to earlier in the evening. Romy's sister had come to the tavern to fetch him home and although Romy had pretended to be annoyed, Bram could tell he didn't really mind. The gruff way he'd greeted her had shown an underlying affection, a familiarity that comes of a deep bond. Right now, Romy was probably at home in a snug living room, while his mother and sister fussed around him.

While I'm sitting here in the cold by myself.

Suddenly, Bram grabbed a plate from the table and hurled it. The plate crashed into the wall a hand's span below the painting and exploded into pieces.

Bram stared at the mess.

You left me alone! He raged silently at his parents. *Don't you dare smile at me!*

Bram shivered. Climbing unsteadily to his feet, he lurched across the living room and staggered upstairs. In his bedroom, he put the candle on the windowsill and collapsed into bed fully clothed, pulling the thick blankets up around his head.

He fell asleep in seconds.

On the windowsill the candle burned on, forgotten.

***

Torches ring the walls, burning sweet incense. Nine robed figures stand in a circle around a dais, chanting in a strange tongue. On the dais, a pentagram has been drawn in chalk and before this, a beautiful young woman kneels with her head bowed. She is naked except for a garland of pink flowers around her neck. The chanting stops and a white light begins to glow from the pentagram. Something is coming.

Bram lurched upright with a cry. His heart pounded. Nightmares flitted at the edges of his vision. In his bedroom dark shapes reared up at him…and resolved themselves into pieces of furniture. He sank back down onto the bed and closed his eyes.

He lay in the darkness wishing for sleep but nightmare images chased each other through his head like leaves blown on the breeze. Finally, he threw back the blankets and staggered to his feet. Hugging his chest, he padded over to the window, pushed it open and leaned out. The city lay before him, dark and empty. A full moon hung overhead, bathing the rooftops in an eerie light. Bram sucked in long draughts of the freezing air, attempting to clear the clinging threads of his dream.

A shadow moved across the moon. Bram looked up and saw a dark shape hovering above the city, blocking out the stars. Bram squinted, trying to make it out. With a gasp, he realized the shadow was a creature, but certainly no bird or beast Bram had ever seen.

As he watched, the winged creature moved, ranging back and forth over the city as if…

It's looking for something! Bram thought.

It dropped lower, over a round silhouette on the skyline: the domed roof of the old temple.

Why was the creature hovering over the temple? And was that a light burning in the temple window?

Disbelieving, Bram scrubbed his eyes, trying to remove the last vestiges of sleep.

When he looked again both the light and the creature were gone.

He shook his head. *Bram, you are a bloody fool,* he told himself. *When will you learn that taverns are no good for you?*

He closed the window, blew out the candle and dropped back into bed. This time, he didn't dream.

***

Slowly, Bram became aware of a pounding in his head. Then, even more slowly, he became aware that the pounding was actually *outside* his head.

What the —?

He pried his eyes open and waited for them to focus. The pounding came again.

"Bram!" a muffled voice cried. "Are you in there? Open up! It's me, Romy!"

Bram levered himself carefully into a sitting position. His head spun. How much had he drunk last night? And what strange dreams he'd had.

"Bram! Let me in, I'm freezing to death out here!"

"All right, I'm coming!" Bram croaked. "Just stop banging. My skull's going to crack!"

Bram pulled the door back to reveal Romy's grinning face. He wore a heavy coat and a hat with ear-flaps tied under the chin.

"At last!" Romy cried. "I've been knocking

for a quarter bell!" He peered closely at Bram and said, "Gods, you look awful. Did we really drink that much last night?"

Leaning against the door frame, Bram said, "It seemed a good idea at the time."

"Bram, my friend, the trick to being a good drinker, is knowing when to stop. A talent you seem to be sadly lacking."

Romy pushed past Bram into the house and knelt by the fireplace. "And letting your fire go out too?" He shook his head in despair. "You really are in a sorry state, aren't you?"

Bram shrugged and scratched behind his ear. His hair felt matted and greasy. "What can I do for you, Romy? I'd best get ready for work."

Romy stood up. "Bit late for that. Don't you know what time it is?"

Bram stared at him, uncomprehending.

Romy rolled his eyes. "Bram, it's past lunch time. That's why I'm here. Rassus sent me to fetch you. He nearly had a fit when you didn't turn up for work."

Bram groaned. He hadn't even noticed that the sun had passed its midday zenith. "Couldn't you have told him I was sick?" he asked Romy.

"Tried it. Think it would've worked as well, except Rassus saw us all in the tavern last night. I don't remember seeing *him* though. Come to think of it, I don't remember much at all."

"That makes two of us."

"Well, come on then, get ready. If you're not on site by the end of the lunch break, I dread to think what Rassus will do to you."

As Bram trudged up the stairs he ran a hundred excuses through his head. He was pretty sure none of them would do any good.

***

The mid afternoon sun was blinding as Bram squinted at the top of the North Wall.

"I'm sure it's fine," Bram said to the hatchet-nosed man in front of him. "The wall's only moved half a degree. That's normal. There's nothing to worry about."

The man, Seffa, scowled at Bram, showing his yellow teeth. "I don't like it. My men are experienced diggers, and if they reckon the wall's moving, then it's moving."

Bram sighed. "All right. Pull your men out and tell Brin to bring over more scaffolding. If the wall has moved we'll have to shore up the tunnel. I'll go down and check it out."

Seffa ran his fingers through his hair, nodded, and stalked off to find Brin and his team of scaffolders.

Bram rubbed his temples. The headache just wouldn't go away. His belly was doing somersaults and his tongue felt like sandpaper. Romy had been right about Rassus being angry enough to spill blood. Bram felt sure the dressing down he had been given could be heard all the way down at the South Wall. Still, it might have been worse. A problem over in the Market Square had called Rassus away before he could finish his lecture.

Bram approached the tunnel entrance. The tunnel was supported by sturdy timber logs hammered into the ground. The site reminded Bram of the open-shaft iron mines on the Isle of Ashon he'd seen as a boy.

He marched down the slope, ducked under the supports and entered the oppressiveness of the shaft. Oil burning lamps, set in glass cases for safety, gave out enough light to see, but not enough to chase away the shadows in the corners.

It felt warmer than outside and the ground consisted of dry, packed earth rather than the slush he had grown accustomed to. As he walked, his stomach muscles tightened with apprehension. If this tunnel collapsed, he would die in an instant.

He hurried down the passageway until he reached the area the men had been working in. Evidence of their hasty departure lay everywhere: discarded spades, shovels, tape measures. Someone's half-eaten lunch.

Bram knelt on the hard floor and went still, listening. Silence.

Then something groaned above Bram's head and there came a long moan like a creaking branch in the wind.

Bram's heart thudded. He listened, praying he had imagined the sound. It came again. Stone grating on stone. The workmen were right. The wall was becoming unstable.

All Bram's instincts screamed, *run!* But he didn't. He closed his eyes for a second, took two juddering breaths, and opened them again. He unclipped the pouch containing his instruments and let it slide to the floor. He took out his tape measure, unrolled it, and swiftly held the tape up to the wall and the ceiling, measuring the height and width of each.

He nodded. All the measurements were correct. Everything seemed in order. The wall should not be moving.

Unless…

Bram uncurled his tape measure again and wrapped it around the nearest of the timbers, measuring the circumference.

It was too small.

With shaky hands, he measured the beam again, praying he had measured wrong.

He hadn't. The timber support was not thick enough to bear the wall's weight.

The groaning came again. This time it was louder and lasted ten of Bram's heart beats before subsiding. As the last creak died away, Bram began to panic. In a rush he measured the next support and the next. Altogether, eight supports in this stretch were not the correct size.

The tunnel could not bear the weight

above. The wall was going to collapse.

Bram grabbed his tool kit and ran. As he reached the end of the tunnel he yelled at the top of his voice, "We need more timber! Quick! The wall is coming down!"

Panic erupted.

People scattered in all directions. The team atop the wall scrambled into the winch baskets, to be lowered to the ground. Foremen along the length of the wall ordered their digging teams out, and people began streaming away from the wall like rats.

Bram didn't follow them. Instead, he ran up to Seffa and grabbed him by the shirt. "Bring your men. We must shore up the timbers before the whole thing comes down!"

Seffa stared at him. "Are you mad? We have to get out of here!"

Bram placed his hands on the man's shoulders, "Listen to me! If the wall collapses, we are finished. Finished! We have to go back!"

"No! The risk is too great!"

"We have to take it!"

Seffa weighed up Bram's words for only a moment before turning to his men and shouting, "Bring timbers, as much as you can carry! Follow me!"

Resolutely he led his men toward the tunnel. Bram kept stride with him, heart hammering. To the naked eye, the wall looked unchanged but Bram knew even a tiny shift could mean disaster. As the tunnel mouth swallowed him Bram felt like he was walking to his doom.

"Quickly," he called, breaking into a trot. "We don't have much time."

He led them to the defective supports where the men dropped their tools and hastily set to work. Bram inspected the supports and saw, to his horror, that three of them had cracked. He heard something grate above his head, and suddenly a thin shower of earth cascaded over his shoulders.

"These three first," he called desperately. "They're splitting and won't last much longer."

Seffa shouldered him out of the way as two of his men hauled an enormous timber log and set it upright against the cracked one.

"How long do we have?" he asked Bram.

"Not long. Maybe a quarter bell."

Seffa called over his shoulder, "Get that overhead support ready. When we get this one into the ground, be ready to slot the overhead into place. Yes?"

Bram watched helplessly as Seffa's team moved about their tasks. In only a short time the workers had the first support hammered into the ground and lashed to the original. As the overhead slotted into place, Bram let out a breath he didn't know he'd been holding. Without pausing, Seffa's team moved onto the next support.

Further down the tunnel something

snapped, and a huge clod of earth and stone went crashing to the floor. Dust flew everywhere.

"Leave it!" Seffa called to his men. "That section can be repaired later, these eight supports are bearing the weight and must be reinforced."

The men obeyed. Sweat gleamed on their brows and their eyes were wide: men close to panic. The second support went into place opposite the first and another overhead slotted in, helping to spread the weight of the ceiling.

But the wall kept on groaning. Bram realized, with a jolt that made bile rise in his stomach, they weren't going to make it. There simply wasn't time. They had to get out now, while they still had half a chance.

A commotion from the mouth of the tunnel caught his attention and people rushed toward him. A big man, flushed and panting, slid to a halt before him and Bram realized it was Rassus himself.

"Which ones?" he barked.

Bram pointed and Rassus turned to the men, barking orders. In seconds three men had been dispatched to each of the defective beams, while a gang of six worked to reinforce the ceiling.

The tunnel became awash with shouts, cries, and the ringing of hammers on timbers.

"Quickly Bram!" Rassus barked. "What was the circumference of these supports when you came down here? Will they hold now?" Bram quickly did the calculation in his head. With the new overheads and the reinforced timbers, they would be able to hold more than twice the weight.

Bram nodded. "Yes. I think they'll hold."

The showers of earth had stopped and the creaking noises were quieter, more irregular — how they should be.

Bram slid down the wall, rested his head on his knees and let exhausted relief wash over him.

Dimly, he heard Rassus saying, "I want teams dispatched to every section of wall. I want every support checked, the measurements written down, and a full report on my desk by the morning."

Bram stopped listening. A terrible suspicion was growing in him. The engineers' plan wasn't going to work.

CHAPTER 8

"Ouch!"

Bram jammed his finger in his mouth and stared defiantly at the half-assembled machine sitting on the table before him.

Where has Falen got to? He wondered. *She should've been here an hour ago! This is a two person job! No wonder I'm getting my hand cut to ribbons!*

It was midmorning and the guild house was quiet. Romy and the other engineers were out in the city, checking the measurements in the digging works but Bram had promised to help Falen finish the modifications to the gas burner before they presented it to Professor

Strand on the morrow. Besides, he wanted to keep as far away from the digging site as possible. Since the near-accident yesterday, a dark cloud had descended over the engineers and Bram felt somehow responsible, as though his doubt was spreading to the others.

He picked up his magnifying glass and examined the contraption. The two small holes he'd bored into the metal looked to be the correct size, but the awl had left ragged edges that could easily catch on something, as Bram's bleeding finger testified. He took a piece of sand paper and began filing down the edges, blowing away clouds of metal dust.

Satisfied, he placed the little glass box Falen had made onto the top of the burner and screwed it into position. He stood back to admire his handiwork. The burner stood about three spans high on little legs. The grill on the front had been enlarged to offer better protection from the flames. The glass box they'd added now protected the pilot light, and once ignited, would burn steadily and safely.

Bram allowed a smile of satisfaction to creep across his face. It was a small but vastly important triumph. The first apparatus to use the new fuel. If the curileum could be pumped successfully into Ral Tora, the possibilities for heating the city were immense. At the very least, the Everwinter would not freeze them all to death.

Falen should be here. He thought. *Where is*

she? And where is Rassus for that matter?

Bram wandered down to the front desk where Seyan, an ancient woman who refused to retire, was on duty.

"Anything come in?"

Seyan rifled through some papers. "We've got a report of a burst water pipe in Saddler Row," she wheezed. "Can you check it out?"

Bram nodded. "Right you are."

After trekking through the busy streets, Bram found that the burst water pipe was actually a fountain that had cracked and flooded the street. Bram closed the sluice feeding the fountain and then left its repair in the capable hands of a mason.

His route back to the guild house took him through the winding streets of Stonetown with its myriad walled gardens and hidden courtyards. Despite living in Ral Tora his whole life, he didn't know this wealthy district, and he soon found himself getting confused.

A deserted intersection lay ahead. Tall villas hemmed in on each side, making it impossible to tell where he was.

The sound of voices drifted to him from somewhere ahead. Bram strained, trying to pick up which direction the voices came from. After a moment's deliberation, he made his way down an alleyway and found himself in a broad courtyard with high walls covered in dead ivy. People filled the square, staring at something at the far end. An excited, jovial atmosphere hung over the crowd as people chatted in small groups. By the well-cut and expensive clothing people wore, Bram guessed the rich of Stonetown had turned out for this gathering. Ladies in velvet robes and elaborate jewels mingled with men wearing pine-marten coats — the height of Ral Toran fashion.

As he made his way around the edge of the courtyard, weaving in and out of the clumps of people, he saw what had caught everyone's attention: a raised platform with steps leading up from each side. A stage, Bram realized, and the crowd must be waiting to watch a play.

Surely nobody would mind if he took a little time out to watch a bit of the play? He found himself a quiet spot near the back and leaned on the wall. A hush fell over the crowd as a man dressed in elaborate finery jumped onto the stage.

He bowed. "Ladies and gentlemen, I'm honored that you've come to witness our humble production. I'm sure you will be enraptured by what we have to show you today."

A round of applause met this statement. As Bram clapped dutifully along with the rest, something nagged at him. He'd seen this man before. The man had a distinctive appearance — bald head with a livid white scar running down the left side of his face.

Bram frowned as he suddenly remembered. This was the man who'd been addressing the Wailer meeting he and Romy had ran into the other day. As Bram recalled, this man blamed the engineers for many of Ral Tora's problems.

What had seemed a light-hearted gathering took on a more menacing atmosphere. Getting back to the guild house suddenly became very appealing.

Gingerly, he threaded his way through the crowd, eager to be away. On the stage, the bald man retreated and a woman began to sing in a high, warbling voice. Bram edged around a group of elegantly dressed young women and found his way blocked by a red-haired youth.

"Excuse me," Bram said loudly.

The youth turned and Bram's mouth fell open in shock.

"Seth!"

"Bram!" His red-haired friend looked like a startled rabbit.

"What are you doing here?" Bram demanded. "Surely you haven't joined these lunatics!"

"Keep your voice down," hissed Seth, making shushing movements. "I've come to watch the play, that's all."

Bram glanced at the stage where the woman was bowing to rapturous applause. "Why?"

Seth planted his hands on his hips. "Because they are putting on *The God's Bride*. Do you know how rare that is? No company in

Ral Tora has produced it in a hundred years!"

Bram scowled. "And you would come to a Wailers meeting to see it?"

"You sound just like Oscar. Look at these people — do they look like loons to you? They're just ordinary Ral Toran folk!"

Bram opened his mouth to reply but Seth forestalled him with a gesture. "Shush. It's starting."

Three women dressed in flowing white robes walked to the front of the stage. One of them said, "We are Mysa, Treyan and Sara. We carry a very sacred duty. Once in every thousand years the king of the gods takes a human bride to strengthen the blood of his people. From we three, He will choose. But first we must call Him."

The women produced colored scarves from their sleeves and began a frantic dance around the stage. A figure rose up through a trapdoor right into the center of this whirling maelstrom. When he was fully revealed, the women's dance ended abruptly and they collapsed to the floor as though their strings had been cut.

The newcomer was tall and broad — clearly male — and wore a headdress that looked like an owl. Yellow eyes the size of spinning wheels surveyed the crowd.

"That's Saiis, king of the gods," whispered Seth with a hint of excitement in his voice. "The maidens have called him and he'll choose one to be his bride."

"Why does he have an owl's head?" For a reason he couldn't quite explain, the sight of it made Bram uneasy.

Seth went up on his tiptoes, trying to see over the crowd. "According to the old legends, the owl was Saiis's familiar. Sometimes he's shown wearing an owl's head but most times he's shown as a powerful young man. That's why this play used to be so popular with young women — because there was always a handsome, scantily clad young man playing the lead role."

Saiis walked around the stage, conversing with each of the three maidens in turn. Then the trapdoor opened again and another figure emerged, this time a woman with flowing black hair and skin covered in white paint so she shone as pale as a moonbeam.

"Here we go!" said Seth. "Saiis won't get it all his own way! That's his wife, Shir, queen of the gods. She'll not be happy about what he's been up to!"

Shir grabbed each one of the maidens by the hair and pushed them off the stage with a wail of rage then began a fierce verbal attack on her husband in a melodic language Bram had never heard.

The people around him were spellbound. Bram shuddered. There was something profoundly unsettling about all this. Why were these people wasting their time watching some silly re-enactment dredged up from the city's ancient past? What was the point to it? He suddenly felt claustrophobic.

"I've got to go," he muttered and pushed past Seth.

"Bram, wait!" Seth cried but Bram ignored his friend and shoved his way through the knots of people. At last he escaped the courtyard and fetched up, breathing heavily, against a wall. His cheeks grew hot with anger. Didn't the city have enough problems without having to deal with the Wailers as well? Curse them!

"What's wrong, Bram?" asked Seth, panting up behind him.

Bram lifted his chin. "I don't like that kind of nonsense. It's creepy."

Seth's brow wrinkled in a frown. "It's just harmless fun."

A memory flickered in Bram's mind. *A shadow moved across the moon. A dark shape hovered, obliterating the stars.*

"I've got work to do," he muttered then hurried away, leaving Seth staring after.

***

By the time he got home later that afternoon it was almost dark. Bram was wet, cold and miserable. His numb fingers struggled with the key, and when he finally got the door open he tumbled gratefully into the warmth of his living room. This time, he'd remembered to bank the fire before he left for work. Bending toward the fireplace, Bram took a log from his carefully rationed stack of firewood and tossed it into the fire. He used one of the embers to light a thick yellow candle.

"I've been waiting for you."

Bram yelped, sending the candle flying out of his hand. He spun around and saw someone sitting in the chair. The face was lost in shadow.

"Who's there?"

A hand reached out to pick up the candle. In its yellow light, Bram saw the trespasser's face.

Tomas.

The hairs on Bram's neck rose. "What are you doing here?"

Tomas gestured to a chair. "Won't you sit?"

Bram didn't move. "I asked you a question."

"There's no need to be afraid. I mean you no harm."

"Really? Just broke into my house for fun, did you?"

Tomas's eyes flicked toward the fireplace and then back to Bram. "I've come to apologize. I didn't mean to hurt you the other day. I'm sorry."

"Right, you've apologized. You can leave

now."

A faint smile flickered over Tomas's features. His deep eyes seemed as black as pits. "I must seem very strange to you. I am not mad, Bramwell Thornley. I told your city fathers the truth."

"The truth?" barked Bram, remembering the Wailers meeting and the strange play he'd seen that afternoon. "And what exactly is the truth? That you are part of some scare-mongering hoax?"

"You don't believe that."

"Don't tell me what I think. You know nothing about me."

"I know you believe science will save you. I know you believe everything your city fathers tell you."

Tomas leaned forward, elbows resting on his knees. The firelight caught his angular features. "Do you ever wonder if you're wrong?"

Anger put an edge on Bram's voice. "I don't want to hear this, Tomas. Please leave."

Tomas surged to his feet, sending his chair clattering to the floor. His shadow loomed over Bram.

"I cannot turn you from your own folly," Tomas said. "Nor can I unblind your eyes or unstop your ears. But you need to stop hiding here in the south. Will you come with me to the north?"

Bram pulled in a shaky breath. "You heard

what the city fathers said. I stand by their decision."

Tomas sagged. He stared at the fire for a moment. "So be it. Know this, Bramwell Thornley. Ral Tora is riddled with untruth, like veins running through rock. Secrets and lies. Layers of meaning. If you would know the truth, read your histories. Find the secrets buried in them."

Then he walked to the door and disappeared into the night, leaving his words ringing in Bram's ears.

CHAPTER 9

The vase exploded against the wall and tinkled to the floor in tiny fragments. Falen stared at the mess, hand frozen in mid-air. Then she spun around, searching for something else to throw. Fury pounded through her veins.

Curse the man! Warrior take him!

She snatched a plate from the table, imagined it as the chief engineer's face, and hurled it against the wall, where it shattered into pieces. Unsatisfied, she scooped up the cups from her cupboard and threw them one by one. As she did so, she imagined each one as the face of a city father, those pompous, useless idiots she had stupidly vowed to serve. The wall became marked with scratches and the floor littered with bits of crockery.

Finally, there was nothing else left to throw so she kicked over her wood pile, sending mess over her carpet. She threw herself into a chair, crossed her arms over her chest and stared at nothing. To Falen's horror, she felt tears welling in her throat, and she squeezed her eyes shut, clinging onto her anger. But her feelings were misplaced, and she knew it. Rassus and the city fathers had only done what they thought necessary.

In the distance Old Rosella chimed. It seemed a lifetime had passed since this morning. This morning she had been an engineer, this morning she had been a success, this morning she had a reason to drag herself out of bed each day and go through the motions of life. But now what was she?

A failure.

Falen's eyes strayed to the map hanging on the wall. On it three mountain ranges enclosed a magnificent city built into the foothills of the Sisters. Variss. Home. Could it really be gone? Could everyone she loved really be dead? Lidda? Harn Yorgesson? Her father?

Four years had passed since Falen had ridden out of the gates of Variss. Four years since her father had banished her. Four years spent waiting for a summons from him that never came. Surely, he would change his mind,

Falen had told herself. Surely, he would come to his senses and send for her. But he hadn't.

In that time, Falen had built a life in Ral Tora. She'd been accepted into the Engineering Guild and risen through the ranks to become one of the most respected engineers in the guild. Ral Tora was everything she ever dreamed. Surrounded by people with interests akin to hers, Falen felt more accepted than she ever had. She had a home, a life, a purpose.

But nothing could fill the hole in her heart where Variss should be.

Falen pushed herself from her seat and stared in the mirror hanging above the fireplace.

What had all her ambitions brought her in the end? The leaders of Ral Tora — the city she now served — had refused to send help to her people. Falen berated herself with a thousand regrets. She should have returned to Variss. She should have left Ral Tora as soon as they realized what had happened. She should have defied her father's banishment and gone home anyway.

And she should have checked the measurements in the tunnel yesterday.

The chief engineer's voice spoke in her memory, "Falen, you are suspended from duty until further notice."

His face had been expressionless as he spoke the words that ended Falen's dreams.

Suspended from duty. Negligence leading to

the endangerment of lives. Gross professional misconduct.

Falen scrubbed a hand through her hair. She'd been so stupid! How had she gotten the measurements wrong? Why hadn't she rechecked them? Somehow, through fatigue or basic incompetence, she'd miscalculated the width of the tunnel supports in her section of the digging works. As a result, the north wall had almost collapsed. Only the quick thinking of Bramwell Thornley had averted a disaster.

There would be an investigation, and when her negligence was confirmed, she would be dismissed from the Engineer's Guild. There could be no second chance for an engineer who'd made such a near-fatal error. It was over.

A small silver box lay on the mantelpiece. Falen gently eased off the lid and tipped out its contents, sending a series of delicate amber hairpins cascading down. Slowly, deliberately, Falen began to tie her hair into the intricate Varisean warrior knots. Lidda had always worn her hair like this. Lidda. Had her old friend thought about Falen through the years?

Falen's fingers worked steadily. It became a ritual. With every braid she tied, Falen reclaimed a piece of her old life and part of her life in Ral Tora died.

Finally, she examined herself in the mirror. The braids resembled tiny snakes, giving her the look of a banshee from an ancient Varisean saga. Falen smiled wryly at the thought. The rest of the pins went into the pocket of her trousers, along with the flint and tinderbox.

Falen knelt on the floor in front of a battered wooden chest and laid her hand on the clasps. She hesitated. The chest had been locked since she arrived in Ral Tora. Steeling herself, Falen sprung the clasps and threw open the lid. Inside were the few things she'd brought with her from Variss.

Falen pulled out her cloak, feeling its soft, heavy texture brush against her skin. With the cloak went a thick winter tunic and trousers. Quickly, before memories overwhelmed her, Falen donned the garments and made her way upstairs to her cupboards. She threw out everything she might need: a small travelling stove, a tent, as much food as she could carry. She stuffed everything into a carry-sack and tied the straps. Into the tops of each boot she slid a dagger and strapped two more to her sides. Swinging the carry-sack onto her shoulder, Falen blew out the oil lamp and closed the door on her empty house.

Ral Tora lay dark and still, full of shadows. Snow was falling gently, dusting the streets like flour. Falen was glad for the darkness as it would help her dodge the patrols of City Watch. The warm Varisean clothes kept the chill air from her skin.

Falen padded silently through the streets of the sleeping city until the north gate came into view. The two massive gates stood closed and barred for the night. Raucous laughter echoed from a hut nearby. Guards. Would they let her out? Not likely. And they would certainly inform Rassus once they figured out who she was.

Falen cursed under her breath. Perfect. Just bloody perfect!

She cast around, trying to think of another way out. Then she had it: the postern gate. Further along the wall, it was small and used only for trade deliveries. Perhaps it would be unguarded.

She turned left, hugging the base of the wall. After a while, the building site came into view and Falen weaved her way in and out of heaps of gravel, soil, timber and rope. Up ahead she saw the dark hole of the tunnel under the wall. The same tunnel that had almost collapsed. Falen hurried past. This area was regularly patrolled at night, both by watchmen and engineers on nightshift checking the digging works every bell. She had no desire to run into any of them.

Something caught her eye. Movement by the tunnel entrance. She paused. Probably a rat, she told herself. She was about to move on when the movement came again. No, much too big for a rat.

Falen's heart quickened. *Get out of here*, she told herself, *ignore it and be on your way*. But she didn't. She stepped noiselessly closer.

Dropping the carry-sack to the floor, she pulled one of the daggers from her boot and moved up behind the shape.

It was a man. His movements were furtive and he kept stopping to look around and listen. What was he doing? Something untoward, surely, or why would he be sneaking around in the dark?

Instinct overtook reason. Falen launched herself. She covered the ground in just a few short strides and went crashing into him, taking them both sprawling to the floor.

The man twisted as he fell and rolled away from her. She followed immediately, her hand curling around the man's wrist. In retaliation, the man sent his other fist swinging toward Falen's face, but she swerved out of the way and took the punch on her shoulder. To her surprise, there was hardly any power in the blow at all. Throwing all of her weight onto the man's chest, Falen managed to wrestle him onto his back where she straddled his chest and pinned his arms to his sides with her thighs. In one fluid motion, Falen pressed her dagger against the man's throat. The man suddenly went limp. Falen leaned down and peered at him. It took a moment before she recognized the features of the Varisean visitor.

"Tomas? What are you doing?" Falen demanded.

Tomas gazed at her with eyes as round as a calf's. His lips wobbled, framing words that wouldn't come. He looked like a stranded fish, all breathless and bloated.

"Let me go," he whispered.

"Tell me what you are doing, curse you!"

"I'm going home. I have to go north even though nobody will help me."

Falen stared at him. Pity and disgust warred within her. When he'd first arrived in Ral Tora, Falen had been terrified Tomas would recognize her but the man seemed too absorbed in his own strange world. Her duty as an engineer, and a citizen of Ral Tora, demanded she turn this man over to the authorities. But she understood how he felt. This man, more than anything else, had convinced Falen to leave Ral Tora. Anyone else would have handed Tomas over to the City Watch. Anyone else.

She got to her feet and hauled Tomas up. With a start, Falen realized he wasn't wearing a shirt, leaving his skin exposed to the chill air. Falen stepped back a pace, suddenly wary.

"Who are you?" she whispered.

"Please, forget you've seen me and let me go. I will return to Variss alone if I must."

A gust of wind swirled Tomas's midnight locks. A terrible sadness lingered in his gaze, as vast as the Everwinter itself.

"Not alone," she said at last. "I'll come with you."

Something moved behind Tomas's eyes, a slight lifting of shadow. He smiled.

"Not alone, then. Let's get going."

Falen nodded. They turned east and followed the line of the wall. It wasn't long before Falen's eyes picked out the postern gate. It was visible only as a silhouette in the wall's base. Falen marched up, gripped the handle, and pulled.

"Curse it!" she whispered. "There's a chain. I don't know any other way out."

Tomas pressed his finger to his lips for silence. He glanced around to check they were alone then took a small hacksaw from his trouser pocket and moved over to where Falen stood. The chain was heavy and rusted. Tomas inspected it briefly before setting the edge of the blade against one of the links.

A deep voice spoke suddenly from the darkness, "I wouldn't do that if I were you."

Falen froze. Tomas gasped.

Four figures detached themselves from the shadows. They wore the crimson and silver of the City Watch.

How will we get out of this? Falen thought frantically. *Think!*

She pointed a finger at the guards and demanded, "What do you think you're doing, sneaking up on us like that? You nearly scared us to death. Who is your captain?"

"I am," said the man with the deep voice. "Now, what are *you* doing here?"

"Isn't it obvious?" Falen snapped. "My colleague and I are engineers and are checking the state of the wall."

"And you need to saw off the lock to do that?"

"Who are you to be questioning us? Take it up with Chief Engineer Rassus, if you don't believe us. He won't be pleased you've delayed our work."

The guard stared at Falen long and hard. For a moment, she dared to hope that her bluff would work. But then the guard began laughing softly and her hopes evaporated.

"He warned me you were a wily one," the guard said. "Did you think I would fall for your tricks? You're coming with us."

Strong hands clasped Falen's arm and twisted it behind her. A voice by her ear said, "Don't struggle and I'll not hurt you, but give me any trouble and you'll wish you'd never been born."

Falen glared at her captor. She briefly considered stamping on the man's foot and seeing how far she could run. Could she dodge four guards in the darkness? But, as common sense got the better of her, she dismissed the idea.

"Fine," she snapped. "But you haven't heard the last of this."

Tomas struggled in his captor's grip and managed to free one of his arms. With a grunt, he rammed his elbow into the man's stomach. The man doubled over. Tomas ran. With a curse, the captain sped after him and caught him in only a few strides. He backhanded Tomas so hard that the Varisean went sprawling into the dirt, where he lay still. The captain picked Tomas up and slung him over his shoulder. When he re-joined the others, his face twisted with anger.

"You've really done it now," he hissed at Falen. "Resisting arrest, assaulting an officer, I'll make sure they throw the book at you for this. You all right, Bant?"

The guard nodded. "Yes, boss."

Falen's cheeks flushed with fury. "Tomas wouldn't have hit him if you hadn't been so rough with us! The Great Father will hear about this!"

The captain smiled at her. "Oh, didn't you know? The Great Father ordered your arrest."

With that, the captain barked his orders and the group moved off, leaving Falen with a sick feeling inside. The Great Father had ordered her arrest? Had he guessed she would try to leave?

The guards marched quickly. The captain led, with Tomas bouncing around on his shoulder. At last, they reached the Forum, turned toward the Father Hall and made their way to the Moot. The captain gave a perfunctory knock on the door, then shouldered it open and ushered his captives inside.

Only a few torches were ablaze, and as a result, shadows filled the corners of the room.

At the head of the table, Great Father Samarin sat flanked by Fathers Erris and Hewin.

Falen glared at them.

The captain dropped the unconscious Tomas into a chair and Falen was pushed into a seat beside him. "We found them where you said they would be, Great Father," the captain said. "They were trying to get out the postern gate. The tall one injured Bant then tried to run away. She came quietly." He fixed Falen with a stare, and said, "Well, quiet*ish*."

The three fathers stared at her in silence. Erris, as always, looked as though he was sucking on a lemon. Hewin's cadaverous face looked even graver than usual.

"Well?" Samarin asked at last.

Falen crossed her arms over her chest. "Well what?"

Samarin's face became stern. "Engineer Falen, you are in a great deal of trouble. I suggest you cooperate."

Falen opened her mouth to reply, but before she could get any words out, Father Erris barked, "Cooperate? That one? You've more chance of getting an Esclede merchant to part with his money! She's a troublemaker. I've always said so. She's gone and proven me right!"

"It must be so nice to be you," Falen snapped. "I wouldn't mind sitting on my fat arse all day, complaining and griping while everyone else does the hard work."

Father Erris's face flushed scarlet. "How dare you speak to me like that? You see, Samarin, this is what we get when we hire northern barbarians! To think we ever trusted her!"

Samarin sighed. "I can see this is going to be a long night. Falen, if you won't tell us what you were doing then we must assume that it is as it looks: you were trying to flee whilst under investigation for professional negligence."

The accusation goaded Falen's pride. "Yes, I was trying to leave, but not for the reasons you suppose. I'm no coward! I don't run from my mistakes. Do your investigation, throw me out of the guild, but let me go home! Please! You say Variss is dead but I must know for sure."

"You see!" cried Erris. "She admits it! Running away *and* disobeying our direct orders. You were told to remain in your quarters were you not, engineer Falen?"

Falen lifted her chin. "I won't obey orders that mean I must abandon my people."

Samarin's eyes flashed with anger. "For shame, Falen. You are a citizen of Ral Tora. Have you abandoned all allegiance to us? Would you leave us when we need our engineers the most?"

"You don't need me," Falen whispered.

"Let me be the judge of that," replied Samarin. "Will you promise you won't try to leave the city again?"

Falen shook her head. "I can't do that."

Samarin sighed. "Then you leave me no choice. You'll be placed under house arrest in the Father Hall until I can decide what to do with you."

Samarin waved to the guards and they took Falen by the arms and marched her out. They took her upstairs and ushered her into a small but comfortable room. The door slammed shut and a key turned in the lock.

Falen slumped to the floor with her back against the door. She chewed her lip, taking in her surroundings. She knew one thing for sure. If those fathers thought she was going to sit here quietly, they were in for a mighty shock.

CHAPTER 10

The woman pointed. "That way. Go to the end of Chandler Street, turn left, cross the courtyard and you'll be on the corner of Wyvern row. You should find it somewhere along there."

Bram gazed in the direction she indicated. "Great. Thanks!"

Following the woman's instructions, Bram soon found Wyvern Row. This part of town was old, perhaps as old as Stonetown and filled with narrow streets and tall buildings that had seen better days. He made his way down the street, looking at each building. A plaque on one wall said, *Headquarters of the*

Knitting Circle. A hastily painted sign hanging from a door handle read, *T. W. Turner, Spoon maker.*

No, definitely not the one he wanted.

At the end of the street, where Wyvern Row met Goose Street, Bram discovered a large, white plastered building. An inscription over the door read, *City Library.*

What are you doing here? Bram asked himself. *You know Tomas is a loon. Why are you following his advice?*

Shaking his head at his own idiocy, Bram pushed through the door into a large, silent chamber filled with dusty shelves. The scent of mildew hung in the air, like wet laundry left to fester.

"Who's there?" came a reedy voice. A woman emerged from behind a shelf. She had weathered skin and black eyes as hard as lead.

"What do you want?" she demanded.

"I've come to find some books, Mistress Librarian."

The librarian peered at Bram suspiciously. "What for?"

"Why does anyone want to read books? To learn."

Her eyes narrowed. "Seems an age since anyone came in here, wanting to *learn.* The only people I get in here are good-for-nothings, who want to sit by my fire and drink my tea. Stealing an old woman's victuals! It's beyond disgraceful!"

"I can assure you I won't steal anything," said Bram. "But a chair by your fire while I read would be nice."

The woman frowned. "What kind of books you after?"

"The histories, everything you've got."

"Phew! You don't do things by half, do you? There must be hundreds of 'em!"

"If you show me where they are, I'll be fine from there."

The librarian grunted and shuffled away. "You'd better follow me, then."

She led Bram to a dark corner of the library with spots of mold covering the walls. A bony hand emerged from her shawl and waved at the top shelf. "There. The ones starting on the left are the oldest, then they continue right down the row. Be careful when you pull them out; they're heavier than they look."

Bram found a rickety ladder and climbed to the highest shelf. Layers of dust lay along the books. It must have been many years since these tomes had last been opened.

The librarian watched him with sarcastic amusement on her face. She did not offer to help. After a while she got bored and wandered off.

Bram pulled out some books at random and then descended the ladder. A small fireplace sat at the head of the room. The librarian, hunched in her shawls, was busy feeding sticks into it. Bram approached her and coughed politely.

"Do you mind if I join you?"

The librarian shrugged. "Do what you like but you're not getting any tea!"

Bram sat in one of the chairs and piled the books by his feet. The librarian leaned over and handed Bram a tome with a muddy gray cover.

"Start with this one."

Bram reached for the book. As he took it, his hand brushed the librarian's papery skin. A sharp tingling flared along his fingers.

The librarian looked at him sharply, black eyes bright. "So, it's started then." She leaned back in her chair. "Yes, read that one first. I think you'll find it especially helpful."

Dismissing her odd behavior, Bram opened the book. The first few pages were missing. As a result the text began midway through a sentence.

"....knew things must change. In those days the people adhered to strange superstitions. The gods guarded their prerogatives jealously and demanded many sacrifices from the people. In Variss, a person was chosen each year to be blinded with hot irons, so they gazed only on the glory of the gods. In Tirsay and Esclede, at midwinter, fifty bulls were sacrificed to Vantaro, Keeper of the Underworld, so he would not unleash his army of ghosts on the world. Here in Ral Tora, women would offer themselves to Saiis, king of the gods, to be his bride and bear his child.

Toran saw that humanity must be servants to the gods no longer. A new age must be forged, an age where humanity was free. The Rift was sealed so the gods were unable to touch the world. As I look out from my window, I see a Ral Tora bright with promise. Three hundred years have passed since the Dividing and its scars have faded. Perhaps in another three hundred years none will remember the names of the gods or their creatures. But Toran's name will echo down the ages as the founder of the greatest city in the world, Ral Tora."

Bram snapped the book shut. The withered title on the spine read, *The Deeds of Great Father Toran, by Elian Stretton, Summer year 355.*

Bram gaped. This text was over nine hundred years old, written at the height of Ral Tora's power. Elian Stretton probably penned this chronicle during the construction of the great aqueduct, First Storm Tower, the Father Hall.

The golden age of Ral Tora. Today's engineers still marveled at what those ancient colleagues achieved.

"I'd like to loan this," he said.

The librarian shook her head. "Can't do that, lad."

"Why not? This is a library, isn't it? Libraries lend books!"

She glanced over at the door, as if to check it was shut. "That's the idea. But lately too many books have been borrowed and not returned. Those damn Wailers keep coming in and taking all they can find about the old rites. Damn near taken a whole bookcase. I'll not lose any more."

"What do the Wailers want with your books?" Bram asked.

The librarian's eyes became hard. "They're looking for something. But they won't find it."

The sudden vehemence in her voice startled him. "I'm no Wailer," he said defensively. "I'll bring the book back."

She reached out and gently took the book from Bram's hand. "It'll be here when you come back."

Bram opened his mouth and then shut it again. The librarian's tone brooked no argument.

"Right. I'll be going."

The librarian watched, unsmiling, as he made his way to the door. She did not say goodbye.

Outside, a storm was brewing. A screeching wind drove flurries of snow across the city. Bram bent his head, pulled his collar up around his neck, and pushed his way through the tempest.

The storm raged all night, howling down the chimney so loudly it kept Bram awake for most of the night. But sometime before dawn it blew itself out and a shaft of sunlight beaming through a gap in his curtains woke Bram the next morning. He considered getting up to close the gap when someone began pounding on his door.

Go away, he thought.

But the knocking continued so Bram staggered out of bed and shambled downstairs. As he opened the door the bright daylight revealed Oscar waiting outside.

"Not got you up have I?" he said with a grin.

Bram grunted noncommittally and moved aside to let Oscar in. He stoked the fire and put the kettle on to boil.

"To what do I owe this pleasure?" Bram asked Oscar.

Oscar frowned. "You've forgotten, haven't you?"

Bram froze. "Er, no I haven't."

Oscar turned a chair around and straddled it. "Don't try lying to me, Bramwell Thornley. You're not as good as Romy, and I can spot his whoppers from a mile off. You agreed to come to the tailor's with me today, remember?"

Bram winced. Oscar's romantic dinner with Ranwey Burr had completely slipped his mind, even though Oscar had talked about nothing else for the last three days. And Oscar wanted *his* advice on new clothes.

"No, I hadn't forgotten. Promise," Bram lied, pouring the kettle. "Just let me get dressed and have a bite of breakfast and then we can get going."

***

"So, where are we going?" Bram asked Oscar, as they turned left out of Bram's street.

"Turner and Son," Oscar answered.

"What? That's down in the Southern Quarter. How about Rowsley's on Traders Square? I've heard he's very good."

"No," Oscar said firmly. "Turner and Son have this gray tunic I like. Ranwey reckons gray sets off my eyes."

Bram shrugged and they began trekking through the city. They were making their way down Cooper's Row when a uniformed officer wearing the black sash of a captain hurried up to them.

"Oscar," he barked. "Urgent orders. We need you at the south gate right away. We have a situation down there."

Oscar snapped to attention. "Yes, sir!"

The captain dashed away.

Oscar shared a look with Bram. "Let's go."

They joined the flow of people flooding toward the south gate. The whole city seemed to have come alive. The orders coming down the chain of command were sketchy. *Incident at the South Gate. All relief units of the City Watch to attend immediately.*

On Nettle Street, Oscar spotted the rest of his unit and hailed them. He and Bram joined the troop, Bram keeping to the back in case they realized he wasn't City Watch and sent him away.

The merchant's houses receded and were replaced by blacksmiths, weapon stores, guardhouses and other paraphernalia of the wall garrison. The south wall was massive, built from solid granite mined from cliffs on the Isle of Ashon. The iron-reinforced gate stood closed.

Steps were carved into the wall on both sides of the gate, leading up to the wide parapet spanning the wall's width. Even at this distance, Bram could tell the top of the parapet was crowded. From the sunlight glinting off armor, Bram realized most of them were guards, but here and there, he saw the yellow robe of a city father.

And was he imagining it, or was that Great Father Samarin himself down by the gate, along with the senior city fathers?

The tall, whiplash thin commander of the South Wall Garrison approached Oscar and barked a few perfunctory orders, before marching off on an errand.

"Come on, lads!" Oscar called. "Up you go! Keep your wits about you but don't draw weapons. We have visitors."

Visitors? Bram didn't know whether to feel excited or afraid. Ral Tora hadn't had visitors since… well, he couldn't remember when.

Oscar grabbed Bram's arm. "Come on. Try to blend in. It's supposed to be guards only up on the parapet."

As Bram reached the top of the wall behind Oscar, an icy wind blasted straight into his face, almost taking him off his feet. Pulling his cloak tighter, Bram cursed himself for forgetting to bring his gloves. Gravel had been spread to make the footing steadier but it was like walking on glass.

Bram followed Oscar along the wall until they stood directly under a watchtower. Archers filled every window of the tower, arrows nocked and ready to fire.

Bram leaned over the parapet and looked out. A dizzying distance below, the Southern Plain stretched as far as he could see.

A long column of people stood in front of the gates. Bram had never seen anyone like them. They were taller and more willowy than the average Ral Toran. Their clothing seemed to be made from a strange fur, dark and silky. And the creatures they were riding!

They looked like… no they couldn't be, could they? They looked like giant otters!

The column waited just out of bowshot. A woman sat at the head of the column, flanked on either side by men with swords. She wore a black robe and had yellow hair spilling down her back. A simple silver circlet sat upon her brow, set with a shining green gem. Sitting astride her mount, she gazed up at Ral Tora's walls.

Something about these people tugged at

Bram's memory, something about their clothing or their demeanor. He just couldn't quite grasp the thought. The breeze picked up, sending the woman's hair streaming out behind her. A standard-bearer held up his pole, allowing the pennant to unfurl and snap in the breeze. It depicted a spread-winged albatross wearing a silver crown.

A shout rang out from the watchtower, "Chellin has come! Open the gates! Chellin has come!"

***

Astrid was beginning to lose her patience. Were they just going to stand there and stare at her? Had she come all this way just to have the Ral Torans hide behind their walls like cowards? Wasn't it obvious to these idiots who she was?

But then she heard someone cry, "Chellin has come! Open the gates!"

About time, she thought.

Slowly, the gate swung open. A group of people rode out, seated on tall gray horses. Two of them were dressed in flowing yellow robes but the others wore armor and carried weapons. They reined in a good distance in front of Astrid. An old man with a bristling white beard seemed to be the leader. Beside him sat a fat man with a bald head who glared at Astrid with open hostility. Rama and Aaron noticed his look and tensed in their saddles. With a minute flick of her wrist, Astrid indicated for them to relax. She wanted no trouble.

The old man nudged his mount forward. His deep eyes swept over the party, assessing. Astrid returned the old man's gaze with her most powerful stare, the one she used on her ministers went she wanted to reduce them to jabbering wrecks.

The old man seemed unruffled by her regard. He smiled. "Greetings, and welcome, strangers. I am Samarin, Great Father of Ral Tora. Perhaps you would gift us with your names?"

Rama growled, "This is the Lady Astrid, Regal of Chellin and all its environs."

Samarin betrayed no reaction to Astrid's title.

He knew who I was already, Astrid thought. *This man is a wily old fox. I must tread carefully around him.*

Samarin said, "Then we are greatly honored. Welcome, my lady."

"Thank you, Great Father," Astrid said. "Your welcome gladdens my heart. I would have sent word of my arrival, but in present conditions I couldn't guarantee messengers would get through."

The Great Father nodded. "I recall the last time a reigning Chellin monarch visited Ral Tora. I was fifteen years old."

She heard suspicion in his voice. Astrid raised her chin. "I appreciate that my visit is out of the ordinary but these are not ordinary times. Don't you think we would all benefit from improved relations between our cities?"

Samarin smiled. "Of course. Now, would you accompany me into the city? Though I warn you, your arrival has caused quite a stir."

Samarin urged his horse to Astrid's side. To her annoyance, he betrayed no reaction to the sight of the dolarchu, as if the giant otters were an everyday occurrence in Ral Tora. Astrid didn't let him see her frown as they moved off.

The streets of Ral Tora were wide and straight. They spoke of planes and angles and geometry. People lined both sides of the street, staring at the Chellin party with wide-eyed fascination. Most faces showed curiosity. Some showed fear. A few held a mix of both. And some stared with open hostility behind their eyes.

Astrid put on her most charming smile, showing all of her gleaming white teeth and waved to the crowds as she passed.

As they moved through the city, Astrid couldn't help being impressed by Ral Tora. It seemed that the world famous Engineering Guild deserved its reputation after all. The curtain walls alone were a marvel. The Goddess only knew how so much granite had been hauled so far into the air and made to stay upright. And then there were the pinnacles and spires, the whole skyline was dotted with them.

Astrid turned in her saddle and surveyed her people. Like her, most of them were staring at the city as they rode through it. Mattack was deep in conversation with the unfriendly city father. What had Samarin named him? Erris? The pair of them looked remarkably similar with their bald heads and ample paunches.

If he strikes up a friendship with that man it could help our cause, Astrid thought. *And perhaps it will keep Mattack out of my hair for a while.*

As they rode Samarin pointed things out. "Over there is where the Great Fire broke out thirty years ago. That house is where Anto Sciro was born. He founded the Guild Council, upon which all our trade is based."

Astrid nodded at Samarin's comments and asked a polite question here and there. On the surface, she was all bland politeness, but she devoured every last scrap of information about the city. Already she had deduced that tension bubbled between Samarin and Erris from the stiff way they addressed each other. Astrid tucked this tidbit away. You never knew when things like that could come in handy. The eyes of her ministers and aides moved constantly, taking in the mood of the crowd, what people were wearing, apparent wealth or lack of it, strategic buildings or landmarks, what the shops were selling, anything Astrid might need.

The hub of the city turned out to be a large square with an impossibly tall tower in its center. Beyond the square, they entered the Forum. Samarin led them to a large gray building, which he introduced as the Father Hall.

"You'll be housed here," he said. "I'm sure you'll find the accommodation to your liking." He glanced at the dolarchu and hesitated. "I'm afraid our grooms won't know how to care for your beasts. We only have stables."

Feeling she had scored a point, Astrid inclined her head gracefully. "Stables will do for now. My people will care for the dolarchu."

The Great Father climbed the steps and Astrid moved in time with him. The big doors loomed ahead. Astrid smiled. In that building the fate of her mission would be decided.

A thrill of excitement wriggled in her stomach. She'd been born for this: intrigue, mystery, and the complex web of politics.

And if she had her way, the web was about to get a lot more tangled.

CHAPTER 11

Falen's ear had gone numb. She'd been listening at the door for so long she was sure her ear would leave an indentation in the wood. But the wait had been worth it. Muffled conversation came from the other side.

"You get off down, Shern. I'll take over. Has she been any trouble?"

"Nah, she's been all sweetness and light since they caught her last time."

Ha! So they think I'm conquered do they? She thought. *I'll give them sweetness and light!*

Footsteps receded down the corridor. Falen settled herself into a comfortable position and waited. After a while, the rasp of snoring came from the other side of the door, just as she expected. For the past two days, Falen had diligently studied her guards' habits and learned the routines of them all. Laria, the dour sergeant was always on the lookout for trouble. Falen had little chance of escape while she was on duty. Shern, the fresh-faced young recruit, was so keen to impress his officers that he did everything by the rules. No chance with him either. But Rollarin, on guard right now, was fat and lazy. As soon as everyone else had left, he would normally settle himself down by her door and go to sleep.

Falen curled her lip in disdain. A Varisean guard who behaved that way would be thrown out on his ear. These southerners were soft.

Falen climbed to her feet and padded over to the only window in her room. Small and at head height, it looked out onto a tiny, enclosed garden. High walls surrounded the garden and the only escape was through the glass-paneled doors on the far side. Falen guessed those doors led to another set of rooms and the garden was for the use of whoever occupied them.

I wonder who's staying there, Falen thought. *One of those fat, useless fathers most likely.*

Frustration was eating Falen up inside. Nobody would listen to her. Samarin had visited her the day after her arrest and she had tried to explain why she so desperately needed to get home. She thought the Great Father might show some understanding but her hopes had been dashed. Samarin was as short-sighted as the rest of them. He had just shaken his head and said how much she'd disappointed him.

That had hurt. He'd sounded too much like her father.

Falen took a twisted piece of metal from her pocket: the clasp of her cloak pin, which she'd hammered straight. A perfect lock-pick.

Carefully, making as little noise as possible, she pulled a chair over to the window and stood on it. Falen inserted the piece of metal into the window lock and wiggled it around.

Nothing. The lock didn't budge.

Falen screwed up her face in concentration, biting on her lower lip. She just had to find the mechanism... if she could just get the right spot...

With a loud click, the lock sprang open.

She pushed the window open as far as possible, tucked the pick into her pocket and boosted herself onto the sill. She poked her head through the window and peered out, checking the coast was clear. Darkness cloaked the garden. Just what she needed.

Silently, she pulled her pack from under the bed, stuffed it through the window and watched it fall into the snow on the other side. Climbing back onto the sill, she thrust her arms through the window, squirmed like a snake and slithered to the ground, where she lay in the snow, listening for any sound.

Eventually, she stood and scanned the garden. Ah, it felt good to be outdoors again! Falen breathed in the crisp night air, savoring the icy feel of it filling her lungs. The position of the moon told Falen it was late. Best get moving. She padded silently across the garden. When she reached the tall windows, she pressed her ear to the glass and listened. No sound came from within.

Falen slipped the pick into the lock. After a few moments it clicked open. Falen crept inside. She found herself in a large sitting room. She saw a fireplace on the opposite wall and the silhouettes of furniture. Three doors opened off the room, one to either side, and one straight ahead.

Falen paused. Which one to take? One of those doors probably led to a bedroom, the other probably a bathroom. And one into the corridor and Falen's freedom. If she made the wrong choice, she would be caught and locked up again.

Falen crept forward. Suddenly a shadow launched itself from the corner and slammed into her. She tumbled to the ground, her assailant on top. A hand tightened round her arms and a knee pressed into her belly, pinning her down. Falen twisted round and heaved upwards. Her attacker went tumbling away and Falen followed. She lashed out, her fist connected with something and she heard a grunt of pain.

A fist flew toward her. Falen tried to move, but she wasn't fast enough and the fist landed in the soft part of her stomach. Gasping, she doubled over. Something smacked into her legs and suddenly she was flying through the air. With a crack, she landed on her back. All the breath rushed from her lungs. Her assailant straddled Falen's chest and something, possibly a knife, gleamed above her.

Falen lashed out, grabbed an arm. They wrestled back and forth, grunting with strain.

Suddenly the door burst open and light flooded the room. Stunned, Falen froze. Two men stood in the doorway with swords in their hands. One of them strode forward, grabbed Falen by the arm and hauled her to her feet.

He pressed the point of his sword against the base of her throat and said, "If you move I will skewer you like a pig!"

The other man ran to Falen's attacker and cried, "Are you all right, my lady? Are you hurt?"

Falen saw her attacker for the first time. It was a woman. She wore a long nightgown and had a red welt on her cheek. The woman climbed to her feet, brushing down her nightdress and tucking a knife up her sleeve. Her long yellow hair, although tousled, fell down her back like a magnificent mane. She had high, sculpted cheekbones and bright blue eyes.

She waved away the man's concern. "I'm fine, Rama. There's no need to fuss."

Rama turned to Falen. "Who are you? Who sent you? You have made an attempt on the life of the Regal. You will hang for this!"

The other man, the one holding the sword, said, "Answer him! Or I'll run you through right now and be done with it!"

Falen felt panic rising in her stomach. What was going on? Who were these people? They were not City Watch. She had never seen any of them before in her life. The woman was making a stifled wheezing sound, and with a jolt, Falen realized she was laughing.

"Come now, both of you!" the woman cried. "Does she look like an assassin?"

The two men frowned at her. "Assassins wear many guises. She attacked you."

"*I* attacked *her*, actually. Now let her go and let's get to the bottom of this. And, Aeron, put that damned sword away."

Aeron stared at Falen with an angry glint in his eye. Then, ever so slowly, he withdrew the sword and returned it to its scabbard. Falen let out a breath.

The blonde woman seated herself in one of the chairs and fixed Falen with a piercing gaze. "Now," she said. "Explain."

Falen pressed her lips together in defiance. She wouldn't play their game. Let them fetch the city fathers. She didn't care.

The blonde woman's gaze hardened.

"You're in no position to defy me. If you won't answer my questions, am I to believe Rama and Aeron are right? That you're an assassin sent to kill me?"

"I'm no assassin!" Falen blurted. "You attacked me, not the other way around."

The woman leaned forward, with a spark of excitement in her eyes. "I recognize that accent! You're from the north, from Variss!"

"And if I am? What's that to you?"

"You don't know who I am? Let me introduce myself. My name is Astrid du Lanstrang Av'Riny, Regal of Chellin and all its domains. These are Rama and Aeron. And your name is?"

Falen goggled. Had she heard right? The Regal? This woman had visited Variss once, when Falen was a young girl. She remembered her as charming and friendly although the tales described her as cunning and ruthless. Falen hoped the Regal wouldn't recognize her. She'd changed a lot in the intervening years.

"I'm Falen, a city engineer."

Astrid nodded. "See. That wasn't so hard, was it? I'm intrigued as to why a Varisean is in Ral Tora?"

Falen pressed her lips together, refusing to answer.

"Fine," Astrid said. "Let's try something else. What were you doing in my room in the middle of the night?"

There was steel in Astrid's voice. Rama

and Aeron stared at Falen with violence in their eyes. Falen realized she was trapped. She would have to tell the truth.

"Trying to escape. They'd locked me in that room opposite but I got through the window. I wasn't going to attack you — I didn't even know you were here."

"Escape? Why?"

Falen glanced at Astrid's guards and then back to the blonde woman. "I had a disagreement with my employers. I want to return to Variss. They had other ideas. What are you going to do?"

Astrid hesitated. "By rights I should call your guards and hand you over to this city's justice. But I sympathize with your plight. I cannot imagine how hard it must be to lose your home. Here's what you will do. Go back to your room, lock the window, and pretend nothing's happened."

Falen opened her mouth for a retort but Astrid held up a hand to forestall her. "I understand your frustration. But I'm asking you to trust me. Things are going to change now I'm here. You only need to wait and you'll get your wish. You will go home."

"What do you mean?" Falen asked suspiciously.

"I will say no more. Be patient, do nothing stupid, and do your best to curb that northern temper of yours, and you may be free sooner than you expect."

Falen frowned. What was this woman up to? Falen suspected that she couldn't be trusted. Yet Falen felt a faint glimmer of hope at her words. And she really had no choice anyway. If she didn't do as Astrid asked, the Regal would call the City Watch and they would probably throw her in a cell. Then how would she escape?

Falen nodded. "All right. I'll do it."

***

Aeron stood by the door, arms folded across his chest, wearing a scowl that could curdle milk.

"Let me guess," Rama said after escorting the Varisean back to her room. "Aeron thinks you should have handed her over to the City Watch but you don't agree."

"How did you guess?" Aeron growled. "As usual, our esteemed lady knows best."

"Oh come now, Aeron," Astrid said. "I have my reasons. Did you get the girl back into her room, Rama?"

Rama nodded. "Yes, although how she managed to get through that window without help I will never know. She must have been *very* determined to escape. Why did you have me take her back at all? Why not hand her over to the City Watch?"

Astrid rolled her eyes at him. "Think.

We'll need a guide to show us the way to Variss. There are none in Chellin. Then, out of nowhere, the Goddess finds us one right here in Ral Tora. And not only that, but this guide comes straight to us! The Goddess is pleased. If everything else on this mission goes so well, our plans will be realized before we know it!"

Astrid's girlish enthusiasm was infectious, and Rama was soon grinning along with her. Even taciturn Aeron managed a tight smile.

"Try and get some sleep," Astrid said. "Tomorrow is a big day, and we'll need our wits about us if we're going to bend these southerners to our will!"

CHAPTER 12

Light was beginning to brush the sky when Astrid rose the next morning. Snow had fallen during the night, covering the garden outside with a soft white blanket. As she gazed across at Falen's room, last night's events replayed through Astrid's head.

She just couldn't believe her luck. Her frustration at the long and difficult voyage melted away. She'd found the Varisean guide she needed. And not just any Varisean either. She'd recognized the girl immediately. Falen obviously thought nobody would recognize her and down here in Ral Tora that might be the case.

But Astrid was the Regal of Chellin and made it her business to know about the ruling dynasties of the great cities. She had spent considerable resources trying to discover Falen's whereabouts after she heard what happened in Variss. She'd never guessed that Falen would hide in Ral Tora. Astrid smiled to herself. She'd go along with Falen's subterfuge. For now.

In the sitting room, Aeron took the kettle from the fire and brewed a pot of tea. "You're up early today, my lady."

Astrid wrapped her fingers around the mug Aeron offered and breathed in the sweet aroma of the drink. "Couldn't sleep. I kept wondering if I'm doing the right thing. Should I have brought us here?"

Aeron's blue eyes flicked up to meet hers. "Only time can answer your question. But you're our queen, and we'll follow wherever you lead us."

To her horror, Astrid felt her eyes fill with tears. To cover it, she jumped up and strode over to the fireplace. "Thank you, Aeron," she whispered.

A maid brought a breakfast of eggs and toast but Astrid left it untouched. Hunger would help to hone her wits. She finished her drink and returned to the bedroom. She crossed to the wardrobe and took out her silver robes of office. The dress had a high neckline that ended under her chin, a tight bodice, and long skirts which trailed on the floor. Over this went a white cloak, secured at each shoulder by an opal and topaz brooch carved into the shape of an albatross.

Teriska, Astrid's handmaid, wore a solemn look as she helped Astrid into the ceremonial robes. Instead of her usual chatter, she was silent as she fastened the tiny hooks on the dress and clasped the cloak in place with the two brooches. Finally, Teriska placed a silver circlet on Astrid's head.

The handmaid sighed. "You look stunning, my lady."

There was a knock on the door and First Minister Mattack entered, accompanied by Father Hewin, the Speaker of Ral Tora's council. Mattack wore his ceremonial robes. Astrid nodded. It was time.

Astrid took Father Hewin's proffered arm and they swept from the room. Her entourage fell into step behind. They headed down a wide, richly carpeted corridor to a lobby area. Black and white tiles covered the floor, polished until they gleamed. At the far end of the lobby, two oaken doors stood closed. Father Hewin approached them and knocked.

From within came a cry of, "Who goes there?"

In response Astrid shouted, "One who would speak with the rulers of this city and take counsel with them."

"Then enter and be welcome!"

The doors swung inwards, revealing the chamber beyond. Great Father Samarin sat at a huge round table. He climbed slowly to his feet.

"Lady Astrid, Regal of Chellin, welcome to the Moot. We'll hear your news and take counsel with you."

Astrid forced her best smile onto her face and swept round the table to the seat Samarin offered. Her entourage seated themselves around her.

Astrid cast a cool eye over the gathering. City fathers in their yellow robes were dotted around the table, mixed with men and women wearing elaborate finery.

They're trying to impress us, she thought. *I only hope we impress them as much.*

When the introductions had been made — a cascade of names she would never remember — Astrid rose from her seat and cleared her throat.

"My greetings to you. My name is Astrid du Lanstrang Av'Riny, by the grace of the Goddess, Regal of Chellin and its domains. I thank you all for your kind welcome." She beamed round at everyone, willing them to trust her. "Many leagues lie between Chellin and Ral Tora but this does not excuse the mistrust that exists between us. After all, are we not cousins? I come then, to nurture friendship between our realms. I fear there is a great reckoning coming. We must stand united to face it."

A rumble of agreement went around the room. The fat city father, Erris, narrowed his eyes in suspicion. "What do you propose?"

Astrid disliked his mistrustful tone. She met his eyes. "An alliance. Together we can find a solution to the Everwinter."

"Fine words," Erris snapped. "But how do you propose we do that?"

Astrid glanced at Mattack. His face had gone bright red with anger. Rama's lips were pressed into a white line and Aeron was scowling.

Easy, she willed them. *We can suffer this man's insolence if it means we get what we want.*

"Before we can defeat the Everwinter, we have to understand it. From the presence of Variseans in your city I assume you know what happened in the north?"

Samarin nodded solemnly.

"I'll get to the point then." She reached out her hand and Mattack placed a tiny scroll in her palm which she held up for all to see.

"This message arrived from Tirsay by bird many months ago. It is a wonder it reached us at all with the terrible weather."

She unrolled the scroll and spoke clearly so none could mistake her words. "From Arnulf, King of Tirsay, to Astrid, Regal of Chellin. We are in dire peril. A dark storm has descended on us. It has raged for weeks. The Star Tarn is frozen and our supply routes are cut off. The hills around the city are full of wild animals driven down from the north. Our outlying villages are overrun. We urgently ask for aid."

A low murmur of dismay buzzed around the room but Astrid pitched her voice to carry above it.

"Chellin stands by its friends. We answered Tirsay's call. Two legions of my finest soldiers were dispatched immediately. I will let my minister tell you what happened."

Mattack stood stiffly. "My name is Mattack Az'Kanar, First Minister for the Province of Chellin. This report is from Captain Ternor of the fifth legion. He was the highest-ranking officer to return from Tirsay." He cleared his throat and began reading from a piece of paper held out in front of him.

"'We journeyed toward Tirsay without incident for five days. But on the morning of the sixth day we awoke to a blizzard. The nearer the city, the worse the weather became. In the end we had to tie ourselves to the person ahead to ensure we didn't get lost. Tirsay had always been a beautiful city, nestled on the banks of the Star Tarn, but we found desolation. Everything destroyed. Buildings toppled, the earth torn and broken, bodies littering the ground. It looked like the result of an avalanche or earthquake, although some of the bodies had obviously been preyed on by beasts.'"

As Mattack finished reading, the listeners

stirred restlessly. Father Erris jabbed a pudgy finger. "What is all this? Why should we believe your report? It sounds like something out of a Varisean saga!"

Mattack bristled. "You should believe me because I have proof." Mattack lifted a wrapped bundle from his chair. He unwrapped it and dropped the contents onto the table with a loud metallic ring.

It was a silver crown with the heron of Tirsay carved into the center.

"The fisher crown!" someone whispered in awe.

"It's true! Tirsay has fallen!"

Great Father Samarin's face paled. "Where did you get this?"

"Where do you think?" Mattack snapped. "My men found it in the ruins of the royal palace. Do you really want the grisly details?"

Astrid stood quickly, trying to defuse the tension. "King Arnulf's last communication to me said he believed this threat came from the north, from Variss or even beyond. I think he was right. I propose we send a joint force to Variss to discover the source of the Everwinter and find a way to counter it. What do you say?"

A hairy, barrel-chested man jumped to his feet. "I say let's do it!"

Astrid turned her gaze on him and the man grew suddenly embarrassed. He sketched her a bow. "My name is Barl, commander of the Panthers. I'm a soldier, not a politician. I reckon the time for talking's done. It's time to fight." He leaned his massive hands on the table and looked round at his compatriots. "I reckon we should do as they suggest. Let's accept the lady's proposal."

Astrid could have kissed him.

Great Father Samarin held up a hand. "Barl, I think it would be prudent to understand all the facts before we make a decision."

"Why? What more do we need to know? These folks have come all this way to offer us help. What else is there to think about?"

"For one thing, we don't know the terms of this proposal," grated Father Erris. "Lady Astrid hasn't explained what she would expect from this alliance. Or what's in it for Ral Tora."

Barl glared at Father Erris. Astrid smoothly cut in, "Father Erris is right. It would be foolish to join an alliance without knowing its terms. My trusted aide, Rama, will describe my proposal."

Rama stood. Even Father Erris looked away as his raptor gaze swept over him.

"People of Ral Tora, my name is Rama Do'Haishan, captain of Lady Astrid's personal guard and commander of Chellin's scouts. The Everwinter seems to have originated around Variss. However, none of the scouts I've sent have been able to get within a hundreds leagues of Ragnar's Gap. The temperatures in the north have fallen fatally low. But our charm weavers have found a drug, a special combination of plant extracts that will help our bodies to endure the cold. We suggest sending a force toward Variss by sea, as far as Whitehaven, and then to approach Variss overland from the east."

The Great Father frowned. "How do you propose to get to Whitehaven? The sea is frozen around the Varisean coastline."

Rama glanced at Astrid. They were getting to the crux of it now. Astrid gave him a minute nod.

Rama turned to the white-haired leader of Ral Tora. "You're right. To reach Whitehaven we'll need an Ice Ship."

Great Father Samarin's frown deepened. "Which you don't have."

"No we don't," Rama replied, fixing Samarin with his hawk's gaze. "But *you* do."

Astrid held her breath. She scanned Samarin's face, gauging his response. Here, then was one of the two reasons she had come south. Would they realize she was only interested in their ship?

A look flashed over Samarin's features. Fear? Or was it something else? At last, Samarin answered. "I'm afraid you're mistaken. Ral Tora has no Ice Ship. I'm sorry to disappoint you."

Rama's eyes narrowed. "It's well documented that twenty years ago an Ice Ship went to the aid of the Chellin vessel, the *Discovery*. And it's rumored that an Ice Ship won the Battle of Gray Rock during your war with Esclede."

"Rumors only. It was the galleon, *Silver Fire* who bested Esclede's fleet: a magnificent warship but certainly no Ice Ship."

Concern creased Samarin's face, but Astrid noticed the quick glance that passed between himself and Father Erris.

So, she thought. *They're lying? What are they up to?*

Astrid needed that Ice Ship. Without it her plan was doomed. "If we don't go north, if we don't find the cause of this winter, I fear the fates of Tirsay and Variss will befall us all. I sent two companies of soldiers to Tirsay and only a handful of men returned. On their return journey, they were beset by terrible beasts, just as King Arnulf described. First Minister, if you will?"

Mattack mopped his brow with a handkerchief and then heaved his ample bulk to his feet. "The soldiers managed to kill one of those beasts although many lives were lost in the process. They took something from the beast and brought it home."

He placed a wrapped object on the table and gingerly pulled back the wrap. Inside lay a cylindrical object, tapered to a wicked-looking point at one end. It was black and shiny like obsidian.

Mattack spoke. "This is a talon taken from the body of the beast that attacked our soldiers. We believe it is the talon of an Ice Dragon."

Nobody moved. Mattack's words hung like shards of glass over the listeners. Nobody breathed. Astrid watched the tableau, not daring to move. She had them!

But then Father Erris surged to his feet and the spell shattered.

"Madness!" he barked. "Are you out of your mind, or do you mock us? We have called this council in good faith, believing you truly wish to help, and you tell us tales of dragons dredged out of your fairy stories! Do you really expect us to believe such drivel?" Erris's face turned purple with rage.

Damn him! The dratted man was going to ruin everything!

Astrid curled her hands into fists. "I assure you, Father Erris, we take this matter very seriously indeed. Do you think I would sail all the way from Chellin on a fool's errand? You insult me! Two thirds of the soldiers I sent to Tirsay were wiped out by this single beast! If you think—"

"What I think, *my lady*, is that you've concocted this tale in order to enlist our aid in one of your convoluted Chellin plots! You Chellins are famed for your deviousness."

"How dare you? I came to offer Chellin's help. I hoped to find friends here but it seems I was mistaken! Would you rather pretend nothing is amiss? To hide in the south, running a city rank with fear?"

"How we run our city is not the concern of a pagan witch!"

Astrid heard the soft ring of steel and turned to see that Rama and Aeron had drawn their swords.

Rama glared at Erris. In a quiet voice he said, "If you insult Lady Astrid again, it will be the last thing you ever say. Apologize or I will cut out your tongue."

Erris opened his mouth and closed it again. He was about to say something when Great Father Samarin banged his fist on the table.

"Erris, be silent! How dare you insult our guests?" He turned to Astrid and spread his hands placatingly. "Please accept my apologies. Nerves are a little frayed. Erris did not mean to offend. Did you, Erris?"

Father Erris inclined his head. "My apologies, Lady Astrid. My tongue ran away with me. Forgive me."

Astrid seethed. If Erris had been one of her ministers, she would have had him publicly flogged. But if she wanted to salvage this situation she must show tolerance. She took a deep breath and motioned for Rama and Aeron to sheathe their swords.

"I accept your apology, Father Erris. We'll forget the incident." Astrid addressed Samarin instead. "I hope that Father Erris does not speak for all of you. We owe it to our cousins in Variss and Tirsay to discover what is really happening in the north. Will you come with me?"

Samarin stared at her for a long time. Conflicting emotions were riding behind the Great Father's eyes. *He believes me*, Astrid thought. *This old man knows far more than he's letting on.*

But then Samarin spoke and Astrid's hopes were dashed. "Alas, I cannot accept your offer. As Great Father, the welfare of Ral Tora's citizens is my responsibility. I won't send any of them into peril. I offer you the full friendship of Ral Tora but we won't join your expedition."

Astrid stared at him. "That's your final word?"

"My final word."

Astrid felt the urge to throw something at him. Instead, she said calmly, "Then I will abide by your decision, Great Father."

Opposite, Erris was smiling to himself.

Smirk all you like, you fat bag of wind, Astrid said to herself. *I will have my way in the end. Oh, yes I will.*

CHAPTER 13

"That went well," said Mattack.

Astrid spun to face him, ready to shout. But one look at his tight, angry expression made her remark die on her lips. Turning to a cabinet, she poured herself a glass of wine and surveyed the people around her.

Mattack was as white as a seagull's breast and he kept dabbing at his forehead with a handkerchief. Rama gripped a stack of papers so tightly they had become a crinkled ball. Aeron hunched his shoulders and tapped his fingers on the table.

Her plan lay dead, hacked to pieces by these white-hearted southern sons of goats. She had been so sure she could win them over. So sure.

"What are we going to do now, my lady?" Mattack asked.

Astrid sat down, indicated for the others to do the same, and then passed around the decanter of wine, making sure everyone poured themselves a drink.

"Today's meeting was an unparalleled disaster. The Ral Torans proved more obstinate than we anticipated. So we must find another way to make them agree with us. Any ideas?"

Rama stared at her. "Excuse me? I'm sorry, my lady, I must have misheard you but it sounded like you are actually thinking of staying here and trying to win the southerners over."

"That's exactly what I plan to do."

"Why? They have already made their feelings plain. I say we cut our losses, go home and leave these southern bastards to rot!"

For a second Astrid was tempted. She would like nothing more than to sail home on the next available tide. But too much was riding on this mission to give up at the first obstacle.

"We need them too much, Rama. How would we get to Variss without their Ice Ship?"

"They don't have an Ice Ship."

"You believed them? Rama, you're better at spotting a lie than that."

Rama narrowed his eyes. "So they were

lying about the Ice Ship. But how does knowing that help us?"

Mattack's glass chinked as he set it down on the table. "I think we're going about this the wrong way. The Ral Torans think they don't need us because they have their own plans to defeat the Everwinter. Somehow, we must convince them that their own plans are flawed and ours is the only sensible solution."

As Mattack's words sunk in, the germ of an idea began to form in Astrid's head. Waving her hands at them she said, "Leave me. I need to think."

They exchanged puzzled glances but did as she instructed. When she was alone, Astrid poured a brandy and sipped it.

This is a test, she said to herself, *I must prove to the Goddess that I'm worthy.*

Astrid stared into the flames. As she watched their intricate dance, ideas formed in her mind. At last, a grin spread across her face. She called Rama in from the next room and handed him a white handkerchief embroidered with the albatross of Chellin.

"Go to Anchor Street and stand beneath the sign of the Boar's Head with this handkerchief sticking out of your pocket. A man will come to you. Bring him to me."

Rama took the handkerchief and studied Astrid's face. His eyes were full of questions.

Don't ask me to explain, she willed him. *The less you know, the better.*

Rama must have read something in her expression because he bowed without a word and left.

It was mid-afternoon and already beginning to get dark. She seated herself by the fire and waited. The logs had begun to burn down when there was a light knock on the door. Rama entered, another man following behind.

Rama blinked. "My lady?"

"I'm here."

He turned at the sound of her voice. "I've done as you asked. What shall I do with him?"

"Nothing. Leave us."

"What? He might be dangerous!"

"I'll be perfectly safe, Rama. Please leave us."

Rama glared at the man, then at Astrid. At last, he stomped from the room and slammed the door.

The man went down on one knee. "What do you ask of me, my mistress?"

Astrid placed a hand on his shoulder. "Ah, Drummond, my faithful servant. I'm afraid I have another task for you. It's time I met the boy."

A thick scarf covered the lower half of Drummond's face, leaving only his eyes visible. "Would that be wise, mistress? It might arouse suspicion."

"Quite right, which is why our meeting will be an accidental one. I want you to arrange it tomorrow."

"I don't think I can, mistress. I'm on shift tomorrow and would be missed. But I can tell you what shift he's on and where he's likely to be."

Astrid considered this. "Yes, that might work. And then I want you to tell me absolutely everything you know of the heating system the engineers are building."

***

Charm Weaver Capella looked as though she had been dragged out of bed. Which, of course, she had.

Her normally luxurious chestnut hair was tousled and her eyes bleary. She yawned. Charm weavers, although powerful in the ways of the Goddess, needed their sleep just like anyone else.

It was late. Astrid had conversed with Drummond all evening and managed to discover the information she required. Together, Astrid and her spy had honed the finer points of her plan.

"Charm Weaver Capella," Astrid said. "I'm going to need your help."

The tattoos covering Capella's arms — runes of power — shone strangely in the firelight. Capella inclined her head and spoke in a deep voice. "I'm yours to command, my lady."

"I need you to weave me an earth charm, but a very potent one. Do you think you can do that?"

Capella nodded. "There's power in the rock of the plateau which I can draw upon."

Astrid smiled. "Good. I *will* get the Ral Torans on board, no matter what it takes."

***

Bram was beginning to wonder why he'd ever decided to become an engineer. Rassus had bawled at him three times so far this morning, his limbs ached from carrying tools, and mud splattered him from head to toe. To top it all, he'd forgotten his lunch.

Now he stood in a queue at the soup tent, waiting for his battered mug to be filled with the brown slop they called food. Eventually he reached the front of the queue and a surly looking woman dished out a scoop of the foul-smelling concoction and handed him a chunk of bread.

Bram mumbled his thanks and shuffled off. Rassus had told him he was not to leave the site, even on his lunch break, so Bram took his mug of soup off to a quiet corner of the site and sat down among the supply sheds. The ground was hard and cold, but at least he was sheltered from the biting wind. He wrapped his hands around the hot beaker, sniffed in the aroma and nearly choked.

What did they put in this stuff? It smelt like offal!

Bram dunked his bread in the soup and tucked in. In a few long slurps, the soup was gone and Bram stared at an empty mug, wishing for more.

The sound of voices wafted on the wind.

"Surely, you don't want to see this part of the site, my lady? It's only our storage areas. Nothing of interest here."

Bram recognized Rassus's voice but it held a simpering tone he hadn't heard before.

A woman's voice answered. "Chief engineer, I asked for a tour of your engineering works, and that is what I intend to get. Your supply area may not seem very important to you but I wish to learn as much as I can of your engineering system before I return to Chellin."

Bram jumped to his feet. But before he had a chance to make his getaway, a group of people rounded the corner and saw him.

"Bram!" barked Rassus "What are you doing here?"

Bram held his mug up apologetically. "Just having my lunch."

He glanced at Rassus's companion and his eyes went wide. She was beautiful. She wore rich black furs, with yellow hair spilling down her back. Her high cheekbones and deep blue eyes gave her a haughty look.

Surely, this must be the Lady Astrid who everyone was talking about? He realized his mouth was hanging open and snapped it shut. He dropped a hasty bow.

To his surprise, Astrid laughed. "Thank you, young man. I'm sorry we've interrupted your lunch. The chief engineer was showing me the work the engineers are doing."

Rassus said, "Bram is one of our most recent graduates from the guild academy. He's been doing some good work."

Astrid lifted an eyebrow. "Really? You must be very proud. "

"Er, yes," Bram stammered. "It's a great honor to serve my city."

"Your city. Of course. I wonder, have you ever thought of visiting Chellin, young man? We're always in need of good engineers."

She smiled, making Bram blush to his hairline.

"I, er, I haven't really thought about it. I don't know much about Chellin."

You idiot! He cursed himself silently. *Why don't you just go and make yourself sound like a witless fool?*

"Oh, I'm sure you'd like it. And you could bring your family along as well. You would be made most welcome."

"I don't have a family, my lady."

She smiled. "Really? A handsome man like you, unmarried? I don't believe it!"

Bram's cheeks went as hot as a furnace.

Lady Astrid laughed lightly, a sound like tinkling bells. "I've embarrassed you. I apologize. But surely you have other family? Parents perhaps?"

"No. My parents died when I was young."

All mirth vanished. Her face became serious and intent. "Is your mother gone, then?"

Bram was a little puzzled by her interest. "Yes."

Astrid's gaze became unfocused, as though she was thinking about something else. "I'm sorry to hear that."

She dug into the pocket of her robe and held out a white handkerchief embroidered with the albatross of Chellin. "I would be pleased if you would accept this token, Bram, as a thank you for your polite conversation."

Bram reached out and took it, not sure what to say.

"It was nice to meet you, Bram. I'm sure our paths will cross again soon." With that, she swept away, Rassus and her entourage in tow.

Bram watched her go then looked down at the handkerchief in his hand. Made from the finest silk, it was probably worth a month's wages.

The lads will never believe this, he thought.

CHAPTER 14

The day had arrived. Bram paced the floor of his living room, belly churning with excitement. Today would be either the engineers' greatest achievement or their greatest failure.

As soon as Old Rosella chimed for midday, Bram threw on his coat and joined the crowds heading to the north wall. On the streets people scurried everywhere, chattering in high, excited voices.

Like Toran's Day, Bram thought.

He hurried through the city and eventually reached the open ground in front of the north wall. Now the network of pipes had been finished, the site had been cleared of building materials so the ground was free of obstacles. Not that a bare patch of ground could be seen, mind you. The crowds made it look like market day. A cordon had been rigged up twenty paces from the wall to give the engineers space to work.

Only the most experienced engineers would take part in the operation. Much to his annoyance, Bram would be a spectator. With this in mind, he strode past the gaggle of engineers standing by the gate and joined his friends instead.

"Good morning!" Romy said cheerfully. "Looking forward to the party?"

"Seems I haven't been invited to the party!"

"Oh my! Do I detect a little bitterness on your part, Mr. Thornley?"

"He's just sore because Rassus won't let him join in," said Seth.

"And why shouldn't I be?" Bram asked. "I've worked just as hard as anyone else. Why do I have to stand here and watch while the other engineers get to do their jobs?"

Seth put an arm around Bram's shoulders. "Because, my hard-done-by-friend, it's a chance for the older engineers to show off. Newbies like us don't get invited to these kinds of things. They're for the big boys."

"It's more fun over here with us anyway," said Oscar in his deep voice. "Enjoy having the day off."

Seth winked at Oscar. "Oh, I know what's really eating at Bram. He's annoyed at missing out on a chance of impressing the ladies. He wanted to strut his stuff in his engineer's uniform, while all the girls go, 'Ooh isn't he brave!'"

"Are you lot gonna shut up, or do I have to drink this all by myself?" Romy asked. He held a green bottle in each hand.

Bram looked at them dubiously, "What's that?"

Romy grinned. "I call it Brain Boiler. My own special recipe. Trust me, you'll love it."

Bram raised an eyebrow. "Romy, the last time I tried one of your home brews I was sick for two days."

"Yes, but I know what went wrong last time. This is perfectly safe." Romy swigged from one bottle and passed the other to Bram.

The liquid inside smelled like a mixture of brandy and lamp oil, and knowing Romy, that might not be too far from the truth. Bram took a sip. He gagged, clamping his lips together to keep from spewing it out as the fiery brew raced down his throat and turned his insides to flame.

"What do you think?" Romy asked.

"Lovely," Bram croaked.

Bram glanced around and noticed that the important people — or those rich enough — had gathered on raised platforms above the crowd to get a better view. On one such platform Bram saw the Lady Astrid. A thin woman with tattoos marching up each arm stood by Astrid's side. The woman's lips moved in a stream of silent words.

Great Rosella began to toll. The signal to begin. The ponderous notes shimmered over the city and the crowd fell quiet.

In front of the gates the engineers had rigged up a great round bowl as wide across as First Storm Tower. The center of this was hollow and connected to the pipes that ran beneath the city. For the purpose of this testing, the curileum would be pumped into this bowl and set alight so it burned like some giant's torch. A symbol of Ral Tora's success.

Out in the plains, engineers had been stationed at each section of pipes to track the fuel's progress from the mine. Engineer Trenak appeared atop the wall waving a blue flag.

"First section clear!" she shouted.

The crowd whooped and applauded. Bram let out a long breath. The first section of pipes had been filled and there was no sign of any problems. Now the fuel would begin pumping beneath the city.

"Section two clear!" came the shout from atop the wall after a few moments. The crowd cheered and people clapped each other on the back.

"Going all right so far, you reckon?" Romy asked Bram.

Bram nodded. "So far."

"I bet old Rassus is feeling smug. You never know, he might even be in a good mood when we turn into work tomorrow."

Bram snorted. "Rassus? I don't think I've ever seen him smile, let alone be in a good mood. If the sun came out, all the snow melted, and we were given a national holiday, Rassus would still complain about sunburn."

Romy laughed. "Anyone would think you don't like the man! I know you've got a soft spot for him really!"

Bram didn't answer. Instead, he turned back to the walls. He could make out Rassus standing by the final sluice. The chief engineer was deep in conversation with Celian. Even from this distance, Bram could see the strain in both men. Rassus's shoulders were hunched and Celian kept running his hands through his hair.

Yet the crowds seemed oblivious to the tension. A bonfire had been lit down by the postern gate and people danced round it. Children rushed about, getting under their parent's feet but nobody minded. An air of cheer permeated the city.

Finally, the call came, "Final section, clear!"

An expectant hush fell over the crowd. Now came the real test.

Celian raised his hand and shouted, "Releasing final sluice!"

He pulled a lever and a deep, subterranean rumble shook the air.

All eyes turned to the great torch.

Silence. A faint moan of pressure as curileum was pumped up through the bowl. Then with an almighty 'whoosh!' a flame ignited, filling the metal bowl like a bonfire.

The team of engineers monitoring the final sluice ran forward, their arms full of instruments and gadgets. They set to work measuring the pressure, temperature and a thousand other things. Then one of them looked at Rassus and nodded.

The chief engineer bellowed, "All sections clear!"

The fuel had been successfully pumped into the city. They could light and heat the city without fear of shortages. The crowds erupted into a cacophony of cheering and hollering.

Oscar threw an enormous arm around Bram's shoulders and said, "Well, it looks as if you engineers have gone and bloody done it. You'll all be heroes after this."

Bram felt a stupid grin spread across his face. After all his worrying, the plan had worked! They'd beat the Everwinter yet!

He yelled out a whoop of delight and threw his arms around each of his friends in turn. Down by the bonfire people had joined hands and were dancing around it in a circle.

Romy held up a bottle of Brain Boiler. "To the future!"

"The future!" the others echoed. They banged their bottles together and downed the potent drink in one gulp.

But then something caught Bram's eye. Celian had left his position by the sluice and moved over to Rassus. Both men bent over the release mechanism as though studying something. Then suddenly, Celian turned and ran back to the sluice at the same time Rassus began bellowing something at the teams on top of the wall. A commotion broke out among the engineers. The teams hurried toward the final sluice, unslinging equipment from their backs as they ran.

The great torch fluttered and went out.

A jolt of fear sliced through Bram's belly. Something was wrong.

"I'm going to talk to the engineers," he said.

His friends trailing, Bram pushed his way through the mob. The crowds were so thick that Bram was pushed off course, and instead of making his way straight toward the wall, he found himself approaching the raised platform on which the Chellins had been watching proceedings. Bram could see Lady Astrid descending the steps, accompanied by her retinue.

At last, Bram reached the front. Celian and Rassus still worked feverishly on the sluices.

Before Bram could take another step, a huge boom sounded from deep beneath the earth. The ground lurched. Bram was thrown on his face in the dirt. People screamed.

"What's going on?" Romy shouted.

A cracking sound filled the air.

Bram had heard that sound before. Stone grating on stone. He looked at the north wall and realized his worst nightmare was coming true.

"Run!" he screamed. "The wall is collapsing! Run! Get out! Everyone get out!"

He scrambled to his feet and pulled his friends up after him. "Run for your lives!"

Celian and Rassus were still working on the sluice. They wouldn't stand a chance.

He took a step toward them but Oscar caught his arm. "No, Bram! We must get away from here!"

Reluctantly Bram followed Oscar. He and his friends joined the crowds thundering away from the wall. Bram threw another look over his shoulder, and to his horror, saw that huge cracks had snaked their way up the wall from its base. The frozen earth in front of the wall had cracked too, and the cracks were beginning to widen even as Bram watched.

"Faster!" he panted, "It won't last much longer."

But Bram knew they were too close, if the wall came down now, they would all be crushed.

Up in front, the ground suddenly caved inwards. People screamed as they were pulled into a gaping hole. Bram cried out in terror and veered to his left, but he was too close. His momentum carried him toward the fissure, its black maw growing larger and larger.

Suddenly a warm breeze brushed against him. It wrapped around his body, slowing his descent. For a second he just hung there, then the breeze pushed him, settling him back on solid ground.

Bram had no time for puzzlement. He and his friends thundered on. Curileum gushed from the hole, flooding the ground with scalding fuel. Smoke rose in great, billowing clouds.

From somewhere ahead Romy shouted, "Follow me and stay away from the edge!"

Bram caught the back of Oscar's coat and ran blindly on, trusting Romy to lead the way. People flitted in and out of the cloud of smoke, as insubstantial as wraiths.

From behind in the chaos, came a terrifying sound.

The groan of falling rock.

The ground shook as the wall collapsed, and suddenly debris flew everywhere. Great chunks of stone and masonry came rolling along the ground with terrible speed, crushing people where they stood, sweeping others into the fissures.

A great gray boulder loomed out of the mist, as big as a cart. Bram screamed in terror. It bounded toward him but at the last moment seemed to hit an invisible barrier and veered off. Bram shook his head in amazement and ran on. The air was thick with tiny stone chips that made Bram cough.

All was confusion. People ran in panic. Some, disorientated in the murk, ran back toward the wall. Bram held his breath and closed his eyes. His grip on Oscar's tunic was the only thing that guided him. He kept his legs pumping and trusted his friend to lead him to safety.

A form materialized from the gloom and grabbed Bram's arm. Bram peered closely and realized it was a man who'd been with the Lady Astrid yesterday.

"Follow me. I will lead you to safety."

He veered to the right and Bram followed, pulling Oscar's tunic to guide him, hoping the others followed.

The man shouldered open a door and Bram was suddenly fleeing down a flight of steps into darkness. The atmosphere was free of dust so Bram pulled in a great lungful of air.

Bram found himself in a wide brick chamber, lit by a fire burning in a brazier. He looked for his friends, and to his relief, found they had all made it, along with three or four other people who had followed them. Romy and Oscar seemed more or less unhurt under the muck but Seth had a huge gash on his forehead that leaked blood into his eyes.

Their rescuer took Seth by the arm and

marched him to the fire. He unceremoniously pushed him to the floor and began cleaning the wound with water from his drinking flask.

The chamber was full of people, mostly the Chellin visitors. By the fire, looking pale and drawn, sat the Lady Astrid. Grime spattered her face and her hair had come loose from its intricate coils and lay in tangled snarls around her shoulders. She stared at Bram.

Bram looked away and ran his fingers through his matted hair. A fatigue like lead flooded his body. He collapsed against a wall, exhausted.

Astrid rose and strode over to him. "Are you all right? Are you hurt?"

She knelt beside him, placing a cool hand on his forehead.

"No," he answered. "Just tired."

She nodded. "We should be safe here. Rama found this cellar. We'll wait here until it's safe to go outside."

Romy and Oscar collapsed beside Bram. Nobody spoke.

Above, the ground continued to boom and creak. Occasionally Rama went to the top of the stairs to look out. Twice, he brought back people who had managed to find the door. Astrid said a prayer for them all to her goddess, and they waited.

After what seemed like eternity, the noises finally died away. Still, the occupants waited. Eventually, Rama told everyone to stay put while he went outside to look around. He returned wearing a grim expression.

"It's safe to leave now."

In silence, they climbed to their feet and followed Rama up the steps.

The space where only this morning crowds had danced and capered, had become a wasteland of jumbled rock and debris. A huge section of the north wall was completely gone, leaving only a pile of broken rocks where it once stood. The collapse had burst the pipes laid in its foundations, and the whole area was flooded with pools of curileum, some of which were ablaze. To the east some of the storage sheds had caught fire and burned fiercely.

Bram put his head in his hands.

This is not happening. This is not happening.

It was over. He looked out on the destruction not only of the north wall, but also of the hopes of the city of Ral Tora.

CHAPTER 15

Someone placed a hand on Bram's shoulder. "Come."

Bram turned to find Lady Astrid staring at him. Too numb to respond, he allowed her to lead him away, Rama and Aeron a step behind. Romy and the others followed.

"This is terrible," Astrid murmured as they stumbled through the wreckage. "A tragedy."

"I don't understand," Bram said. "How could this happen?"

Astrid shook her head, sending dust flying from her hair. "Who knows? But your people must move on from this mistake."

Bram stared at her. "Move on? To what?

What can we do now?"

Astrid's gaze turned hard. "You don't give up. You find some other way to beat the Everwinter."

She placed her hands on Bram's shoulders, looking him in the eyes. "Bram, I offered an alliance to the city fathers and they refused. Now things are different. I will make my offer again and would like your support. Can you give me that?"

He opened his mouth to ask why she needed him but Seth staggered over. Blood and grime caked his red hair and his eyes looked startlingly white in his dirt-smeared face. "Bram, we're going to head home now. We need to check our families are all right."

Bram squeezed Seth's shoulder. "I'm sure they'll be fine."

Seth, Romy and Oscar moved off, picking their way through the debris. Watching them go, Bram felt loneliness seep into his bones.

I have no family to worry about, he thought. *There will be nobody searching the rubble for me.*

Astrid watched him, her blue eyes calculating. "Bram? You still haven't answered my question."

He shook his head. "I'm sorry. I have to go."

Before Astrid could reply, he hurried away.

***

Astrid watched him stagger through the rubble. Damn the boy! Why must he be so difficult? She took a step but Rama laid a hand on her arm.

"Let him go, my lady. There'll be time to win him over."

Astrid gazed at Bram's retreating figure for a second then nodded. "We'll go to the Father Hall. That's where everyone will congregate."

They made their way through streets choked with people. Some stood calling the names of friends and family while others chanted loud prayers.

Funny, Astrid thought, *how people of science immediately turn to prayer when something goes wrong.*

A large crowd had gathered at the corner of Goose Street and a man was bellowing, "The old gods have spoken! We are cursed for our sins! We must turn back to the old gods now, before it is too late!"

He wore smart clothes like a merchant and his eyes, as they raked over the mob, were like vultures eyes. He reminded Astrid of the Chellin high priest.

At last, they arrived at the Forum. On the steps to the Father Hall, a squadron of the City Watch desperately tried to hold back the crowd. The mood tasted ugly. Rama and Aeron drew their swords as they pushed through the mob. The watchmen recognized

Astrid's party, and let them through without comment.

Suddenly a man staggered up behind them, panting, and Astrid turned toward him. Rassus. Mud and blood covered the chief engineer's clothes.

"Chief Engineer," she began, "I thought you were —"

"Dead?" He laughed sourly. "No such luck." He pushed past Astrid and stomped into the Father Hall.

Astrid shared a look with Rama before they made their way through the doors and down to the Moot. The dozen or so people seated at the table looked haggard. Nobody spoke above a whisper, as though to do so would be to break some unwritten rule.

Rassus stalked over to a vacant seat and threw himself into it. Astrid took a seat opposite, where she could watch the chief engineer. He should not be alive. He might yet ruin her plans.

Great Father Samarin sat with his eyes closed. His beard and eyebrows were full of dust, giving him the look of a wild hill-man from the western deserts. Commander Alara of the City Watch had a bandage around her head and her face was as white as bed linen. She gripped the edge of the table with both hands, as though it was the only thing keeping her upright.

At last, Great Father Samarin stirred

himself. He nodded at the guards and they swung the heavy doors shut, leaving the room in silence.

The Great Father seemed to have aged. As he pulled himself to his feet he winced in pain and the skin around his eyes had grown thin and stretched, brittle as paper. One gnarled hand grabbed the arm of his chair to steady himself.

"I won't waste time telling you what's happened," he began. "The whole city must be aware of this disaster by now. What we need to do is decide how to deal with it." His pale eyes fixed on Rassus. "Chief Engineer, report please."

Rassus's mouth twitched as though about to make an angry retort, but in a quiet voice he said, "What do you want me to say? Isn't it obvious? We made a mistake somewhere. The tunnels beneath the wall couldn't take the weight. The wall collapsed. The pipes exploded. People died."

Astrid let out a slow sigh of relief. They didn't suspect.

The Great Father stared at the chief engineer. "How could this happen?"

"Because we're human," snapped Rassus, fixing on the Great Father with a baleful stare. "We're just people, doing our best in a bad situation. Our best wasn't good enough. We all knew the plan held risks."

"I was assured they were acceptable."

"Curse you, Samarin!" Rassus shouted. "If you'd listened to me none of this would have happened! I told you not to turn it into a public spectacle! It was an engineering project, not a carnival!"

"Are you saying this is *my* fault?"

"You're the one looking to blame! So blame me if you like, I already do. I am chief engineer. People are dead because of me. Celian, my second in command, and the best engineer I've ever worked with, is dead because of me."

"I've heard of Celian's death," the Great Father said in a quiet voice. "We all mourn his passing. He was a brave and much loved man."

Rassus glared at Samarin. "I know. He should have been chief engineer, not me. I resign my commission. I want no part of this anymore."

It was Samarin's turn to glare. "What? You would resign now, when we need you most?"

"You don't need me."

"But who will replace you? With Celian gone, who is left?"

"After Celian, Falen is the best. But I doubt she'll work for you after the way she's been treated."

Samarin pushed his lips together. His eyes held an angry glint. "I do not accept your resignation, Chief Engineer. You will remain at your post and help to put right this disaster."

The two men stared at each other. Rassus's eyes were bright with fury. Samarin held the chief engineer's gaze and Rassus looked away.

"Very well."

The Speaker of the Council, the somber-faced Father Hewin, now cleared his throat and stood up, eager to forestall any further arguments.

"I've been getting reports in from all over the city and I feel we can draw an accurate picture of what is happening. A four hundred meter section of the north wall and gate collapsed, as well as two watchtowers. As we speak, teams of rescuers are being sent to start digging through the rubble for survivors. Fire crews are dealing with several fires. Most have been contained but two threaten the Cotton District. The area has been evacuated and cordoned off.

The engineers, under the command of engineer Trenak, have begun the process of shutting the pipes and stabilizing the excavation works on the rest of the wall. In addition, many of the pipes beneath the city have ruptured and caused explosions in the merchant's quarter and Saddle Row. So far, we know eighteen people have died. It is sure to be more once updates start coming in."

Samarin nodded, then turned to the City Watch. "Commander Alara?"

Alara did not stand. The bandage around her head had turned crimson. Nevertheless, she held her back straight and her voice held a military crack as she reported, "My lord, as you would imagine, the city is close to panic. I have turned out all units of the City Watch in an effort to keep order. I fear this will not be enough. I ask permission to impose an immediate curfew. Under the circumstances I think this will be the easiest way to bring normality back to the city."

Samarin thought for a moment. "All right. Make the preparations."

Alara nodded and then climbed unsteadily to her feet. Two of her officers took her elbows to support her and tottered toward the door.

"Commander?" Samarin called after them. Alara turned back to look at the Great Father. "As soon as you've given the commands, take yourself straight to the healers and don't leave until they tell you to. That's an order."

Alara gave a tight smile and then made her way out of the meeting hall.

Samarin surveyed the room. "So, what now?"

Astrid saw her chance. "May I speak, Great Father?"

"Of course, my lady."

Astrid cleared her throat. "You all know why I came to Ral Tora and what I offered you. When last we met you turned down my proposal because you were certain you had a better way. Your way has ended in tragedy. I make my offer again. Will you not now consent to come north with me?"

Father Erris answered, "I might have guessed you would use this disaster to further your own plans. Don't listen to her, Samarin."

Samarin ran his hand over his face. "The council isn't in full session. No decision can be made until—"

"Do as she asks!" Rassus barked suddenly.

Father Erris swung his bald head around to glare at the chief engineer. "And just when exactly did you start agreeing with the foreigner?"

"When I realized she talks a lot more sense than the overpaid, fat bags of wind we call city fathers!"

"Chief Engineer!" hissed Great Father Samarin. "You overstep yourself! I will not have this insubordination! Do you understand?"

Rassus didn't answer. Samarin slammed his fist down on the table so hard the sound echoed around the room. "Do you understand?" he bellowed.

"Fine!" barked Rassus.

"Very well. Who else agrees we should send a force north with the Lady Astrid?"

Astrid held her breath.

Rassus raised his hand and then, one by one, the dozen or so people in the room raised their hands until only Father's Erris and Hewin remained.

"Are you all insane?" cried Father Erris.

"You would follow this northern witch to your deaths?"

Father Hewin, who had remained stony faced and silent, now said, "Erris, I think you're swimming against the tide." Slowly he raised his hand.

"You can't be serious!" Erris said. "Hewin, you know what this woman stands for! Her heathen beliefs go against everything we in Ral Tora believe. How can you even contemplate this? Have you taken leave of your senses?"

"We do not live in normal times, Erris. Perhaps it is time you put aside your apprehension and support us."

"Never!" Erris's eyes flashed as he turned to Samarin. "You cannot do this, Great Father. You need a unanimous agreement and I will not add my vote to this idiocy."

The Great Father turned pale eyes on Erris. "You're wrong, Erris. When the city is under an emergency curfew, the Great Father's vote overrides the council. It's agreed. We will accept the alliance Chellin offers and send a force to the north."

Erris let out a howl of fury. "You won't get away with this insanity! Do you think the people will accept you making an alliance with these heathens? You haven't heard the last of this!" With that, he stalked out of the meeting chamber and slammed the door behind him.

"Charming man," Astrid said dryly.

"Erris won't be the only one upset by this

decision," said Father Hewin. "Perhaps it would be prudent to keep this discussion to ourselves."

Rassus snorted. "What, with that bag of piss, Erris, blurting his poison to any who'll listen? The news will be all over the city by morning."

"Rassus is right," Samarin said. "And besides, I think there will be more that support rather than oppose us. At least we will be seen to be doing something positive, rather than sitting on our behinds doing nothing."

"Something positive?" said Father Hewin. "Make no mistake, Samarin, many people won't be happy. They won't see it as something positive, but as something dangerous. My apologies to Lady Astrid, but a lot of people regard the Chellins with suspicion."

"There's no need to apologize to me, Father Hewin," Astrid said. "Many of your people think I am a witch, just as many of my own people think you are ignorant bigots. This is because of prejudice and ignorance. This alliance will help change that."

Father Hewin nodded. "I hope you're right. I'm looking forward to seeing the delights of your city. I've heard your architecture is exquisite."

Astrid blinked at him. She had not expected this. "You intend to come with us?"

"Of course, you'll need a representative

from Ral Tora's government, and who better than myself? I am Speaker of the Council, I can speak for the city fathers and we can hardly spare Samarin himself at a time like this."

Great Father Samarin raised an eyebrow at Hewin. "Did you think to discuss this with me before you made this announcement, Hewin?"

Hewin blushed. "I'm sorry, Great Father, but I'm the obvious choice."

Samarin sighed. "You're probably right. All right. You will go with the Lady Astrid as the representative of the city fathers, although I shall miss your support on the council. Erris will be more troublesome than ever after this."

Astrid bowed. "Welcome aboard, Father Hewin. I'm sure your wisdom will prove invaluable on this trip."

Samarin said, "You will have ten of our best soldiers, picked by Commander Alara herself to accompany you. I will put Barl in charge of them. He is the best tracker we have and a veteran of the war with Esclede. If anyone can find your road to Variss, he can."

Astrid nodded. "Good. But I must make a request of my own. I wish to take the Variseans Falen and Tomas with me as well."

Samarin's eyebrows shot up. "I cannot agree. Engineer Falen is awaiting the outcome of an investigation for professional negligence and Tomas is with our healers. Besides, what possible use could they be to you?"

"Both Falen and Tomas are from Variss,"

Astrid replied. "They will be my guides. I beg your indulgence in this, Great Father."

Samarin looked over at Hewin. A silent agreement seemed to pass between the two men. "Very well. I doubt the case against Falen would stand now anyway. It's clear she was not responsible for the flaws with the tunnels. And our healers have not had much success in treating Tomas's condition. Perhaps you will do better."

"The next high tide will be in two days," Astrid said. "That's when we sail."

***

Bram wandered in a daze. Tomas's words kept running through his head.

Secrets and lies. Layers of meaning.

He had believed so wholeheartedly in the engineers. He had believed science would save them. Now he felt bereft, shaken, as though the prop supporting him had collapsed. Perhaps Seth had been right all along. Were they fools to put so much faith in their scientists?

So many questions.

Snow had started to fall. Big, fat flakes fell lazily through the windless air to settle on the tops of walls and the skeletal branches of trees. Bram let the flecks catch in his hair and slide down his face, unnoticed.

Secrets and lies. Layers of meaning.

What was really going on here? He felt as

though the truth was some elusive stranger who disappeared round a corner each time he caught sight of them.

He walked mechanically and it was not until he saw the large, dilapidated building looming through the snowfall that he realized he had come to the Old Library.

A rueful smile played across his lips.

Inside, the library hadn't changed. The same antiquated, musty smell assailed Bram's nostrils and the same dim light flickered through the room. The librarian looked up from her seat by the fire as the door opened.

"Ah. You're back. I wondered when I would see you again."

I bet she has no idea what's been happening in the city, Bram thought. *This library is her whole world.*

"I didn't find what I needed last time," he said. "I thought I'd try again."

The librarian grunted. "Well, I hope you can remember what you were reading. I certainly can't."

Bram's eyes wandered over the shelves. So much knowledge hidden away. Thousands of years of history, left to gather dust. Bram took a seat next to the librarian.

"What you said to me last time, about the city being based on lies? What did you mean?"

She turned to regard him with eyes full of knowledge. "Why have you come here?"

Bram hesitated. "To find the truth."

"A dangerous word," she replied, turning away and staring into the fire. "Be sure you are ready for it or you might find more than you bargained for."

"What do you mean?"

"Exactly what I say. There is truth to be found here, but first you must peel back the layers of lies and be prepared for what you find beneath. Are you ready for that?"

Bram took a deep breath. "Yes."

The librarian waved her hands at the space around them. "Then you've come to the right place. Good luck."

Bram sighed, pulled himself to his feet and made his way through the shelves, filling his arms with the books he had been reading the last time he came here. When he had as many as he could carry he sat down at a dusty desk and began to read.

Some time later, an odd grating noise made him look up from the page he was studying. The librarian had fallen asleep. She was leaning back against her chair, mouth hanging open, snoring loudly. Wisps of her hair rose and fell with her breath.

Bram snapped the book shut with a dull thump and rubbed his eyes. How long had he been here? All evening?

A log crackled in the fire, sending up a plume of red sparks. The librarian grunted and then turned over.

Bram leaned his chin on his hands. This

was getting him nowhere.

What exactly do you expect to find? He asked himself. *A miraculous answer to all of Ral Tora's problems? Go home, you idiot. This is a fool's errand.*

He pulled himself to his feet and began piling up the books. But as his eyes scanned the room, looking for the shelves he wanted, he noticed a shadow on the wall at the back of the library. He left the books on the table and moved closer. A door, Bram realized, no higher than himself, reinforced with bands of rusted iron. A heavy-looking lock secured the handle.

Bram turned around, surveying the library. Silent as a crypt.

Bram padded back to the fire and found the librarian still asleep. A bunch of keys dangled from her belt.

He hesitated. Curiosity got the better of conscience. He leaned forward and, ever so gently, unclipped the librarian's keys.

She groaned.

Bram froze.

She stretched and turned over. After a few of Bram's heartbeats she began snoring again.

Bram breathed out slowly.

Wrapping his hand around the keys so they wouldn't jangle, Bram returned to the door. He brushed the worst of the cobwebs from the padlock and inspected it. The mechanism was old and rusty. Bram put the first key into the lock and struggled to turn it.

The lock wouldn't budge. He inserted the next key. Still no luck. He tried a third key and the lock suddenly clicked open.

To Bram's relief, the hinges did not squeal as he pushed the door open but it made a dull scraping noise as its base pushed through layers of dust and grime. Spiders scuttled out of the way. A cold wind blew through the opening, carrying the scent of damp to Bram's nostrils.

Darkness lay beyond the door.

Bram unhooked one of the small oil lamps hanging on the library wall and held it up. A stone corridor ran off into the distance. Bram hesitated, looking from library to corridor and back again.

What are you doing? he asked himself. *Lock the door and go home!*

But he didn't. He took a step into the corridor and then another. The walls were made of large, mortared bricks angling up into an arched ceiling. His boots clicked on the flagstone floor as he walked. After a time Bram reached a flight of steps that angled steeply downwards.

The lamp illuminated only the first few steps of the stairwell. Bram placed each foot with care, mindful of the black tumble ahead of him. The descent seemed to go on forever and Bram had the distinct feeling he was descending into a bottomless pit. At last, however, the steps came to an end. Another corridor stretched off into darkness.

How deep does this go? Bram thought. *I must be well below the foundations of the library now.*

As he descended this time, something caught his eye. Friezes decorated the wall of the stairwell, scenes of flowers and trees. The carvings were old and decrepit but they must have once been exquisite. Tiny patches of color remained, giving them the look of withered things still trying to cling to life.

He moved on. The temperature dropped and Bram thought wistfully of the fire burning in the library. No sound reached his ears except his own footsteps.

Bram reached the bottom of the stairwell and found himself at an intersection. The main passage carried straight on, with two others splitting off in different directions. Torches were spaced at regular intervals along the wall. Bram opened the glass case of his oil lamp and pressed its flame to the wick of the first torch.

With a *whoosh* the torches along the passages sprang into life as though this first one was connected to all the others.

He paused to consider his options. A part of him wanted to get out of here as quickly as he could. But another, more insistent part, demanded he carry on. He began walking.

The air in these depths carried a strange smell, not of rot or mold, but of something else. *Age.*

At length, Bram reached a dead end. A

solid wall blocked the end of the corridor. Bram shook his head, wondering why anyone would build a corridor that didn't lead anywhere.

A frieze of a large, reptilian beast covered the wall. It had large wings, a long neck and tail, and an elongated head with bright fiery eyes. Intrigued, Bram reached out and ran his fingers along the carving, feeling the smooth stone under his fingertips.

A voice. A whisper. So quiet as to be almost beyond perception.

Who are you? Why do you disturb our sleep?

Slowly the wall swung inwards.

Bram's heart pounded. *Get out of here*, his instincts screamed.

Instead, he stepped through the door and stood in the darkness, his breath coming in ragged gasps. Bram pressed his lamp to a torch on the wall.

As light flared, Bram's jaw fell open. A massive room spread out before him, its ceiling so high it was lost in shadow. Countless shelves crammed with books filled the chamber.

As he stepped inside, Bram felt as though he was trespassing on an ancient secret. He approached one of the bookshelves and peered up at it. The books were large and heavy with leather bindings. Gently, he reached up and pulled one out, coughing at the plume of dust that came away with it.

Bram carefully laid the book down on the floor and then sat down cross-legged in front of it. He lifted the cover. The pages were yellow and as brittle as charcoal. There was no date on the title page but from the strange, spiky script Bram could tell this book was old, far older than anything in the library above. He squinted at the faded gray writing, trying to make it out.

On the War of Dividing and the Creation of the Rift.

Inside, the text had faded into illegibility. Holding his lamp as close to the page as he dared, Bram found a passage still readable.

In the ninety seventh year of the War of Dividing, the Fire Dragon Teranan and her allies finally brought an end to the conflict. With heavy hearts, the survivors enacted the Dividing according to the Treaty of Vaspara and the world was split. All creatures with the Gift were imprisoned forever in the Quiet Land, never again to walk with mortals.

He closed the book and returned it to the shelf. He took down another and opened it.

Rituals of the Gods by Elisha Vaz Kirwan

Mantaro, the Warrior, has always been most protective of his rituals. Blood will appease him and make sure his benediction is bestowed upon you. In battle, the wounded must be slain by the survivors and their hearts burnt in the sacrificial brazier if your next victory is to be assured. Mantaro will accept no less.

Saiis, king of the gods, is a lover of women. Once in every thousand years he will choose a human wife. That wife will bear his child so the blood of the gods flows in the veins of mortal kind. Saiis's child will be a great leader of men, for he will be both mortal and immortal, god and human. But Saiis can be cruel. If he does not approve of the child, he will strike him down. For this reason, the children of Saiis are pitied as well as revered.

Shir, Lady of Sorrows is gentle. She asks only that we pray by her pools and remember our dead. If we do so, she will care for our loved ones in the afterlife.

Bram paused. Pray by her pools? Remember our dead? Was this where the Ral Toran tradition of the memory pool came from?

He turned the page but found nothing else he could make out. Sighing, he closed the book and returned it to its place.

In the far corner of the library Bram found another stone door with the reptilian beast carved into it. The door swung slowly inwards as he brushed it with his fingertips. Beyond, he found a vaulted vestibule with four passages leading off in different directions.

Conscious that if he got lost he might not be able to find his way out again, Bram stopped. Apprehension and excitement churned in him. At some deep, primeval level, Bram knew he should not be here. He was a trespasser, walking paths that had not been trod for years uncounted. But another part of Bram knew he had to go on, had to discover whatever secrets were being kept in the ancient bowels of Ral Tora. So he took the left passage, lighting the torches as he moved.

At length he arrived at another stone door. Unlike the others, this one had cracked down the middle and half had fallen inwards, obscuring the picture carved into its surface. In front of the door, like a guardian, sat a statue of a dog. Its face still bore a snarl and the last vestiges of red pigment could be seen in its eyes.

Bram shuddered, feeling the hair on his neck rise. Why did that dog seem to be staring at him?

Steeling his courage, Bram stepped through the door. He found himself in one of the largest and most ornate chambers he'd ever seen. Gone was the pale stone of the earlier corridors, this chamber was carved from pristine white marble. A ceiling carved into the semblance of many magnificent beasts stretched overhead. They had huge glorious eyes that seemed to be staring down at Bram.

But other than its decoration, the room stood empty.

Bram walked wide-eyed through the chamber and beyond it to another, just as grand as the first, but also empty. He soon realized he had found his way into a complicated series of interconnecting chambers, each carved of the same beautiful marble. All empty.

As he moved Bram found himself becoming more and more uncomfortable. His mind kept straying to the statue of the dog guarding the entrance to these chambers and the way its eyes seemed to glare at him. It had felt like a warning.

Stop being a coward, he told himself. *You haven't seen anything untoward since you came down here.*

At last, Bram came to the end of his search. He stood in another empty chamber like the ones he had already passed through, except there was no way out of this one. A dead end. He must retrace his steps.

Then a slight discoloration on the wall caught his eye. Stepping closer, Bram realized it was another stone door bearing a faded frieze that looked like a tall man. The man's head seemed oddly misshapen.

Bram paused, licking his lips. What was he doing here? *Get out*, he told himself. *Get out now.* But a strange compulsion lay on him. Curiosity burned inside. Bram reached out and touched the carving. The door swung inwards and Bram stepped through into pitch darkness.

A strange odor reached his nostrils. For a moment, he couldn't put a name on it, but then it came to him.

A graveyard.

Swallowing, Bram ran his hands along the

wall looking for a torch. His oil lamp only lit the tiny space around him and revealed nothing of his surroundings. Soon he had moved several paces into the room but had found no sign of any torches.

Behind him, something grated. Bram whirled round to see the door swinging shut. Bram yelped and flung himself at the diminishing gap. Too late. The door closed with a thud.

Bram thumped the door with his fists. He pushed and pulled and heaved as hard as he could. It wouldn't budge. Panic rose in his throat.

"Let me out! Help!"

His words faded to nothing in the dead air.

Bram sagged against the door. Hysteria began to build in his belly. He took a deep breath and let it out slowly.

Think, he told himself. *Try to find another way out. There must be one somewhere.*

He needed light. Bram placed his hands on the wall again and began following it. He had no idea how far he'd moved into the room when his fingers brushed something cylindrical attached to the wall.

A torch!

Mouthing a silent thank you, Bram lit the torch, sending blazing yellow light through the room. Bram looked around then screamed in terror.

A huge beast stood looking down at him.

It had a narrow head with gaping, many-fanged jaws. Its massive body had a vicious, barbed tail and wings that stretched almost the whole width of the chamber.

Bram gulped in terror and waited for those terrible jaws to descend and tear him to pieces.

But the beast didn't move.

Bram pulled in a steadying breath and looked closer. The light glancing off its hide created strange shadows...

Bram gasped as realization hit him. A skeleton.

What Bram had taken to be dark eyes were actually staring sockets in the beast's skull. The torchlight had cast the skeleton into shadow, masking the fact that it was long dead. The bones had faded to a muddy brown and gleamed dully in the flickering light.

Bram had no idea how it was still articulated. Time and gravity should have reduced the skeleton to a pile of bones.

Questions tumbled through his mind. Who knew about this beast? Samarin? The librarian? Who had put it here? And why?

A raised platform sat in front of the beast, and, Bram realized as he squinted at it, something was lying on it.

Bram took faltering, fear-driven steps toward it, terrified and captivated.

Another skeleton.

Not a beast this time. A man. He was tall, exceptionally so, and the remnants of fine clothing clung to his skeletal frame. His hands clasped a magnificent sword to his chest. It had a golden pommel and strange symbols carved into the blade. A shield lay by his side, but the design on it had long since faded away. Bram moved around the platform, examining the skeleton. He reached the skull and stopped, staring. The eye sockets were mere slits, tapering to a sharp point. The jaw angled sharply downward, giving the whole face an elongated look, like melted wax.

The hair rose on the back of Bram's neck. His heart pounded.

He glanced around the chamber again, at the marble floor and walls, and the elegantly carved ceiling. Then his thoughts returned to the statue of the dog. It had seemed to be guarding something…

A tomb, he realized. *These are the old catacombs.*

He heard the step behind him too late. Something slammed into him and sent him crashing to the ground. A hand grabbed a fistful of hair and jerked his head backward. A knife pressed against his throat.

"What are you doing here?" a voice hissed.

"I, I'm sorry!"

The knife vanished and Bram was pulled roughly to his feet. Hands spun him around and he came face to face with the librarian.

"I asked you a question."

Bram stared, mouth hanging slack. Gone

was the doddering old librarian. She had thrown off the shapeless gray shawl and wore a tight fitting leather tunic and trousers, with a brace of knives strapped to her waist. The hard, dark eyes were ablaze with power and anger. The way she stood — weight balanced and knife poised — suggested she knew how to fight with a blade.

"I, er, I couldn't find what I wanted in the library," Bram stuttered, knowing he was in deep trouble.

The librarian's gaze flickered from Bram to the platform behind. Fear flitted across her face. "Did you touch the bones?"

"No."

"You're sure?"

Bram nodded.

The librarian turned to face the skeleton. She held her hands over the skull and closed her eyes. Her lips moved but Bram could hear no words. After a moment, she fixed Bram with a hard stare.

"We must get out of here. Now."

She took Bram's shoulder and pushed him roughly through the door ahead of her. The door swung closed behind, sealing the tomb.

The librarian bowed her head, letting her hair swing forward to curtain her face. Bram could hear her mumbling strange words. Mesmerized and fearful, he watched in silence. After a moment, she looked up and nodded then moved off, Bram following in her wake.

They hurried through the series of interconnecting marble chambers — chambers Bram now realized were empty tombs — and came to the broken stone door. They ducked through it and then the librarian halted in front of the statue of the dog. She raised the knife and slashed it across her palm.

The librarian closed her fingers so the blood welling from the cut dripped through her fingers onto the statue's head. As the blood hit the smooth stone surface, it hissed and then disappeared as though absorbed. After a moment the dog's faded red eyes began to glow with an eldritch power.

"It's done. None shall pass through here again, broken door or not."

Without waiting for an answer, she turned and strode off.

Bram stared at the dog. He'd sensed its power before, a slumbering, brooding presence. But now that presence had been awoken. Bram felt sure if he reached out his hand, the dog would bite him.

In sudden fear, he turned and fled after the librarian.

Silence as heavy as a blanket hung between them as the librarian led them back through the catacombs. Bram wanted to apologize but couldn't find the words.

The damp, musty odor of the library came as a relief as he stepped at last from the corridor. The librarian swung the door shut and snapped the padlock into place.

She held out her hand. "Keys."

Bram dug into his pocket and sheepishly dropped the keys into her palm.

As the librarian tucked them into her pocket, the look she gave Bram could have melted stone. Bram opened his mouth to speak but she stalled him with a curt, "Come."

Obediently Bram followed her to one of the smaller bookshelves.

"Grab that end."

Together they dragged the heavy shelving across the floor and placed it in front of the doorway. When it was in place the librarian wiped her brow and sighed.

"That was too close. Do you have any idea of what you could have done?"

Bram didn't know what to say so he kept silent.

The librarian stomped over to the fireplace and slumped into a chair. She shook with fury.

"What are you going to do?" Bram asked her. "Are you going to tell the Great Father?"

Her black eyes seemed like bottomless pits as she stared at him. "What would be your punishment if I did?"

"I don't know."

Her lips pressed together in a thin, disapproving line.

"What were those things?" Bram asked.

She regarded him for a long time, head cocked to one side. "You said you came here looking for the truth. You've found it. Are you ready to face it, Bramwell Thornley?"

Bram nodded slowly. "Secrets and lies. Layers of meaning. I think I'm beginning to understand."

The librarian reached out and grabbed Bram's wrist. "Know this, engineer, there is far more to our world than the academies of Ral Tora can teach you."

Bram glanced over at the bookcase now blocking the door. *So many secrets.* "Do the city fathers know what's down there?"

"Some of them. But they ignore it, and hope by doing so, it will go away."

Bram stared at the librarian, at the shabby clothes, stringy hair, the persona. "Who are you?"

"All you need to know is I guard Ral Tora's secret, and I will kill any who betray it." Her gaze sliced through him. He had no doubt she would carry out her threat. "What I need to know," she said, "is what you plan to do now."

"I won't tell anyone what's down there," he said quickly. "Nobody would believe me anyway."

For the first time, she smiled. "Perhaps. I don't think Ral Tora is ready to face its past just yet. But that time approaches."

"What do you mean?"

"Look around you. Change is coming. The north is moving. You know this already, I think. Ral Tora's time is almost here. Her people must be ready to face the truth or die. There is no other choice."

Bram shivered. He felt as if the icy hands of winter had put its fingers round his heart and squeezed. He swallowed a few times, working up enough saliva to speak. "So, you won't tell the Great Father I was trespassing?"

The librarian shook her head. "I will make a bargain with you, Bramwell Thornley. I will keep your secret if you keep mine. Agreed?"

"Agreed."

She held out her hand. Bram shook it.

As Bram trudged home through the dark streets he realized something. The librarian had called him Bramwell Thornley.

But he'd never told her his name.

CHAPTER 16

Bodies were always heavier than one expected. As he let this one slump to the ground, the man grimaced. This was not how he liked to do business. The body would be found and questions asked. Murdered watchmen did not go unnoticed in Ral Tora. If only the fool man hadn't challenged him, he would still be alive to return home to his family tonight, not lying face down in some forgotten alleyway.

Nobody got in the way of Roishan Darry, nobody who wanted to live.

He stooped and pulled his knife from the watchman's back. Killing was sometimes necessary but deaths out of place attracted attention and he could do without such complications. Wiping the blade on the watchman's tunic, Darry returned it to the plain scabbard hanging at his side and strode away, melting into the shadows.

The streets were dark and empty. Only watchmen and footpads would be abroad tonight and no footpad worth his salt would try anything on Roishan Darry. He mulled over his new name. Over the years he had used so many pseudonyms he could barely remember his real one. Not that it mattered, of course. Names were a convenience, allowing a man to change his identity at will. This name would serve him well enough until the time came for a new one.

As he walked the silent streets he kept his hand on the hilt of the dagger, just in case, but he felt no fear of what might be abroad in the night. This was his domain. This was where he belonged.

At length he reached his destination. For a while, he stood in the shadows, studying the building. A light shone deep within the ruins of the old temple, so faint as to go unnoticed unless you knew to look for it. Roishan Darry waited, still as a statue. Nobody moved in the Forum, no soldiers, no citizens hurrying home. As still as death.

He stole up the steps and knocked on the broad oaken doors of the old temple. A spy-hole slid open and two eyes peered at him. They narrowed with dislike. The slot slammed shut and bolts groaned. The door creaked open and Darry pushed his way through.

He entered a reception chamber that would have once been grand. Friezes of the gods were carved into the ceiling and the remains of a mosaic covered the floor. Most of the mosaic's tesserae were missing and the friezes had cracked.

Ral Tora no longer honored its gods. They had forgotten them, like so much else.

"You're late."

Sesaille Masa's voice dripped venom. Some might call her beautiful, with those high cheekbones, raven-dark hair and large, blue eyes. But those blue eyes were full of contempt and the full mouth perpetually turned down in a sneer.

Darry had no love for her lofty attitudes. If he had his way, he would gut the bitch and be done with it — he had killed many women for less — but Sesaille stood high in the Assembly and Darry suspected the Masters had given her the Gift. If so, Sesaille could kill him in a heartbeat. Until he was bestowed with the Gift himself, Darry knew he must tread warily around Sesaille.

He smoothed the scowl from his face and said, "Lateness applies only to those who are governed by others. I am not the Assembly's lapdog, Sesaille. I come when I choose to."

He knew he stepped close to the line, but Darry wanted to see how far he could push her. Sesaille's mouth tightened, but she didn't reply. Instead, she crossed the entrance hall and disappeared beyond. Darry followed. Sesaille led him along a dark corridor, lit only by weak candles fixed into brackets on the wall. At the end of the corridor a short flight of stairs descended into the gloom.

Sesaille did not take the stairs, but stood watching Darry with eyes like ice crystals. Darry walked down the stairs and laid his hand against the door at the end. After a moment, heat formed beneath his palm and the door swung silently inwards.

Darry entered a cellar; a cramped, low-ceilinged room lit with many stand-lamps and candles. A battered table occupied the middle of the room with seven people seated around it. The air was warm, which meant one of the seven must be using the Gift. Darry felt a faint tingle at the thought. Soon, the Gift would be his.

The door swung shut. Darry remained silent, surveying the people before him. As usual, all seven wore masks. Only their eyes were visible through the fabric veils, each dyed a different color, to identify them to the other members. Only the Speaker knew the identities of everyone but Darry was sure he had discovered the identity of at least three of them. All three had the Gift. They must stand very high in the Assembly of the Old Way.

"Roishan Darry," a deep voice said from behind the red mask. "The Assembly welcomes you. Be seated."

A chair pulled itself back from the table without being touched. Darry made a point of meeting the speaker's eyes before he sat down. He would show them he was not disturbed by displays of the Gift.

"I have taken risks coming here," Darry said. "If my absence is discovered my position will be compromised. Say what you have to say."

"Events have changed. The plan must be changed accordingly."

"You mean the arrival of the Chellin bitch? She's unimportant."

Yellow turned to Darry. A woman's voice came from behind the mask. "Do you think so? Then you are a fool. She brings complications with her. The Masters are not pleased by her interference."

"You wish me to deal with her?"

"No. We have another task for you. The Chellin queen must be watched. You will be our spy. We have arranged for you to accompany the group sailing north. You must watch everything that goes on and make contact with our agent in Chellin. Once there, you will follow his orders to the letter: he will have further instructions from the Masters."

Darry scowled. "An excellent plan, with

only one drawback. I've been seen regularly in the position I've adopted here and were I to suddenly turn up in the journey party I would be recognized — my face is not one you can easily forget." Absently he ran his hands along his scar. It was an old wound he'd picked up in a fight, a thick white line that ran down his forehead, through his left eye, and halfway down his cheek.

Yellow said, "It can be disguised. You will assume the identity we give you, everything has been prepared."

"What's in this for me?"

Yellow shared a glance with Red. "If you perform your task well, we will petition the Masters to give you the Gift."

"Has my work here not been enough? I've done everything asked of me: orchestrated riots, sown dissent and tripled the number of people joining the Wailers. Is this not sufficient? I have done more to weaken the government of Ral Tora than any of you, and still you want more from me?"

This time Blue spoke. His voice sounded petulant. "Who do you think you are to question us? We are the agents of the Masters and we will decide when you have done enough!"

Darry bit back a retort. *The city fathers would be mightily interested to know who you really are*, he thought.

"If you think you can just walk in here and

demand—" Blue began but trailed off. His eyes moved upwards, to a spot in the air above the table.

A shimmering cloud appeared, like heat haze from a fire. It coalesced into a face. The hooded visage had a large mouth and eyes of pure white.

Instantly, the Assembly of the Old Way prostrated themselves on the floor. Darry stared, wide-eyed, at the face of the Master. His heart hammered against his ribs. Never before had he been in the presence of such an all-consuming power.

The blind eyes fixed on Darry. *Roishan Darry*, a voice said in his head. *Are you ready to serve me?*

Darry nodded. A lick of flame shot from the Master's mouth and touched Darry's forehead. In that instant, Darry knew he'd given his soul. He crossed his hands over his heart and bowed low. "My lord."

The Master's eyes narrowed in satisfaction then flicked toward the Assembly, where they lay on the floor.

"You may rise."

Slowly the Assembly resumed their seats, but their eyes remained fixed on the Master. Over the years Darry had become adept at reading emotions and in the eyes of the Assembly he saw a strange mixture: Red's small black eyes held guarded respect; Yellow's gaze was filled with awe. But Blue's deep eyes were sparkling with joy. No fear, only a calm self-assurance, an acceptance of the power of the Master. Yes, Blue definitely held the real power in the Assembly.

"What would you have us do, Master?" Blue asked.

The Master began to speak in a language Darry didn't understand. The Assembly listened avidly. Darry was excluded, not yet trusted to be part of the Master's plans. A small knot of frustration tightened within Darry's chest. He might not be Gifted with the speech of the Masters but soon he would be. This new mission held the key. If everything went according to plan it would bring him what he sought: the power that lay beyond the Rift.

Darry smiled in anticipation.

***

Charm Weaver Capella looked ill. Her skin was pale, with dark smudges beneath her eyes like bruises. Astrid bade her take a seat and then sat down opposite. They were alone. Even Rama and Aeron had been dismissed.

Capella would not meet Astrid's gaze. She fiddled with her dress, wiping away imaginary dirt. Leaning forward, Astrid took hold of Capella's tattooed hands, forcing the charm weaver to look at her. A dark pain clouded Capella's features.

"I have failed you, Mistress," she croaked.

"Nonsense," Astrid replied. "You've performed your task admirably. As always, the Goddess smiles on us."

Capella looked at Astrid incredulously. "How can you say that? People died! I released too much power and many of the Goddess's children were killed. I am surely cursed!"

Astrid dropped Capella's hands and leaned back in her chair. She must tread warily here. Choosing her words very carefully, Astrid said, "Your compassion does you credit, Capella. You are indeed a worthy agent of the Goddess's will. It's unfortunate people lost their lives, but you know there is always a price to pay for the use of power. Look at it this way; we had to get the Ral Torans to agree to our plan. If they didn't then many more would have died when the Everwinter consumed them. Now, they have a chance to change such a fate. A few may have died, but isn't that a price worth paying to save thousands?"

Capella ran her hands through her curly brown hair. Emotions shifted behind her eyes. At last she said, "Yes, Mistress, you're right. I'll pray to the Goddess and seek Her guidance."

Astrid smiled as Capella rose from her chair, bowed to Astrid, and quietly left the room. When the door had closed, Astrid's smile turned into a frown. The charm weaver seemed oddly affected by the incident at the wall. She must be watched in case she betrayed her mistress's secrets. Astrid stood and made her way into the next room.

Rama frowned as Astrid walked in and resumed an earlier conversation. "I don't see how this mission has suddenly become a success, my lady," he said. "We may have gotten the alliance you wanted but we still don't have an Ice Ship, and that's what we were really after."

"That's where you're mistaken, Rama." Turning to Mattack who sat by the fire, Astrid said, "First Minister, would you enlighten Rama?"

Mattack, who had been dozing, came to attention. He fumbled in his pocket and pulled out a small piece of parchment. He unrolled it and held it up for all to see. Rama and Aeron leaned forward to get a better look.

"What's this?" Aeron asked.

"A note from Great Father Samarin, written in his own hand," answered Astrid. "And written hurriedly too, by the looks of it. He passed it to me just after the meeting ended. Read it aloud, Mattack."

The First Minister fished around in his breast pocket and pulled out his spectacles. He perched them on the end of his nose and read, *"Don't mention the Ice Ship, we'll speak of this later. Wait in your room. I'll come to you."*

"What does that mean?" asked Rama.

Astrid stared at him as if he was stupid. "Isn't it obvious? They *do* have an Ice Ship. He's as good as admitting it but he doesn't want it to be common knowledge. We have our alliance and soon we'll have our ship. It's all starting to come together."

There was a knock at the door. Aeron opened it and allowed Great Father Samarin to sweep into the room. The old man had changed his clothes and managed to wash the worst of the mud from his hair and beard. He wore a heavy fur coat with a high collar. His eyes swept the room, taking in all the details in an instant.

"Lady Astrid," he said smoothly. "I trust your people have all been accounted for?"

"Yes, Great Father," Astrid answered. "Goddess be praised."

"Good. You know why I'm here?"

Astrid nodded.

"Then you must come with me. Ask no questions. Bring no others. You'll have to leave your people behind."

Rama raised an eyebrow. "My lady does not go anywhere without Aeron and myself. We will not leave our queen unprotected."

Samarin waved a hand irritably. "Fine. But be quick. Hewin is looking after things at the Father Hall but it won't take long before people begin to notice I'm gone." He cast an appraising eye over their clothes. "And wrap up warm."

Astrid exchanged a look with Rama and then grabbed her thick, pine marten coat and threw it around her shoulders.

To her surprise, instead of heading down the main staircase into the Father Hall, Samarin turned left, and led her along a landing and into the area housing the servant quarters. They passed many doors on either side. Samarin set a brisk pace, and Astrid had to step quickly to keep up with him. At length, they came to a set of narrow steps.

"Watch your footing," Samarin warned. "The steps are small and the fall is long."

Astrid grabbed the rail with one hand and held her dress up with the other as she picked her way down the stairs. It was so narrow they had to descend in single file, with Samarin first, followed by Rama, then Astrid, with Aeron bringing up the rear. Astrid guessed this must be the servant's access to their chambers.

Samarin quite clearly did not wish to be seen.

At the bottom stood a door with a heavy padlock. Samarin pulled a key from his robe and unlocked it.

"Quickly, before someone comes," the Great Father whispered.

Beyond the door lay darkness. Astrid baulked. Was this some kind of trap? Determined to show no apprehension, Astrid strode resolutely through and waited in the darkness for Samarin to close and lock the door. A spark ignited, outlining Samarin's features as he lit a torch.

They were in a tunnel of mortared stone.

The stench of mold and long disuse filled the air.

Samarin set off down the tunnel and the rest stepped into line behind. "This is a bolt hole," Samarin explained as they trudged along. "It was constructed when the Father Hall was first built. We are passing beneath the city, lower even than the sewers. If the city was ever under attack — as happened frequently in days gone by — the leaders of the city could escape to the sea this way. I think there is only Hewin and myself who are even aware it's here."

Astrid nodded. She could appreciate such measures. The promontory on which Chellin stood was itself riddled with secret passageways and bolt holes. They always came in useful in times of siege or social unrest, or if you wanted to make a political rival disappear.

Silence fell. The only sound was the creak of Rama's sword belt and the echo of footsteps. The temperature fell and Astrid found herself shivering, despite her thick coat. The tunnel stretched in a straight line. There were no markers to show which direction they were travelling or how far they had come. It seemed like they walked all day.

Finally Astrid heard a noise coming from up ahead.

"The sea!" she exclaimed. "I can hear the sea."

"Yes, we're not far away now," Samarin

answered.

The crash of waves grew louder. The air became thick with the smell of salt water. Then light appeared in the tunnel ahead and Astrid found herself walking out onto a golden sandy beach.

She found herself in a sea cavern in the cliffs of the Ral Toran Plateau. The sea lapped against a beach that curved around the back of the cavern.

A tall ship bobbed on the water. She had three masts, each carrying pristine white sails. The ship's material was strange; too smooth to be wood and a strange milky pink color, like the inside of a seashell. At the prow two huge blades stuck out, for cutting through ice. The figurehead was carved into a mermaid, so intricate that she looked like a living creature, patiently waiting for her passengers.

"She's beautiful," Astrid breathed.

"Yes." Samarin agreed. He led the group down to the water's edge and pointed. "It's very cold down here. See the chunks of ice in the sea? Now look at the ship. Do you see any ice on her? On the rigging or the sails?"

Astrid squinted at the ship. Her rigging and sails looked as strong as if they had only just been fitted.

"Such is the power of an Ice Ship," Samarin said. "Nothing can touch her. While you are aboard you will feel nothing of the Everwinter that surrounds us and she will cut through the frozen sea as if it were butter."

"How is this achieved?" Astrid asked in amazement.

The Great Father shrugged uncomfortably. "We don't know. Our scientists have examined her many times. At first, we thought she must carry some sort of internal heating system fixed to a relay so it renews itself as she moves, but we could find nothing. The secrets of the Ice Ships are lost to us. The ship is almost a thousand years old but she is as sound as when she was first built. She needs no maintenance. She has been in this lagoon since before I was born and there is not a barnacle nor a frayed rope or a torn sail on her. We don't know why."

So this is why he doesn't want his people to know the ship exists, Astrid thought, *because they can't explain its powers with their science. What I could do with a ship like this in my fleet. What fools these southerners are. As soon as we are out of Ral Tora's waters, they will never see their Ice Ship again!*

CHAPTER 17

Bram rubbed his hands together and held them out toward the small blaze burning in his fireplace. It was very late. He'd been falling in and out of an uneasy doze, with images of skeletal monsters playing through his mind. Finally, he'd risen from bed.

Secrets and lies. Layers of Meaning.

Nothing made sense any more. He had so many questions he could barely list them all. What was the thing beneath the library? What was the creature he had seen flying over Ral Tora? What was happening in the north?

He had no answers.

A log rolled out of the fire, sending sparks

into the air. The flames cast dancing shadows across the walls. Above the mantelpiece, Bram's parents gazed down on him with a look Bram couldn't read.

What should I do? He asked them.

Astrid's words from earlier came back to him. *You do not give up. You find another way.*

Realization dawned on him slowly, like sunlight rising over the horizon. He knew what he must do.

Pausing only to bank the fire and throw a coat across his shoulders, Bram went out into the night. The snow had frozen, forming a treacherous film on the ground. With wary steps, Bram made his way through the sleeping city. He reached the Forum without encountering a soul.

Ahead, the tall buildings of government loomed, like silent sentinels. Across the plaza lay the Father Hall. To the left, in a forgotten corner, squatted the ancient temple. A thought struck him. The temple was the only building in the Forum whose occupants had played no part in Ral Tora's troubles. No, it was science, not the old gods, who'd let the city down.

Bram squinted at the dilapidated building. What things must the old temple have seen during its lifetime? Around it, Ral Tora had changed beyond recognition, while it waited, silently watching its power erode. Bram blinked. Was that a light shining in the temple's depths? But when he looked again, he saw nothing.

At the top of the Father Hall steps, the two guards looked Bram over and nodded at him to go in. It wasn't unusual for engineers to be called to meetings in the middle of the night. But once inside, Bram did not go to the Moot. Instead, he crossed the vestibule and climbed a staircase. After passing through many opulent galleries, he reached a wide landing that housed a suite of rooms.

A man stood guard by the door and he came instantly to attention when he saw Bram approaching.

Bram had seen the man before. Pale blond hair brushed his shoulders and his crooked nose looked like it had been broken many times. His confident bearing spoke of a man used to wielding weapons. Bram searched for the man's name. Aeron. Astrid's bodyguard.

Aeron placed his hand on his sword hilt and watched Bram. Now he was here, Bram's courage faltered. What did he have to offer Lady Astrid?

But he'd made his decision and couldn't back out now.

"I apologize for the lateness of the hour," Bram began. "But I wish to speak with the Lady Astrid."

Aeron frowned. "Wait here."

The blond man disappeared through the door and muffled voices came through the wood. The door opened and Aeron said,

"Come."

Bram entered a plush sitting room lit with many lamps. Lady Astrid sat in a seat by the fire. Her hair was pinned up for bed and she wore a long silk robe.

"This is unexpected, Bramwell Thornley," she said. "How can I help you?"

Since he'd not been offered a seat, Bram stood uncomfortably before her. "I've heard Ral Tora and Chellin have formed an alliance and that a force is being sent to Variss."

He paused, waiting for confirmation.

After a moment, Astrid inclined her head. "You heard correctly. But what has that to do with you waking me in the middle of the night?"

Although she sounded annoyed, laughter danced in Astrid's eyes.

Bram suddenly found himself struggling to speak.

"Yes?" Astrid prompted.

"I want to come with you," Bram blurted. Then, before Astrid could refuse, he rushed on, "I'm an engineer and my skills could come in useful. I'm good at fixing things and I don't mind fetching and carrying or anything else you ask me to do…"

He faltered as he realized Astrid was beaming at him as though she knew something he didn't.

"So, may I come?" he asked warily.

Astrid's face became serious. She rested

her chin on her hands as she considered. At last she said, "You raise a valid point. Your skills would be very useful on the journey ahead. Very well, Bramwell Thornley, you may accompany us. We leave in two days."

A strange feeling filled Bram's chest. Relief, fear or perhaps a mixture of both. Not trusting himself to speak, he bowed and scurried from the room.

As he left, he saw Astrid grinning like an excited child.

***

Falen looked up into the night sky. The stars were bright and the moon hung above, fat and yellow. She breathed deeply. It felt so good to be free.

She stood in the middle of Jarrom Street, in front of her house. She held the key in her hand, but for some reason, she hesitated in opening the door. Falen hadn't expected to come back here. The last time she left, she'd planned on it being for good.

The lock was stiff but finally gave way under Falen's efforts. Once inside, she had to feel her way in the dark, but eventually managed to find her tinder and flint and light a few candles. Her living room was just as she'd left it. Evidence of her last fit of temper lay all around. The vase still lay in pieces on the carpet. Books lay strewn around the floor, where she'd swept them from the bookcase in her anger.

Nothing had changed.

Everything had changed.

Three long weeks had passed since her house arrest in the Father Hall. In that time, events had rattled along without her. When Father Hewin had come to release her earlier in the evening, the reports of the disaster at the wall had rocked her to the core. Then close on the heels of these terrible tidings came the news of the approval of Lady Astrid's plan and that she, Falen, would accompany the expedition. The professional negligence case against her had been dropped. Falen's hopes had come true. She only wished it hadn't come at such a cost.

When would she learn to be careful what she wished for?

A tear ran down her cheek and she dashed it away irritably. Time to set things in motion. There'd been too much delay already.

She knelt by the fireplace. One of the bricks on the left side was loose. Falen took hold of this brick, gently worked it from side to side, and slid it out. A small cavity lay inside. Falen stuck her hand in and came out with a brown bag that smelled damp. Falen opened the bag and took out a book.

This was the last thing Lidda gave her before Falen left Variss. Falen ran her hands over the book's surface.

On the Treaty of Vaspara and the sealing of the Rift.

She hadn't touched the book since she left Variss. It held painful memories.

"Are you still alive, father?" she said to the empty air. "And you, Lidda? Harn?"

She pushed down a surge of despair and steeled her courage. "I'm coming," she said in a strong voice. "Hold on. I'm coming."

Falen tucked the book under her arm and went upstairs to begin packing.

***

Bram chewed his lip, surveying his belongings. On the floor lay his rucksack next to a mound of clothes and other essentials that he was busily trying to pack.

They were leaving tomorrow. Bram could hardly believe it. Leaving. Leaving Ral Tora.

What was I thinking? Bram demanded of himself, as he folded up his second thickest coat and stuffed it into his rucksack. *What do you think you will achieve? You will probably get yourself killed.*

A knock came at the door. As he pulled it open he saw Romy, Oscar and Seth waiting impatiently outside. They shouldered past him as soon as Bram had the door open.

"Let us in will you, Bram, we're freezing!"

Romy said. He carried a large sack on his shoulder.

They huddled around the fire in the living room.

"Almost finished your packing?" Oscar asked.

Bram nodded.

"So you really are going?" Seth asked. "I thought you would've seen sense by now and decided to stay."

"We've been through this," Bram replied patiently. "I know you all think I shouldn't go, but it's something I have to do. I'll be fine, don't worry about me."

"Let it go, Seth," Oscar said, placing a hand on his brother's shoulder. "We won't talk him round."

"No, you won't, so let's talk about something else. How's your head, Seth?"

Seth put his hand to the bandage. "Ah, fine. The doctor said I've got nothing inside but rocks anyway. Have you heard about poor old Toby though? He broke both his legs."

"Did he?" Bram asked, dismayed to hear of his class-mate's injury. "Is he going to be all right?"

"Yeah, I think so. It was touch and go for a while though. They thought he might lose a leg."

Bram whistled under his breath. "Anyone else we know hurt?"

Seth shook his head. "No, thank the gods."

"How's Commander Alara?" Bram asked Oscar.

Oscar's face turned grim. "Not good. Although she's resumed her duties, she still isn't well. She's been having seizures which leave her incapacitated. The surgeons are saying she has swelling on her brain. They want to operate but it's really dangerous and Alara isn't very keen on the idea. The command is falling to that turd, Marchant. I don't like it, Bram, I really don't. Marchant isn't a strong commander, and right now, strong leadership in the Watch is what we need, with all the trouble that's stirring."

"People not happy about our alliance with Chellin?"

"Unhappy isn't the word. There's mass hysteria brewing. People are calling the Lady Astrid a witch and saying she put a curse on the city."

"What? That's ridiculous!"

"I know, but it's amazing the stories people will believe when they are looking for someone to blame. Especially when that damn sect is stirring things again."

"The Wailers?"

"Yup. Now the city's in turmoil, they're more numerous than ever, spreading their poison. And intelligence is suggesting they may have a new leader — Father Erris."

"Erris!" Bram cried. "Surely not! I know he didn't approve of the alliance but he wouldn't join the Wailers! They go against everything he believes in!"

"Who knows? There's only rumor at the moment, but I tell you this, if someone as respected as Father Erris has joined them, it won't be long before others start doing the same. I don't like it at all. I can smell trouble brewing."

"Oscar, you can always smell trouble brewing!" Seth put in. "Everything will die down, you'll see. As soon as the expedition has gone and the repairs begin, everything will go back to normal."

Oscar snorted. "Normal? I've almost forgotten what that's like."

"What are you doing, Romy?" Bram asked.

Romy looked up guiltily from where he'd been rummaging in his sack.

"Well, is this a farewell party or not?" he asked. He took out a large round object, wrapped in muslin. A second object followed, then a third and fourth. Romy set them on the table and pulled the wrappings off. He revealed a huge roasted ham, a side of beef, a mound of chicken legs, and a dish piled high with roast potatoes. He reached back into the sack and pulled out a couple of bottles of brandy and three bottles of Brain Boiler. He grinned smugly.

"Where did you get all this?" asked Seth.

Romy tapped his nose. "Never you mind. A master like myself never reveals his secrets."

"You mean you stole it!" Oscar said.

"No I never! I called in a few favors is all. You're not on duty now, Oscar, so you can stop acting the guardsman." Romy turned to Bram. "Throw some more fuel on the fire, my friend, and fetch some glasses. We're having a knees-up!"

Later that evening, thoughts of his bed, the sheets being gently heated by a warming pan, filled Bram's head as he battled his way through the darkened streets of Ral Tora. Bram would have liked nothing more than to lock his front door, climb into bed, and not venture out again until the storm blew itself out. But after he had ushered his friends out of his house earlier, after eating and drinking all afternoon, he'd found a note pushed under his door.

Come to see me. I have something for you.

There had been no name, but Bram knew instinctively who'd sent it.

An icy blast buffeted him, sending sleet driving into his face. He blinked rapidly and wiped his eyes with mittened hands. Pulling his hood back into place, he wrapped his arms around his body and trudged on.

Although already dark, it was not particularly late, and Bram passed small pockets of people hurrying home from work and trades people shutting up their businesses for the night. Nobody gave him more than a perfunctory glance as they rushed past. The thick slush made Bram's trek across town long and tedious and by the time he arrived at his destination his feet were soaked and his hair was plastered to his head despite the hood.

With relief, he placed his hand on the library door and pushed his way inside. A fire burned in the hearth but the librarian was nowhere in sight. Bram's eyes flickered toward the door to the vaults and dark, frightening memories began to surface. Pushing them down, Bram concentrated on the task at hand.

"Hello?" he called.

No answer. Shrugging, Bram peeled off his sodden coat and hung it near the fire to dry. He sank into one of the easy chairs by the fireplace and held his hands out to the warmth. Where could the librarian be? Surely, she had not left the library unattended? Bram felt a stab of annoyance. After he'd trekked all this way through the snow to see her, she could at least have the decency to be here!

A pot of tea bubbled gently on the fire indicating that the librarian probably wasn't far away. Bram eyed the pot longingly. He knew how protective the librarian was about her tea but he decided he'd earned it, so he grabbed a cup from a tray on the mantelpiece and filled it from the kettle. Setting the cup to his lips, he sighed appreciatively as the hot, sweet liquid sank into his stomach. Stretching out his legs and leaning back, Bram settled down to wait.

Except for the crackle and hiss of the fire,

the library was as quiet as a tomb. The books stood in dark, silent rows. Bram looked down at the flagstone floor. Who would have guessed what lay hidden down there, right beneath his feet?

The bones of a huge beast, head as big as an ox-cart, teeth as long as an arm. And beside it, the skeleton of a man, exceptionally tall, with an elongated face.

"They're here, I tell you!"

Bram jumped, slopping tea all over his knee. Setting his cup down, he got to his feet and wove his way among the dusty shelves. At the back of the library, he came upon a door which stood slightly ajar. A sign on the door read: *Librarian's study. Private. Keep out.*

Voices were talking within. Bram tiptoed closer and peered inside. A tiny room lay beyond. The librarian stood in the center of the room, speaking to someone Bram couldn't see.

"You're sure?" a voice asked. A fleeting recognition passed through Bram. Where had he heard that voice before?

"As sure as I can be, Old Heart," the librarian replied. "I've felt the use of the Gift many times. It's in the city. Who else would be using the Gift but an assembly of the soul-sworn? You know what they must be searching for."

Silence. Then the other voice said, "They must not be allowed to find it. All could be lost if they do. Every day the Rift grows wider, it won't be long until a way is opened. We can't let them find what they're looking for."

The librarian shook her head. "They won't find it. The sisterhood will stop them. We will keep the weapon safe until the quest can succeed."

"You are brave, Young One, and a worthy servant."

The figure moved. Bram gasped in shock as he saw a face he recognized. Tomas. The Varisean placed his hands on the librarian's shoulders and bent to kiss her forehead. In response, the librarian fell to her knees and bowed her head to the floor. "I swear my soul to your guidance, Old Heart."

Bram's jaw fell open. The librarian was kneeling to Tomas!

As if sensing the thought, Tomas's eyes shifted toward Bram's hiding place.

"Come here," he commanded.

Despite himself, Bram shuffled sheepishly through the door, unable to disobey that command. The librarian scrambled to her feet and glared at Bram.

"Have you been listening?" she demanded.

Bram swallowed, glancing at Tomas. "I didn't mean to, I heard raised voices..." he trailed off as he realized that Tomas was staring at him. Only, it wasn't Tomas. Something looked out from Tomas's eyes, something with power that crackled in the room like sparks from an anvil. Bram stepped back a pace. He had seen this once before, in Tomas's room the night he arrived.

"Who are you?" he whispered.

Tomas didn't answer. His eyes moved to the librarian and a silent communication seemed to pass between them. Tomas blinked and when he looked at Bram, his eyes had returned to normal.

"I must be going," he said in Tomas's usual voice. "Time is getting on and it's a long walk back to the Father Hall." Without another glance toward the librarian or Bram, he left.

The librarian and Bram regarded each other in silence.

A thousand questions crowded into Bram's mind, but he said only, "I got your message."

The librarian nodded. She moved into the main library, Bram following. The windows rattled in their casements and the door suddenly blew open, sending snow swirling inside. The librarian closed the door and shot the bolt. She made her way over to the fireplace and took a seat, indicating for Bram to do the same.

When Bram had first met the librarian he'd thought her an eccentric old woman but had soon discovered it was just a façade to hide her true identity. Now, as Bram looked into her blue eyes, he wondered what mysteries she protected.

Secrets and lies. Layers of meaning.

"I know you must have many questions,

Bramwell Thornley, but I need you to listen and trust me. You must forget all that you have seen here tonight and never speak of it again."

"Then tell me what is going on!" Bram said. "Who is Tomas?"

"He is who he says he is."

Bram shook his head. That was no answer and she knew it. "You're asking me to trust you, yet you tell me nothing. Why should I believe anything you say?"

A wry smile crossed her face. "A fair question. Search your heart. What does it tell you?"

Bram pressed his lips into a tight line. This woman and Tomas were enigmas. Mystery surrounded them like a shroud. Yet, for reasons he could not explain, Bram found he *did* trust her. Something about the clear honesty of her gaze compelled him.

Leaning forward, she took both of his hands in hers. "Know this: Tomas has his task, just as you have yours. He can be trusted and you'll discover this, I think, in the months ahead."

She withdrew her hands and Bram realized she had deposited something in his palm. Bram held up the object. It was a whistle, about six inches long and made from bone. Strange symbols marched along its length. They reminded Bram of the carvings on the walls of the catacombs below the library.

"What's this?"

"Take it with you when you leave. It will bring help when you're in danger. Promise me you'll take it with you."

Bram closed his fist around the whistle. "I promise."

CHAPTER 18

"Take care of yourself," Romy said, clasping Bram by the hand. He placed a bottle of Brain Boiler in Bram's hand. "For the journey."

Bram took the bottle and smiled in gratitude.

"Bring me back some of those famous Chellin sagas will you?" Seth asked as, behind them, the rest of the party began boarding the boats. "I've heard they're the best in the world."

"Of course I will," Bram answered. Seth's face creased with worry. "I am coming back," Bram promised. "I will see you all again."

Bram blinked and his thoughts came back to the present. *Can I keep that promise?* Bram wondered. *Will I ever see Ral Tora again?*

Beneath his hands the smooth wood of the

ship's rail made him remember where he was: aboard the Ice Ship *Regalia*, with the three other ships of Astrid's fleet following. Ral Tora lay far behind and the gray sea stretched out on all sides.

An icy rain fell and a steady breeze blew from the north. On *Stormdancer*, *Scimitar* and *Mystery*, nobody except the crew were on deck and they were going about their duties with heads bowed against the elements. But on *Regalia* Bram felt nothing of the wind, rain or cold. The power of the Ice Ship wrapped her in a cocoon of warmth so that no weather touched her decks. Bram struggled to adapt to these new experiences.

Bram glanced down and saw, in the sea to either side of *Regalia*, two long shapes leading the ship.

The tashen.

Astrid summoned the serpents as soon as the ships were safely away from Ral Tora's coast. Bram had thought he might wet himself when the huge beasts reared up out of the water. Father Hewin had fainted.

But Astrid explained that the tashen were needed to guide the ships through the dangerous straits on the way to Chellin.

Looking at them, Bram grabbed the rail tightly to steady himself.

Astrid's crew carried on their duties, oblivious to him. Since they had come aboard Bram had seen little of the other members of the party. Falen and Tomas had been sequestered with Father Hewin and Lady Astrid most of the time, recounting everything they knew of Variss and the north.

The contingent of Panthers, elite guards from the City Watch that commander Alara had assigned to the mission, had kept to themselves. Bram had been left in his own company. Even at mealtimes, which they all shared in the tiny dining room, talk centered on the necessities of the expedition and since Bram had little of value to add, he had mostly been excluded from the conversation.

He was already homesick. He missed his friends. Although he never thought he would admit it, he even missed Rassus. He felt useless and alone.

"You all right, lad?"

Bram jumped. Barl, commander of the Panthers, strode toward him. He was a big craggy man, with wild red hair and beard to match, and hands so huge they looked as though they could crush a man's skull.

Bram searched for something to say. "I was just, you know… thinking."

"Thinking? You don't want to do that. It was thinking that got us in this mess in the first place!"

The big man took a place next to Bram and leaned on the rail, looking out to sea. "Roast my behind, this is strange aint it? If you'd told me a month ago I would be aboard a magical ship, being guided by sea monsters, on my way to Chellin, I would probably have thought you were drunk out of your skull. But here we are."

"Here we are," Bram agreed. They stood in companionable silence for a while, until Bram said, "Have you been to Chellin before?"

Barl snorted. "Nah! Nobody from Ral Tora has been to Chellin for years, except the traders. Strange place by all accounts. Full of witchery and weird goings on. They can turn themselves into birds and fly away over the sea."

Bram was about to laugh at such a preposterous notion, but saw the dark shapes of the tashen in the water and sobered abruptly.

Barl clapped Bram on the shoulder. "Come with me, lad. You need some company."

Bram allowed himself to be led below deck and through the warren of low passages until they came to a wooden door. From behind the door came the sound of raucous laughing. Barl pushed the door open without ceremony and led Bram inside. The ten people inside the cabin jumped up when Barl entered and clapped their fists to their hearts in salute.

Barl stood facing the group, hands on hips. "I know what you've been up to." He stooped and pulled something out from below the table: a small ale barrel that had already been broached. He put the barrel on the table and glared round at his Panthers. "Well?"

The group shifted uncomfortably. A tall woman with blonde hair in a long braid down her back said, "Sir, it's my fault. Everyone's been getting bored and restless. I thought it would boost morale — "

"To get steaming drunk?"

"Well, I —" the woman stammered.

Barl's face broke into a grin. "Sergeant Saskia, I think it's the best idea I've heard today. Make room for one more. We have a guest. This is Bram and he's going to be joining us."

The Panthers banged their fists on the table and cheered. Sergeant Saskia moved along the bench and Bram squeezed in beside her. The room was small, with barely an inch to spare around the table, but nobody seemed to mind. Cups were passed round and ale served from the barrel.

Saskia handed Bram a cup and said, "Cheers!"

Bram set the cup to his mouth and drank. It felt good to be in company. He looked around at the Panthers. There were six men and five women, including Barl. They all had lithe figures and muscular arms. Oscar had often talked about the Panthers. It was the ambition of every City Watchman to get into the elite squad. Only the finest got into the Panthers. They were the best in their fields: trackers, logistical analysts, weapons experts.

EVERWINTER

Commander Alara herself had been in the Panthers, before she had been promoted, and rumor had it that every one of the Panthers had to best her in single combat before they were allowed into the regiment.

To Bram's left sat a man with a shaven head and strange, swirling tattoos covering his forehead and the left side of his face. A herring-bone earring dangled from the man's ear. Bram tried not to stare, but the strange tattoos fascinated him.

The man saw him looking and said, "I'm from the Isle of Ashon. These are my clan markings."

"I'm sorry, I didn't mean to stare," Bram said, flushing.

The man grinned. "Don't worry. Everyone stares. That's what they're for, so everyone can see I'm from the Eagle clan, the best fighters on Ashon."

"The puppy dog clan more like!" Barl shouted from the head of the table.

"Well at least I know what clan I'm from, Barl," the man replied. "With a mother like yours, there's no telling who your father might be!"

Barl saluted with his cup. "Too right there. I propose a toast. To mothers everywhere, be they whores or queens!"

Everyone raised their cups. "Here, here!"

The tattooed man held his hand out to Bram. "I'm Corban by the way."

Bram took Corban's hand. "Nice to meet you."

Saskia leaned over. "I'd be careful of shaking hands with that one if I were you, Bram. He's a brilliant pickpocket."

Bram turned back to Corban, only to find the tattooed man holding the handkerchief Astrid had given him. "Did I say the Eagle clan were the best fighters? We are the best thieves as well."

Bram stared at him, unsure. Corban laughed good-naturedly and punched Bram on the shoulder. He handed back the handkerchief and said, "Only joking. Come on, drink up, it's going to be a long night."

The laughter was at Bram's expense this time but he soon found himself joining in.

"A song!" someone called from the corner.

Barl winked at him. "How about it, Bram? Sing us a song!"

Heat flushed into his face. All eyes were on him and he didn't want to let his new friends down. He remembered a bawdy tune Romy had composed that might go down well. He cleared his throat and sang.

"Oh Elsie the farmer's daughter,
If you've never met her you oughta
I'd chase her night and day,
To get a roll in the hay,
But sadly I never caught her!"

After a few verses the Panthers began to pick up the words and join in. Soon "Oh Elsie the farmer's daughter!" was ringing out so loud Bram was sure the crew could hear them above deck. Maybe this wasn't so different to being at home after all. How many times had he and his friends drunk ale and sung songs in a tavern?

"Right, Panthers," Corban said. "I think it's time we showed our young friend what fine composers we are. How about one of our own songs? Say, *The Soldier and the Magpie?*"

There was a round of agreement. Corban launched into a song about a soldier who fell in love with a girl with a pet magpie. The magpie got jealous and every time the soldier went to see her, the bird would steal a piece of his clothing until eventually he had to go and see her naked. At which point the magpie promptly pecked his manhood off.

By the end of the song Bram was joining in with the chorus, even though his words were beginning to slur. He grinned as Saskia topped up his mug.

***

Bram was thankful that Saskia had accompanied him. Without her he would have difficulty standing up. His arm hung over her shoulder, while she gripped his waist and helped him to wobble down the corridor. The small trek to Bram's cabin had never seemed so long and arduous. He had already bumped his head twice on the low beams and smacked his shoulder into the wall as he staggered from side to side.

At last, they reached the door. Bram stumbled and went crashing to the floor, pulling Saskia down with him so they ended up in a heap, with Saskia on top.

At that moment, Falen stuck her head out the door of her cabin. Her eyes alighted on Bram and Saskia in the compromising position on the floor, and widened in surprise. Her expression turned cold.

"Don't let me interrupt you," she hissed, striding past them to the ladder that led above deck.

Saskia extricated herself from Bram and got to her feet. She pulled Bram up behind her. "What's wrong with her?"

Bram shrugged. "Damned if I know."

"Well, goodnight, Bram. I hope you don't feel too bad in the morning."

Bram gave her a wry smile and Saskia threw him a mocking salute as she strode back down the corridor, flicking her blonde braid over one shoulder. Bram drew a deep breath. The motion of the ship was making his stomach churn.

Falen's reaction puzzled him. He'd not spoken to her in days and the first time she saw him she snapped at him. What had he done? He made his way to the ladder she had taken and climbed onto the deck. The balmy night air felt good in his lungs and helped to clear his thoughts. The only crewmember above deck was a lone man standing at the wheel.

Falen stood at the stern. He could see her outline against the sky. Bram walked over. She stiffened at his approach but did not turn.

"Falen?"

"What do you want?"

"I just came to see if you were all right."

She spun to face him. "Why wouldn't I be?"

"I don't know, you seemed a bit angry."

She stared at him with an unreadable look in her eyes. At last she said, "What you do, and who you do it with, is no business of mine."

"Do you mean Saskia? She was just helping me back to my cabin."

Hang on, Bram thought. *Why am I justifying myself to her?*

"Like I said. It's no business of mine," Falen said. Then she stalked off without a backward glance.

Bram stared after her. What just happened? Why was she upset with him? He rubbed his eyes and ran his hands through his hair. He yawned. Definitely time for bed. He staggered off.

Bram's cabin was a tiny space no bigger than a broom cupboard with a narrow bed along one wall, a washstand in the corner, and hooks nailed into the wall for clothing. Bram fell into bed and pulled the blankets up over his head. The warmth of the Ice Ship and the rolling motion of the sea soon pulled him into sleep.

Who is he? You are sure?

Yes. Can't you feel it? There, buried deep in him.

Ah, yes. I feel it. Can he hear us? Talk to him.

You are near brother! We can sense you. What is your name? Answer us!

Bram opened his eyes. Darkness filled the cabin. There was silence but for the creak of the ship.

But those voices....

Bram strained his ears, sure he could still hear them speaking. But they did not come from within the ship, it seemed more like they were outside, deep in the depths of the ocean, like a whisper just beyond the edge of hearing. He remained still for a long time. No sound reached him. Eventually, certain he'd been dreaming, he drifted back into a dreamless sleep.

***

The next morning the sleety rain stopped and the wind moved round to the south. The fleet dropped anchor to allow the captains of

Stormdancer, Mystery and *Scimitar* to consult with Astrid about their course.

About mid-morning Father Hewin knocked on Bram's door and entered to find Bram lying on his back in bed, with a wet towel over his face.

"Bram? Are you well?" he asked.

"No." Bram muttered from beneath the cloth. "I think I'm dying."

Hewin plucked the towel away and sniffed Bram's breath. "You've been drinking haven't you? In that case, I have no sympathy."

Bram opened one eye and looked at Hewin. He'd ditched his yellow city father robe and wore simple cotton trousers and a shirt. He looked much younger.

"You're looking well, father. Is the sea air agreeing with you?"

Father Hewin ignored the compliment. Instead, he went over to the basin and poured Bram a glass of water. "Here, drink this."

Bram levered himself up onto his elbows. He squinted at Hewin until the glass came into focus then gingerly reached out and took it. He gulped the contents down and fell back onto the bed with a groan.

Hewin frowned at him. "I have never understood the urge of the young to drink so much alcohol it makes them ill."

A thought managed to penetrate Bram's foggy brain. This was the first time Hewin had visited him in his cabin since the voyage had begun. Bram levered himself onto his elbows again. "Did you want something, Father Hewin?"

"I came to keep you abreast of developments. The Lady Astrid and I have managed to beat out the finer points of our quest. We'll reach Chellin in nine days. We'll stay there for a week while the ships are provisioned. We will then sail north to Whiteharbor and disembark. We'll approach Variss from the south, through Ragnar's gap."

"And then?"

"And then Tomas and Falen will guide us to Variss and we will see what we can see."

"Great plan."

Hewin stiffened at Bram's sarcasm.

Bram held up his hand. "Sorry, I don't mean to be so negative. I'm not at my best today."

Hewin scowled. "Then I suggest you get some sleep and stay off the liquor in future."

He bade Bram good day and left.

Late that afternoon Bram felt sufficiently recovered to leave his cabin. He made his way above deck and stood squinting whilst his eyes adjusted to the light.

On the foredeck a group of Panthers were practicing their swordplay. Bram made his way over. Commander Barl and Sergeant Saskia leaned on the railing, watching Corban and another panther, Demas, go through their paces. Barl scratched his red beard and then grinned at Bram.

"Ah, here's our young friend. Feeling better now, Bram?"

Bram smiled wryly. "You could say that. I'm sorry you had to take me back to my cabin last night, Saskia, I made the mistake of thinking I could match the Panthers pint for pint."

Saskia waved his words away. "No apology needed. We've all done it at some time or other, haven't we?"

Bram smiled his thanks and turned to watch Corban and Demas. They were stripped to the waist, showing that Corban had more clan tattoos on his chest and arms. Both men were sweating with exertion as they spun and rolled and jumped, clashing their blades together and then whirling apart. They thrust and parried and swung again. The ring of steel filled the air, the swords moving so fast they became a blur.

Bram was mesmerized. How could they fight so quickly and accurately without cutting each other to ribbons?

The two men were evenly matched and so for a long time they moved backward and forward along the deck, one having the upper hand for a while, before the advantage swung back the other way. Corban made a feint to Demas's left. Demas followed with his blade, leaving his right side exposed. Corban spun back and swept his sword around in a wide arc. It caught ⸱Demas's blade and sent it spinning out of his grasp to go skittering across the deck.

Corban raised his sword point until it was level with Demas's throat. "Do you yield?" he panted.

Demas nodded. "I yield."

Corban lowered his sword and the two men clasped hands.

"Not bad, Corban," Barl said. "But that feint is a dangerous one. If he'd not fallen for it, your back would have been exposed and that would have been the end of you. Remember; never turn your back on your opponent."

Corban saluted with his sword. "Yes, boss." He looked at Saskia and Barl. "Who's next?"

"I'll do it," Bram blurted.

They all stared at him.

"You?" Barl asked. "You know how to fight?"

"Well no, not exactly. But I'm eager to learn."

Corban shared a look with Barl. "All right." He picked Demas's blade up from the deck and handed it to Bram. It weighed more than Bram expected. He had to hold the hilt with both hands, just to keep the blade level.

"Keep the tip of the blade up, like this."

Corban took a two-handed grip and stood with his feet shoulder-width apart. He held the blade level with his eyes. "Feel the balance of the sword, get used to its weight. Swing it from side to side, like so."

Corban made it look easy, but Bram found himself swinging the blade clumsily from side to side like a sweeping brush. Even so, Bram began to get a feel for its weight and find its center of gravity.

"Good," said Corban. "Now bring it in an arc in front of you."

Bram swung the sword and Corban brought his own blade round so that they collided with a sharp clang.

"You've just learned your first blocking stroke," said Corban. "That's what you'd do if someone brings their blade toward you from above. Now, do the same again."

This time, as Bram swung his sword round in the arc, Corban brought his blade up from below, the opposite direction to the one Bram expected. Corban's blade went straight through Bram's defense and whistled past his ear. Bram staggered back.

Corban smiled. "That's your second lesson. When in a fight, think on your feet, vary your moves, and try to surprise your opponent, because you can be sure he will be trying to do the same to you. Now, blade up again."

They carried on like this for an hour or more. If it had been a real battle, Bram would have died a dozen times over, but Corban was a patient teacher, and every time Bram overstepped, left himself unguarded or made a clumsy stroke, Corban would point out what he'd done wrong and make him do it again. Bram seemed to spend most of his time picking himself or his sword off the deck and had to endure Barl and Saskia's laughter every time.

Eventually, the sun began to sink below the horizon and Corban called a halt for the day. Bram ached all over. He knew he would be as stiff as a pole in the morning. But he felt good. He was actually doing something at last, instead of just being a piece of baggage.

Corban took Bram's sword from him and placed a hand on his shoulder. "You did well, Bram. You have natural balance and agility. With a bit of training I think we could make a swordsman out of you."

"Really? Would you teach me?"

"Why not? It's not as though I have much else to demand my attention whilst we are on board this tub."

Bram clasped Corban's hand and went below decks to get something to eat. Fighting was hungry work. In the galley he managed to beg some bread and cheese, went back to his cabin and sat cross-legged on his bed while he ate his supper.

As he chewed, he thought back to the voices he had heard last night. With so much ale in his system, surely he must have imagined them? But they had seemed so real and stirred up a vague recognition he couldn't quite place.

Don't be stupid. You imagined it, he told himself.

Of course. He'd been drunk. That was all there was to it.

He swallowed the last piece of bread and cheese and put his plate down on the table. As the ship moved, the plate slid along the table and clattered to the floor. The raised lip along the table's edge was wholly inadequate.

Bram frowned. Leaning forward, he examined the table. If he'd been in Ral Tora he could have used some sort of magnet to anchor the plates to the table. But seeing as they didn't have any magnets, he'd have to come up with something else to stop his plates sliding about. And while he was at it, he was sure he could come up with a better way of controlling the oil lamp swinging from the ceiling. At the moment it could either light fully, or not at all. With a few modifications Bram was sure he could rig up a switch to allow him to control the amount of oil coming through, and thus the lamp's brightness.

Eagerly, he pulled a bit of paper and a pencil from his pack, leaned against the table and started making plans.

***

"We bail it out, just like on any other ship," the captain said with a scowl. The sour-faced man clearly didn't like being asked questions.

Bram held out the bit of paper for the captain to see, filled with diagrams and sketches. "But it must take an awful lot of man power to bail it all out by hand. If you've got some spare rope and some buckets I can rig up this pulley system which will mean you are able to bail the same amount of water in a fraction of the time, with a fraction of the effort. All it will take is one man turning the winch."

The captain squinted at the paper. From the way he mouthed the words as he read them, it was obvious he didn't read well, but he seemed to understand the diagrams well enough.

He rubbed his stubbly chin. "So you're saying you can build us some kind of machine that will help clear the bilges?"

Bram nodded. "Like I said, all I'll need is some rope, buckets and any tools you might have."

"That would certainly help us out in a storm. When the weather's rough, it's always the bilges that fill first, although we've no idea whether the same rules will apply on an Ice Ship. All right, you can have whatever you need. See the first mate, he'll sort you out."

The captain stalked off, and Bram grinned. He was finally doing something useful!

He got what he needed from the first mate and went off to find Corban. Despite the bruises he'd gained yesterday, he was eager to

272

continue his training. He'd be on this ship for another eight days, he may as well make use of the time.

Corban was going through some intricate patterns on *Regalia's* deck, moving from one pose to another with a grace and agility that left Bram gaping.

Barl and Saskia were leaning on the ship's rail, as usual. In one meaty fist Barl held a haunch of beef, which he tore at like a dog worrying at a rabbit.

"Morning, Bram!" he bellowed, dribbling juice down his chin. "Fine day to get a pasting, eh?"

Bram smiled, but didn't respond to the commander's jest.

Corban raised his sword in salute as Bram approached.

"We're going to work on balance today," he announced as he handed Bram a sword, hilt first. "When fighting with a blade, balance is your greatest weapon. If you overbalance, you'll expose yourself and you'll die. You need to be able to move quickly and still keep control of your sword. Now, blade up."

Bram brought the blade up in front of his face.

Corban swept his left leg back and pivoted on it, keeping his sword perfectly balanced in front of him. "Copy me."

Bram did so but found that when his weight moved, the tip of the sword dipped down, despite his effort to keep it level. He went back to the start and tried again. Before long, Bram's calves and shoulders were burning with pain. He could understand why it took years of training to become adept with the sword. Muscles he'd never used before were straining under the onslaught.

Gradually, it became easier to move whilst keeping the blade under control. When Bram had mastered this move, Corban moved onto another. From their position with the left leg back, Corban brought his sword round in an arc while simultaneously spinning around to face the opposite direction.

Bram, determined to get it right, concentrated as he swung his sword and twisted his body. But as he moved, his legs got tangled and he went staggering sideways. With a cry he threw his arms up and his sword caught Corban's with a clang. The blade was ripped out of Corban's hands and flew into the air. Bram watched as the blade reached its apex and came flying down again, straight at his chest.

Barl shouted something. Saskia cried out. The blade spun as it fell, catching the sunlight.

Bram had no time for fear. He had no time to cry out.

As the sword dropped toward him he threw up his hand to meet it —

— and the blade stopped in mid-air.

Corban gasped. Barl and Saskia hurtled

over and skidded to a halt, gaping.

The sword hung blade downwards, an inch from Bram's outstretched hand.

He scuttled out from under it and the sword crashed to the deck.

Corban approached the sword slowly, as though it was a viper that might strike. Carefully he bent and picked it up. Barl and Saskia leaned over him, examining the blade.

"I've never seen anything like it," Corban said, turning the blade over. His eyes fixed on Bram. "What did you do?"

Bram's heart pounded. "I, I don't know," he stammered.

Corban exchanged a look with Barl that Bram couldn't read. They were silent for a time. Eventually Barl said, "Well, whatever happened, it saved your life. Otherwise you would have been skewered like a pig, my young friend."

Bram ran his hands through his hair. "I don't understand."

Corban sheathed his own sword and placed the spare one back in its scabbard. "We need to work on balance, Bram. Meet me back here tomorrow and we'll carry on."

Bram nodded, not trusting himself to speak. Barl ruffled his hair and the three Panthers moved off along the deck.

Bram returned to his cabin, thinking about what had happened. Why had the sword stopped in mid-air like that? Surely it must be something to do with *Regalia's* strange power. He latched on to the explanation. Yes, that made sense. Nothing to do with him. Nothing at all.

***

On a bright morning eight days later Bram was playing nine-bobs with Barl when the lookout on the main mast shouted, "Land ahoy!"

Everyone came above deck and clustered along the rail. Far in the distance, Bram saw a strip of white coastline.

Bram glanced to his side and realized Astrid had come up beside him. She stared straight ahead with a look of joy on her face.

"Home," she breathed. "Chellin at last."

CHAPTER 19

Chellin, a beautiful and ancient city, lay along a rugged, craggy coastline. Several headlands reached out into the sea like fingers and the city had been built into the sides of them, clinging to its precarious perch like a giant seabird colony. Some of the headlands were separated from the mainland, connected only by high bridges.

Bram gulped as he looked. Those bridges were high. Very high.

As they drew closer to the city, Astrid ordered the ships to drop anchor while she performed the farewell ritual to the tashen, a ritual the Ral Torans watched with wide eyes and slack jaws. As soon as the serpents had disappeared into the open sea, the fleet sailed into one of Chellin's deep harbors.

Once he had finished with his packing, Bram left his cabin and climbed on deck. Nerves wriggled like worms in his belly. How would the Ral Torans be received in Chellin?

On the deck of *Regalia* the crew were securing the ship whilst a team of docks men unloaded the party's luggage.

Bram spied Father Hewin and the Panthers standing by the rail, staring out at Chellin. It was a cold, clear day and the sun made the white stone of the city sparkle. Footsteps echoed on the planks behind him and Bram turned to see Tomas approaching. He stood beside Bram in silence, staring out at Chellin.

Bram watched the Varisean. Tomas's face bore an unreadable expression, but his eyes roved over the city as though looking for something. He stiffened and then grabbed Bram's shoulder. Bram flinched.

"There is peril here," Tomas breathed. "Knives in the dark... flickering shadows. I cannot see clearly. They are close now." Shuddering, he passed a hand over his face. When he looked up again he smiled thinly at Bram. "I know you find it hard to heed my advice, Bramwell Thornley, but you must be careful here. The place stinks of treachery." He squeezed Bram's shoulder and then stalked off.

As they disembarked and started moving toward the city Bram fell into step with Falen and Tomas. Father Hewin walked beside Astrid, while the Panthers brought up the rear. The soldiers looked wary. A number of them had hands on weapons and even though Barl was loudly making conversation with Saskia, his eyes darted everywhere, alert for danger.

They left the harbor and entered a wide thoroughfare that snaked its way up the side of the cliff. Streets ran off at intervals on either side, and the buildings were tall and elegant, carved from white stone. Hardy coastal plants grew everywhere: hanging from window boxes, framing doorways, standing in planters on street corners. It seemed as if the very rock was alive.

Bram stared like a child. Chellin was so different to Ral Tora. There was no uniformity to the buildings, as though the builders had chosen their design according to their mood at the time. Many of the houses had been carved into the semblance of natural things. Some resembled the craggy, bare rock of the cliff, while others looked like waves or a pebble beach. The streets ambled in long curves, wherever the natural contours of the cliffs took them. The tangy odor of the sea and the haunting cry of gulls provided a perfect backdrop.

The road they followed led to the top of the cliff. The Chellins, used to living in such steep places, seemed unaffected, but the Ral Torans were soon panting. Bram's muscles were screaming by the time the track leveled out. They were high above Chellin now and the wind plucked at Bram's clothes and hair.

Ahead of them was one of Chellin's many headlands. Over the millennia the sea had pounded its base until it had become separated from the mainland and now formed an island. On the headland's crown sprawled the royal enclave of Chellin, a complex dominated by a huge, many-turreted palace with pennants snapping in the breeze. A bridge ran between the promontory and the mainland, a high, narrow span of stone stretching across the gap.

Bram gulped. Was there no easier approach to the palace?

A group of guards wearing black doublets barred the entrance to the bridge on the mainland side. As Astrid approached, one of the guards blocked the way with his sword.

"Who approaches the royal enclave?" he asked in a strident voice.

Astrid drew a white knife and held it out. "It is I, Astrid du Lanstrang Av' Riny, Keeper of the Silver Knife, protector of the Seals, by the grace of the Goddess, Regal of Chellin."

The guard saluted with the sword. "We, the Royal Guard of Chellin, recognize and welcome you, Regal. May the Goddess smile on you."

The guards swept aside and Astrid walked

confidently out onto the bridge. Gritting his teeth, Bram moved along with the group. The bridge narrowed in the middle, forcing Bram to walk beside the parapet. Unbidden, his eyes traveled downwards. An impossible distance below, the sea crashed against rocks, throwing spray and foam thirty paces into the air before falling back again with a boom.

Looking at the drop, memories began to surface in Bram's head. Suddenly he was on First Storm Tower again, losing his grip, falling, falling, falling....

"Are you all right, Bram?" said Falen, regarding Bram with concern. "What is it?"

Bram moved his tongue in his mouth. "I don't think I can do this."

"Do what?"

"Cross this bridge."

Falen straightened. Her voice took on a commanding tone. "Nonsense. You can do anything you set your mind to. Now, let go of the parapet and look straight ahead."

Bram fixed his eyes on the palace. He clasped Falen's outstretched hand tightly, and followed as she led him in careful, measured steps. After twenty agonizing paces, they reached the other side of the bridge. Bram had never been so relieved to feel solid earth under his feet. Letting out a huge breath, he smiled at Falen.

"I've made an idiot of myself, haven't I?"

Falen snorted. "Bramwell Thornley, you

say some stupid things. Anybody would be a bit nervous after your fall off First Storm Tower. It will pass in time. Besides, everyone is scared of something — I'm terrified of spiders."

Bram laughed and, feeling reckless, squeezed her hand in thanks. Since the incident on the ship, Falen had barely spoken two words to him, and Bram, to his surprise, realized he'd missed her.

Astrid and the rest of the party had halted on the palace steps. The gilded doors stood open and a group of people in white robes waited to greet Astrid. At their head stood a tall, handsome man. He had a strong jaw line, deep eyes, and long blond hair held back by a silver circlet. His stance spoke of confidence as he moved forward and bowed to Astrid.

"Bright blessings, Regal. My thanks to the Goddess for bringing you safely home to us."

Astrid inclined her head slightly. "High Priest, Tamardi. I trust you have been keeping things in order while I've been away?"

"Of course. The senate and I have been running things very smoothly. Why, we could almost believe we had no Regal at all!"

Astrid's mouth tightened. "But you *do* have a Regal, high priest. She has returned and will take up the rule again."

"Of course, of course," he said, smiling. "And may the Goddess guide your hand and bring wisdom to your rule." His eyes moved beyond Astrid to the Ral Torans. "You have brought companions. May we be introduced?"

Astrid stiffened almost imperceptibly. "Of course."

The high priest moved over to Father Hewin, and after being told his name, took his hand and said, "I look forward to conversation with you, father. I will be fascinated to learn all you can tell me about your southern city."

Father Hewin shook the high priest's hand heartily, eager to make friends. "And I will be glad to learn from you, high priest. Your ways and beliefs seem strange to us, and I would gladly learn all I can about them."

A smile played across the high priest's handsome features. "The Goddess smiles on those who wish to learn her ways. You are very welcome in Chellin, father."

The high priest turned to Tomas, but the Varisean shrank back, hands held out in front of him as if to keep the man away. A slight widening of the high priest's eyes betrayed his surprise at this reaction, but he was far too polite to comment. Instead, he turned away, took Falen's hand, and kissed it.

"I'm honored to meet you, daughter of warriors."

Bram felt a twinge of irritation as Falen blushed. Surely she wasn't impressed by such easy charm?

"This is Bramwell Thornley," Astrid said, "an engineer from Ral Tora's famous guild."

Tamardi's eyes flicked to Astrid and then back to Bram. "Welcome to Chellin, Bramwell Thornley. I'm sure we'll get to know each other in the days to come."

Bram didn't know what to say, so he kept his mouth shut. The high priest grinned and turned away, offering his arm to Astrid.

The party passed through the open doors, the palace swallowing them like a hungry mouth. Inside, an army of servants waited. Bram found himself being ushered down a long, echoing corridor. He glanced over his shoulder as he went, and saw the high priest staring at him.

He shivered then followed his guide deep into the mysterious heart of Chellin.

***

High Priest, Tamardi Di Goron, sauntered off toward his apartments, and Astrid ached to plunge a knife into his back. Oh, how she hated that man! In the weeks away from home she had almost forgotten how much his grin infuriated her, how much his insidious voice made her want to garrote him. The Goddess alone knew what poison he had been pouring into the ears of the senate while she had been away.

Teriska, her handmaid, came over and curtsied. "Mistress, if it please you, perhaps you would like to retire to your apartments now and I will help you into your state robes."

Astrid sighed. She longed to climb into a hot bath, soak for a long, long, time and then climb into bed. But politics left no time for such niceties. There were reports to be given, judgments to be made, policy to be debated, and of course, the senate to be placated. She allowed herself to be led away by her handmaid, waving away a multitude of questions her ministers fired at her.

At the entrance to her quarters, she paused and took a breath. Servants scurried everywhere, like an army of mice, eager to make everything ready for their mistress.

In Astrid's private bathroom, a room big enough to accommodate a large family, Teriska began running Astrid a bath. Astrid pulled off her garments and let them fall to the floor. Gratefully, she sank down into the hot water and let it soothe her tired muscles. Teriska scrubbed Astrid's back and then washed her hair, all the while chattering like a bird about the latest fashions in the court, and which lords had shown an interest in which ladies. Astrid paid the girl no heed. What did she care if her courtiers had taken to wearing satin instead of silk?

Pulling herself at last from the haven of the water, Astrid wrapped a towel around herself and sat by the fire. The flames writhed and hissed. Thoughts of the senate crept into her mind. How would they receive her? Many of them had hoped she would never come back from Ral Tora. How would they react now she'd returned? If the senate had their way, they would abolish the monarchy and turn Chellin into a republic. Not one of them would admit it to her face, but Astrid's spies had overheard many discussions and witnessed many secret meetings.

"Who do you think would be president of a republic?" she asked aloud. "One of you? Hardly. The high priest would seize power and destroy you."

For all their supposed wisdom, the senate couldn't see what was in front of their noses.

Feeling the need to be alone, she dismissed Teriska and donned the white robes of her office. A servant brought a crystal decanter of pink wine, which she snatched greedily, pouring herself a glass and gulping it down.

She seated herself in the main reception room and looked out of the tall window. The wind had picked up again, rattling the casements and whipping the flags atop the palace towers into a frenzy. A fitting backdrop to her thoughts.

A knock on the door signaled the arrival of First Minister Mattack. His bald pate shone with sweat. "No rest for us yet, eh, my lady? I barely had time to change my clothes before the summons came from the senate."

"The senate forgets we've been at sea for almost two weeks. We're not allowed human weaknesses such as fatigue. Remember, Mattack, nothing is to be said of the subject we discussed. I don't want that information reaching certain ears."

"Of course, my lady. The senate will only hear what we want them to hear."

"Excellent. Lead the way."

Rama and Aeron fell into step behind Astrid and Mattack as they left the royal apartments and descended into the lower levels of the palace. A contingent of royal guards escorted them through the winding corridors until at last they reached a wide reception chamber with a floor of polished red and white flagstones. The seal of Chellin had been embossed into the black marble door at one end: a spread-winged albatross.

Astrid halted in front of the doors.

The guards bowed. "Welcome to the senate, Your Majesty."

They pushed the doors open and Astrid strode through. The room had been hollowed out of the rock of the plateau and the door Astrid used lay halfway up one wall. Steps led down to the center, where a raised stand, like a pulpit, had been placed. Tiers of stone seats curved around the walls and were crowded with people in white robes. The High Priest Tamardi sat in the front row, smiling up at her. Astrid held his gaze for a second, before indicating for Mattack to take his seat next to the high priest. Steeling her resolve, Astrid marched down the steps and assumed her place in the pulpit. She pulled her face into as haughty and regal an expression as she could, and glared down at the senators.

Rosenthay, leader of the senate, bent his spindly old legs and stood. Sketching a creaky bow he said, "Lady Astrid, on behalf of all the senate, I bid you welcome. It's been a long time since you stood in this chamber and conversed with us. We've missed both your beauty and your wit."

Oh, I'll bet you have, Astrid thought. *You've had it all your own way while I've been away, I'll warrant. Things are going to change now I'm back, you two-faced old goat!*

Astrid flashed Rosenthay a brilliant smile. "Your welcome gladdens me, senator. I have missed our... sparring."

Rosenthay smiled at her choice of words.

Astrid forced her face to remain impassive, but her stomach tightened in annoyance. Why didn't he ask about her mission? Obviously, the senate's spies had already told him what happened in Ral Tora.

Rosenthay ran his tongue around his lips. "So, it would seem that your trip has been a success —"

Someone interrupted, "That would depend on your definition of success."

Astrid narrowed her eyes at the speaker. She should have known Senator Nerie would not keep quiet. The woman never could.

"What do you mean, senator?" Astrid asked politely.

Senator Nerie ran a hand through her thick yellow hair. With her rosebud lips pressed together in a pout, she regarded Astrid with large blue eyes that had snared many a man. Nerie's outfit was hardly decent for a senator — her dress cut so low it left little to the imagination and her fingers glittering with many rings. But only a fool would be duped by Nerie's porcelain-doll appearance. Those big blue eyes were hard enough to chip diamonds and hid the cunning of a snake. Many of Nerie's rivals had ended up dead with no evidence to implicate the senator in their downfall. She was too clever for that.

"Let's look at the facts," Nerie said. "What's been achieved? We have an alliance with Ral Tora. That sounds very grand but what good will it actually do us? Will they trade their technologies with us? No. Will they send us their engineers? No. Have they found a way to combat the Everwinter? No. We have raised taxes to fund a trip that has been of no benefit to Chellin whatsoever."

Rumbles of agreement went around the room. Nerie fixed Astrid with her gaze, and a tight smile crossed her face. "What say you, Regal?"

Astrid wanted to slap the woman. Instead, she said calmly, "Your concern for Chellin does you credit, senator. However, I feel you are mistaken. An alliance with Ral Tora will bring a sharing of knowledge that can only be of benefit to Chellin."

"Which brings us to another point," said Nerie, glancing round at her colleagues. "We have a bunch of foreigners roaming freely around our city. How do we know they can be trusted?"

"What concern is that of yours, senator?" Astrid said. "They are my guests, under my protection, and I will vouch for them." Her voice held a threat that was not lost on Nerie. The senator smiled at the rebuke.

"Senator Nerie raises a valid point," said the high priest suddenly. "These people are non-believers, ignorant of the Goddess's ways. We cannot have them polluting our people with their tales of science and logic."

Astrid glared at him. The senate was no place to start prattling about the Goddess. "We agreed, right here in the senate, to the terms of the alliance before I even set foot outside Chellin. Did you expect the Ral Torans to hand over their Ice Ship and then wave me on my way?"

The high priest didn't answer. He smiled thinly and nodded, as though conceding the point.

Senator Nerie frowned, her big eyes growing dark. "You won the vote for your trip to Ral Tora by the slimmest of majorities. And your...persuasive...talents played their part. I for one have never been happy at the prospect of having strangers in our city and I know many in this chamber agree with me."

Astrid's cheeks grew hot with anger. She gripped the pulpit so hard her fingers ached. The damned woman had all but accused Astrid of intimidating the senators to vote her way. How dare she? Especially when Nerie had half the senate in *her* pocket, through promises of power or of sharing her bed.

In a cold voice Astrid said, "I have not come here to bandy pointless words with you, senator. The fact of the matter is we have an alliance with Ral Tora and they will be given all the courtesies due to diplomatic guests."

"Bringing armed soldiers into the city was never part of the agreement," Nerie said smoothly, ignoring Astrid's rebuke. "Yet you bring these 'Panthers' into the palace and allow them to keep their weapons! It seems pleasing your new friends is more important than the safety of your own people."

"That is a fair point," Rosenthay said before Astrid could reply. "It goes against all protocol to allow these Panthers to go armed about the palace."

Astrid glared at Rosenthay and the old man gazed blandly back at her. *What's going on? They are arguing over trivialities.* She sensed a plan at work here, somehow the senate was shepherding her in the direction they wanted her to go, like terriers worrying at a bear.

Determined not to play their game, she said, "You've done nothing but whine and complain since I arrived in this chamber. I've fulfilled my part of the agreement — I've secured the Ice Ship and the alliance with Ral Tora, which is more than any Regal before me could achieve, and yet you carp like village fishwives! What have you been doing to keep your end of the bargain?"

The senators bridled at that, sending telling glances at each other. She may be the Regal, but the senate still expected her to speak to them with the deference they were sure they deserved.

After a moment's silence, Astrid snapped, "Have you all gone deaf? What progress have you made in finding a solution to the Everwinter?"

Senator Rerkan, a barrel of a man whose robe was pulled tight over his sagging paunch said, "The city's best scholars are still working on the problem."

Astrid had to stop her lip curling in disgust. Rerkan was a greasy slob of a man who had a reputation among the servants for being a vindictive bully. If he had not held important estates to the north of Chellin, and had an enormous family that would undoubtedly want revenge, Astrid would have disposed of him years ago.

Addressing her comments to Rosenthay, she said, "And what of our efforts in the north?

How go the preparations for my expedition? Has there been any success in corroborating the reports of the scouts?"

Rosenthay deferred to Nerie once more, and the yellow-haired harlot smiled coldly. "I have good news my lady — as it turns out, you will not have to journey to the north at all."

Astrid's heart thudded. What scheme was this?

"While you were away Captain Ternor and his company retracted their statements. They admitted that the Ice Dragon talon they brought back with them was a hoax. They made it all up."

"What are you talking about? I was present when Captain Ternor made his report. He was not lying!"

"I'm afraid you were duped, just like the rest of us. Captain Ternor and his company turned out to be accomplished liars."

Astrid felt a trap closing around her. She could not possibly think what Nerie was up to, but the blue-eyed woman somehow held the upper hand. Astrid glanced at Mattack, hoping the minister would speak in her support. But Mattack was studiously avoiding her gaze. She glared at him. What was wrong with the man? Surely Nerie hadn't gotten to him?

She fixed the blonde harlot with an icy stare. "Why would they lie about their mission? They are trained soldiers of Chellin, sent on a vitally important task. They are oath-sworn to tell the truth!"

Nerie's face folded into a look of concern, as though what she was about to say pained her. "They failed in their duty, my lady, and broke their oath. They told us the truth eventually, when they were questioned in more detail. It turns out that Ternor's company began arguing and ended up in a fight that got out of hand. Nine of the company were killed. The rest made up an elaborate tale to cover this up and escape a court martial."

Astrid stared at Nerie. The woman's blue gaze was hard.

"How dare you stand in the senate and lie to me?" Astrid hissed.

Muttering broke out around the room and a number of senators surged to their feet. Nerie didn't flinch.

"I do not like being called a liar. I demand an apology." She turned her gaze on Rosenthay.

Rosenthay cleared his throat. "It's true, my lady. I heard it from Captain Ternor myself."

Nerie all but smirked. "So you see, I am not a liar. I will have that apology now."

Fury churned in Astrid's belly. If Nerie had been within distance she would have struck her.

You simpering bitch! I will wipe the smile from your face!

"I don't know what game you're playing, but I will have the truth of this. I will speak to

Captain Ternor and his company myself. And when I get the truth, you will be apologizing to me on your knees!"

Astrid had hardly expected Nerie to crumble into weeping at her threat, but the look of triumph that erupted over Nerie's features shocked her. "That may be a little problematic," she purred. "Captain Ternor and his company are dead."

Astrid froze. She could feel the ground shifting beneath her feet.

"What do you mean?"

"They could not face the disgrace of a court martial. Two weeks ago they requested the Breath of the Goddess. They were not refused."

The trap had been sprung. Astrid spun to stare at the high priest. "You did this? You allowed such an abomination?" She could not keep the disgust from her voice.

"You know the law better than anyone, my lady," Tamardi answered. "Any condemned prisoner may request the Breath of the Goddess. As Her high priest, it is my duty to administer the final rite. I did not shrink from my responsibility." His eyes challenged Astrid to dispute him.

You murdered them! Astrid thought. *You black-hearted son of a whore!*

The Breath of the Goddess. Chellin's oldest law. Anyone facing trial could take their own life if they chose, thereby throwing themselves on the judgment of the Goddess.

But Astrid knew Ternor and his men had done no such thing.

They'd been murdered, made to look like suicide.

It took all of Astrid's will to stop her voice from shaking as she said, "You really expect me to believe that trained Chellin soldiers asked you to help them kill themselves?"

Tamardi's eyes narrowed. "Of course. Do you doubt me?"

Astrid paused. It was one thing to call a senator a liar but quite another to call the high priest of Chellin a murderer. Besides, the senate had already swallowed whatever lies he and Nerie had told them, they would be unlikely to listen to a word Astrid had to say. So, the soldiers had been silenced. But what did Nerie and Tamardi have to gain by discrediting them?

Sounding almost uncomfortable, Rosenthay said, "In light of this development, the senate has decided your expedition to the north will not go ahead, my lady."

The *senate* had decided? As if they had the right to tell her what to do! Astrid took a deep breath, willing herself to calmness. "This changes nothing," she said, raking her eyes across the senate. "Nothing. I will sail for the north as planned."

Rosenthay opened his mouth to speak but the high priest cut him off. "Agreement was only given to your northern expedition on the basis of what the soldiers reported. Now we know we cannot trust their testimony, it is the decision of the senate that an expedition to the north no longer has merit. The senate will not finance it."

Astrid stared at him. Why was he trying to stop her going north? He should be glad to get rid of her!

"Lord Tamardi is correct," Rosenthay said. "In times of crisis it is the duty of the senate to decide on the best course of action to keep the city safe."

"And what, in your infinite wisdom, has the senate decided to do?"

Rosenthay's gaze was steady as he said, "It is the duty of the Regal to remain here and lead her people. We will look to our own. All outside influences within the city are to be banned. Only the true religion will be tolerated and all foreigners will be asked to leave. The Goddess will save us if we are true to her ways."

Astrid stared, open-mouthed. "This is your plan?" she exploded. "To do nothing and hope the Goddess will save us? Are you out of your minds?"

The high priest's chest puffed out at the insult. "May I remind you, my lady, that our secular laws are closely entwined with our ecclesiastical ones. In times of crisis, we turn to the Goddess, just as we always have done. And as her Voice, I have the power to make decisions concerning the welfare of Her people."

One of Astrid's fingernails snapped and she looked down in surprise. She hadn't realized she was gripping the pulpit so hard. So, here it was at last then, the high priest's plan. He wanted to undermine her authority by citing religious law. And he was right. Under Chellin law, the Voice of the Goddess — the high priest — held responsibility for the safety of the people if they faced any form of spiritual danger. And the Everwinter certainly posed enough danger.

But by quoting religious law, Tamardi had fallen into his own trap. He had underestimated her, believed he knew the laws better than she did.

Astrid could barely keep from smirking. Instead, she fixed Tamardi with a hard stare and said, "You're quite right, high priest, and your knowledge of the Goddess's laws is impeccable. Tell me, what does section seventeen of the third canon say?"

The high priest stiffened. Silence filled the senate.

Astrid put on a puzzled expression. "Can't you remember what it says? I could have someone fetch a copy if you'd like."

Everyone was looking at the high priest. He could not refuse to answer without making himself look foolish.

In a strained voice he said, "Section

seventeen of the third canon says, 'There shall be two champions on earth: the Voice of the Goddess and the Sword of the Goddess. Although the Voice will pass on the Goddess's wisdom, it shall be the Sword who will lead Her people. And if ever dispute comes between the Voice and the Sword, the Sword will take precedence, for first and foremost the Goddess is a warrior, and so shall Her people be.'"

Astrid smiled. "And who is the Sword of the Goddess?"

The high priest's eyes were full of venom. "You are."

"I am. And I claim right of precedence. All decisions made in the senate in my absence are hereby made null and void. My expedition will go ahead. Any who dispute my decision are disputing the will of the Goddess and will face the justice of the Sword. What say you?"

Astrid turned full circle in the pulpit, looking each senator in the face. Senator Nerie's eyes burned with a fire as bright as the high priest's.

So. They had planned this together. Why did they want to keep her in Chellin? Surely, their plans would be better served with Astrid out of the way? She must solve this riddle if she wanted to keep her city and her life.

The senators knew they'd been beaten. They couldn't argue with her without undermining the very reasoning they had relied on.

You should know by now never to underestimate me, she said to herself.

"What say you?" she asked again.

At last, Senator Rosenthay gathered himself. "We acknowledge your rights as Sword of the Goddess. Your wishes will be carried out."

Astrid inclined her head. As she turned and left the senate, the high priest stared after her with eyes as dark as a grave.

CHAPTER 20

A blue silk jacket and matching trousers had been laid out on the bed. Bram, dripping from the bath and clad in only a towel, scanned around for his normal clothes. They were nowhere to be seen. Some industrious servant had taken them away while he had been bathing and left these garments in their place.

Shivering in the cold air, Bram shuffled across the room and examined the arm of the jacket. Tiny white dolphins had been stitched around the cuffs and the lace at the collar had been gathered up into a semblance of stylized flowers.

If they thought he was going to wear this,

they'd better think again. He'd rather freeze!

A small glass bell sat on a side table. He shook it, smiling as a high-pitched 'tink-link' filled the room. Not quite up to Old Rosella's standards! A moment later the door opened and a blonde serving girl entered and stood staring at Bram expectantly.

Bram jumped, startled. To his horror, the towel unwound itself from his waist and slipped to the floor. He yelped and grabbed it awkwardly, yanking it back around his waist. His face burned as hot as the fireplace.

The serving girl showed no reaction. "How can I be of service, my lord?"

Bram spluttered, trying to think of something to say. "I, yes, I... er...thank you for lighting the fire."

The girl inclined her head. "Was the bath water to your liking?"

"Um, yes, very nice. My clothes have disappeared though."

"I laid them out on the bed for you, sir."

"No, I mean the clothes I was wearing when I arrived."

"Oh, those...items," she said, wrinkling her nose slightly, "have been taken to the laundry. Are the garments I provided not to your liking?"

"Yes, they're lovely," blurted Bram. "It's just that I would prefer my own clothes. Could you bring them back when they're ready?"

"As you wish. sir. Will there be anything

else?"

"No. Thanks."

After the girl had left Bram retired to the bedroom and gingerly donned the jacket and trousers. He stood back to look at himself in the mirror and cringed.

I look like a jester, he thought. *If Romy and the others could see me now, they would probably die of laughter.*

Bram stomped over to the window, leaned his elbow on the sill and stared out. A walled garden lay below, where rows of leafless trees rattled in the wind. A group of ladies were valiantly trying to play skittles, even though their hair was being whipped into their faces, and dead leaves swirled around them.

Bram had been given clear instructions by Father Hewin to remain in his rooms.

Don't go poking your nose into trouble, the father had said.

But curiosity plagued him. He was in a foreign city, with so many things to explore, and he'd been told to stay indoors! He wandered round his rooms, inspecting the paintings and the tapestries, and then, for the sake of something to do, he pulled open the big wardrobe in the bedroom and peered within. To his delight, he found a heavy coat and a pair of stout boots inside.

Thinking of the garden outside his window, Bram grinned. *Excellent! I haven't played skittles in ages!*

There was nobody in sight as Bram left his rooms. A large door with a heavy iron handle stood at the end of the corridor. Sure he would find the garden on the other side, Bram pulled it open and stepped through, only to find himself standing in a small gallery with a staircase winding upwards.

The thick runner hugging the middle of the stairs silenced Bram's footsteps as he climbed. Another long corridor stretched into the distance with high windows along one side and suits of armor along the other. Two servants appeared ahead, carrying a large wickerwork basket between them. Bram turned on his heel and strode in the other direction, hoping he would eventually find a door to take him outside.

Bram found himself in a circular chamber with five arched corridors leading off. He stopped and looked around, assessing each of the exits in turn. He was no longer sure which way the garden lay. If he kept on wandering around he was likely to get lost, which would prove Father Hewin right, and earn Bram another ear-bashing. He was just about to give it up as a bad job, and retrace his steps back to his room when he heard voices coming toward him.

"Silly girl! Can't you follow simple instructions, Samsa? The Regal will want the Tiara dining set for tonight's dinner, not the Regal set. We aren't entertaining royalty."

"I'm sorry, Hetty, but you said she wanted the best so I just assumed —"

"Well there's best, and there's *best*, isn't there?"

Bram dived through the nearest entranceway just as an old woman with a tight gray bun on the back of her head and a young girl with a trembling lip came into view. They halted in the circular chamber while the older woman gave the younger one a thorough dressing down, complete with wagging of her finger. "If you want a job done in this place do it yourself…"

Bram hurried away. A flight of stairs faced him, and unless he wanted to come face to face with the old harridan and her cowering helper, he had no choice but to take them. As he climbed, Bram realized that these stairs did not lead up to another level of the palace as he expected, but began to loop round and round in a spiral.

Face it, Bram said to himself, *you don't know where you are. You have been in Chellin less than a day and you've already gotten lost! Turn around and go back!*

But stubbornness kicked in. He'd come this far, he'd bloody well find out where these stairs led! At last, he reached a door. A large glass panel in the middle let through the afternoon sunlight, flooding the stairwell with light. At last! He'd finally managed to find his way outside! Feeling a little smug, Bram pulled the door open and stepped through.

His mouth fell open in shock. He'd found a garden all right. But this was no manicured palace garden with ladies playing skittles. This was a high, wild garden with ivy growing over the stones and jamming its fingers into crenellated battlements. The wind howled and, far below, the palace roofs sparkled with ice. He stood atop one of the palace's many towers with a dizzying drop on every side.

Bram's heart thudded and he stumbled a few paces, clutching desperately at the wall. From behind him came a terrible cry, "Kar-ark!" and something huge hurtled toward him. Bram threw himself to the ground in terror.

"Whoa! What are you doing, lad?" somebody shouted. "You shouldn't scare Eobrus like that. He could have taken your head off!"

Bram breathed heavily, smelling the moldy scent of damp stone and ivy. He looked up. The most enormous bird he had ever seen sat on the parapet, no more than six paces from where Bram cowered. It had magnificent silver-gray plumage and a long pink beak. It stared at Bram with intelligent little eyes.

A man rushed over and pulled Bram to his feet. "You all right, lad?"

"I think so," Bram stammered, keeping his eyes on the bird. "What is that thing?"

"You never seen an albatross before?"

"No. I'm from Ral Tora."

The man snorted. "So I'd guessed. No Chellin would come bursting up here like that. Not when we have albatrosses nesting."

"They nest on top of the palace?"

"Aye. Not on this tower though, lucky for you. If he had been guarding a nest, he might have killed ya."

Bram stared at the bird nervously. As if sensing Bram's unease, it opened its beak and bellowed, "Kar-ark!"

Bram backed away.

"No need to worry now," said the man. "He won't hurt you. You startled him, that's all."

Bram pulled his gaze from the bird and took a look at his rescuer. The man wore a coat similar to Bram's own. He had a large nose and gold hoops dangling from his ears. The man held his hand out, palm facing toward Bram, in the Chellin way of greeting. "I'm Serz, falcon master to Lady Astrid."

Bram copied Serz's gesture. "I'm Bram. Pleased to meet you. I'm sorry for barging in on you like this."

Serz waved the apology away. He bent over and reached into a bucket by his feet. The pungent smell of rotting fish reached Bram's nostrils and he crinkled his nose in distaste. Eobrus picked up the scent and fixed his black eyes on Serz expectantly. Serz pulled a large silver fish from the bucket and tossed it into the air. Eobrus's head darted out, catching the fish in his beak and swallowing it whole.

"Is he tame?" Bram asked.

Serz raised an eyebrow. "Hardly. Nobody can tame an albatross. And why would we want to? Their wild spirit is what makes them beautiful. They're creatures of the Goddess. Masters of the air and the ocean. We feed them when they nest on our towers to help them get through this harsh winter. Fewer chicks survive each year, so we do what we can to help them."

"He's beautiful," Bram breathed.

"Watch this," said Serz. He pulled another fish from the bucket and threw it over the side of the tower.

Eobrus launched himself after it. Bram gasped. Eobrus's wingspan was incredible. Ten or eleven paces by the looks of it. Eobrus dived, caught the fish in mid-air, and banked to the right. He flapped those magnificent wings once and rose up on the air currents, pushing higher and higher, far above the tower.

Bram leaned over the parapet, watching. How must it feel to have the freedom of the skies? To see the world spread out below…

and feel the wind brushing through his feathers. There, an updraft catches his body and he spreads his glorious wings and lets the thermals carry him up, up, until the puny people on the tower are mere specks and he can see the beautiful ocean stretching out before him, calling to him, beckoning him home…

Bram lurched, grabbed the parapet. A wave of dizziness swamped him. Squeezing his eyes shut, he fought to get his bearings. He stood on the tower, on solid stone. But for a second it had almost felt as though he was up there with Eobrus, sailing through the skies.

He looked up. Eobrus glided majestically and circled, down, down, and landed back on the parapet exactly where he had left it. The giant bird cocked his head to one side and regarded Bram with his black eyes.

Come fly with me, brother.

"What?" Bram asked Serz.

The falcon master squinted at Bram quizzically. "I didn't say anything."

Bram glanced at Eobrus. The albatross gazed at him. He ran a hand through his hair and grabbed the parapet for support.

"You still haven't told me what you're doing up here, lad," Serz said.

Bram took a deep breath and concentrated on the falcon master. "I was looking for a garden I saw from my window. There were ladies playing skittles. I got lost."

Serz barked a laugh. "Ha! I would say so! That'll be the winter garden you're thinking of, a favorite haunt of Lady Yasmeen and her cronies. It's over yonder." He pointed over the palace rooftops, back the way Bram had come. "It's easy to get lost here, even if you do know it. The palace is a maze. Still, why did you go out on your own, why not get a guide?"

"I thought I might get into trouble for wandering around."

"There are only certain parts of the palace that are out of bounds, and they are heavily guarded. We have guides to show visitors around so they don't get lost."

"Oh," said Bram, feeling foolish, "I didn't know that."

"Come on," said Serz, throwing the last fish to Eobrus, "I'll take you back to your rooms — where did you say they'd put you?"

"I think the serving girl said it was the Pearl rooms."

"The Pearl? A strange choice. They're stuck out in the south wing, miles from anywhere. Come on then, I'll show you a bit of the place on the way."

Serz opened his palms wide to Eobrus to show he had no more fish. The albatross cocked his head, kar-arked loudly, and launched himself into the air, soaring over the rooftops and out to sea.

"He'll be back tomorrow, no doubt. Old Eobrus is getting lazy in his dotage and won't turn down a free feed."

Bram watched the albatross until he was out of sight then followed Serz down the tower steps.

They soon found themselves back in the bustling heart of the palace. Servants in blue livery scurried about, hauling water, carrying platters of food, sweeping floors, polishing armor, dusting tapestries. The gray-haired harridan Bram had narrowly managed to avoid earlier appeared in the distance, admonishing a footman.

Serz bowed politely to her and said, "Good day to you, Mistress Hetty."

The old woman paused in her haranguing of the footman and frowned at Serz. "A good day? Hardly! You try organizing a state dinner with only this lazy rabble to work with!"

Serz grimaced and moved off before she could say anything else. Bram hid a grin behind his hand but Serz saw it.

"You can smile all you like, young Bram, but after you've been on the receiving end of the housekeeper's temper, you'll realize why I made a quick exit! The palace is very busy today. I think I'll take you by another route."

He led them into the cloisters: a square garden open to the sky, with covered walkways along each side. A statue in the middle of the garden caught Bram's eye. It was carved into the semblance of a woman, with a raven sitting on her shoulder and a lamb by her side. A group of women knelt by the base of the statue, heads bowed in prayer.

Nodding toward the women, Serz said, "The Daughters of the Moon, priestesses of the Goddess. They're nervous at the moment because the high priestess is close to giving birth. There's rumors she's carrying twins.

That will cause some fun for the succession!
One of the babes must be a girl — the high
priestess always bears a girl — but if the other
is a boy, High Priest Tamardi's position will be
threatened, a situation he will certainly
dislike."

Bram studied the knot of women. Their
heads were bowed to the floor as they chanted
in low voices. Beyond the cloister, Bram saw a
large white building nestled among the bare
trees. It had a domed roof and four high
pinnacles on each side.

Following Bram's gaze, Serz said, "That's
the temple. It's big enough to fit the whole
population of Chellin inside. It's a little city of
its own really, with the politics to match. In
there the high priest and priestess are the
rulers."

"High priest and priestess? They are
married to each other, then?" asked Bram.

Serz shook his head. "By the Goddess, no.
Don't even suggest such a thing in the high
priestess's presence, she would likely have
your head! The high priestess's husband is
Lord Simeon, commander of Chellin's navy,
and a more devoted couple you'll never see. I
hope the second baby *is* a boy, for his sake, I
know he would dearly like a son."

Bram soon realized his good fortune in
bumping into Serz. The man gossiped like a
fishwife and his knowledge of the palace was
incredible. In short order Bram had been

shown the kennels, the stables and finally, the tourney ground. Here, much to Bram's delight, they stumbled upon the Panthers being put through their paces by Barl.

"By my belly!" Barl thundered, clapping Bram on the back. "It's our young apprentice! How're you finding our host's hospitality, my friend?" He winked at Bram conspiratorially and said, "Just between you and me, I think this place is grand. True, the locals are a little odd, but you should see the room they've given me, fit for a king it is! And the barracks this lot have got will have them all fat and lazy in no time!"

Bram laughed. "I don't think there is any danger of that with you in charge, Barl."

Bram left the Panthers with a promise he'd find them later for some sword practice. From the tourney grounds Serz took Bram back through a series of courtyards into the palace proper. By this time Bram was completely lost. He and Serz were making their way down a lavishly carpeted gallery with shields and weaponry hanging on the walls, when they encountered a group of people coming the other way.

Serz bowed. "Your Eminence."

Bram recognized the high priest at the head of the approaching group. Copying Serz, he quickly sketched a bow.

"Ah! What do we have here?" exclaimed High Priest Tamardi Di Goron. "Serz! I haven't seen you for many days. Tell me, how's that little sparrow hawk of mine coming along?"

"Very well, Your Eminence, "Serz replied. "She'll be ready for her first hunt in a few weeks."

"Excellent. And who is this? The Regal's young guest? Bren isn't it?"

"Bram," Bram corrected, belatedly adding, "Your Eminence."

"Bram. Of course," the high priest smiled and flicked a strand of blond hair out of his eyes. He took Bram by the shoulder and began walking him back the way they'd come. This close, the man smelled of sweet perfume.

"So tell me, Bram, how are you enjoying your stay?"

Bram groped for something to say. "Um, the palace is lovely."

"Yes, the jewel in the Goddess's crown. Did you know it took two hundred years and thousands of slaves to build this place? The bones of those slaves form the foundations of the place, so the tale goes. Not that I believe any such nonsense! Good granite is what keeps the palace standing, as old and solid as time. But you would know all about that kind of thing being an engineer, wouldn't you?"

"Well—" Bram floundered.

"Don't be modest! I hear the city of Ral Tora is a sight to behold and it's the skill of the engineers that have made it so."

"Perhaps. The people who built Ral Tora

originally were the real masters though. We just repair and maintain what they built all those years ago."

"Your Eminence," one of the high priest's cronies cut in. "Forgive me, but Senator Rosenthay will be waiting."

Tamardi glanced at his associate, a flicker of annoyance crossing his face. He turned back to Bram, all smiles, "I have to go. We must meet again soon though, and I will show you a little of Chellin."

Not knowing what else to say, Bram murmured. "Thank you, Your Eminence."

"Until our next meeting then." He clapped Bram on the shoulder and strode away.

When the high priest's party was out of sight Serz whistled under his breath. "Well, it seems you have friends in high places. First the Pearl rooms, now being noticed by the high priest himself."

Bram pondered this as they walked. He took his leave of the falcon master when they reached his rooms and pushed his way through the door. He found the blonde serving girl pottering around inside.

She curtsied when Bram entered. "Good afternoon, my lord."

Bram paused. "Oh. Hello. Er, how are you…?"

"Marijke my lord, my name is Marijke."

Bram held out his hand. Marijke stared at it. Bram turned his palm toward her in the

Chellin greeting. "Nice to meet you, Marijke. I'm Bram. And please don't call me lord."

Marijke looked at him strangely. Then she slowly reached out her hand and turned the palm out toward him, "As you wish... Bram."

"Good. Would you like a drink?"

Bram poured two glasses of wine from a decanter and offered her one.

"It is not permitted, my lor— Bram." Marijke said.

Bram shrugged and sipped at the drink. He took his coat off and slung it over the back of the chair.

Marijke frowned. "What have you been doing in those clothes?"

The knees of his trousers were ripped where he had thrown himself across the tower roof to escape the diving Eobrus. He smiled in what he hoped was a conciliatory way. "I ran into a spot of trouble."

Marijke tutted. "This will never do. You have been invited to Lady Astrid's banquet tomorrow night, what will you wear?"

"Can't I just wear my own clothes?"

Marijke's eyes widened as if he had muttered a profanity.

"What do you think I should wear?" he asked.

Marijke pursed her lips. "I will get the seamstress to measure you up. We will have something suitable run up in no time."

Although Bram's face was all polite smiles,

inside he was cursing his big mouth.

***

Astrid had not realized how knotted her hair could become in such a short space of time. She had dismissed Teriska but was now regretting sending the maid away. She had been diligently doing battle with her yellow mane for the last quarter bell, brushing it out to its full length and pulling out the snarls the sea wind had put in it.

She had changed from her robes of state into a simple nightdress and sat at her dressing table. Her jewels lay in a tangled pile on the table, and her staff of office had been lazily tossed onto the bed. A glass of wine and a good book awaited her by the couch in the sitting room.

Tonight, she would relax and be just Astrid. She relished the thought. It had been too long since she had been able to spend time by herself.

There was a knock at the door. Her heart sank. Could they not leave her alone for an instant? Frowning, she shouted 'enter' and turned back to the mirror and began combing her hair again.

"Ah, so beautiful, like a cloth of molten gold."

Astrid froze, hairbrush raised, then

whirled round. High Priest Tamardi stood in the door to her bedroom, smiling. The blood rushed to Astrid's face. More calmly than she felt, she placed the brush on the dressing table.

"I see your manners haven't improved while I've been away. Has nobody ever told you it is inappropriate to enter a lady's bedchamber?"

The high priest cocked his head. "Many apologies, my lady, but you did say 'enter'. I assumed that meant I was free to come in."

She felt a stab of annoyance at his smooth sarcasm and covered it by crossing over to the wardrobe and throwing a shawl across her shoulders. She tilted her chin up. "What can I do for you?"

"Shall we retire to your sitting room? As far as I am aware, it is not customary to conduct state affairs from a bedroom."

Feeling he had outwitted her again, she gestured impatiently for him to precede her from the room. She took a deep breath before she followed him. Tamardi waited for Astrid to seat herself before he sat down in one of the chairs before the fire. Although she did not feel hospitable, custom and manners demanded Astrid offer her guest a drink.

"May I offer you a cup of tea?"

"Yes, thank you. It is most cold tonight."

Astrid leaned over to the pot positioned on a little table and began pouring. Again she wished she had not dismissed Teriska. Her maid would have normally done this job, but Astrid had to do it instead, as though she were a common tavern wench.

Tamardi steepled his fingers and watched Astrid pour the drinks. Astrid tried not to look at him, but she felt those deep eyes boring into her and it was all she could do not to spill the tea.

As the high priest reached out to take the cup, he gently brushed Astrid's finger with his own. Startled, Astrid looked up to find him staring at her with hunger in his eyes. She quickly withdrew her hand, but her skin tingled where he'd touched her.

"You haven't answered my question," she snapped. "What can I do for you? Is there some matter of state you wish to discuss with me?"

He remained silent, his eyes locked on hers. At last he said, "Must it always be a matter of state? Can the Regal speak of nothing but duty?"

"You should know the answer to that better than most, high priest. You have sacrificed much for your ambition. We both have." She fixed her eyes on him, determined she would show him no weakness, and was rewarded when he looked away.

"That's true. A position of influence brings certain....responsibilities, even though we would sometimes wish it otherwise."

Uncertain of what he was getting at, Astrid remained silent. Tamardi took a sip from his cup, "I merely wished to know of your adventures in ₂Ral Tora. Is the city as magnificent as they say it is?"

"Why bother to ask me, Tamardi? I'm sure your spies have told you all you need to know."

A half-smile crossed his face. "Your tongue remains as rough as ever."

"I only speak the truth."

"In as blunt a fashion as I've come to expect from you. That was quite a performance you put on in the senate this afternoon. You outmaneuvered me very skillfully."

"Is that why you've come? To continue arguments that should be left in the senate?"

Tamardi grimaced. "No, you misjudge me. We dance a complicated dance in the senate, a game with many rules. You won the game today, and I will accept it."

"Then what do you want? Did you expect a welcome? After all that's passed between us?"

She immediately regretted her words. In this game of false courtesy she had been the first to falter. He showed no sign of it though. He shook his head sadly.

"Ah, Astrid, have we come so far we can barely be civil to each other?"

The use of her name instead of her title was another breach of courtesy and it irked her, but more disturbing were the memories that came unbidden, when he said her name.

"Yes, we have come that far. The whole city knows we cannot abide one another."

"Then they are fools who don't know the truth."

"What truth would that be?"

Tamardi stared at her. "You know what I'm talking about."

Astrid felt a flutter in her belly. She quickly looked away. "You're talking nonsense."

"Am I? There was a time when you did not think so."

Her eyes snapped up. "That was a long time ago. Much has changed."

He nodded. "Much has changed. We have changed."

"Do not tar me with your own brush, Tamardi!" Astrid hissed in sudden anger. "You were the one who became a stranger, like a snake shedding its skin."

Tamardi's eyes blazed with defiance. "Like I said, much must be sacrificed for position."

"You did more than make sacrifices, Tamardi. You destroyed everything that might divert you from your path. I know you're involved in something. Something dark. Do you think I don't know of your secret rites beneath the temple? What have you got hidden down there?"

A look of pure fury crossed Tamardi's face, the same look Astrid had seen in the senate that afternoon. The high priest did not like the fact that Astrid's spies had penetrated his secrets. "Sword of the Goddess or not, you have no right to pry into the business of the priesthood. What goes on within the temple is my business."

"*Your* business? The high priestess carries as much authority as yourself! Or had you forgotten Ravessa?"

Tamardi's mouth twitched. "While the high priestess is with child she cannot fulfill her duties. It falls to me to oversee the spiritual well-being of our people. I should not have to explain this to you."

There was a dangerous tone to Tamardi's voice. He did not like being questioned about matters he saw to be none of Astrid's business. Astrid was tired and in no mood for another argument so she said nothing and stared into the fire. Tamardi's expression softened.

"Why must we always argue, Astrid? There was a time when we used to talk and debate and enjoy each other's company."

"Does Nerie not satisfy you then? Not talkative enough on the pillows for your liking?" Astrid knew she sounded like a petulant girl, but she could not keep the acid from her voice.

Tamardi made no effort to deny his involvement with the senator. Instead he said, "Nerie has many talents, and no doubt can keep most men satisfied. But she is no challenge, no poison that gets into a man's blood and spreads like wildfire. Like you."

Astrid stiffened. "I think you should leave now."

"You don't really want me to."

Astrid surged to her feet, sending her cup flying. "Get out!"

Tamardi put his cup down and rose to his feet, standing very close to her. "I'm glad I can still arouse such passion in you, Astrid."

She slapped him hard across the face. His head snapped to the side. Suddenly he lunged forward and grabbed Astrid's shoulders. Before she knew what was happening, his mouth had descended onto hers, kissing her hungrily. Despite herself, she gave in and returned the kiss, slipping her arms around his waist to pull him closer.

Years fell away and she was young again, in the arms of her lover...

She pushed him away. "What are you doing?"

"What you want me to do."

She regarded the high priest. His face, although a little older, was as handsome as it had always been, his smile as disarming as ever. But his eyes, which had once been so full of joy and laughter, were now dark and untrusting, full of secrets. He was no longer the man she had known. He was her enemy, and she had no doubt he would bring her down if he could.

"You play games as well as any court lady, high priest. Sweet words drip from your forked tongue. But I am no starry-eyed wench. You know as well as I, there can be no reconciliation between us. You have chosen a path that makes you my enemy."

The look on Tamardi's face melted into a mask of contempt. "This is your final word?"

She nodded.

"Then it seems we really have come too far. Let the Goddess witness that I tried to reach accommodation with you. I have stated my case. Now we must walk the paths we've chosen. Be warned, my lady, I will show you no mercy when I bring you down." He strode to the door and slammed it behind him.

Astrid slumped into a chair. She had never realized the Regalship could be so lonely.

CHAPTER 21

Much to Bram's annoyance, Father Hewin and Barl had managed to evade the seamstress's attention. Father Hewin had again donned his habitual yellow robe and Barl wore a plain linen shirt and black trousers. Falen, for a wonder, was wearing a dress, and Tomas wore a ridiculous red outfit that made him look like a jester.

Marijke had been true to her word and had enlisted what seemed an army of seamstresses to furnish Bram with some new clothes. As a result, he now wore a tight blue tunic picked out with yellow flowers and a pair of baggy trousers that made him look as if he was wearing a skirt. After this dinner, he was definitely going to find his old clothes.

Bram scanned the hall. Astrid sat at the high table with her ministers and officials. High Priest Tamardi sat at one end of the table with a heavily pregnant red-haired woman at the other. The High Priestess Ravessa, Bram guessed.

He fiddled irritably with the collar of his shirt. All the frills and lace chafed his skin.

They were seated in the Grand Hall awaiting the first course of the state dinner to welcome Astrid home. Bram supposed he should be honored but all he really felt was out of place. Romy would have been more at home here, with his charm and his smooth tongue, but Bram didn't understand all the intricate rules of court etiquette, and would rather have stayed in his rooms.

"Burn my beard! I feel like a goldfish in a bowl!" Barl grumbled to Bram's left.

Bram was inclined to agree with the big man. Although the courtiers of Chellin were far too civilized to stare openly at the Ral Torans, every now and then a covert glance was aimed in their direction, before quickly being diverted again.

The doors at the far end of the hall suddenly burst open and an army of servants marched in carrying trays and plates and pushing little trolleys piled high with food. The first course was served in short order. A servant placed a platter in front of Bram, and pulled off the cover to reveal a whole red crab on a bed of some strange green stuff.

Bram stared at it. What was he supposed to do with this?

Falen picked up one of the claws, wrenched it open with both hands, and sucked out the insides. The others stared at her for a second, and then copied her. Next, Falen picked up a small metal implement that looked like a pair of nutcrackers, and proceeded to crack the crab's shell and pluck out the meat with a little silver fork. Everyone else followed her example.

"Where did you learn such fine manners?" Bram asked in a teasing voice.

"Not all of us have the manners of a goat," she replied tartly. "Some of us are a little civilized." To emphasize her point she stuck her tongue out at him.

As the guests ate, a dazzling array of performers kept them entertained. A troupe of jugglers dressed in garish red and yellow costumes juggled with little crystal spheres, so perfectly formed they were like flashes of sunlight flying through the room. The diners oohed and aahed in appreciation.

Bram picked the last of the flesh out of the crab shell and dropped the fork onto his plate. A servant materialized from nowhere, whipped the empty plate out from under his nose, and replaced it with the second course.

This time, slabs of pink meat covered in a creamy sauce filled the plate.

Bram leaned over to Falen. "What's this?"

"Bull Shark."

"What?"

"Bull Shark. Have you never eaten it before? It's a common meat in the north."

By the time the third course arrived, Bram felt as though his shirt buttons might pop. Barl ploughed through the meal as if it was his last. The big man had juice dripping down his chin and little splotches down his chest.

"Roast my behind, but these Chellins know how to throw a party, don't they?"

Bram nodded. "I don't think I've had this much food in years. Or drank so much wine either."

Barl bellowed a laugh. "Ha! I'll drink to that!" he raised the glass in a silent toast and drained it. A servant stepped from behind Barl's chair and filled his glass from a crystal decanter.

"Did you see that?" Barl said when the servant had departed. "I'm sure these Chellins are trying to get us drunk!"

"And you're doing your best to help them," said Father Hewin from Barl's other side.

Barl grinned at the father. "I'm just doing my bit for political relations. It wouldn't do to insult their hospitality would it?"

Father Hewin frowned and went back to

demurely picking at his food. Falen hid a smile behind her hand and Tomas giggled shrilly.

Bram, feeling a little fuzzy, leaned back in his chair and surveyed the room. People finished the meal and began pushing back their plates and loosening shirts and kirtles. Conversation hummed around the hall.

As the meal finally came to a close, the speeches started. One of the senators made a long and elaborate speech to welcome Astrid home, and to welcome her guests. Next, High Priest Tamardi stood and spread his arms wide to the gathering.

"My friends," he began with a grin, "the Goddess has indeed been kind, to deliver our Regal back home safe to us. I have offered up many prayers in thanks. Now, as my own contribution to tonight's festivities I would like to offer something for your entertainment." The high priest waved his hands at the door where a garishly dressed man entered and strode purposefully to the high table.

"Ladies and gentleman, may I introduce Laslon Do'Kamrim, the greatest bard Chellin has seen for many a year," announced the high priest. "He's going to sing one of the old tales for us tonight."

Laslon Do'Kamrim bowed with a flourish. "Many thanks, Your Eminence," he said in a high, feminine voice. "Lady Astrid, lords, ladies and guests, for your entertainment tonight I will recite for you the tragedy of

Queen Arisha and her ill-fated pact with the Goddess."

A murmur broke out around the room. Some people clapped excitedly. Astrid went very still and stared at Laslon Do'Kamrim without blinking.

The bard picked at the strings of his lute and began to sing.

> "I will tell you of a noble queen,
> As wise as she was fair,
> I will tell you of the elder days,
> Of Arisha Golden-Hair.
>
> With wisdom, grace, and justice true,
> She ruled our lives, our land,
> And, smiling, we held faith in her,
> Followed her guiding hand.
>
> But what thoughts were hers, alone at night,
> Sleeping in her bower?
> A longing gnawed at Arisha's soul,
> A greed, a need for power.
>
> Dominion over sea and land,
> Over air and fire and earth,
> These were hers by right she said,
> By lineage and by birth.
>
> She conquered all that lay before her,

And swept all else away,
Control of sun and stars were hers,
Control of night and day.

But the Goddess turned and said to her,
Daughter, stay your hand,
It is not for you to decide the fate,
Of air and sky and land.

The world is mine, lest you forget,
Made from my body, my breath, my heart,
And you, my daughter, are only one,
Small and lowly part.

But Arisha would not heed the words
The Goddess spoke to her,
Believing she was as powerful,
As the One who gave her birth.

So the Goddess smote her daughter down,
Her world she broke and tore,
Because of greed and power and pride
Arisha was no more.

The last strains of Laslon's song lingered in
the air, gradually dying away, to leave a thick,
heavy silence.

Nobody spoke.

The singer bowed his head and let his hair
swing over his face, breathing heavily. A
smattering of clapping began in the far corner
of the room, and eventually everyone followed

suit, although it soon trickled into silence.

What is going on here? Bram thought. *Does the song mean something to the Chellins that we don't understand?*

The high priest stood up and dismissed the bard with many words of praise. When the doors had closed behind Laslon Do'Kamrim the high priest said, "I would like to add my own blessing to the Regal's return. In this time of dire trial, I feel it is fitting to find inspiration from the teaching of the Goddess Herself, so I will read a few passages from the Book."

He reached down onto his seat and picked up a heavy-looking tome. He opened it to a page marked with a strip of red leather and ran his tongue around his lips before speaking.

"This passage is from the Edicts of Termanius, First Disciple of the Goddess, and tells of his confrontation with the Gray Witch who tried to turn him from the Goddess and pollute his heart with evil ways.

'After many days and nights of strife, when brother turned against brother, and friend against friend, all was at last made plain to the servant of the Goddess. And Termanius, seeing that the Witch meant to ensnare him spoke thus, 'Your words are poison dripped into the ear like sweet nectar. You are a snake that lies invisible in the grass. But no more! Soon all will know you, for I am a servant of the Goddess, and I curse you! I will smite you, I will smite you down and ruin you utterly until your tears water the earth and your line is destroyed!' "

The high priest fell silent and lifted his gaze from the book. He stared straight at Astrid. The Regal's face was emotionless, like a carved mask. But something danced in her eyes that Bram had not thought to see there.

Hate.

***

A fire crackled in the hearth, chasing away the worst of the night-time chill, but the blood in Astrid's veins remained like ice. Her sitting room was warm and inviting; her mood as dark and threatening as a storm. It was late. The palace slept, but not Astrid. She sat straight-backed by the window, staring out at the heaving sea.

She might have been that way all night; she had long since stopped taking any note of time. At first, after the high priest's performance at dinner, she had been consumed with a white-hot fury. In the privacy of her rooms she had shouted, she had screamed, she had thrown things, and sworn vulgarly enough to shock even the most battle-hardened soldier. Now though, the fury had passed and left in its place a cold, black anger that shriveled and gnawed at Astrid's insides.

Her mind played a million scenes over and over. In each one Tamardi Di Goron was screaming. In each one he died a more horrible death than the last.

There was a light rap on the door.

Astrid's eyes flicked in that direction but she didn't move.

The knock came again.

Astrid blinked. She took the ball of black hatred, wrapped it up and locked it away in her mind. There it would keep and fester until she was ready for it.

She pulled herself to her feet and went to the door. The man she had been waiting for stepped inside and began looking around nervously.

"Don't worry, Serz," Astrid said. "We're alone."

The falcon master smiled thinly. "I wasn't sure whether you wished others to know of your plans—"

"No!" Astrid said sharply. "None must know."

"As you wish. You can trust me."

"Yes, Serz. You've served me faithfully for many years." Astrid indicated for him to sit down. She poured two cups of mulled wine and passed one to the falcon master. She seated herself opposite and wrapped her fingers around her mug.

"What do you have to tell me, my friend? Does the boy show promise?"

"Ah, my lady, I wish I could tell you what you want to hear. The simple truth is, I'm not sure. I did as you asked. The charm worked well; the lad was drawn to the tower just as we planned. I had Eobrus up there, waiting."

Astrid leaned forward eagerly, "What happened?"

"I felt nothing from the boy. On that alone, I would say he is not a quentarc but I could hear Eobrus trying to speak to him, and Eobrus would not have done so if he didn't sense something in the boy."

"So, what does that mean?"

Serz paused. He looked like a man bearing ill tidings. "Are you sure you aren't mistaken? There could be hundreds of lads in Ral Tora who match Bram's description."

"I'm not mistaken!" Astrid snapped. Then in a softer voice she went on, "I've had my eye on the boy for many years. Trust me, Serz, he is the one we're after. My spies worked very hard to find him. His mother hid herself very well. I don't think the Ral Torans had any idea who she was. There may be none in Ral Tora who realize the truth of the boy's ancestry."

Serz took a sip from his cup and shook his head. "But there are so many rumors surrounding his mother. How do we tell which are true? Some say she never left Chellin at all, that she hides here still. Others say she killed herself and her son to stop them being found. Why are you so sure she went to Ral Tora?"

"Where else would she go? If she remained here she would surely be found. And what better place to hide than Ral Tora? A city of science where her gifts would never be discovered, and even if they were, would not be believed?"

"But if Bram is the person we're after, then surely he would have exhibited signs before?"

"Why would he? His mother would certainly not have taught him. She wanted to protect her son. Better for him to grow up as a scientist and never suspect what he is."

Serz looked skeptical. "Then what are we to do?"

"I want you to watch him, become his friend, get close to him, and report anything of interest straight to me."

"As you wish. But the high priest seems to have taken an interest in the boy. I think he's suspicious and is wondering why you've brought Bram to Chellin. He's been asking all sorts of questions about me as well. The stable master said he wanted to know of my background, how I train the falcons, everything. My lady, if he discovers I am a quentarc, you know what the priesthood will do to me."

Astrid scowled. "By the Goddess! Does that man miss anything? Blind his eyes!" She gathered herself, took a deep breath. "I will let no one touch you. How long have you been here now? Fifteen years? And in all that time nobody has suspected your gift. I will be dead before I see Tamardi Di Goron take you."

Serz paused. Finally he said, "I will do as

you ask. It will be easy to befriend the boy: he is too trusting. But I cannot watch him every hour of every day."

Astrid nodded. "Just do your best. I will keep an eye on the high priest. If he makes a move against Bram, I'll be waiting."

After Serz had left, Astrid sat by the window. Her mind worked furiously, turning over plans and schemes. The moon moved across the sky and sank beneath the waves. The first peach blush of sunrise was touching the horizon when she finally reached a decision.

She went into her bedroom and crossed over to a wardrobe standing in the corner. Inside were a few old gowns she irritably pushed aside. She fumbled around the back until her fingers found a tiny switch. She flipped it and the back of the wardrobe slid away to reveal a dark passage. Astrid scrambled inside and closed the door behind her.

She stood in a rough stone corridor stretching away to either side. It was dark and dank, stinking of mold and the sea. She clicked her fingers and lamps sprang into life along its length, casting flickering orange light on walls of gray granite, stained and weathered by time.

The tunnel formed part of a network of secret passages built into the walls of the palace. Astrid had spent years getting to know the tunnels intricately. They had proved invaluable on many occasions: for spying on her enemies or for the odd assassination.

As she set off heading roughly north, she wondered how many Regals before her had trod these silent ways, alone with the ghosts of the past and the soft sighing of the sea. Other than Astrid, only one person knew of these secret ways; the person she was going to meet. Her councilors, ministers and all the other important people of the city had no idea that for years she had been walking these paths, spying on all of them.

At length she came to a short flight of timeworn steps. At the top of these she paused, listening to the sounds coming from the other side. Beyond lay the chambers of senator Rosenthay, a hotbed of plotting and insurrection. Many times Astrid had stood here and listened to the scheming that had gone on within.

This time though, nothing could be heard except the soft grunt of snoring. She moved on. The tunnel undulated, dipped, and climbed again as it followed the contours of the palace. Finally, she reached her destination.

On the wall to her left was the faint outline of another secret door. A slot was carved into it at eye level, which Astrid slid slowly aside. Carefully, she leaned forward and pressed her eye to the slot.

"Are you going to come in or just stand there?" came a voice from inside the room.

Astrid smiled to herself. She tripped the latch on the secret door and stepped through. "There's no catching you out is there?"

"You should have learned that by now," said High Priestess Ravessa. She sat by the fire, dressed in a thick white robe. Her keen brown eyes studied Astrid with the intensity of a hawk's.

"Close the door will you, Astrid, you're letting in a draft."

Astrid did so and took a seat opposite Ravessa. "You knew I was coming?"

"After what happened at dinner last night? Of course you would come; I knew you'd need someone to help you plot your revenge."

Astrid shook her head. "You'd left the table before Tamardi got up to his tricks. Is there nothing that escapes you?"

Ravessa smiled. "You're not the only one with spies, Astrid." She leaned forward, a movement hampered by her swollen belly, and poured Astrid a cup of tea. She passed it over to Astrid and said, "So, tell me."

Astrid accepted the cup and blew on the hot liquid. At length she said, "It was a challenge, declaring that shortly he will depose me. Whatever the high priest is planning, it will come soon. We must be ready or we will lose Chellin. I will die before I let Tamardi Di Goron take my city!"

Ravessa regarded Astrid steadily. "You knew this would happen. We sat in this very room and discussed it when we planned your trip to Ral Tora. You knew when you left the city he would get to work on the senate and begin to take control. A risk we both decided was worth taking. Have you changed your mind about your quest? Will you stay here and fight Tamardi for control of the senate? After all we have planned?"

"I will never do that! We have come too far to back out now! But it is hard to watch Tamardi take control of Chellin from me."

"Don't you think I know how that feels? Every day I do battle with the dratted man in the temple. He has undermined my authority at each opportunity but I have held my tongue, and put up with his arrogance. Will you let your pride jeopardize our plans?"

"Do you think this is just about pride?" Astrid snapped, stung by Ravessa's words. "You, who know better than any, the sacrifices I've made? You insult me, Ravessa!"

The high priestess didn't reply. Between them, the fire crackled. Ravessa absentmindedly placed a hand on her belly. Finally, she said, "Pride has always been one of your faults, Astrid. Yet, it's one of mine as well, so I have no right to criticize you for it. Accept my apologies."

Suddenly moved, Astrid caught Ravessa's hands in both of hers. "For all you have done for me, sister, you have earned the right to speak to me as you please. You need never apologize to me. I owe you too much."

Ravessa squeezed Astrid's hands. "I've only done what any sister would. We've come a long way haven't we, Astrid? Twenty years ago you were a scullion and I was the lowliest acolyte in the temple. Now look at us. Between us we rule the greatest city in the world."

Astrid grinned, feeling a strange elation. "If my mission to the north is successful we'll rule much more than that. Nobody will stand against us. Nobody. I will be empress, and you will be supreme mistress of the church. We'll rule the continent."

Ravessa nodded, her eyes shining. Very softly she said, "And when that happens, I will draw a knife across Tamardi Di Goron's throat and watch him bleed."

A knock came at the door, and both women jumped.

"Who is it?" Ravessa called.

"Tania, Your Eminence," came a muffled voice.

Ravessa blew out a breath. "Very well, come in."

A young serving girl entered. She startled at the sight of Astrid, and dropped a curtsey. "I'm sorry, Your Eminence, Your Majesty. I didn't mean to interrupt."

Ravessa waved away her apology. "I will take breakfast now. Bring enough for two: Lady Astrid will be dining with me this morning."

Tania curtsied again and scurried from the room.

Ravessa said, "How goes your battle with the senate?"

Astrid scowled. "As it always does. Why do you ask?"

Ravessa pursed her lips. "My spies saw Mattack talking with Senator Nerie yesterday."

"Curse that dratted woman!" Astrid cried, thumping the arm of her chair. "Is there nowhere she will not sink her claws?"

"Will Mattack remain loyal?"

Astrid thought back to Mattack avoiding her gaze in the senate. "The first minister is a coward. He will do the bidding of whoever scares him the most."

"Then you will have to make sure you scare him more than Nerie. That shouldn't prove a problem for you."

Astrid shook her head. "It's not that simple. He might have already given Nerie vital information. I made sure only Rama and Aeron knew the truth about Bramwell Thornley, but what if Mattack found out? What if he's told Nerie and Tamardi?"

"You can't know that for sure."

"No, but I will have to watch the first minister carefully, all the same."

Ravessa clicked her fingers. "That reminds me. I have something to show you."

Awkwardly, she levered herself from her chair and waddled over to a cabinet from which she took a small object. She flicked it over to Astrid, who snatched it from the air and held it up to get a better look.

In her hand lay a white lily carved from bone. Astrid's breath caught in her throat.

"Is this what I think it is?"

Ravessa nodded solemnly. "A Death Lily. One of my spies found it in a disused warehouse by the docks."

"What does it mean?"

Ravessa looked at Astrid long and hard. "You know what it could mean. The Death Lily is the symbol of the Children of the Old Way. It could mean they are present in the city again."

"No. I don't believe it. They wouldn't dare set up a sect here, not after they were outlawed. The penalty for doing so is death. No, this is just a hoax, somebody scare-mongering."

"I wish it really was that simple. But in the warehouse where the lily was found, a circle had been drawn into the floor, a circle of blood. That's how they open their rites. The Goddess will tell me nothing. I fear we're walking into the unknown."

"Then my mission becomes even more urgent." Astrid looked down at the white flower lying in her palm and a shiver went through her.

Am I blind? she asked herself. *Am I missing something? Something important?*

But then stubbornness reasserted itself. She

had always known her plan was dangerous. She and Ravessa had weighed the risks and found them acceptable. If Astrid didn't do this, if she abandoned her quest and remained in Chellin, then Tamardi Di Goron would gain control of the senate and put into place his ultimate goal: the abolition of the monarchy, and the imposition of religious law. There would be no stopping him, and the chaos that would ensue would send Chellin spiraling into anarchy.

Then eventually, the ice would come south and devour Chellin just as it had devoured Variss and Tirsay, and all the magics of the priestesses and the charm weavers wouldn't be able to stop it.

But if Astrid went north, if she achieved her goal, she could break the power of the Everwinter, and become the most powerful woman in the world.

Astrid smiled to herself. The risks were worth it.

She cupped her hand around the flower, felt its chill bite into her flesh. "I will go north as planned, and when I return with the thing we seek, you will rejoice!"

Ravessa grinned like a child. "Ah, it's a sweet dream isn't it? What I wouldn't give to see spring flowers again and feel a warm breeze in my hair."

"You will, sister. Your child will know summer, just as we did when we were young."

Ravessa stroked her belly. "Child? Children, you mean."

"You're sure it's twins?"

"As sure as I can be. I should have expected it: twins run in our family."

Astrid remained silent, letting all the scenarios and implications of this news run through her mind. Finally, she said, "Is one a boy?"

"I don't know. I hope they're both girls because they'd both go into the temple and neither would be in danger. If one's a boy he'll be a threat to the high priest. The last boy born to a high priestess disappeared soon after his birth." There was a tremor in Ravessa's voice, betraying her fear.

Astrid clasped Ravessa's hand. "I promise I'll protect you, sister."

Ravessa smiled. "I think it's time we had some breakfast. Then you must return to your rooms before Rama and Aeron realize you are missing and tear the palace apart."

Astrid nodded, smiling. "Some sleep would be welcome as well."

CHAPTER 22

The sun rode the pale sky high above and a wind as sharp as glass blew through the city. Falen had pulled a woolly scarf round her neck and a thick, heavy coat wrapped close about her. Her hair whipped and snaked around her head, even though she had pinned it back meticulously.

Falen stopped and looked around, taking a moment to get her bearings. The palace lay behind her, the city ahead. Falen glanced around to make certain nobody was following. To her relief, the road was empty. She hurried off, hugging the sides of the cliff in an effort to keep out of sight.

She found the steep, undulating streets odd. In Variss, streets were wide and straight to better accommodate groups of mounted warriors and Ral Tora had been similar, though for different reasons. Here in Chellin everything wound around the cliff in curves and the buildings pressed close on either side. It made for a strange atmosphere and Falen felt as though she was being watched.

As the Ral Toran party had been making their way to the palace two days ago, a random glance down a side street had revealed something Falen had never thought to see again.

Today, in the cold light of a new day, in an alien city, surrounded by strangers, she was unsure of her recollections. Had she really seen what she thought she had? Or had she just imagined it?

She had to know the truth.

At length she reached an intersection with a statue of a rearing horse in its center.

Her pulse quickened. She was near. She took the path to the left, and soon came to a white-plastered house with Sea Ivy growing over the outside. The plaster was peeling and a cyrin tree had been allowed to grow so tall its branches hung over the building, spilling its sharp green leaves across the roof and walls. The house looked forlorn, a lifeless husk.

A vase of red flowers stood in an upstairs window. Falen's stomach twisted with apprehension. The flowers had bell-shaped heads and were strikingly bright against the white plaster. They were a beacon. They had drawn Falen like a moth to a flame.

There was no sign of life. No footprints marred the dirt around the door, no movement betrayed life within.

Maybe she was too late. Maybe whoever had placed the Ochre Flowers was long gone. But she had to know.

Falen glanced up and down the street. She took a deep breath and pushed open the door. It swung forward on creaking hinges and led into a hallway thick with dust and cobwebs. The once expensively tiled floor had fallen into decay, with the droppings of rodents and the discarded feathers of pigeons forming a stinking carpet.

Silently, Falen moved through the house. The ground floor was deserted, only a crumbling divan in the living room betraying the fact that anyone had ever inhabited this place. From the hall a flight of rickety stairs climbed upwards into gloom. Falen laid her hand on the banister and peered up.

A shadow moved at the top.

Falen jumped back, heart thudding. "Who's there?"

No answer.

Falen drew her dagger and placed her foot on the first step.

"Come no closer!" a voice screeched.

Falen froze. "I mean you no harm."

"Begone! Or I will blast you! I am a powerful wizard! Begone!"

"I just want to talk to you," Falen shouted.

There was a pause then the voice shrieked, "Begone, foul demon! You won't trick me!"

"This is no trick. May I come and speak with you?"

Another pause. "Go slowly, and if I do not like the look of you, I will blast you to pieces!"

Falen sheathed the dagger and resumed her climb, careful to move slowly with her hands visible to show she carried no weapon. At the top of the stairs a figure crouched in the shadow of a doorway.

"Glory to you," Falen said in the Varisean greeting.

The figure shifted further back into the shadows. "Are you a demon come to punish me?"

"I'm no demon. My name is Falen Godwinsson. I saw the Ochre Flowers in the window and came to answer their call."

The figure sucked in a huge breath, like a sob. "That's not possible. Oh, by the Great Warrior, do not torment me! She's dead, like the rest of my people. May the Mother take me, I should be dead too. I deserve punishment! Take me then, demon!"

"I'm not here to torment you, I'm telling you the truth," Falen snapped, feeling her irritation rise.

The figure remained silent for a long time. At last it said, "Come into the light so I may see you."

Warily, Falen crept forward until she stood in a small patch of sunlight. A sharp intake of breath and the figure rushed across the landing and grabbed both of Falen's hands. "Warrior be praised! It *is* you!"

Falen gasped. She recognized this man. Deep lines surrounded green eyes and a fringe of white hair hung down over the forehead.

"Dagur? Is that you?" she stammered.

The man's face contorted into a look of delight and terror. "Aye. By the Mother, I never thought to see your face again." He pulled her close and Falen let herself be enfolded by his arms. Pushing him away, she held him by the shoulders and stared into his haunted eyes. "What are you doing here, Dagur?"

Dagur glanced away and back again. He took her hand and pulled her toward one of the rooms off the landing. "Come with me. I'll tell you everything."

The large room at the back of the house had been turned into a makeshift camp. A pile of rags that must have passed as Dagur's bed filled one corner, with a tin cooking stove in the middle of the room. Clothes, food, fuel and a few weapons were scattered around the place. Dagur seated himself cross-legged by the stove and bade Falen do the same.

"It's been too long since I had guests," he said in a melancholy voice. "Too long since anyone graced my table."

Falen glanced around the room at the clutter and debris, and at the unkempt, tired man before her. "What's happened to you?" she asked in a choking whisper. "You are the Varisean Royal Ambassador. Why are you living like this? Have the Chellins mistreated you?"

A spasm passed across Dagur's dirty face. "They don't know I'm here. Nobody does. The Varisean Royal Ambassador returned home long ago, at the call of his sovereign, like any loyal subject would." He laughed bitterly. "Except this loyal subject never made it home. He turned back, too afraid of what he might find in Variss and too eager to save his own skin. He returned to Chellin, in disgrace and shame, knowing he had betrayed his people."

Falen's stomach tightened. Coldly she said, "So, rather than seeking the protection of the Regal, you chose to hide here like a beggar, too ashamed of your cowardice to show your face."

Dagur flinched as if Falen's words struck him. Miserably he said, "Yes. I've been hiding here for what seems a lifetime. In desperation, I placed the Ochre Flowers in the window, never really hoping anybody would recognize them. But here you are, alive and hale. You don't know how much that gladdens me, princess."

"Don't call me that!" Falen hissed. "That title isn't mine anymore. I am Falen Godwinsson, City Engineer to Ral Tora."

Dagur raised an eyebrow. "Is that where you've been? I'm glad. I remember how much you wanted to see Ral Tora. We were all shocked when your father banished you. Now though, it seems he may have saved your life."

He passed her a cup of weak wine. She swirled the contents around, contemplating its depths. "I should have fought harder to make my father see sense. I should have stayed and stood up to him. The *Sorah* is upon me, Dagur. I must return my blood debt."

Dagur looked at her sharply, "You owe no blood debt, Falen. The *Sorah* does not bind you."

"You don't understand. I have grave suspicions about my father, Dagur. Of what he might have done." She unslung the bag she'd been carrying and pulled a book out of it. She ran a hand over the leather cover, remembering the day when Lidda had given it her.

Falen had scoffed at the so-called history contained within this book. It had sounded like children's fairy-stories to her. Now she was no longer sure.

"What happened in Variss after I left?"

Dagur looked at the floor. "Your father was an honorable man. Many good works were done by his hand."

"What happened, Dagur?"

Dagur sighed. "I only heard rumors. Your father abandoned the Mother and the Great warrior and adopted the gods of the monk, Nashir." He glanced at Falen, his eyes troubled. "And his rule began to fail. He became obsessed with the mountains, taking trips up into the Sisters as if looking for something. Unrest in Variss grew. There was talk of finding you and putting you on the throne."

Falen gasped. "What? Variss would depose its king?"

"When a king abandons his people is he entitled to their loyalty?" Dagur held out a hand as if to forestall her answer. "It doesn't matter anyway. The Everwinter destroyed Variss."

Grief twisted Falen's mouth. "When the monk came, my father changed. He became someone I didn't recognize. He was so eager to embrace these new gods. What was so terrible about his life that he would give it all up? That he would abandon us?"

Tears were suddenly running down her cheeks as grief she had kept tightly locked up inside worked its way free.

Dagur put an arm around her and she buried her face in his shoulder. "What are you doing here, Falen?" he asked softly.

She wiped her face with her sleeve and straightened. "I'm going back to Variss."

He digested this in silence for a moment. "Why? What do you expect to find?"

She didn't answer for a second, instead reaching out and clasping the book to her chest. "Have you heard of the Rift, Dagur?"

A look flashed across his face. It was gone so quickly she could have imagined it. It looked to Falen like fear.

"Well?"

"Why do you ask?"

"Could it have been what Nashir and my father were looking for in the mountains?"

"The Rift is a legend. One most have forgotten," Dagur replied. "Surely your father wouldn't give credence to such stories."

Falen shook her head. "The way he changed, Dagur, anything is possible. Could they have been looking for the Rift?" There was an edge of panic in her voice she couldn't quite control.

Dagur regarded her for what seemed an age. He nodded. "Yes, I suppose so."

Yes, I suppose so. She had wanted Dagur to tell her she was being ridiculous. She had wanted him to say the words that would allay all her fears. Instead, he had confirmed them.

She nodded. "Now you know why I must go north. I have to discover what happened to our people and pay the blood debt my father has laid on me."

Dagur shook his head. "There's nothing in the north but horror and death. Falen, I don't think you can survive such a mission."

Falen nodded. "If that's the price the *Sorah* asks of me, then so be it."

The sun was setting outside and shadows began to gather in the room. Falen stood and said, "I must be getting back to the palace. Will you come with me? A royal ambassador should not be living like this."

Dagur shook his head. "No. I don't wish to broadcast my cowardice and shame. And I don't want to see you leave on your quest."

Falen stared at him for a long time. At last she nodded, "I understand. Farewell, my old friend, perhaps one day we'll meet again."

"I will pray for that." Dagur folded his arms about her once more, then she turned and left. She did not look back.

The streets of Chellin had become a cold, dark maze. The sun was a red ball, sinking into the sea and just casting enough light for Falen to find her way. She barely registered the climb back to the palace. A ball of ice surrounded her heart.

At the top of the cliff, she spoke the password to the guards on the bridge and made her way across. She turned left, avoiding the busy main entrance to the palace compound and entered through one of the side gates leading into the grounds. Small oil lamps in round glass cases had been lit along the paths in the gardens. Falen hurried, eager to find her rooms and lock her door on the night.

Suddenly she heard voices on the path ahead, "Burn my beard! If you keep this up, you'll be a Panther before you know it, my lad!" Falen stopped. That was Barl's voice. Bram answered, "Are you offering me a job, Barl? What will Rassus say when we get back? Poaching his staff! It's disgraceful!" Laughter erupted.

Falen glanced around for somewhere to hide. She was in no mood for conversation. A path on the left led to the temple. The doors of the large, ornate building stood open so Falen trotted over, ran up the steps and stepped into the dim interior. She pushed the doors shut, hoping her companions hadn't seen her enter.

From the many wooden benches in front of the altar Falen guessed that a service must have just finished. There was nobody in sight though, and the cavernous, columned chamber lay quiet. Standing lamps gave off a little illumination and iron braziers stood at intervals on the floor, giving a tiny amount of heat.

Falen's eyes flicked toward the statue of the Goddess standing above the altar. She was not Falen's goddess, but from the sword She held aloft and the look of triumph carved into Her marble face, Falen guessed the Great Warrior would be proud to have Her by His side.

Falen moved deeper into the temple. She passed through an archway that led into a series of smaller inter-connected chambers. She found a secluded alcove and sat down on a bench to think. Thoughts and emotions chased each other through her head.

She felt a deep joy that Dagur was alive. Despite the dire conditions in which he'd chosen to live, the ambassador was hale, and it eased Falen's loneliness to know at least one person from her past had survived. But on top of this joy was a terrible fear, so powerful that if she thought about it too long it threatened to overwhelm her.

What have you done, father?

She became aware of conversation nearby. "You're sure of this? We must not move too early and risk showing our hand." A woman's voice.

A man answered, "Of course I'm sure. The boy must be dealt with. He could be a threat to our plans."

Falen's ears pricked up. She was sure she recognized the voice. She got to her feet and walked toward the sound. Cautiously, she peered around the corner. Just ahead lay a small alcove not unlike the one she had just vacated. Three people huddled in the small space. The man who'd spoken was High Priest Tamardi. Next to him stood a blonde woman in a low-cut dress and another man with his back to Falen.

"What are you suggesting?" the blonde woman asked.

"If he can't be turned to our cause he must be disposed of," said the high priest.

The second man laughed. "At last! Let me do it. It would give me great pleasure to cut the throat of the trusting little fool!"

"No!" barked the high priest. "I'll deal with him. You must keep playing your part."

The man snarled. "For how long? I have fulfilled my part of the bargain. When will I get what was promised?"

Anger blazed in the high priest's eyes. "*I* decide when the bargain is met. You would do well to remember that! Our plans are yet far from fruition."

"Then stop all this jabbering and act! You say the boy must be silenced: I say stick a knife in his ribs and be done with it. You say the Regal must be prevented from going north, I say slit her throat as well. Why make it more complicated?"

The blonde woman flashed an angry glance at the man. "It's because of such rash talk you don't stand higher in the Assembly! You will not speak again in this meeting and you will follow our instructions! Is that clear?"

The man growled under his breath but eventually grated, "As you wish."

The blonde woman stared at him for a moment before turning back to the high priest. "Do you think the boy could be turned?"

"Possibly. But it will be dangerous to try. Astrid has him watched like a hawk and anything we tell him will doubtless reach her ears."

"Then it seems clear what must be done."

The high priest nodded. "Yes. Bramwell Thornley must be killed."

Falen gasped.

The high priest's eyes snapped toward her. She spun round and ran.

"After her!" the high priest bellowed.

Falen bolted through the temple, slipping and sliding on its smooth marble floor. Footsteps pounded behind her. Something smacked into her calves and she went crashing to the ground. Her chin struck the flagstones, smashing her teeth together. Blood flooded her mouth. She scrabbled along the floor, fingers trying to find purchase on the stone. Something grabbed her legs and began pulling her backward. She was flipped onto her back and found herself looking into the face of the high priest's colleague, the man who had talked of killing Bram.

Falen's eyes widened in recognition.

"You!" she gasped.

"Hello, Falen."

His fist descended and everything went black.

CHAPTER 23

The blade whizzed past, mere inches from Bram's ear. He spun around, only to be confronted by the weapon coming at him from the other side. Just in time, he managed to bring his own sword up, narrowly avoiding his midriff being sliced open. Then the blade was gone again, and Bram had to spin around to keep track of it, following its silver blur in the air.

He rammed his weapon upwards, only to be met by his opponents jarring riposte that sent shudders of impact snaking down his arm. He staggered backward, panting, hoping to get a little respite, but something collided with

Bram's legs and took them out from under him. The ground came racing up to meet him with a smack. The sword flew out of his hand and landed with a thud in the dirt. A sword-point jammed against his chest.

Bram looked up into the face of his attacker.

"That was good," Corban said. "Not only were you moving well but you were even beginning to anticipate my next attack. A definite improvement."

Bram grimaced. "I'll have to take your word for that, Corban. Your beatings hurt just as much today as the first time I sparred with you."

Barl, who was watching nearby, bellowed, "You need to distract him, Bram. Next time, tell him there is a cheap Esclede whore waving at him, that should have the desired effect!"

Corban made a rude gesture at his captain then addressed Bram. "You've mastered the basics and there is not much more I can teach you. It is all down to practice. Just remember to never expose your back and always keep your vital organs covered. Never be enticed into a stroke you don't want to make. Fighting with a blade is about bluff and counter bluff: to win the battle of the mind is to win the fight."

Bram got to his feet and stood panting, hands on knees. "It's all very well saying that, but if I was ever in a real fight I would probably forget everything you've taught me."

"Which is why practice is so important. The more you practice the moves, the more they become ingrained and the responses become automatic, instinctive. You would be surprised how easily it comes to you when you are fighting for real. Now, I'm off for a spot of breakfast, and I suggest you do the same, training this early makes a man hungry!"

Clasping Corban's hand briefly, Bram bid him farewell and returned to the palace. Servants were bustling about carrying breakfast trays and armloads of freshly laundered linen. Bram managed to commandeer one of the trays for himself and carried it back to his rooms. He placed it on the little table by the fire and began to tuck in.

He had barely finished his meal when there was a knock on the door. Before he could answer it, Marijke, who had been busy cleaning, hurried over and pulled the door open, admitting a young serving boy dressed in gold and black.

"A message for you, sir," he said, handing Bram a rolled parchment.

Bram unrolled it and read the contents.

His Eminence, Tamardi Di Goron, High Priest of Chellin, humbly invites Bramwell Thornley to take refreshments with him this morning in his private apartments.

Bram's stomach turned over. The high priest wanted to see him? An uncomfortable feeling stole over Bram's skin. There was something about the high priest that unsettled him. Although the man had been friendly and welcoming, there seemed to be something else riding behind his pleasant words.

Nevertheless, Bram was not blind to the honor he'd been offered. With a tight smile he said to the boy, "Please tell his Eminence I would be delighted to meet with him this morning."

As the door closed behind the serving boy, Bram threw himself into a chair and pulled in a shuddering breath.

"You should be honored his Eminence has taken an interest in you," said Marijke from where she had knelt to tend the fire. "Many would give their back teeth to have a private audience with him. He is a great man."

Perhaps he is. But he gives me the creeps all the same, Bram thought.

Another knock came at the door. Bram's heart leapt. Maybe it was the serving boy come back to say the high priest had changed his mind. But when the door swung open it revealed Father Hewin in his yellow robes.

"Forgive my interruption, Bram. I've not got you out of bed, I hope?"

Bram shook his head. "Is something wrong?"

"I'm not sure yet. I was wondering if you have seen Falen recently?"

"Not since breakfast yesterday. Why?"

"I can't find her, and her maid tells me she

didn't sleep in her bed last night."

The hairs rose on Bram's neck. "She's missing?"

Father Hewin held out placating hands. "I didn't say that. No doubt she will turn up."

Heat flooded through Bram's body. "We have to find her! Anything could have happened!"

He strode to the door. Father Hewin blocked the way. "Where exactly are you going? Falen is a grown woman and perfectly capable of looking after herself. There's no need to go running through the palace like a loon! If she hasn't surfaced by midday I'll send the Panthers out looking for her."

"Midday is an age away! I'll go now!" He tried to push past but Father Hewin held him back.

"No you won't. I hear you've been invited to an audience with the high priest. You will go to this audience, is that clear?"

"But—"

"Is that clear?"

Father Hewin's gray eyes were like chips of stone. There would be no arguing with him.

"Fine!"

"Good. I want a full account of your meeting with the high priest when you get back."

Father Hewin departed and Bram slumped into a chair again and rested his elbows on his knees. Falen missing? The thought made his stomach knot. What could have happened to her?

Anxiety gnawed at his chest as he donned the clothes Marijke set out for him, clothes appropriate for a meeting with one of Chellin's most important people. When the serving boy returned to fetch him, Bram was almost glad. At least it would distract him from worrying.

He followed the boy to the high priest's quarters. Bram found himself in a large, sumptuous room. A man and a woman sat on divans, talking.

The boy stepped forward and coughed delicately. "Your Eminence, may I introduce Bramwell Thornley of Ral Tora."

They swiveled round. Bram didn't recognize the high priest's companion, she had long yellow hair and a dress cut so low that Bram found himself blushing. She fixed Bram with an unfriendly stare.

High Priest Tamardi's handsome features broke into a smile, showing perfect white teeth. "Ah, Bram! So glad you could make it. Won't you come and sit down? We are having spiced wine and cakes."

Bram mumbled his thanks and sat on one of the chairs near the fire, feeling uncomfortable. The high priest crossed his legs, lounging back on the divan. The woman watched Bram curiously.

"Let me make introductions," Tamardi said jovially. "Bram, I would like you to meet

Senator Nerie. She has a special interest in meeting you: she used to be ambassador to Ral Tora."

"Really?" Bram asked, surprised.

"Oh, many years ago now," said Nerie. "Probably before you were born."

"Oh, I see."

Silence descended. Bram fidgeted.

"So, how are you finding Chellin?" Tamardi asked eventually. He indicated for the serving boy to pour some wine and passed a glass to Bram.

Bram accepted it gratefully. "Chellin is like nothing I have ever seen before," he answered honestly. "It's so different to Ral Tora, but beautiful all the same."

Tamardi smiled. "Our ways must seem very strange to you, as yours do to us. To learn, we must embrace new ideas. Don't you agree?"

Bram wasn't sure what he was expected to say. "I think it's good to share ideas if that's what you mean. I remember when Falen joined the Engineer's Guild, some didn't like it because she was from Variss and they have totally different techniques to us, but it turned out she had loads of different skills which she shared with us and we all benefited from them."

Why did you just say that? He's not interested in your prattle! He berated himself.

Bram took another sip of the wine. It really

was lovely.

The high priest fixed him with a probing stare. "You must be very pleased at being chosen to accompany our Regal on her mission. Of all the excellent engineers in Ral Tora, it was you whom she chose."

"And Falen too, of course," Bram corrected. "But to be honest, I don't think it's because of my engineering skills, there are far better engineers than me in Ral Tora. Engineer Trenak is the best, now Celian is gone. I don't think she'd have come though, she's got a new-born daughter."

The wine seemed to be loosening Bram's tongue. *You are gossiping like a fishwife!* He took another gulp of wine. To his surprise, he found he had finished the glass. The serving boy refilled it.

"Really?" Tamardi sounded surprised. "You must have other skills Lady Astrid thought would prove useful?"

Bram shrugged and took another gulp. "Maybe it's just because I'm such excellent company." He chuckled at his own joke.

The high priest smiled indulgently. A look passed between him and Nerie. "The weather is good today," Tamardi said brightly, pointing to the window. "Let's take advantage of it, and take a walk. How would that suit you, Bram?"

Bram needed no prompting. "I'd love to," he said. He got to his feet, stumbled and caught himself on the arm of the chair. Bram's legs seemed wobblier than they should be. Through the hazy fog filling his brain, a voice shouted at him, *get a grip! You're showing yourself up in front of the high priest!*

Tamardi held the door open and waited for Bram politely. Bram took a deep breath, got his legs moving and followed Senator Nerie out. Outside the high priest's apartments they turned into the grand gallery, through the cloisters where the Daughters of the Moon were praying at their statue, and finally left the palace precincts and made for the bridge over to the mainland.

"Where are we going?" Bram asked.

Tamardi put a fatherly arm around Bram's shoulders. "I told you I would show you more of the city, and that's what I intend to do. There are far more delights to behold in Chellin than just the palace."

Bram said nothing. All his thought was bent on the bridge, on making sure he didn't freeze like last time and make a complete idiot of himself. Curiously though, as they set foot on the high stone span, the panic didn't come. The warm, fuzzy feeling in his stomach was growing and with it came a sense of calm, as though nothing really mattered.

The streets were busy. A gentle breeze blew in off the sea, bringing with it the scent of seaweed. People moved out of the way as soon as they recognized the high priest, and many of them called out greetings or benedictions.

Occasionally, Tamardi would call out blessings, "The Goddess keep you, my child."

They emerged onto the waterfront. Ahead of them was Chellin's harbor, with the Ice Ship *Regalia* bobbing gently at anchor.

Tamardi ignored the Ice Ship, and turned right; leading them past warehouses and shipyards until eventually they reached a beach. Bram found himself scrabbling unsteadily. A voice in Bram's mind was shouting, *where is he taking you?* but the voice drowned in the sludge of his thoughts.

At last Tamardi stopped. He turned to Bram and flashed a wide grin. "Here we are then, Bram. One of the treats of Chellin, as I promised you."

Bram looked around. They had rounded a headland and were standing on a crescent beach sheltered on both sides by curving cliffs.

The high priest took Bram by the arm and steered him down to the water's edge. Nerie hung back, watching the pair with interest.

"What are we doing here?" Bram asked.

Tamardi turned his gaze on Bram and there was a look in his eyes that made Bram's heart beat a little quicker. "Bram, my young friend, I wish to introduce you to one of the wonders of Chellin: we are here to meet the tashen."

Tashen? The word penetrated Bram's thoughts slowly, like a rock sinking through mud. Alarms started ringing.

The tashen! Sea serpents!

"Hang on!" he cried, "I don't want—"

"What you want does not matter," Tamardi said and all traces of friendliness were gone from his voice. The deep eyes stared at Bram, and the joviality of earlier had been replaced by suspicion and anger. "Why does the Regal have such an interest in you?"

Bram's vision swam. "What are you talking about?"

Tamardi's face twisted into a snarl. He took a couple of steps toward Bram with fists clenched and for a second Bram thought he would strike him. But instead he said, "Do you think I don't know of your meetings with Serz? Or that the falcon master is a quentarc? Astrid thinks she has been so clever to hide him from me. The fool! I have known about him for years! And now, my young friend, we have you, who Serz has been following like a shadow! Mattack has told me all about you. I know who you are, even if you don't know yourself. And you won't be allowed to fulfill your part in this story. I've come too far to let a boy ruin my plans."

"I don't know what you're talking about!" Bram cried, fear making his voice shrill. "I'm just an engineer!"

"You young fool! Do you think Astrid would've brought you to Chellin if there was nothing in it for her? Both you and the Varisean witch are in league with Astrid. I will deal with you like I dealt with her!"

Warnings exploded in Bram's head. Varisean? He must be talking about Falen! She had been missing since yesterday.

Taking a few tottering steps forward he demanded, "What have you done to her?"

The high priest watched Bram with contempt. "The bitch was spying on me. She has been dealt with."

"What do you mean?" asked Bram in a voice tight with fear. "If you've harmed her I'll—"

"What? Avenge her? I don't think so. Look at you, a trusting fool disabled as easily as a babe. What do you think you can do to me? Me, the highest servant of the Masters! Compared to me you are but a moth against a hawk! It would have been a pleasure to slit the little bitch's throat and feed her to the Masters, but I haven't. She's very beautiful. Perhaps I'll make her my concubine."

"I'll kill you if you touch her!" Bram shouted.

He surged toward the high priest but had not taken three steps before his knees folded beneath him and he pitched into the sand. Struggling limply, he tried to rise but his limbs had become weak and useless.

The high priest curled his lip in disdain and then turned away. He walked until he was standing ankle-deep in the sea. Raising his hands high above his head, he began singing in a harsh language. The sound reminded Bram of the cries of seabirds, high and lonely.

Bram tried to push himself up but his legs wouldn't obey him. He felt woozy and disorientated, as though he was half asleep.

The bastard has drugged me, he thought.

Bram managed to stagger to his knees and crawl a few paces before he collapsed again at the edge of the water. Cold breakers swirled around him.

Out in the bay, beyond the high priest, something was happening. Two white-crested waves were zooming toward the shore. Then, not more than thirty paces from the high priest, two of the tashen broke the surface of the sea. Their alien, reptile-like heads reared upwards out of the water and their massive blue eyes fixed on the high priest.

In response, Tamardi changed his song. Its pitch became higher and its beat faster. His words moved to a different rhythm, becoming a chant, repeating a phrase over and over.

The tashen responded. They started weaving their heads from side to side, in time with the high priest's words. Then they circled around each other in a strange and bizarre dance. At the same time, they began to sing. There were no words, but the high, fluting sounds sounded almost like speech, as if they were trying to communicate…

Hear us!

Bram looked around wildly. Who had said

that?

The tashen circled faster and faster, churning the sea into a frothing white mass.

Who are you, cold one? Answer us!

Bram stared, bewildered. *What is going on? Hear us, cold one!*

Bram covered his ears with his hands. He was going mad.

Answer us!

Tamardi fell silent and stared at Bram. There was a hunger in his eyes; and Bram suddenly knew that the high priest wanted something from him. Bram tried to back away. He wanted to run, he wanted to get as far away from this man and these creatures as he could.

But his brain had lost control over his body. As much as he screamed at himself to flee, his body remained mired in the surf.

The tashen danced.

Answer us!

The great serpents were a blur now, two coils of darkness whirling round and round.

Answer us!

Bram tried to shut it all out.

Answer us!

Suddenly, like striking vipers, the tashen lunged at him, massive teeth flying toward his throat.

Desperately he cried in his mind, *I hear you!*

There was a flash of light and a woman's voice shouted, "Back, Old Ones, this is no place for you!"

The tashen fell back, crashing into the sea and were gone. The sea seethed and swirled where they had been.

"You've done it now," the woman said to the high priest. "You'll hang for this."

Briefly, Bram caught a glimpse of the woman and recognized the tattoos spiraling up her arms. He groped for the name. Capella?

"This is church business," the high priest snarled, "nothing to do with you."

"Murder is now church business? The senate will be most interested to hear that."

Bram looked around desperately. He had to get away. Capella and the high priest were staring at each other, taking no notice of him. A blue glow surrounded the charm weaver's hands. The high priest eyed her warily.

"Would you use the Gift on me?" he asked. "Would you strike the Goddess's disciple?"

"You are no servant of the Goddess," Capella replied. "And I know you have the Gift yourself."

In answer, the high priest stretched out his arms. The same blue glow surrounded them. A bolt of power flew from the high priest's palm and struck Capella full in the chest. She went spinning through the air and landed in the sand with a dull thud. The high priest advanced on her but she raised her own hand and a shaft of energy sent the high priest staggering backward.

Bram scanned the beach and cliffs. There were no dips or hollows, no clumps of vegetation that might hide him. His eyes alighted on a dark smudge in the cliff face. A cave perhaps? He got to his feet and staggered toward it. The ground tilted crazily and Bram flung his arms out to keep his balance.

Glancing back toward the sea, he saw the high priest and the charm weaver grappling with each other. They were so intent on each other they hadn't yet missed him, but his advantage would not last long. The tashen had disappeared into the sea. Senator Nerie too had fled.

The cave was a few paces ahead now, just a little further and he would be safe. His legs folded beneath him and he collapsed onto the beach. Sand filled his mouth.

Get up you fool! He screamed at himself. *Get up!*

Wobbly arms braced on the beach, Bram heaved himself to his knees. With a head full of fog and limbs as shaky as saplings, he crawled up the final part of the beach and into the mouth of the cave. As the darkness swallowed him, he fell onto his back.

One thought shone in his mind: Falen was in danger, and somehow he must find her.

CHAPTER 24

Sweat dripped from High Priestess Ravessa's brow and was hastily mopped away by the anxious nurse. The high priestess's face had turned pale as milk and her breathing ragged.

The midwife placed a hand on Ravessa's distended belly. "It won't be long now."

Ravessa made a growling noise deep in her throat. "It can't be soon enough for me!"

Astrid shared a look with Ravessa's husband, Simeon, who sat on the other side of the bed. The Lord Commander of the Chellin Navy looked terrified.

"What are you smirking at?" Ravessa

snapped.

Astrid startled. "I wasn't smirking."

"I suppose you find all this highly amusing? Pregnancy is by far the most horrible experience of my life!"

Ravessa's face folded up in pain as another contraction racked her body. The midwife placed a piece of wood between the high priestess's teeth and Ravessa bit down on it hard.

A sharp knock sounded on the door and Charm Weaver Capella burst into the room. Her hair was disheveled and a bruise was forming over her left eye.

"I apologize for intruding," she blurted, "but I must speak to you right away! It is most urgent!"

A jolt of fear thudded through Astrid. What had happened? Astrid hastily excused herself and hurried Capella out. In the corridor, Capella wrung her hands in frustration.

As soon as the door closed she cried, "It's the high priest, my lady! I've been following him, just as you asked, and you were right! He tried to kill Bramwell Thornley!"

Blood pounded in Astrid's head. A wave of dizziness swamped her. Grabbing Capella's shoulders, she croaked, "Is Bram all right? Tell me everything!"

In a rush, Capella told of how she had spotted the high priest taking Bram into the city and followed them, of how Tamardi had called the tashen, and the terrible consequences.

Astrid listened grimly to Capella's tale. "Where is Bram now?"

"I don't know!" the charm weaver cried in dismay. "He must have run away while I fought with Tamardi!"

"But he *did* get away? You're absolutely sure the tashen did not reach him?"

Capella nodded. "I got there in time. The boy wasn't harmed. I called the Royal Guard and had Tamardi arrested. He is in the cells."

Astrid blew out a long breath. "That's something, at least."

So, Tamardi had made his move. The game was in motion.

Thoughts tumbled through her head like grains of sand in an hourglass. She had so many things to do: find Bram, protect Ravessa and her children, warn the Ral Torans.

First, though, she must finally take care of the high priest.

"Come."

With Capella at her side, Astrid strode purposefully through the halls of the palace. Servants groveled, ministers bowed as she passed, but Astrid didn't acknowledge any of them. Her mind whirled with possibilities.

The high priest had discovered Bram's secret. Who had he told? The senate? The Ral Torans? And how long before somebody told

Bram himself?

Astrid flinched away from the possibility. If Bram learned she had been keeping the truth from him, his trust in her would be shattered, and she wanted to avoid that at all costs. But at least Bram lived. Somewhere. Tamardi had failed, and there was no way she'd let him wriggle out of what he'd done. Astrid listed the charges she would file against the high priest: attempted murder, kidnap, conspiracy.

Oh yes, Tamardi would be swinging from the rafters after she had finished with him.

She reached the senate. The doors stood closed, showing it was in session. Astrid indicated for Capella to wait outside and then flung the doors open and walked in without being announced. The senators paused mid-sentence and looked up in surprise. Astrid ignored their questioning stares and marched down to her pulpit in the center of the room.

She climbed into it, placed her hands on the sill, and stared malevolently down.

"You know why I am here."

Nobody spoke.

Then Senator Rosenthay cleared his throat. "My lady, honored as we are by your presence, we were not expecting you. We are debating the levies of the dockmen's guild. If we had known you were coming—"

"High Priest Tamardi Di Goron has been arrested. He tried to kill Bramwell Thornley. He'll face the full force of the law. I want him executed."

Rosenthay glanced around at his colleagues. A look passed between them. "My lady," Rosenthay said eventually, "the high priest has already been dealt with."

Astrid narrowed her eyes. "What do you mean?"

"The high priest was brought before us less than a bell ago. He was cleared of all charges."

"What?" Astrid exploded. She sprang down from the pulpit and strode over to Rosenthay. "By the Goddess, you had better be joking, senator!"

Rosenthay backed away hastily. "No, my lady, the high priest has been released."

Astrid slapped Rosenthay across the face. The blow sent the old man sprawling.

"You have gone too far this time!" Astrid raged. "I will have you hanged for this!"

Rosenthay laid a hand on his cheek and then glared at Astrid with venom in his eyes. "It was a unanimous decision! The high priest did nothing wrong!"

Astrid stepped into the middle of the floor and glowered at the senators. "I hope you all have your pensions in place because after this I will see all of you out on the street! *I* am queen of this city, *I* rule here. How dare you undermine my authority?"

Senator Nerie rose to her feet. "I'm puzzled by this outburst, my lady. You have no reason to complain. After all, we have only been following the law."

Astrid spun to face the yellow-haired harlot. "What are you talking about?"

"The High Priest Tamardi Di Goron is a member of the senate. I'm sure I do not need to remind you that all criminal matters relating to a member of the senate are the sole affair of the senate. It is written in the constitution, just as the law that makes you Sword of the Goddess is written. Surely you are not saying your rights should be respected and ours should not?" Nerie stared at Astrid, daring her to argue.

Astrid's fingers twitched. She longed to throttle the woman.

"I see." Astrid said at last, her words cold. "So, you have taken a prisoner out of *my* custody, from *my* cells, guarded by *my* soldiers and set him free without even consulting me?"

"He should not have been in your custody in the first place!" Nerie snapped. "If a member of the senate is charged with a crime, he or she should be placed under the Senate Guard. It is not a royal matter!"

"This is treason!" Astrid hissed.

Nerie laughed. "Really? Tell me, how can following the law be treason? You seem quick to enforce the law when it gives you an advantage but a little more reluctant when the advantage is not yours! The law giving us this right was written into the statute book hundreds of years ago. If you wish we can have it brought here, so you may see—"

"I know my own laws!" Astrid shouted.

Here was the crux of it then. The senate was flexing its muscles because she had outwitted them in their previous meeting.

"Why did you release the high priest? What lies did he tell you?"

Rosenthay frowned. "We agree the high priest was foolish to call the tashen and to take a diplomatic guest out of the palace without going through the proper channels. But we don't think there was any ill intent. The high priest explained that he called the tashen because he'd promised to show the boy our ways. He was trying to aid our diplomatic cause."

Astrid shook her head in amazement. "You fools! How can you believe such rubbish? Does it not strike you as an odd thing for the high priest to do? Is it usual for guests to be introduced to the tashen?"

"Well, no," Rosenthay admitted, "but he is the high priest and is closer to the creatures of the Goddess than we are."

"So that qualifies him to summon some of the most dangerous creatures of the ocean? Only myself or the charm weavers know the proper ritual for calling the tashen."

"The high priest assured us he knew the proper ritual as well. There was no risk to any of the people present."

"So why did they attack Bramwell

Thornley?"

Rosenthay fidgeted and looked uncomfortable. Nerie stood once more.

"I was there and saw what happened. The tashen were agitated and restless. I think they were bothered by the recent storms. Nobody could have predicted their reaction. It wasn't the high priest's fault."

Astrid smiled at her. "Of course you were. I should've guessed."

Astrid turned her back on the blonde woman before she could reply. "So, the high priest is to go unpunished?"

Rosenthay answered, "No. He will pray for guidance at the temple three times a day for a week, and will make reparations to Bramwell Thornley personally."

By the Goddess, he will not! Astrid said to herself. *If that man goes anywhere near Bram, I will blind him.*

Aloud, she said, "So, that's it?"

Rosenthay stood his ground. "The matter is closed. The senate has spoken."

Astrid said nothing. A blood vessel twitched in her temple. "Then where is the high priest now? I see he does not sit in session with you?"

"Of course not," Nerie answered. "He has other duties to perform."

"What duties?"

"Why, the high priestess of course! She has gone into labor. The high priest has gone to bless the birth."

Astrid gasped. What a fool she had been! While she had been here arguing with the senate, Ravessa and her children had been left unprotected!

Heart hammering, Astrid hiked up her skirts and ran from the senate.

"What's wrong?" Capella cried, as Astrid rushed past.

"We must hurry!" Astrid cried in anguish. "The high priest has Ravessa! You know what he will do to the babes! Come on!"

The two women charged through the palace. Servants dived out of their way and then stared after them in astonishment. As they reached the high priestess's apartments, Astrid saw to her horror that the door stood open. She burst into the birthing room. Empty. The bedclothes were rumpled and soaked with sweat, and one of the chairs had been overturned.

There was no sign of Ravessa or Simeon.

The sound of weeping came from the next room. Astrid strode through to find a blue-robed priestess kneeling on the floor, head in hands. She looked up as Astrid entered, showing the red crescent moon tattooed on her cheek that marked her as a Daughter of the Moon. Astrid stalked over to the girl and pulled her roughly to her feet.

"Where is your mistress?" she demanded.

The girl heaved in great breaths, trying to

control her sobs. "She...the Goddess.... It's all gone wrong!"

Astrid shook her by the shoulders. "Get a hold of yourself! Where is Ravessa?"

"The high priest came. He took her. He said she is cursed. We all are! Oh, how have we so displeased the Goddess? What is to become of us now?"

"What are you talking about?"

The priestess stared at Astrid with huge round eyes. "The babes!"

"What about them? Tell me!"

"They were delivered, right here in front of the high priest. He said some words over my mistress and then the babes came."

Capella strode forward and asked anxiously, "What words? What did he say?"

The priestess shook her head. "I don't know. I've never heard the language before."

Capella looked at Astrid grimly. "The Gift. He has used the power to speed up the birth."

Astrid bit down the panic that clutched at her. Turning back to the priestess she said, "What happened to the babes and their mother?"

"That's when we knew we were cursed!" she wailed. "The high priest saw them and denounced us all. The Goddess has shown Her displeasure. The high priestess gave birth to twin boys!"

Astrid's heart thudded. For a wild second she thought the girl must be trying to play some sort of joke on her, but a look at the fear in the priestess's eyes made her realize this was the truth.

She swallowed. "Boys? How can this be?"

The priestess had no answer for Astrid. She just shook her head and then closed her eyes, as though uttering silent prayers to the Goddess.

Astrid bowed her head. *Is this my punishment, my mistress? Am I cursed?*

The import of the priestess's words slowly sank in.

Twin boys.

This had never happened before. The high priestess *always* bore a girl child. Always. It was a sign of the Goddess's favor. The daughter would go into the temple and become high priestess in her turn. Sometimes twins were born, and occasionally one of those twins was a boy. These births were thought to be a double blessing: a girl to become high priestess and a boy to become high priest. But never, ever, had the high priestess given birth only to boys. It was a sure sign the high priestess had lost the goddess's favor.

And if Ravessa is cursed, then surely I am too.

Astrid clutched at Capella's arm for support. All of her plans seemed to be collapsing at the foundations.

"Where is Ravessa?" she croaked.

"I don't know!" the priestess wailed. "The high priest took her."

Astrid forced herself to think. Where would Tamardi take Ravessa? Somewhere his power was strong.

The temple! Of course!

Spinning on her heel, Astrid charged from the room, with Capella two steps behind. "Find Rama and Aeron," she screeched as she ran. "And summon the guard!"

***

Bram retched for the umpteenth time. His body had long since expelled everything it had, but still Bram's stomach contracted, determined to rid itself of every vestige of poison. Bram rolled onto his back and looked up.

A rock ceiling closed high over his head, gently dripping water onto the floor. From the cave's entrance came the sound of waves lapping against the sand. He must have passed out and had no idea how long he'd remained unconscious.

He needed to move before the tide came in and flooded the cave. Gingerly, he flipped himself over, clambered to his knees, and splashed some of the dripping water onto his face. Shakily, he got to his feet. His legs still felt like water but the dizziness had passed and now the nausea seemed to be receding. Bram carefully picked his way through the jumbled rocks and standing pools of water toward the back of the cave. The tangy iron-smell of seaweed stung Bram's nostrils.

Brilliant! Caught between a madman and the sea, both of which will kill me given half a chance!

He sat down on a barnacle-encrusted rock. All was silent. Even the sound of the waves had become a distant hum. Bram looked around, letting his eyes adjust to the gloom. A crab scuttled away from him, hiding itself beneath a rock. A runnel of seawater ran down the roof and landed in a standing pool with a plop that echoed loudly in the stillness.

Bram put his head in his hands. His brain churned up memories, trying to piece together the afternoon's events. Images of the high priest and the tashen flashed before his eyes. Bram blanked them from his mind. He wasn't ready to think about that yet. He leaned back and sucked in a deep breath. He had to think, formulate a plan, but his thoughts slipped away like oil.

His eyes roved the cave, hoping to find courage among the shadows. Something caught his eye: a tall rectangular shadow on the wall, too regular to be a natural part of the cave. With an effort, he pushed himself from the rock and made his way over.

A door. Tall and narrow, it was made from bleached wood and reinforced with bands of iron. Orange spots of rust encrusted the metal. The door had a twisted iron ring as a handle which Bram pulled. The door swung open, letting through a draught of freezing air.

Bram's heart began to beat a little faster. What had he stumbled on? He peered through into darkness.

No sound came from beyond the door, but the steady breeze told Bram it must lead somewhere. Tentatively, Bram took a few paces through the door. Ahead, steps climbed into the heart of the cliff.

Toward the city! Bram thought. *This must be an old smuggler's route.*

Thanking his good fortune, Bram began to climb.

CHAPTER 25

The door slammed open so hard some of the plaster fell from the wall. A servant, who had been busy polishing, looked up at the clamor.

"My lady," she said, curtsying low enough for her skirt to touch the floor.

Astrid glowered at the servant as though she were the cause of all her woes. "Where is Lord Tamardi?"

The servant stared at her. "I, I don't know."

Astrid glared for a moment and then stalked off. Her heart pounded with fury. She pulled the knives from her sleeves and marched on.

Rama and Aeron had soon joined her and Capella, and now the party came out into the cloisters, where a full moon hung in the dark sky. Its eerie illumination showed the statue of the Goddess in the center, and at the statue's base a group of the Daughters of the Moon bent in supplication. They were weeping.

Astrid strode over and cried, "You there!"

The women looked up and horror crossed their faces. Many of them made the sign of the star on their breast: the sign to ward off evil. The women shrank away from Astrid and huddled together in the shadow of the statue.

They think I am cursed, Astrid realized.

"What are you doing?" she demanded. "You should be attending your mistress. Has she not just given birth?"

The Daughters of the Moon looked at each other uncertainly. A raven-haired girl stepped forward and said, "We are not allowed to attend the high priestess. The high priest has sent us here instead, to pray for forgiveness from the Goddess."

"Forgiveness? For what?"

"For the injury we have caused Her. Why else would she curse us and our mistress?"

Astrid baulked. The Daughters of the Moon were Ravessa's closest followers and if they believed their mistress to be cursed what hope would there be for the rest of the people? Tamardi's poison was already beginning to spread.

"Where is your mistress now?" Astrid asked.

"The high priest took her. We don't know where."

Astrid took a deep breath. Turning to Rama, Aeron and Capella, she said, "Come."

They moved into the heart of the palace, to places normally alive with the hubbub of government and society. Something had subtly altered; servants gasped and stared as Astrid hurried by. Fear permeated the air.

Astrid and her party were crossing the ballroom when a shout came from behind.

Whirling around, Astrid saw a squadron of guards spilling into the room. The commander called, "My lady, wait!"

Astrid recognized the commander: Talerick, a level-headed young man who had risen up the ranks through hard work and dedication. Relief washed through her.

She waited for him to catch up then said, "Well met, captain. I have some work for you. I want you to send one of your men to find Captain Samuel of the Royal Guard and tell him to meet me in the Great Hall. The rest of you are to come with me: we are going to make an arrest."

She stalked off across the hall and came to an abrupt halt as she realized the guards had not followed her. "Captain?"

Captain Talerick shook his head. "I am

sorry but you won't be going anywhere. We've been sent to arrest you."

Astrid stared at him. *Arrest me? But you are my guards!* "I beg your pardon?"

"You are under arrest for breaking the laws of Chellin by colluding with foreigners and bringing down the wrath of the Goddess upon us. The senate has spoken."

Astrid's fists tightened around the handles of her knives. "Captain Talerick, may I remind you that I am your sovereign and just by drawing weapons against me you are committing treason."

Talerick swallowed, clearly uncomfortable. "Forgive me, my lady, but we have our orders."

"Your orders? What orders can possibly override the will of your sovereign? May I remind you that when you joined the guard you swore an oath to protect the Regal and to follow her to the death! What has happened to your honor?"

The captain looked at Astrid steadily. "My honor remains intact. I am an officer in the Senate Guard now, and my oath of loyalty to them must supersede all others."

"Damn you, Talerick!" Astrid snarled. "I have known you since you were a sniveling boy hanging onto your mothers skirts! How dare you betray me like this?"

Talerick's gaze didn't waver. "I'm sorry you see it like that. Now, you must come with us."

There was the sharp ring of steel and Rama and Aeron pushed Astrid out of the way to stand between her and the guards. Capella came forward also and Astrid could see the blue glow of the Gift in her eyes.

"Step back, my lady," Aeron said softly. "If they want you they must come through us."

Astrid quickly scanned the room. There were eighteen guards blocking the exits. Eighteen against four: not good odds. She sighed and tucked her knives back into her sleeves. She instructed her people to put their weapons away.

To Talerick she said, "We'll come quietly."

The captain bowed. "I swear you won't be harmed."

"You young whelp," Rama growled. "Do not make promises you cannot keep. You are signing your queen's death warrant."

A shadow of uncertainty crossed Talerick's face. "The senate will make any further decisions regarding Lady Astrid. Now, come."

"Do as he says," Astrid grated. "The three of you are no good to me dead."

She followed meekly as the guards led her from the room.

"Where are you taking us, captain?" Astrid demanded as they marched down the hunter's gallery.

"You are to be presented to the senate,"

Talerick answered. "They await us in the Great Hall."

"What is to become of us?"

"I don't know. That's the senate's business."

How did it ever come to this? Astrid thought. *I am a prisoner in my own palace!*

A group of people suddenly burst into the hunter's gallery. "Are you all right, my lady?" one of them cried.

Astrid's heart soared. Captain Samuel! The Royal Guard!

Talerick pushed his way to the front of his troop until he stood face to face with Samuel. "The Regal is in good health, Captain," he said stiffly. "She is being escorted to the senate."

Captain Samuel, a thick-set, middle-aged man who had spent all his adult life in the Royal Guard, looked Talerick up and down.

"I don't think so," he said quietly.

Talerick bristled. "Stand aside, captain. This is none of your concern."

Samuel placed his hands on his hips. "I am a captain of the Royal Guard and anything that concerns the Regal's safety concerns me. Unlike some, the Royal Guard remains loyal to Chellin."

Talerick's hand tightened on the pommel of his sword. "Stand aside or you will be arrested as a traitor."

With a whoosh of steel, Samuel drew his sword. "It will be you who stands aside."

Behind him, the rest of his men drew swords.

The hunter's gallery crackled with tension. Astrid froze, her heart thumping. Something crashed into her back and she fell to the floor. Next thing she knew, the gallery was filled with shouting and the sound of steel ringing against steel. Astrid struggled to get up but something pinned her down. A second later, someone pulled her up and she found herself face to face with Rama. He had a graze along his temple and his sword in hand.

"Quickly!" he bellowed at her. "Go!"

Fighting filled the whole of the hunter's gallery. Comrade against comrade, friend against friend.

Oh Chellin! Astrid cried silently. *What has become of us?*

Someone grabbed her wrist and yanked her forward into the custody of the Royal Guard.

Capella shouted, "For the high priestess!"

A blinding blue flash lit the corridor. Astrid covered her eyes just in time, and opened them to see guards staggering around blindly. Capella stood in the middle of the hunter's gallery, arms outstretched, with a blue glow fading around her. She strode over to the soldiers of the Royal Guard and passed her hands over their eyes. Whatever charm she had weaved on them fell away and they could see again.

Captain Samuel quickly took control of the

situation and ordered his men to disarm the rest of the Senate Guard and round them up. This done, he approached Astrid.

"Are you hurt, my lady?"

Astrid placed her hands on the captain's shoulders. "I am well, thanks to you, Samuel. You and your men will be handsomely rewarded for this bravery. Now, tell me, how many units of the Royal Guard remain loyal to me?"

"All of those stationed in the palace, my lady — we do not bow to the senate or the high priest."

"How many units are here in the palace?"

"Thirty five at present, my lady."

"And how many units of the Senate Guard?"

"Seventy three, counting these here."

Astrid frowned. "We are heavily outnumbered."

"Outnumbered maybe," Samuel replied, "but each one of my men is worth three of those sniveling cowards of the Senate Guard. We have another forty-two units stationed in the city. They will come immediately if I send out word. But there is something else. The senate has ordered the arrest of the Ral Torans. I don't know whether they are yet in custody. What are your orders?"

Astrid leaned against the wall. Everything was happening so quickly she barely had time to think. The Royal Guard was loyal to her. The

Senate Guard was not. It was just possible that with the support of Captain Samuel Astrid would be able to regain control of the palace, and defeat the high priest.

But that would risk civil war.

Tamardi not only had weight of numbers on his side, but also the weight of righteousness. By now, his messengers would have gone out into the city bearing the tidings of Ravessa's twin boys and subsequently, tidings of the curse the Goddess had placed upon her. Many would rally to the high priest's call, believing it to be the will of the Goddess and the only righteous path. If she fought the senate and the high priest, Chellin would become a blood bath.

I will not start a war, she thought. *I will go north as planned, but first I have to find Ravessa. I have to free the Ral Torans. I have to find Bram. I have to do a thousand things.*

She dropped her head into her hands, the weight of responsibility feeling like an iron cloak around her shoulders.

What would Ravessa want me to do?

And then she had her answer.

Ravessa's voice echoed in her mind. *Would you destroy Chellin for me? Nothing is more important than the quest.*

"Captain Samuel," Astrid said, straightening, "have these traitors taken to the cells and then come with me. We go to free the Ral Torans."

Now she'd decided on her course of action, a cold resolution filled her. Even though her grip on Chellin was sliding away, at least she had a purpose.

The palace was deserted. Nobody walked its corridors. Even the servants had disappeared. They knew that something was afoot and had no wish to get caught up in it. Astrid's party moved in silence, weapons drawn, the only sound was the tramp of boots on the polished floors.

The runner Captain Samuel had sent on ahead reported that Father Hewin, Falen and Tomas were not in their rooms. Astrid took this news grimly. The Ral Torans may already have been arrested. If that was the case, they would be in the senate's cells, and there would be nothing Astrid could do to help them. She clung onto hope. The Panthers would not have gone without a fight and it was possible they hadn't yet been taken.

So, with grim determination, Astrid led her people to a little used servant entrance and out onto the tourney fields.

The palace grounds were a dark pool of shadow. Frost-hardened grass crunched underfoot. A line of light smudged the eastern sky, indicating it would soon be dawn. They moved quickly, conscious of being out in the open and in the pre-dawn stillness every sound seemed magnified a hundred-fold; the creak of leather, the scrape of sword on scabbard.

Astrid gritted her teeth and hurried on, Captain Samuel at her side. The Panthers' barrack building was located on the far side of the tourney ground, amidst a jumble of buildings designed to accommodate the needs of the palace guards.

As they approached the barracks Astrid noticed a commotion outside. People moved in the shadows and weapons glinted.

"Damn it!"

She called a halt and her party darted behind a stable before they could be seen. Rama poked his head around the corner and surveyed the building.

"It's the Senate Guard," he whispered. "They've surrounded the barracks".

Samuel leaned out and followed Rama's gaze. "The door's closed. That means the Ral Torans must still be inside."

Astrid felt a tiny spark of hope. "How do we get them out?"

Rama and Samuel shared a look. "If Talerick and his men are anything to go by, I don't think the Senate Guard will give up without a fight."

Grimly, Astrid drew the knives from her sleeve. "Then we must do what we must."

Samuel hurriedly whispered orders to his men. Surrounded by a ring of guards, Astrid stepped out from behind the stable and approached the building. The guards spotted her immediately. They spun to face the advancing soldiers. Astrid's men fanned out in a line and halted ten paces from the Senate Guard. The two groups regarded each other. The officer in charge, a pale man with the mark of a lieutenant on his shoulder stepped forward and bowed.

"Lieutenant Sorl of the Senate Guard, my lady."

Astrid inclined her head. "I don't need to tell you why I'm here, lieutenant."

Sorl looked beyond her to the soldiers, assessing their strength. His eyes flicked over the grim faces of the Royal Guard and his hand tightened on his own sword. "I beseech you not to interfere in this," he said to Astrid. "We've been ordered to arrest the Ral Torans and must do our duty."

"Your first duty is to Chellin. Do you really think she will be served by her people fighting among themselves?"

"I have no quarrel with you, my lady, and I have no desire to match weapons with your men. But I have sworn an oath to obey the orders of the senate. I cannot stand aside. Chellin will not be served if her officers abandon their oaths."

"Even if those oaths help to turn her into a pit for tyrants? Have you stopped to ask why the senate has ordered the arrest of the Ral Torans? What reason did they give you?"

"It is not my place to question—"

"It is your place to think, man! The Ral

Torans have committed no crime other than being foreigners. When did we begin arresting innocent people in Chellin? Have we sunk so low? Your orders do not come from the senate but from the high priest; the senate is his tool now."

The men behind Sorl began shifting restlessly. "I didn't join the guard to end up serving the high priest!" someone cried. There were rumbles of agreement.

Astrid spotted her chance. Evidently, some in the Senate Guard were not happy. If she handled this right, they may all get away without bloodshed.

"You are worthy servants of Chellin," she said loudly. "Make the right decision now. Stand aside and let me take the Ral Torans out of here. The very future of Chellin may depend on it."

Sorl looked at his men and an unspoken communication passed between them. Very deliberately, Sorl's men sheathed their weapons.

Astrid breathed a sigh of relief.

"May I make a suggestion?" Rama asked. "If Sorl and his men will agree to having their hands bound and being sealed within the barrack building it will look as though they put up a fight and that way they will not face punishment for letting us go."

Sorl considered this for a moment and then nodded. The senate guards parted and Astrid strode purposefully up to the door of the barrack building. She rapped on it with the handle of one of her knives.

From inside a voice bellowed, "By my belly! How many times? We are not opening the door, and if you try to come in here I will crack the skulls of each and every one of you!"

"That won't be necessary, commander," Astrid shouted. "The Senate Guard has stood down."

There was silence for a moment and then Father Hewin's voice said, "Lady Astrid? Is that you?"

"Yes, it's safe to come out now."

The door opened a crack and Barl peered out. He clutched a battle-axe in one meaty fist. When he saw Astrid and her soldiers his face broke into a grin and he threw the door open all the way.

"You came just in time!" he bellowed. "We were about to come out here and give these young whelps a thumping!"

Father Hewin pushed past Barl and approached Astrid. His normally somber face was mottled with anger. "What is going on here? These people said we were under arrest!"

Astrid quickly filled them in on what had happened. Hewin listened in silence.

"So you see," Astrid concluded. "The high priest holds the upper hand. It is no longer safe in Chellin."

Tomas pushed his way through to Astrid.

"Where is Bram?" he asked. "And Falen? I don't see them with you."

Astrid grimaced. "After his confrontation with the high priest, Bram disappeared and I have no more knowledge of Falen's whereabouts than you do."

Tomas swore loudly. "I must find them." Before anyone could stop him, he pushed through the soldiers and ran off across the tourney ground.

"Damn it!" spat Barl and made to chase after but Astrid put a hand out to stop him. "No! He is going back into the palace, we can't go that way, we will be caught!"

"But we cannot leave him," said Hewin. "Nor can we abandon Bram and Falen! They must be found!"

"I know!" said Astrid desperately. "But if we don't secure the Ice Ship, the quest is doomed! I will send my people to find the others, but we have to move!"

After a moment, Father Hewin reluctantly nodded. Rama and Samuel quickly bound Sorl and his men and shut them in the barracks as agreed.

Astrid led her people across the tourney field toward the main entrance. For a second she dared to believe that they would make it to the bridge unchallenged but suddenly people began spilling out of the palace ahead of them and blocked their path. They were all guardsman dressed in the green and gold of the senate. They heavily outnumbered Astrid's party. Senators Rosenthay and Nerie were with them.

"Halt!" Nerie shouted. "You are all under arrest!"

Astrid's heart sank. She knew these soldiers, under Nerie's command, would obey every order. Still, she had to try.

"Stand aside!" she shouted. "You have no authority over me."

In answer, Nerie nodded to the commander and his soldiers drew swords and began advancing.

"If it's a fight they want that's what we'll give them," growled Barl.

Astrid chewed her nail, thinking. They couldn't win this fight. Rama's eyes found hers; he knew it too. Aeron's eyes glinted with anger and the blue glow of the Gift surrounded Capella. They were ready to fight. To die.

"No," she said suddenly. She asked Captain Samuel, "How long can you hold them here?"

Samuel's expression was determined. "As long as you require, my lady."

Astrid clasped his hand. "Then, may the Goddess forgive me, I ask you to hold them. I hope we meet again, Captain Samuel, so I can repay this debt."

Samuel held Astrid's gaze, understanding the unspoken command. *Give your lives if you have to.* He turned to his men and shouted,

"Company advance!"

In a rush, the Royal Guard sped across the ground. They crashed into the line of the Senate Guard with an audible impact. The clash of weapons and the roar of fighting enveloped the air.

Astrid ordered the Ral Torans, "Follow me quickly!"

"What are you doing?" bellowed Barl. "We must help them!"

"To what end?" hissed Astrid. "Follow me, unless you wish to die here!"

She turned east and ran across the open ground toward the palace, the rest of the group following. They entered the cloisters, a silent place that seemed eerily abandoned without the Daughters of the Moon praying in the center. Astrid hurried into the middle of the lawned garden and put her fingers to her lips. She let out one long, shrill whistle and waited, eyes turned heavenward. After only a moment, a dark shape came spiraling down from the sky and landed on the statue of the Goddess.

Eobrus.

Astrid bowed her head to the albatross. "Thanks be to you, Old One," she said. "I need your help." She closed her eyes and tried to communicate her needs to the bird.

You must get a message to Serz. Bramwell Thornley has disappeared. Ask Serz to find him; if anyone can find the boy, it will be him. The future of Chellin depends on it.

Astrid was not a quentarc but she hoped that Eobrus could hear. The great albatross cocked his head and regarded her shrewdly, as if he understood every word. After a moment, he let out a loud 'kar-ark!' and then took to the air. He wheeled round the garden once before he disappeared over the rooftops.

There was no more time to lose. Bram's fate, for the moment, was out of her hands. She had to get the Ral Torans to safety.

She strode over to a dark corner of the cloisters. Here, ivy covered the wall and the area smelled of moss and wet plants. Astrid placed her hands on the wall and ran them along it, searching. Her hands alighted on a slight protuberance, like a handle in the rock. Gratefully she took hold of it and pulled downwards.

A soft rumble shook the air and then a section of wall slid sideways, ripping ivy from the wall and sending showers of dust into the air. Beyond lay a dark space. In the dim, pre-dawn light, Astrid could make out a set of steps descending into darkness.

"Capella, come here," she instructed the charm weaver. "I need you at the front, you will have to light our way."

Obediently Capella stepped toward the opening. She raised one hand into the air and a ball of blue light surrounded it.

Father Hewin crossed his arms over his chest. "What in the name of sanity are you doing? Do you expect us to blindly follow you down there?"

She had no time for this. With as much patience as she could muster Astrid said, "You have to trust me. This passage leads to the secret tunnels that riddle the palace. It will take us down to the base of the headland, and from there we can get to the harbor."

"Trust you?" spat Hewin. "Why should we trust you? This damned alliance has led to nothing but trouble!"

"If you stay here, Father Hewin, the high priest will capture you. Your fate would then be sealed."

"He would not dare to harm us! We are diplomatic guests!"

"Do you think that matters to him? He would risk war with Ral Tora rather than let the alliance stand! You must come with me!"

Hewin's eyes were full of suspicion. He opened his mouth to speak but a clamor outside the cloisters made them all turn around.

"Guards!" cried Astrid. "Quickly! Follow Capella down the stairs."

Hewin gave her a withering stare but then ducked into the opening. The Panthers followed until only herself, Rama and Aeron remained outside.

"I hope you know what you are doing, my lady," Aeron muttered.

So do I, Astrid thought.

She followed Rama and Aeron through and closed the door behind them. Heart hammering, Astrid followed as Capella led them into the deep heart of the promontory.

CHAPTER 26

After climbing steadily, the tunnel that Bram walked began to descend again. A flight of steps, smooth and well cut, angled steeply downwards toward who-knew-what.

A torch was fixed to the wall with a rusty bracket. Bram reached out to touch the metal casing and jumped back in alarm as it ignited with a whoosh. Seconds later, other torches spaced along the walls ignited also, illuminating the steps.

The hairs rose on Bram's neck. He had seen this before. In the vaults beneath the library in Ral Tora the torches had lit of their own accord, as if by...

What? He asked himself angrily. *Magic? Don't be so absurd, they must be connected by pipes in the wall.*

Reaching hands out to either side to steady himself, Bram made his way down the steps. At the bottom, he found a narrow corridor with walls of roughly-hewn stone. From above him came an odd sound, like someone sighing over and over.

The sea! I'm under the sea!

Trepidation rose in him. From what he knew of Chellin engineering, they did not have the skills to successfully drill the seabed. Was this passageway safe?

But, looking around, Bram realized that the structural design of the place was nothing like the architecture of Chellin. In fact, it looked more like something he would see in Ral Tora; a ribbed ceiling with pillars spaced at regular intervals to support the roof. The tunnel's sturdy, angular features were alien to the flowing, curving style of Chellin.

This must have been built by Ral Toran engineers, Bram realized. But to Bram's knowledge, no engineers from Ral Tora had visited Chellin for many years. This tunnel must be ancient.

A stout wooden door blocked the way. Bram pressed his ear to the wood and listened. No sound came from beyond.

The door swung open easily as Bram pushed it and he carefully stepped through. He stood in a vast room crammed full of all sorts of artifacts. Old benches, rolled up carpets, battered picture frames, tables with legs missing, chipped statues and moldy tapestries. An earthy, rotten smell filled the room. Dust covered everything.

Carefully, Bram began picking his way through, trying not to disturb anything. Beyond this first storeroom, Bram found another, this one filled with books. Some were piled in tall columns and some were scattered across the floor as though a child had thrown them there in a tantrum. Bram thought of the librarian back in Ral Tora. She would be appalled at such a sacrilege.

A noise came from ahead. Bram froze. It sounded like breathing. His heart thudding in his chest, Bram crouched down behind a stack of books and waited. He held his breath. A soft 'swish' filled the air. Pages being turned.

Slowly, Bram edged out from his hiding place, taking tiny, hesitant steps toward the sound. He poked his head round a pile of books and saw a man seated in an old rickety chair. He had his back to Bram. On the man's lap rested a small age-yellowed book.

The man had a shaven head and wore a dark uniform. A herringbone earring dangled from one ear. Recognition hovered on the edges of Bram's memory. He was sure he'd seen that earring before...

"Corban!"

The Panther jumped up with a yelp and spun round, sword drawn in a flash. His eyes narrowed.

"Bram?" he said. "What by all that's holy are you doing down here?"

Bram felt giddy with relief. He wanted to run up to Corban and throw his arms around him. Instead, he said, "I might ask you the same thing!"

Corban glanced behind him. "I, er, went to the temple to pray to The Mariner. Took what I thought was the right door but ended up in some underground chambers. I'm a bit lost."

Bram slumped to the floor. "Corban, I need your help."

He told Corban everything that had happened with the high priest. Corban listened silently.

"I have to find Falen," Bram concluded, gesturing weakly. "I have to find her."

Corban ran his hands over his bald scalp. A sheen of sweat made his skin shine. The title on the spine of his book read, *Uses of the Gift*.

"Of course we must find her," Corban said. He held out a hand and pulled Bram to his feet. Bram noticed something odd about Corban's face.

"Your tattoo is smudged."

Corban raised a hand to the clan markings that covered his forehead and left cheek. Blue paint came off in his palm. "Never mind," he said, turning away. "I'll re-apply it later. Come on."

They moved out of the storeroom and into a confusing network of passages. Something on the wall caught Bram's eye and he moved closer. A faded, barely recognizable painting adorned the wall. A lion perhaps, except it had the wings of an eagle.

Unease squirmed in Bram's belly. He had seen these types of paintings before, under the library in Ral Tora.

Reluctantly Bram followed Corban. At length they reached an intersection. One corridor went left and began to climb while the other ran off to the right.

Bram blew out a breath. "At last! This must lead up to the entrance!" he started up the left path but Corban put a hand on his shoulder.

"No, we must go this way."

"But this way leads upwards. Surely the entrance must be this way?"

Corban snarled in anger. "I said no! Do not make me pull rank on you, soldier! We go right." Roughly, he grabbed Bram's shoulder and pushed him forward.

"There's a door ahead," Bram said suddenly.

"That's right. Just go straight through."

Beyond the door, Bram found a large chamber with a heavy round table in the middle. A man sat in one of the chairs staring at Bram expectantly.

The high priest.

Bram staggered backward. Corban's strong hands seized him and propelled him into the room. The Panther pulled the door shut and leaned on it.

Bram whirled round. "The high priest!" he hissed urgently. "We have to get away."

Corban didn't answer. He addressed the high priest. "I've found something you lost."

The high priest's eyes glinted hungrily. They had the look of a predator. A smile twitched the corners of his mouth.

"Where have you been?" the high priest said to Corban. "You were instructed to prepare for the ritual."

"You cannot give me orders!" Corban snarled. "I'm not your servant! If I hadn't found this young whelp he would have gotten away from us! It is I, not you, who have served the Masters' plans!"

"Corban?" Bram said. "What's going on?"

Corban's dark eyes flicked toward Bram and they were full of contempt. Suddenly he grinned and put his hand to his forehead. He wiped away his clan markings to reveal a white, puckered scar. It ran from his forehead, through his left eye and half way down his cheek. Bram had seen this man before, what seemed a lifetime ago now, addressing a Wailer's meeting in Ral Tora.

"Who are you?" Bram whispered.

Corban let out a cracked laugh that carried no mirth. "Why don't you tell him, high priest?

Why don't you tell him how I've been watching him from the start? Why don't you tell him how I've been your spy?" Seeing the look that formed on Bram's face, Corban said, "Ah! Have I upset our little puppy? Don't worry, little one, you won't feel this way for long. In fact, soon you won't feel anything."

"Traitor!" Bram cried as understanding filled him. "Barl will have your guts for this!"

"Barl? Do you really think that fat hunk of meat is any threat to me? I could kill him in my sleep." Corban leaned forward and the look in his eyes made Bram step back a pace. "And I *will* kill him, be assured of that. When I am done, each one of the Panthers will lie stinking in an open grave. Except Saskia, I might let her live — at least until I've had my fun with her."

"I trusted you!" Bram bellowed. "We all trusted you. How can you betray us like this?"

Corban sprang forward and grabbed Bram by the throat. Fingers like steel squeezed, cutting off Bram's air. "Trust is a luxury you cannot afford."

"Enough!" cried the high priest.

Corban threw Bram to the floor.

"A merry dance you've led me since you arrived here, Bramwell Thornley," said the high priest.

Bram scrambled to his feet and backed away. High Priest Tamardi Di Goron regarded him with lidded eyes. "You were not expecting to see me?"

"As I am sure you were not expecting to see me," Bram hissed in response. "I'm not floating face down in the harbor as you clearly expected me to be."

The high priest's face took on a look of surprise. "I've no idea what you're talking about. Do you, Darry?"

"You instructed the tashen to kill me," Bram said. "When Astrid finds out, you're finished."

"I doubt that very much," Tamardi said. He rose from his chair and stood facing Bram, hands tucked behind his back. He wore a long blue robe and his thick blond hair lay unbound to his shoulders. "After tonight Astrid du Lanstrang Av' Riny will no longer hold power in Chellin."

There was something in the high priest's calm arrogance that set Bram's hair on end. "What do you mean?" he asked carefully. "What have you done?"

"I have done nothing," the high priest replied. "The Goddess Herself has spoken, and in doing so, has denounced the Regal."

"And She's chosen you to seize power I suppose?"

This time the high priest smiled. "Of course. Would you care for some wine?" He moved over to the circular table and poured out a glass of honey colored liquid. "This is the last of the Ashon Gold. An excellent bouquet. It is truly delicious I can assure you."

Bram stared at Tamardi as though he were a predator.

"I'll take that as a "no", shall I?" the high priest said brightly. He seemed to be enjoying himself.

"If you want to kill me, I'll make sure you have a difficult job of it."

The high priest smiled. "If I wanted to kill you, do you really think you could stop me?"

"What do you want with me?"

The high priest sipped his wine and regarded Bram over the rim of his glass. "I wish you to join me."

Bram narrowed his eyes. "Join you? Then why try to kill me?"

The high priest put the goblet down on the table. "That was a mistake. I have seen my error since then and I apologize. You are a very rare individual, Bram Thornley. Together you and I could command immense power. Have you never suspected why Astrid brought you here? What her interest in you is?"

Bram stared at the high priest. The high priest stared back.

At last, Tamardi said, "I do not blame you for suspecting me. I have done little to earn your trust. I am not a monster, Bram, despite what Astrid has told you. I seek only to serve my people. Time is turning full circle. Soon the past will be upon us once again. Only those who have been loyal to the Old Gods will be spared once they return. I seek only to show my people the true path so that their souls may be saved."

"Old Gods?" Bram asked. "There were people in Ral Tora who talked of them. You are one of them aren't you? A Wailer!"

The high priest raised an eyebrow. "A what?"

Corban shifted his position by the wall. "It's what the Ral Torans call our kind."

A frown creased the high priest's features. "We prefer to be called the followers of the Old Way," he said to Bram. "Once you understand, you will join us."

Bram scanned the room, looking for a way out. There were two exits but the high priest blocked one, Corban the other. He fought to keep his legs steady: he would not show fear in front of these men. As long as he kept the high priest talking, he stood a chance. "What do you mean?"

Tamardi pursed his lips, tapped them with his finger, thinking. "Long ago, when people still worshipped the Old Gods, there were many strange customs. Most were superstitions, empty, meaningless. But one of those rituals was real. It took place in this very room. Can you feel it, Bram?"

The chamber felt old. Memory filled it. Something tingled on Bram's skin. There was something here, he could almost see it...

Torches ring the walls, burning sweet incense. Nine robed figures stand in a circle around a dais, chanting in a strange tongue. On the dais, a pentagram has been drawn in chalk and before this a beautiful young woman kneels with her head bowed. She is naked except for a garland of white flowers around her neck. Abruptly, the chanting stops and a white light begins to glow from the pentagram. Something is coming. A blaze of light flares and when it dies, an opalescent figure is standing within the pentagram. The young woman looks up and says, "Saiis, my lord. Will you take me to wife?" The figure of light towers over the young woman. Then it reaches out a hand and raises her to her feet. The young woman's face is full of joy as the figure pulls her into its embrace.

"I knew it!" cried the high priest, grinning as wide as the doorway. "You see it, don't you?"

Bram shook his head. "I don't know what you're talking about."

"Tut-tut, Bram. You are a terrible liar. All right, let me continue the story. There is a rumor, a whisper that dare not be uttered aloud. This rumor says that a hundred years ago the Bride of the God was performed here in Chellin and that Saiis chose a young woman to be His bride. It is rumored that following the ritual, the young woman gave birth to a daughter, and in time, the daughter gave birth to a son. The daughter was a powerful priestess within the hierarchy of the Old Way but twenty years ago, both the priestess and her infant son disappeared. Some say they were murdered. Some say they still hide somewhere in Chellin. Some say they fled south. To Ral Tora."

Tamardi Di Goron's eyes were like drills, boring into Bram. "What power that child must hold. The blood of a god flowing in his veins. The perfect tool for a greedy queen who wishes to extend her power—"

"Shut up!" Bram shouted.

"Who knows how the story is going to end?" said the high priest with a wry smile. "I see two possible outcomes. Either the child will fulfill his destiny and ally himself with the servants of the Old Gods. Or he will die. The question is Bram: what do you believe?"

Bram's breath came in heavy, ragged gasps. "I am Ral Toran. I believe in science and reason. I will have no part in your madness."

Corban moved so quickly that Bram didn't even see him. His fist slammed into Bram's cheek and sent him sprawling onto his back. White hot agony flared through his skull.

"Such a shame," the high priest said conversationally. "It seems the story will be a tragedy after all."

Bram staggered to his feet. He would not face the high priest on his knees. "You have tried to kill me once and failed," he rasped. "What makes you think you will do any better this time?"

The high priest laughed. "A fighting spirit, I like that. Darry, bring him."

Corban grabbed Bram's arm and twisted it up behind his back. "If you struggle I will break your arm," Corban hissed.

The Panther propelled Bram after the high priest, through into another room.

As the chamber came into view, Bram whimpered in fear.

In the center of the room lay a marble slab with a tall skeleton atop it. The figure clutched a metal staff in its bony fingers, and its long, slanted eye sockets stared sightlessly up. High, high above reared the skeleton of a massive, winged beast with teeth as long as an arm.

In an instant Bram's mind went spiraling back to the vaults beneath Ral Tora's library and what he had discovered there. He'd never thought there might be more of the terrible creatures, but here he was, staring at another.

Bram fought to control his fear. He felt suddenly like a fly, caught in the web of something far bigger and far more powerful than he was.

Secrets and lies. Layers of meaning.

"Bram!" a voice shouted.

Falen sat slumped on the far side of the chamber, chained to the wall. The High Priestess Ravessa hung by her side, and in a small, makeshift cot, two tiny babies.

"Falen!" Bram yelled.

He wrenched himself out of Corban's grip and launched himself across the room. Before he had gone two paces, a force smacked him across the face and he went crashing to the floor. The high priest lowered his hand, a blue glow slowly fading.

"Yes, your little witch is here, Bramwell Thornley. As I told you, she has not been harmed."

Bram pulled himself to his knees and looked at Falen. Her black hair was a matted mess but she seemed to be unhurt. The high priestess though, was another matter. Her dress was torn and stained with fluid. She was barely conscious, with her head hanging down listlessly and her skin as pale as bone. Seeing the two babes lying asleep in the cot, realization dawned on Bram. The high priestess had just given birth.

"What have you done?" Bram said to the high priest. "What have you done?"

"Nothing yet," snapped the high priest. "In fact, you're just in time."

"Let them go," Bram begged. "You have me, let the others go."

The high priest shook his head. "I don't think so. You really haven't figured out what's going on here, have you?" He moved over to the skeleton and ran his hands over the age-darkened bones lovingly. "Isn't she beautiful?" he crooned. "Beautiful and deadly, like poison ivy. It's time to begin. Darry, bring the brats."

Corban, or Darry, or whatever his name really was, approached the crib and picked up the two babies. They started bawling and

Ravessa roused herself at the sudden din. "My sons! Don't hurt them!"

Falen pulled at her chains. "Take your hands off them, snake!"

Darry took no notice of the women. He placed the squalling infants on the marble slab, by the head and feet of the skeleton.

The high priest looked on with rapture. "It won't be long now, my mistress. Soon you will live again!" He drew a long, curved knife and advanced toward the squirming children. Ravessa screamed. Bram watched in horror. The high priest raised the knife high into the air.

"No!" howled Bram. He flung himself at the high priest.

Tamardi turned toward him, the knife in his hand. Bram's eyes widened in shock as he felt the cold of the blade slide between his ribs, deep into his chest. Blood sprayed as the high priest wrenched the blade out.

Falen howled. Corban laughed.

The high priest looked down at Bram. "Such a pity."

Bram's legs folded beneath him. Blood ran through his fingers where they pressed against his chest.

No. No. No. Not like this.

Bram sucked in a deep breath and felt something tear inside him. His lungs heaved and a great gout of blood exploded from his mouth. He struggled to breathe.

The high priest raised the knife over the new-borns once more.

Bram struggled weakly. *Get up! Get up!* But his bloody hands slipped on the floor and could find no purchase. Tamardi didn't even glance in his direction. He was a fly, small and insignificant in the spider's web.

The babes squirmed on the slab and cried in fear, somehow sensing the danger.

"By the blood of the new-born you will have life, my mistress!" Tamardi cried. The blade flashed as it descended.

Footsteps pounded outside. Tamardi spun round, fire blazing in his eyes.

"Someone is coming! Stop them, Darry!"

Corban drew his sword and marched toward the door just as two figures burst into the room.

Serz and Tomas.

"Thank you," Bram whispered.

Tomas spotted the high priest and let out a bellow of rage. He threw himself across the room and yanked the knife from the high priest's hand.

The high priest hissed with fury. He raised his hand and sent a ball of blue fire spiraling toward Tomas. It cannoned into Tomas's chest, sending him spinning through the air to land in a crumpled heap in the corner.

The high priest smiled in triumph. He moved to retrieve his knife but as he did so, a strange sound stopped him in his tracks. The sound came from Tomas. Laughter. A gust of wind blew through the chamber as though a door had been opened and closed.

Slowly, Tomas climbed to his feet.

"You are an abomination," he said to the high priest. "You have broken your oath. You have sought to use the Power here, beyond the Rift where it should never be used." The voice was not Tomas's own. It was as deep and strong as bedrock. Bram had heard it before, a lifetime ago, on the night Tomas had arrived in Ral Tora and then again when he spoke to the librarian.

A muscle twitched in the high priest's jaw. "Fool!" he spat. "Do not try to stop me. I am the agent of the Goddess and She has chosen me to be the vessel of her power!"

Tomas approached the skeleton, his lip curled in disgust. "Is this what you worship?"

"She is the Goddess!"

"She is not what you think."

"What would you know — a sniveling wretch from a dead land?"

Tomas glared at the high priest with eyes that burned wildly. "I know more than you could ever imagine. You are meddling with forces that will consume you."

Tomas turned and in a swift movement swept his arm over the stone slab. The bones went clattering to the floor.

Tamardi howled in fury. Snatching up the knife, he lunged, but Tomas grabbed the high priest's arm. Tamardi wailed in sudden pain. Where Tomas had touched him, the high priest's skin carried a raw, red welt.

The high priest gaped at his forearm in horror. "Who are you?"

"A servant of Teranan and your enemy," Tomas replied.

"Really? Then you will die as such." A jet of blue fire slammed into Tomas. The force of the blow sent the Varisean staggering backward but he caught the bolt in his hand and then sent it careening back toward the high priest. Tamardi leapt to the side and the bolt crashed into the wall, sending chips of stone flying.

Bram forced his body to move. Inch by painful inch, he began to crawl across the floor. By the door Corban and Serz were circling each other. The falcon master did not look used to holding a sword. A sly grin twisted Corban's face; a cat playing with a mouse.

Corban lunged at Serz and the falcon master took a cut to the temple. Laughing, Corban backed off and began circling. Serz crouched, eyes wide and sword outstretched.

Serz stood no chance against the Panther. Corban danced forward, blade snaking toward Serz's stomach. The falcon master brought his own blade down and managed to deflect the blow. Warily, he backed away.

Don't back yourself into a corner, Bram thought, *that's what he wants you to do.*

Bram dragged himself forward. At last his hand closed around the hilt of the sword Corban had discarded. Digging its point into the floor, he used it to pull himself up and stood, swaying drunkenly.

Corban was slowly pushing Serz backward. A lightning series of attacks forced the falcon master further and further into the corner and a hundred tiny cuts began crisscrossing Serz's limbs.

Bram tottered toward them. Corban brought his sword round to clash against Serz's weapon. The sword went flying out of Serz's hand and landed with a clatter on the floor. Serz backed off but found himself pressed against the wall.

Corban let out a wild laugh. "Is there nobody who can offer me a good fight?"

Corban pulled his sword back, ready to plunge it into Serz's heart. Bram threw himself toward the panther and brought his sword smashing down onto Corban's arm, cleaving through skin, bone, and sinew. The traitor's hand flew off in a spurt of blood.

Corban howled and went crashing to the floor, writhing in agony.

Bram's energy was spent. He fell to his knees and his head sunk to the floor. Serz rushed over.

"Bram!" he said urgently. "Are you all right?"

"Get the children," Bram managed to

whisper. "Help Ravessa and Falen."

Serz nodded and moved away.

Bram's lungs strained to pull in air. His heart struggled to pump blood round his body, only for it to be lost through the rent in this chest. Gradually his organs were failing. The floor felt cold against Bram's forehead. The cold spread, seeping through him like water soaking into parched soil.

I'm dying, he thought.

A dark pit opened up before him and Bram teetered on the edge. The darkness promised an end to pain. He longed to plunge into it.

"Bram," a strong voice said. Hands seized him by the shoulders and pulled him to his knees.

"Help him!" Falen's voice cried.

"I cannot. He is beyond all help."

Bram's eyes began to dim. Only shadows moved before him, gray, indistinct.

He tried to reach out, to clasp his friend's hand one more time, but his limbs would no longer move. He had no strength left.

Suddenly, his blood began to pound. A scalding pain raced through his veins, as though hot irons had been pressed against every part of his body. Bram gasped, arching his back and writhing on the floor. The searing agony lasted for ten heartbeats before subsiding, leaving Bram cold and dazed.

His sight cleared. Falen leaned over him, eyes wide with fear.

"Falen?" he gasped. "What's wrong?"

Falen pointed and put her hands over her mouth.

Bram placed his hand on his chest. Where the wound had been only a tight, tender scar remained.

"What have you done?" Falen whispered.

Bram rubbed his hands over his eyes. *What is happening to me? Why am I still alive?*

Tomas knelt in front of Bram, staring intently at him as though he understood everything that had just transpired. But they were not Tomas's eyes. They were eyes that looked back over thousands of years and thousands of miles to an immense creature, old and powerful, and sad beyond reckoning.

Come to me, a voice whispered in Bram's head. *We will ride the winds together as we once did. I will show you who you are.*

Yes, Bram answered. *I will come.*

"We have to go," said Tomas, rising to his feet.

Falen got up and pulled Bram after her. "Can you walk?"

Bram nodded and looked around. The chamber was a scene of carnage. Cracks and rents split the walls. Bones lay scattered around like discarded toys. Blood, both Bram's and Corban's streaked the floor and in one corner, lay Corban, gripping the stump of his right arm.

Falen strode toward him. "Traitor!" she

snapped. "I'll kill you!"

"No!" Bram said urgently, "Leave him. We'll not become like him."

Serz stumbled over, supporting Ravessa who clutched her two screaming children. "There is chaos in the palace," he said. "Astrid was making for the harbor, and so we must try to get there if we can."

"Where is the high priest?" Bram asked.

"Fled," said Tomas. "But I don't think this is over, he won't give up easily. We have to hurry."

They stumbled from the room, leaving the skeletal beast to guard the scattered bones of its mistress.

CHAPTER 27

How did it ever come to this? Astrid asked herself as she fled through the tunnels of Chellin. *How did I become a fugitive in my own city?*

Astrid pressed her lips into a tight line and stumbled on. Capella's light showed a steep, featureless tunnel angling downwards into the heart of the promontory. Long ago Astrid had discovered this bolt hole, built for Regals who needed to escape the palace.

She had never dreamed she would be one of them.

"My lady, there is light ahead," said Capella suddenly.

The sound of waves echoed up the tunnel. A ring of pale light appeared, one that grew steadily bigger as they approached. The iron tang of the sea filled the air, the smell of salt and seaweed. They reached the end of the tunnel and found it blocked by a rusted iron grille fixed into the rock walls with heavy bolts.

Capella leaned forward, using her light to examine it.

"It's locked."

The rusted mechanism looked to have been untouched for years, centuries even. Astrid reached into the neck of her dress and pulled out a chain. On it hung a key, which was supposed to unlock all of the secret doors within the palace.

Astrid prayed that it would work on this one.

Squinting in the light, Astrid placed the key in the lock and slowly turned it. The lock snapped open with a click. Breathing a sigh of relief, Astrid pushed the grille aside and stepped out into the dawn.

Before her was a curving bay at the base of the headland with high, sheer cliffs rearing above. A shingle beach reached down to the water's edge where the sea pounded the rocks with fury, sending plumes of freezing spray into the air. It was a wild, lonely place and matched Astrid's mood perfectly. She turned into the wind and let it slice through her, savoring its icy touch.

Father Hewin looked around in dismay. "What now?"

Astrid marched to the water's edge and pointed. An old iron bridge arched out over the sea to the mainland.

"You cannot be serious!" Barl bellowed. "You want us to cross that thing? It would collapse if a gull landed on it!"

"There is no other way. Would you rather return to the palace and take our chances there? I'll go first to make sure the bridge is safe."

"Not a chance," said Rama. "I will go first."

Rama's gray eyes brooked no argument. Astrid nodded.

Quickly, Rama jogged up to the bridge and placed his hand on the railing. It swayed and creaked as the wind whistled through its bars. Rama stepped out and walked steadily, eyes fixed ahead. Astrid held her breath.

Rama jumped onto the beach on the far side and waved. Astrid signaled for the others to begin crossing. Barl insisted on going last.

"If anyone is going to make this thing collapse, it'll be me!" he said. "I'm not known for my trim figure!"

Father Hewin approached the bridge. He hesitated, staring at the sea in terror. The city father bit his lip and scurried as nimbly as a cat across the swaying span. Next went the

Panthers, Aeron and Capella, leaving only Astrid and Barl waiting.

The big man bowed grandly. "After you, my lady."

Astrid hiked up her dress and clambered over the rocks to the head of the bridge. From here, the sea looked like an angry monster that could swallow the slender iron bridge in a heartbeat. Astrid gulped. She glanced at Barl and then at Rama who waited for her on the far side.

Grimly, she stepped out. A mighty wave crashed beneath her, sending freezing spray over the bridge, drenching her in its icy grasp. Astrid gasped and clutched at the railing.

Fixing her eyes firmly on Rama, Astrid walked onto the bridge. Time seemed to last forever on the dangerously swaying span, but at last, Rama grabbed her wrists and she found herself stumbling down the beach. Capella ran over and caught her, and the two women sank into the sand in relief. Only Barl remained on the other side. The commander screwed up his face and raced across. The bridge creaked and groaned under his weight but held firm.

Once they were all assembled on the mainland, Rama took control.

"There is a cliff path behind us," he said. "It will take us to the lower levels of the city. From there we may be able to get to the harbor unmolested."

Astrid let him lead the way. She glanced

up to the palace perched high on its lonely promontory. It seemed distant and unthreatening but Astrid knew things were happening in there that would decide the fate of them all.

Where are you, Bram? She thought. *Where are you, Ravessa? Are you even still alive?*

The cliff path was steep and they were forced to go in single file. The sun was rising above the sea, promising a crisp clear day and the wind moved round to the south, giving them some respite.

They had not been climbing for long when the first signs of habitation began to appear at the side of the path: piles of fishing nets, lobster pots, small gardens with hardy plants. Whitewashed houses began to dot the cliff face and they soon found themselves passing between a row of cottages into the city proper.

Rama peered round a corner and looked out. Satisfied, he indicated for the others to follow him. It was early. The streets were all but deserted, yet Astrid knew that soon people would begin waking: fishermen going to catch the morning tide, shopkeepers setting out their stalls, thieves on their way home from a night's work. As swift and silent as shadows, the party stole through the streets, moving steadily downhill toward the harbor.

Just as Astrid began to hope they would get there undetected, the booming of a gong split the quiet stillness of the morning.

"The alarm!" hissed Astrid. "They know we've left the palace! Run!"

They fled. Heavy footfalls began to echo along the streets behind them.

"There are many," Rama panted. "We can't outrun them."

"We must!"

Already Father Hewin was beginning to tire. "I can't run all the way to the harbor," he gasped.

Barl pulled the father's arm over his shoulder and half carried him. "You can do it."

Astrid risked a glance behind. Soldiers were pouring through the streets. Ahead, the thoroughfare began to widen and the buildings to recede. The cries of gulls echoed on the wind.

The harbor! They were almost there!

The party burst out from the city and onto the waterfront. *Regalia,* lay at anchor not more than two hundred paces away. The crew peered over her side in alarm and saluted crisply as they saw who approached.

We're going to make it! Astrid thought. *We're going to reach the ship!*

But Astrid's joy turned to ashes in her mouth as guards suddenly spilled onto the quayside and fanned out, blocking the path to the Ice Ship. Astrid's party skidded to a halt and spun around but more guards blocked the way back.

They were surrounded.

Rama and Aeron drew their swords. Astrid glanced at them, then without a word, pulled the knives from her sleeves.

The captain of the guard stepped forward. Talerick. "It seems we are fated to keep meeting like this, my lady," he said. "What was left unfinished at the palace will be finished now. You have nowhere to go. You must surrender and come with me."

Astrid faced the young captain. "You know I can't do that."

"That's your final word?"

"My final word."

Talerick sighed and his shoulders slumped. "Take them," he said to his men.

The guards marched forward. Astrid's party formed a circle. The Panthers rocked onto the balls of their feet, weapons raised. Capella's hands glowed with the Gift.

Bellowing a battle cry, the Senate Guards broke into a run and crashed headlong into Astrid's party. Astrid staggered as she caught a blade on her knife. She pushed the blade away and followed it with her own. The knife sank into something soft. A soldier crumpled to the ground at her feet, blood pumping onto the quayside.

Oh, Chellin! She cried silently. *Forgive me!*

"Get behind me!" Aeron bellowed, trying to push her out of the way.

Astrid was surrounded by fighting. The weapons of the Panthers were a blur as they jumped and spun and kicked. Astrid had never seen such skill. They moved with the grace and fluidity of the animal that gave them their name. Shots of blue power rained down on the guards as Capella summoned the Gift. Rama and Aeron worked in unison, slicing through their opponents in their efforts to protect Astrid.

Her throat tightened. She had brought them to this. The fire of guilt kindled within her. If her people were to die, she would die with them, weapon in hand.

Whirling her knives above her head, Astrid jumped into the fray.

***

With Tomas leading, Bram and his companions quickly emerged from the underground passages and into the temple. A massive gilt-encrusted statue of the Goddess stood watch above the altar, but Bram turned his gaze away as they passed its towering form. He had had his fill of gods and goddesses. The temple seemed deserted but to be certain Tomas led them into a dusty, disused area and over to a window that rattled in the wind.

"This is where Serz and I came in," he said.

He placed his hands on the sill and vaulted

through. After landing softly on the other side, he turned back and helped Ravessa clamber out. Serz gently handed through the children. One by one, the party climbed through and gathered on the lawn outside.

Dawn was beginning to break. Streaks of red and pink were glimmering over the ocean but shadows still clung in thick clumps beneath the trees.

Tomas moved over to Ravessa, who clutched one of her babes in the crook of each arm. He gently placed his hands over their eyes and they fell immediately asleep. Tomas's eyes darted from side to side, checking for danger.

When he was satisfied, he reached up a finger and beckoned the others after him. In single file, they flitted from shadow to shadow and paused behind a hedge to look out. The tourney ground lay ahead, an open space with little cover. Beyond the tourney ground, silhouetted against the lightening sky, was the bridge that led over to the mainland. As always, guards were patrolling the entrance.

Serz swore under his breath. "Trapped like rats! How are we going to get across?"

"Isn't there another route?" Bram asked.

"Not that I know of. The palace was built here for defense with the bridge being the only access. Trouble is, that makes it exceptionally difficult to get out!"

"Ridiculous Chellin engineering," Falen

said. "Who would build a place with only one way out? If you were under siege you would all be trapped in here."

"Well, it seems we have no choice," said Bram grimly. "It's either the bridge or nothing."

"And how do you propose we get by those guards?" asked Falen.

"Get down!" said Ravessa suddenly.

They threw themselves to the ground.

A column of men wearing green and gold uniforms was crossing the tourney ground. They marched past the entrance, over the bridge and down into the city. As they disappeared, a gong began to sound from the palace.

Serz let out a low whistle. "The Senate Guard has been turned out, there must have been eleven units there at least."

"What are they after?" Bram asked.

"Isn't it obvious? We must get across that bridge!"

Bram searched his brain for a plan, any plan. "We need to draw the guards away from the bridge somehow. Wait! I've got an idea! Serz, do you have your flint and tinder with you?"

Serz nodded. "What are you going to do?"

Grabbing the tinderbox, Bram said, "I'm going to create a diversion. When the guards leave you must run as fast as you can across that bridge, I'll follow as soon as I can. Clear?"

Bram looked at Ravessa's pale, drawn face. "Can you manage this?"

Ravessa nodded. "I'll manage."

"Be careful, Bram," said Falen, grabbing his arm.

Bram nodded and darted out of their hiding place and headed toward the gardens. The tall hedges hid his movements and he soon found what he was looking for. A dead tree stood in the center of a lawn, long-since blasted to death by the Everwinter.

Bram reached up and broke off small twigs and branches to use as kindling and arranged them at the base of the tree. He knelt down and struck the tinder but the hard, frozen wood did not take the spark. He tried again. The flames spluttered and died as soon as they touched the cold wood. Bram gritted his teeth in frustration.

At last a tiny yellow flame flared. It snaked through the shavings, gaining height and strength as it devoured the dry wood. Bram leaned forward and blew on it, sending it gushing against the tree trunk. The flame spluttered as if it would go out but then found purchase and began licking its way up the base of the tree. The sea breeze took hold of it and fanned the fire gently. The flames grew higher, snaking up into the branches, hissing and crackling.

Bram packed the tinderbox away and ran back the way he had come. He ducked behind a hedge and carefully peered through the foliage. The guards on the bridge had seen the fire and were pointing animatedly.

Suddenly a branch came crashing down from the tree and landed with a thump at the base of a hedge which went up with a whoosh. The heat was getting close now, and Bram began to get nervous — one strong gust of wind and the fire would come in his direction.

Four of the bridge guards ran toward the fire, one of them shouting, "Get water! We have to stop the fire from reaching the palace!"

The guards came racing past Bram's hiding place and a second later, Serz and the others sprang up and pelted toward the bridge. Bram jumped to his feet and ran after them. There were still two guards on the bridge but they were so preoccupied with watching the fire that they didn't see Tomas and Falen until it was too late. Tomas knocked one guard down with a deft punch to the stomach, while Falen elbowed the other in the face so hard he fell unconscious. They rushed across the bridge but Falen stopped and turned round, waiting for Bram. He caught up and grasped her outstretched hand. Together they sped across and down into the city.

"We must keep away from the main street," Serz shouted. "I know a back way to the harbor, follow me."

They turned into a street lined with trees. Ravessa began to struggle. Her breathing was labored and her legs were starting to buckle beneath her. Falen and Serz took the children from her, while Bram and Tomas pulled her arms over their shoulders to support her.

They ran on. People were beginning to appear on the streets as the sun rose. Before long, the party had to dodge their way through the paraphernalia of a city waking up: supply carts, fishermen carrying nets, shopkeepers opening up for the day. Serz led them unerringly and as they rounded a corner they found themselves suddenly at the harbor.

They skidded to a halt and gaped.

A battle raged. Astrid and the Panthers were fighting furiously against a ring of armed men. Bram's eyes widened as he saw Father Hewin in the middle of them swinging a sword.

"Quickly! Get away before we're seen!" Serz hissed.

But it was too late. Talerick pointed. "Arrest them!"

A group of guards broke off from the fight and ran toward Bram and his companions.

"Follow me!" Serz cried.

They raced along the waterfront and down some steps onto the beach. Glancing over his shoulder, Bram saw that the soldiers were following them, and worse, Ravessa was falling behind. The high priestess slowed and then crumpled into the sand.

"I can't go any further," she panted.

The others ran back to her. Serz handed the child he was carrying to Falen and drew his sword. Bram did the same. They fanned out in a line in front of Ravessa and waited for the guards.

At Bram's side Tomas said, "Don't let them take us. Death is preferable to what Tamardi will do to us."

There were too many guards for Tomas to handle alone. Bram stepped to Tomas's side. It was time he tested the skills he'd learned. His heart fluttered wildly as a guard pelted toward him and his grip on his sword was slippery with sweat.

The guard swung the sword wildly and Bram ducked under the blade, spun away, as Corban had taught him, and smacked the man on the temple with the hilt of his sword. The man fell unconscious in the sand.

A second guard approached. A stinging slash missed Bram's throat by an inch. Bram spun away from the arcing blade, using his momentum to carry him out of its reach. In a flash, he answered with a riposte of his own, sending his blade singing high toward the man's face but the man ducked under it and backed off. He jumped forward and slashed at Bram who threw himself hard to the left and rolled out of the way just in time. He scrambled to his feet and jabbed the sword up in a desperate attempt to deflect the blow. Bram's blade passed through the guard's defense, stabbed into the man's neck just below his chin and carried on travelling upwards into his brain with a sickening wet noise.

The man jerked once and collapsed backward, ripping the blade from Bram's hand. The other guards advanced on him. The children had awoken and were screaming, despite Falen's attempts to shush them.

Bram's sword lay in the sand a few paces away. He threw himself toward it. His hand closed around the hilt just as a blade came swinging down to stab him. He rammed his sword up just in time, connecting with the guard's blade, ripping it from the man's grasp and sending it flying away where it landed on the beach beside Falen. She passed the children to Ravessa and grabbed the sword.

"Variss!" she cried as she charged forward. Falen ducked under the first man's attack and slashed at him with her sword. The man grunted and a deep gash opened up along his arm. She spun away and, pulling her knife from her belt, hurled it with pinpoint accuracy. It buried itself in the man's leg.

Then suddenly the guards retreated down the beach. Panting, Bram leaned on his sword, watching them.

Tomas growled deep in his throat. Following the Varisean's gaze, Bram saw three figures standing on the quayside looking down at them. Senator Nerie stood on the right of the group with a white-bearded old man on the left. Flanked by these two, looking resplendent in his blue robes of office, stood High Priest Tamardi Di Goron.

The high priest's eyes raked the scene before him. His gaze settled on Astrid and the Panthers beginning to take control of the battle with the Senate Guard and then on Bram and Ravessa's twin boys. Anger twisted his face.

"Enough!" he shouted. "I will end this once and for all!"

He jabbed his fingers into the air, splayed like a claw, and jagged streaks of blue light jumped across the sky. The wind picked up, thrashing the high priest's silken cloak about his knees. He began chanting strange, foreign words. He held a knife in one hand, which he suddenly slashed across his bared wrist. Blood welled from the cut, the droplets scattering on the wind.

"By blood I have called you and by blood I command you!" he bellowed at the sky.

Something cold and wet landed on Bram's cheek. He looked up in surprise and saw that snow was falling. The flakes were small but grew heavier in seconds, falling in thick clumps. The wind turned into a freezing gale that whirled through the harbor, almost taking Bram from his feet. In response, the sea churned. White waves sawed against each other, rearing up, falling back, and crashing down onto the beach. Falen's hand found his and he clung on as the world turned white.

"He has called a blizzard!" Falen screamed into the wind. "We must protect the children!"

Bent double, Bram staggered over to where Ravessa was desperately clutching her sons and pulled off his coat. He wrapped it quickly round the squalling twins, trying to give them some protection, any protection from the freezing wind. On the harbor the battle had come to a standstill, the soldiers withdrawing lest they strike one of their own in the chaos.

On the wind came the sound of drums.

Bram looked to the north, into the wind. Tears squeezed from the corners of his eyes, and he could see nothing except the swirling snow. But the drums grew steadily louder.

Suddenly the wind died. The sea turned as smooth as polished glass. The temperature plummeted. Goose bumps pricked Bram's skin. His breath turned white.

A coat of rime formed beneath Bram's feet, a silver layer of frost that raced across the ground, sealing everything it touched beneath a crystal covering. Icicles grew on the cliffs, like thousands of tiny daggers. The ships in the harbor became marooned, stuck at awkward angles in a sea of ice. Only *Regalia* was unaffected. She bobbed in a small circle of unfrozen ocean, her sails and rigging untouched while those around her went stiff with frost.

Bram felt drops of ice form in his eyebrows and cling to the hairs inside his nose. He shivered, teeth clattering. The air became painful to breathe.

The drumming grew louder, a steady *dum-dum-dum*. Nobody moved, as though they too were frozen. Waiting.

A screech of fury split the sky and a terrible creature burst out of the clouds.

As Bram took in the plated blue scales, the merciless eyes, the curved talons and the ice that shone on its hide, he felt his world shift under him. These creatures did not exist. They were monsters out of a fairy tale. He remembered the skeletal beasts in the vaults beneath Ral Tora and Chellin and realized he was looking at another but one very much alive.

"Goddess save us," whispered Serz.

The creature descended on cold winds into the harbor and hovered in front of Tamardi. The high priest's face was enraptured.

"Take them all, Mighty One," he cried.

The beast opened its mouth and shrieked hideously, ripping the morning asunder. It beat its heavy wings, *dum-dum-dum*, and climbed into the air.

The soldiers on the harbor scattered in terror. The dragon swooped and plucked up Captain Talerick. Its talons sliced through him, raining down blood and gore.

"Draw your bows!" Barl shouted. "Bring it down!"

A volley of arrows arced into the air but

ricocheted harmlessly off the creature's hide. Angered, it dived again and Bram yelled in anguish as he saw Saskia swept aside by its claws.

Tomas ran to the edge of the sea. Raising his arms, he screamed, "Over here!"

The beast swiveled its massive head around and glared at Tomas. Letting out a bellow, it dived with outstretched claws. Tomas raised his hands and a shot of blue power sped at the creature. With amazing agility, the dragon swerved in mid-air and the bolt crashed harmlessly into the sea. The beast hissed and began to circle Tomas, careful to keep out of range.

Seeing Tomas in danger, Serz dropped to his knees in the sand. He closed his eyes, placed his hands on his forehead and began muttering words under his breath. A white cloud appeared from the direction of the city, moving quickly against the wind. Hundreds of sea birds, Bram realized as the cloud grew closer, with Eobrus in the lead. The birds flocked around the dragon, scratching and pecking.

The dragon howled in fury and swiped at its tiny assailants with its vast talons. Eobrus led the birds away and they banked to the left and dived from the other side. The dragon opened its mouth and a great gout of air blasted into the flock. Birds plummeted to the ground, frozen. Eobrus climbed, taking the flock high above the dragon, and they dive-bombed, aiming for the beast's eyes. The dragon twisted, lashed out with its tail and cut through the flock in an explosion of feathers.

Tomas placed a hand on Bram's shoulder. "We have little time. The birds won't hold the ice dragon for long. I had no idea the priest held this much power. I need your help."

"Anything!" Bram cried desperately, as he watched the dragon snapping at Eobrus. "Tell me what I can do!"

Tomas's eyes were filled with yellow flame. "You must call the tashen. Set them free of the waves."

"*What?* I can't call the tashen. Only Astrid can do that."

Tomas did not blink. His eyes were like living pits of fire. "Astrid has a pact with the tashen. They do her bidding because it suits them. But only you can command them."

The dragon snapped its jaws and another bird dropped from the sky. Only a few remained.

"I can't command the tashen anymore than I can command those birds up there!" Bram said, exasperated. Why was Tomas talking such rubbish?

"Then see!" Tomas snarled. He lunged forward and grabbed Bram's head in his hands.

—He is on a ship. The creak of waves fills the cabin. Beneath, deep in the ocean there are voices.

"Hear us! Will you not answer us, master? We have waited for centuries. Will you not answer us?" –

– Torches ring the walls, burning sweet incense. Nine robed figures stand in a circle around a dais, chanting in a strange tongue. On the dais, a pentagram has been drawn in chalk and before this, a beautiful young woman kneels with her head bowed. She wears a white robe and has a garland of white flowers around her neck. Abruptly, the chanting stops and light begins to glow from the pentagram. Something is coming. Suddenly an opalescent figure is standing within the pentagram. The young woman says, "Saiis, my lord. Will you take me to wife?" The figure of light towers over the young woman. Then it reaches out a hand and raises her to her feet. The young woman's face is full of joy as the figure pulls her into its embrace. "What is your name?" the God asks. The young woman looks up. She has blue eyes and hair the color of sand. "Elyria Thornley, my lord." –

Bram gasped. From far away, he heard the librarian's voice saying. "Are you ready for the truth, Bramwell Thornley?"

Secrets and lies. Layers of meaning. It was him. He was the lie. She had known all along.

Something had stopped him falling into a fissure when the wall had collapsed in Ral Tora. Something had stopped the sword-blade from descending when he'd had that accident with Corban. The tashen had spoken to him. He had survived a sword thrust to the chest that would have killed a wild boar.

"Elyria Thornley was my grandmother's name. She was the bride of a god. What does that make me?" he whispered to Tomas.

The Varisean didn't answer. Instead, he reached out and pulled something from around Bram's neck. Looking down, Bram saw it was the bone flute the librarian had given him.

"Call the tashen."

Slowly, Bram reached out and took the flute. It felt oddly warm in his hands and he could feel the indentations of tiny runes carved into its surface. As he set it to his lips, it was as though he'd owned it his whole life. His fingers moved easily across the holes, coaxing a melody from the whistle that was at once terrible and beautiful. The high, lonely notes went floating out across the sea, and far, far away, over the waves.

The ice dragon bellowed in fury. With a wide swipe of its massive claws, it destroyed the last of the sea birds, leaving only Eobrus alive.

On the edges of his hearing Bram heard Eobrus say, *"For you, brother."* And Serz answered, *"Goodbye, my old friend."*

The albatross launched himself at the dragon, battering the creature's neck with his sharp beak. But the bird never stood a chance. The dragon whipped its head around as quickly as a snake and brought its massive jaws down on Eobrus's body. With one last 'kar-ark' Eobrus's spine snapped and he died.

Serz wailed in horror.

The dragon fixed its ice-blue gaze on Bram. Its orbs, devoid of iris or pupil, glowed with a cold intelligence. It dived.

In terror, Bram watched as the great beast came for him. Bram threw himself out of the way, but the creature's sharp talons bit deep into his shoulder, ripping through flesh and sinew. Bram desperately stabbed at the underbelly of the giant creature with his sword. It hissed in pain and began to climb, ready for another dive. It banked to the left, tucked its wings behind it and plummeted earthwards again.

Serz ran to meet it. He waved his sword wildly above him. The dragon's tail whipped out and caught Serz across the chest. The falcon master went flying through the air and crashed against the cliff with a sickening crunch. He fell to the ground and lay still.

Falen and Tomas staggered to either side of Bram, determined to defend him, but the dragon's tail snaked out again and caught them both hard against the chest, sending them flying.

The dragon hovered in the air, vapor drifting from its nostrils.

It lashed out with its foreleg and cracked Bram across the head so hard his vision went black and hot blood began pumping down the side of his face. Bram lurched and the dragon curled the talons of one huge paw around his chest.

An arctic cold trickled into Bram's body. He looked up into the burning blue eyes of the dragon and it looked back at him. In the depths of its gaze was a cold, iron will and not the faintest scrap of compassion or mercy. The dragon hissed and the talons squeezed.

Doom-boom. Doom-boom.

Something was smashing at the sea ice, trying to break through. Chunks of blue-green ice went flying into the air and two serpents reared out of the hole.

The tashen.

They saw the ice dragon and howled.

"Help me," Bram tried to say but his chest was so constricted his words were barely more than a whisper.

And yet the tashen heard him. The fins along their back rose up and fanned out to reveal large, leathery wings. Bony protuberances on their body began to grow and extend until they revealed themselves into legs. The sea dragons flapped their wings and heaved themselves ponderously out of the water with an almighty bellow.

The ice dragon threw Bram to the ground and circled the tashen. The serpents veered away, one in either direction so the dragon couldn't follow them both, and slashed at the dragon's scaly hide with their claws. The ice dragon climbed higher. The tashen followed.

Ice dragon and sea dragon became embroiled in a deadly dance. The tashen were smaller than the ice dragon so they joined their strength and attacked it from both sides. One of the tashen bit deep into the dragon's shoulder and the other came snapping down from above and raked a deep gash down the ice dragon's neck.

The ice dragon snapped its huge jaws and lashed at them with its tail but the tashen used their lesser size to their advantage and dodged the dragon's attacks. The dragon climbed higher, trying to outrun its adversaries, the tashen deftly followed. The ice dragon suddenly fled northward with the tashen in pursuit.

Bram watched until they were specks in the distance.

I live in a world where ice dragons live and sea dragons do my bidding, Bram thought. *The world is not what I thought. I am not what I thought.*

Weariness filled him. His bones felt like lead. Surely, it was not possible to feel so tired? He felt stretched and thin like a hide pegged out in the sun.

Falen, Tomas and Ravessa were watching him warily. Something new shone in their eyes. Respect? Or was it fear?

He couldn't bear their scrutiny. Stumbling, he turned away and approached the spot where Serz lay.

The falcon master's eyes were open, staring up at the frozen sky. Grief welled in Bram's throat, a choking lump that made it hard to breathe. Serz had been his friend. Gently, Bram leaned forward and closed Serz's eyes.

He stood. "Where is the high priest?" he asked.

"Fled," Tomas answered. "No doubt gone to seek reinforcements. He'll soon return with more soldiers. We must go."

Bram pulled in a deep breath, trying to draw strength from somewhere, anywhere. He felt numb. Mechanically, he let his companions lead him from the beach.

On the quayside, the Panthers were busy tending to the wounded. Saskia's body was wrapped in a blanket and taken on board *Regalia*. She would be given to the sea.

Bram fought back tears. Why was this happening? Why had Saskia and Serz, and all the soldiers who lay unmoving on the quayside had to lose their lives? For what purpose?

There were no answers in the cold bite of the breeze.

Bram stumbled along the gangplank and on to the ship. Astrid was the last to board. She stood facing Chellin, an unreadable look on her face. At last, she turned away and made her slow way onto *Regalia's* deck.

The crew cast off and steered *Regalia* out

into the frozen sea. Such was the power of the Ice Ship that she needed no wind to fill her sails. As soon as the steersmen laid a hand on her wheel she moved off, cutting through the ice-covered ocean as if it were butter.

Nobody spoke to Bram.

Alone at the bow, he stared out at the sea stretching away like a polished mirror.

How was he to face an enemy with such power? How was he even to begin?

Bram's eyes wandered to the northern horizon. Dark clouds were gathered there. What was he sailing into? What awaited him in the north?

The ship sailed on.

THE END

ABOUT THE AUTHOR

Elizabeth Baxter was born and raised in England. In her spare time she enjoys reading, hiking, traveling the world and watching England play cricket. She's been writing since she was six years old and plans to continue for as long as she's able to hold a pen (or a keyboard). If you are interested in more information about the author and forthcoming books, visit her at:

Website/blog:
http://elizabethbaxter.blogspot.com

Printed in Great Britain
by Amazon

14461387R00267